Praise f<

"... an impressive debut and a promising start to a smart new mystery series." — Kirkus Reviews

"If you've ever wondered what Stephanie Plum would be like with a little experience in life under her belt, Nanci Rathbun has the answer. ... Her heroine is flawed and complex, her plot perfectly constructed to bring out all of the facets she's created. For mystery lovers, or fans of romantic suspense, Nanci Rathbun is one to watch." — Shelf Awareness, October 8, 2013

Praise for *CASH KILLS*

PI Angelina Bonaparte "reminded me at times of Parker's Spenser in her detecting, her sense of humor, and her flamboyant sartorial style. ... *Cash Kills* is a first-rate mystery that combines police procedural with private detection and it features a compelling lead character and a marvelous cast. It's entertaining, fast-paced and suspenseful, and is highly recommended." — Reviewed By Jack Magnus for *Readers' Favorite*

"To find justice in the midst of lies and cover-ups, Angie must face her own fear of trusting another. Readers will relate to her humor, vulnerability and dedication to the truth." - IBPA Benjamin Franklin Silver Honoree for digital ebook excellence — September 2014

Praise for *HONOR KILLS*

"I found *Honor Kills* an extremely satisfying read. It ticks all the boxes of a good detective mystery, and the lead character Angie is extremely easy to empathize with. It's not often you come across a middle-aged PI hero, who is also female. The plot was intricate and full of twists and turns as befits such a mystery story. Having read *Honor Kills*, I am motivated to read the other books in Rathbun's series, which is probably as high a praise as a reviewer can give an author. — 5* Review by Grant Leishman for *Readers' Favorite*

"Nanci Rathbun takes the time to explore why her characters doggedly pursue their objectives; and this too makes *Honor Kills* a superior read in a genre that too often focuses on the 'whodunnit' over the 'why pursue this inquiry' question. The result is another spirited Angelina Bonaparte mystery that requires no special familiarity with predecessors in the series in order to prove satisfying to newcomers and prior fans alike." — Reviewed by Diane Donovan for *Midwest Book Review*, April 2018

CASH KILLS

Angelina Bonaparte Mysteries #2

Nanci Rathbun

Published by Dark Chocolate Press LLC
http://darkchocolatepress.com

This book is a work of fiction. All characters, events, and organizations portrayed in this novel are the product of the author's imagination or are used fictitiously. Any resemblance to actual events, locales or persons—living or dead—is entirely coincidental.

SECOND EDITION
ISBN: 978-1-9867628-8-5 (Print)
ISBN: 978-0-9987557-3-1 (Digital E-book)
Library of Congress Control Number: 2017903142
Rathbun, Nancianne.
Cash Kills / Nanci Rathbun
FICTION: Mystery/Suspense

Cover design by Nathaniel Dasco
http://BookCoverMall.com

Formatting by Polgarus Studio
http://www.polgarusstudio.com

Author photo by Michele Rene Chillook, Dubuque, Iowa

Published by Dark Chocolate Press LLC
http://darkchocolatepress.com

Dedication

This book is dedicated to my daughter Leah and my son Matt. You've both made your mother proud. I hope I make you proud, too.

Acknowledgements

I wish to thank my critique partners in Waukesha, Wisconsin, where this story began, and the Murfreesboro Writers Group in Murfreesboro, Tennessee, where it came to fruition. A very special thank-you is due to Susan Anthony Michael, beta reader and friend, for helping me cut away the dross so that the heart of the story could shine.

Chapter 1

Don't put your trust in money, but put your money in trust.

—Oliver Wendell Holmes

My office partner, Susan Neh, walked into our shared conference room, slowly pulled out a chair and, brows furrowed, sat facing me. "Angie, there's a woman here complaining that her parents had bank accounts worth millions and she doesn't want the money." Susan leaned across the table. "Can you imagine?"

"Maybe." I thought about the illegal ways that my papa probably accumulated wealth and how I would feel if I knew the details of my eventual inheritance. "What's her story?"

Susan opened her mouth, but abruptly shut it. "I think you should hear it from her directly. She's agreed to talk to you."

"I'm not sure that's legitimate, Susan, unless she wants to retain me."

"She might. I'm trying to convince her that she shouldn't ditch the money until she knows more. Come on, Angie, at least listen to her."

I pulled my five-foot-three frame up and checked myself in the small mirror that hung on the back of the door. A private investigator has to present a professional appearance in order to be hired. The days of tough guy Sam Spade have been replaced by the era of techno-geeks and corporate types. It's hard for a woman to be taken seriously. Clients expect a man. And for a fifty-something woman like me, it's twice as hard. So I ran my hands through my short, spiky white hair, checked my teeth for lipstick and straightened my Donna Karan business suit. When we entered our common office, I grabbed a legal pad and pen from my desk and waited.

Susan and I share office space on Prospect Avenue, on Milwaukee's east side. I'm AB Investigations, she's Neh Accountants. The "s" on the end of both our firms can be misconstrued. We each run one-person companies.

Susan made the introductions. "Adriana Johnson, this is Angie Bonaparte."

I smiled at the Sicilian pronunciation coming from my Japanese-American friend's mouth: Boe-nah-par-tay. I'd taught her well. Don't get me started on Napoleon. The little general was a French wannabe from Corsica, who ruined the name with his attempt to Gallicize it.

"Adriana, it's nice to meet you," I said. "Susan filled me in a little. Before we talk, I need to explain what a private investigator does and how it might affect this conversation. Then if you decide that you'd rather I wasn't privy to your information, I'll bow out with no hard feelings."

I assessed her as she nodded in response. She sat scrunched tight against one side of the client chair, taking up as little space as possible. The only way to describe her was nondescript: brown hair, light brown eyes, slightly olive complexion, slender, dressed head to foot in discount store beige. Bland and quiet. She hadn't moved or spoken since I entered the room.

I gave her a brief rundown on my services: tracking information and people. I explained that, under Wisconsin law, nothing she told me was private unless I was working for her attorney. In that case, whatever she shared with me would come under attorney-client privilege.

"May I please use your phone?" she said in a surprisingly sultry voice that contrasted sharply with her image. I handed her my cell phone and she placed a call. "Uncle Herman, this is Adriana." She pronounced it Ah-dreh-yah-nah. "I'm with the accountant you recommended. Yes, Susan Neh. She introduced me to a private investigator, whom I wish you to hire on my behalf. I understand that the investigator would then be covered by attorney-client privilege." She paused and listened, her face not showing any expression. Then she spoke again. "I mean no disrespect, Uncle Herman, but if you cannot accommodate me in this way, I will find someone who will."

Hmm, the mouse has teeth, I thought.

Then she handed the phone to me. "Ms. Bonaparte, this is my attorney, Herman Petrovitch. He was a friend of my parents and I've always called him Uncle. He'd like to speak with you."

I knew quite a few lawyers in the city, but I'd never heard of Herman Petrovitch. I took the phone. "Attorney Petrovitch, this is Angelina Bonaparte. I share office space with Susan Neh. She thought I might be able to help Ms. Johnson with her concerns about her inheritance."

When he spoke, his voice was rich and his accent middle-European. "I wish to retain you, Ms. Bonaparte. Anything which Adriana tells you must be kept confidential. I'm very concerned that when her inheritance is known, she might become the object of the press or even fortune hunters. She is a very good girl, but naïve in the ways of the world. I've told her that she can provide you with basic information, but I would like to meet with you personally once you and Adriana have talked. Is one hundred and fifty dollars an hour, plus expenses, acceptable?"

"That will be adequate, if I agree to pursue the matter, Attorney Petrovitch." Actually, it was a bit more than my usual fee, but I wasn't going to argue with the attorney of a brand new millionaire. "I'll be in touch once we finish here." He gave me his address and phone number and rang off. I leaned back in my chair and waited.

Adriana's story began in the late nineties, in what was then Yugoslavia. She handed me three faded visas, for Jan, Ivona and Adrijana Jovanović. The visas were issued in 1994. Then she handed me citizenship papers for John, Yvonne and Adriana Johnson, issued in 1999. "My parents came to the U.S. near the end of the Bosnian War. I was four."

That surprised me. I'd taken her for no older than twenty-one.

"They wanted more than anything to be Americans, so we went to classes to learn English and Americanized our names. Uncle Herman settled here about three years earlier. He helped my parents get visas and citizenship by sponsoring us. He even helped Papa with money to start our little hardware store on the south side of Milwaukee. We felt comfortable there, among so many Poles and even some Serbs."

She paused. "Papa was a carpenter and mason in the old country. He could fix almost anything, even engines. So the store was a good fit for him. Mama helped out when I was in school. They sent me to parochial grade school, but there wasn't enough money for a Catholic high school, so I went to the public school then."

She leaned forward. "There was never enough money, Ms. Bonaparte. We rented a two-bedroom bungalow at the back of a two-house lot. My dresses were homemade or from the thrift shop. I didn't go to prom because it cost too much. Mama cut my hair at home. We never went on vacation. Our big treat was to rent a movie and watch it on our second-hand TV. I never owned a video game or a cell phone.

When I graduated from high school and wanted to attend the university, there was no money then, either. So I got a job at a supermarket and helped my parents at the hardware store from time to time."

As she spoke, she twisted and clenched her hands and her voice got quieter. Then she paused and her gaze fell to her lap. "Last week, my parents died in a botched burglary attempt at the store. There was nothing stolen—the police think the robbers panicked and ran after they shot my parents. I would have been there, too, to help with inventory after closing, but I'd begged to be allowed to spend the weekend with a friend. The police have yet to find the ones responsible. Of course, in our little store, there was no recording equipment, and no one saw or heard a thing that night. A neighbor called the police when she got up to use the bathroom and noticed that the lights were still on in the front of the store. I buried my mother and father two days ago."

The account was given without emotion, flat, as if she'd recited it so often that it no longer had impact.

"They always told me there wasn't enough. No matter what I wanted or asked for, there wasn't enough to have it or do it." Her jaw firmed. Tension radiated from her. "Yesterday, Uncle Herman showed me their will and their accounts. They had millions, Ms. Bonaparte." Her voice rose. "Millions. All those years of scrimping. All those years of not enough. I thought they loved me, that they would do anything for me, if they only had enough. And all that time, they did."

She stood and walked over to the window, her back to me and Susan. Her shoulders tensed and she remained there, stiff and unmoving, for several moments. Then she turned. "I told Uncle Herman that I didn't want the money, that if they never cared enough to give me the education I longed for and the nice things that others had, I didn't want their d-damned money!"

The mild profanity was obviously foreign to her. Susan moved forward in her chair, but I motioned her to stay still and let Adriana finish.

"How can I take it? I don't even know how they got it. We lived simply in the old country. We weren't rich there, either. And the store never produced that kind of income. I don't know what to do, but I know that I don't want ill-gotten money."

She'd wound down enough that I felt I could approach her without stifling her story. I stood and walked over to her and took her hand in mine. Hers was icy cold and I could feel the small tremors of her body. Her eyes were slightly unfocused. "Adriana—" I deliberately pronounced it the way she had on the phone, not the Americanized way that Susan used when she introduced us—"I think you're in a mild state of shock right now." I turned to Susan. "Would you brew us some of your fantastic tea? With plenty of sugar." She nodded and slipped out. "Susan makes the best tea, Adriana. No tea bags, she brews it from real tea leaves or herbs." As I soothed her, I led her to the conference room, sat her on an upholstered love seat and covered her legs with a throw. Susan came in with the tea and we watched while Adriana sipped and seemed to relax. When she set the cup down and leaned back, closing her eyes, I motioned to Susan to follow me from the room.

Susan and I met when we both worked for PI Jake Waterman. She conducted his financial investigations and I did his legwork—computer searches, tails, background checks. It didn't take Susan long to earn her CPA and go out on her own. Wisconsin requires that a person applying for a PI license be employed by a private investigator. I worked for

Waterman long enough to learn the ropes—significantly shortened since I already had a degree in library science and understood the tenets of research. Then Susan and I decided to lessen expenses by sharing office space. Most of Susan's clientele are of Japanese descent, but lately, she's expanding her base and has made inroads into the Hmong and Vietnamese communities, as well as starting to get referrals for Caucasian clients.

Once in the outer office, I whispered, "Did you do the books for her parents' store?"

"Yes," Susan whispered back, "and there was no income there that would account for millions in the bank."

"Poor kid. Not only to lose her parents, but then to find out that they lived a lie all those years and lied to her, too."

We heard Adriana stir a bit and went back into the conference room. She was huddled under the throw, but her eyes seemed alert. I pulled a chair over and sat close, again taking one of her hands. This time, it was warm. I felt I could go a bit further.

"Adriana, what did your attorney tell you about the money? He must have some sort of explanation."

"He said that my papa had sworn him to secrecy, and that, as Papa's attorney, he couldn't tell me anything, even though Papa is dead now." She stopped, closing her eyes again.

I mulled over the legality involving attorney-client privilege. Usually, an attorney cannot divulge information about a client, even after death, unless there was suspicion of fraud or intent to commit a crime. But in the case of wills, there was wiggle room, because the beneficiary had the right to understand the testator's intentions. However, that only applied if there was a dispute. Disputes over wills generally involved someone wanting more, not less. I needed to check my understanding before I met with Petrovitch.

I was ready to tiptoe back out when Adriana spoke. "If your papa and mama had behaved that way, would you want the money?"

"I honestly don't know," I replied. My father was a typical Sicilian father—protective, hard-working, and fairly chauvinistic about what his only daughter, and only child, should know. But to hide that much money while pretending that we didn't have enough for me to even go to college—no, no way would Papa do that to me. So how would I feel if I found that out? "If you don't accept the bequest, will you have enough to live on?" I asked her.

"Not for long. I have about three months' savings in the bank. And the store income has been steadily declining for years. I doubt I can salvage much from it, maybe a year's worth of living expenses—if I'm frugal. Of course, I've always been frugal, so that's not a burden that I've never carried before."

"We don't know if the money came from legitimate sources or not, so I think it's premature to decide to discard it. Let's take a small step back and consider options. If you decided to keep it, or some of it, what would you want to do? You mentioned college. Would that appeal to you now?"

Her eyes sparkled a little. "I've always felt that God intended me to be a nurse. But they said we couldn't afford the schooling." She stopped for a moment. "It's not too late, is it? People who are much older than I am go back to school."

"Yes, they do, and no, it's not too late, if that's what you want. So maybe keeping the money to finance your education and give you a start in life is not such a terrible thing, even if we're not sure yet where it came from." I smiled at her obvious excitement at that idea.

"Maybe not. Of course, I don't need that much. But there are lots of ways to put it to good use. I could talk with Father Matthieu at our church. He works with a lot of charities. He would know."

"Let's take it one step at a time, Adriana. First, are you still living in the same house?"

"Yes, but I've been staying with my friend, Jennifer, since my parents were killed."

"I think it might be time for a change of residence, at least until we know more about the money and about the persons who were involved in the killings."

"You think I'm in danger?" Her face, already pale, lost its remaining color.

"Probably not. But it won't hurt to be cautious, especially since nothing was taken in the burglary." She nodded. "What did Attorney Petrovitch tell you about drawing on the funds?"

"He said there's an account for living expenses and gave me a checkbook for it. He also said there are several other accounts for investments and things, that aren't so…um, liquid?"

Susan nodded. "That means that the investments aren't as easy to convert to cash in a hurry."

"I see," Adriana responded. "Well, there's a quarter million in the account I can draw on. I've never been that liquid in my whole life!"

We all giggled a bit. It was good to hear Adriana joke in the midst of her turmoil. It made me realize that she might be plain, but she had spunk. That would carry her far.

Now I needed to get her to a safe place. I called Anthony Belloni, aka Tony Baloney, a real estate mini-mogul who owed me big time for saving his butt when he was suspected of murdering his girlfriend, Elisa Morano. The dog had a wife and four kids, now five. I swallowed hard over working on his defense team—my own ex pulled the same shopping-around routine on me—but ultimately, Tony didn't deserve life in prison for infidelity. He agreed to rent a nice two-bedroom apartment to Adriana, furnished and ready to move in. The building manager would be waiting whenever we arrived.

While Adriana filled out paperwork for me, Susan and I conferred. She would start digging into the accounts that Attorney Petrovitch disclosed to Adriana. I would take Adriana to her parents' home to pick up whatever clothing and other belongings would fit in my Miata convertible. I didn't want Adriana to drive her own car, in case anyone had her under surveillance. My mind ticked over on ways to get from her home to Tony's apartment building with less chance of being followed. Paranoid? Maybe, but as the saying goes, just because you're paranoid, it doesn't mean there's nobody after you.

Chapter 2

Sex is emotion in motion.

—Mae West

It was four o'clock by the time I got Adriana settled in her temporary apartment, purchased a pre-paid cell phone for her, gave her a cautionary talk about not contacting anyone she knew until I gave her the green light, and arranged for her car to be delivered from my office to a friend of my papa's who owned several downtown parking lots. I called Attorney Petrovitch, but his secretary informed me that he would be away for the remainder of the day. She made an appointment for us to meet at his office the next morning at nine. I still had an hour before I planned to meet my guy at the gym, so I called Bart Matthews, a Family attorney—and I mean Family as in *The Sopranos*. Bart was the one who hired me to investigate on Tony Baloney's behalf. I figured that Bart owed me, considering the flesh wound to my waist that the real murderer inflicted. First, though, I had to get past Bart's secretary, Bertha Conti.

Bertha was an inveterate chain smoker, like Bart. "Law offices of Bartholomew Matthews," she rasped.

"Bertha, it's Angie Bonaparte. Any chance I can get ten minutes of

Bart's time? I know how busy he is, but I figured you would find a way to squeeze me into his schedule if anyone could." It always helped to schmooze Bertha, who ran the office with an iron hand—and it wasn't enclosed in a velvet glove.

"Ms. Bonaparte, it's rather late in the day for favors like that." She paused. I remained silent. Eventually, her minuscule better side kicked in. "But considering your recent injuries on behalf of our client, I'll see what I can do. Hold, please."

In a few seconds, Bart was on the line. "Angie, what's up?" I heard the click and flash of his lighter, followed by the intake of breath as he lit up yet another cigarette. In addition to smoking, Bart's got to weigh three-fifty. A walking heart attack or stroke. His motto: *Eat right, exercise, live healthy, die anyway.*

"Bart, I need some legal advice."

"You in trouble?"

"Nope. I'm doing some digging for a client. She's the beneficiary of her parents' estate. The attorney is named as the executor. They left a lot of assets she didn't expect. He doesn't want to tell her how they accumulated so much. Claims attorney-client privilege. Is he entitled to withhold the information?"

"Hmm. Offhand, I'd say no, not if she wants to protest the terms of the will."

"Right now, she seems more worried that the assets are tainted. It's not that she wants more. She's not sure she wants it at all."

"Geez, Ange, tell her to take the money and run. Regardless of how the parents got it, it's hers now. She can be a do-gooder with it, if she wants to. But if she turns it down, where will it go? Maybe to someone who won't want to do good with it?"

Why didn't it occur to me to ask Adriana who would be next in line if she refused the bequest? It was so basic. I felt pretty embarrassed. "I'm not sure, Bart. I'm meeting with the attorney in the morning. I'll ask. For now, I'm more interested in whether my client has the right to insist on knowing how her parents built such a large estate in secrecy."

"I don't do much complex estate planning, Angie. Mostly simple wills for Family. I'd say she has grounds to dispute the terms, if she wants. But that's off the cuff. You may want to consult a specialist. I can give you a couple of names."

I took the information, even though I'd already decided to approach Petrovitch as if the assumption was a fact and see how he responded. Bart sent greetings to my papa and we rang off. Time to hit the gym.

You won't see sex kittens in thongs at Rick's Gym. There were mats on the floor, a boxing ring, treadmills, and bags and weights. His regular clientele was mainly firefighters, police officers and private security personnel. I like it there, despite the lingering odor of sweat socks. It's real.

It's also the place where I first noticed how attractive my guy was. I met W. T. "Ted" Wukowski while working on the Belloni case. He was investigating for the prosecution, I for the defense. I thought him an uptight, humorless chauvinist, until the day I ran into him and his partner, Iggy, at Rick's. The day I noticed Wukowski's fine body encased in workout sweats. The day I thought, tough-guy detective Dana Andrews in the film noir classic, Laura. The day he smiled and made all my assumptions about him start to burn up in the fire of my—okay, I'll admit it—lust.

It took us a while to get past our individual hang-ups: my trust issues, his fear about a woman's vulnerability in a dangerous profession. After my near miss with the real Morano killer, there were a few bad days when I thought Rick's was the only place I'd ever see Wukowski.

But he came around. Thank God, because I was a sniveling basket case, the kind of woman I detest, when I thought he'd written me off.

I shook off the memories and pulled into Rick's parking lot, where Wukowski waited, leaning against the front fender of his Jeep Wrangler, arms and ankles crossed. "What?" I glanced at my watch. "I'm not late."

"Nope, you're not, Angie. I'm early. I already worked out and cleaned up, so I could make a last-minute meeting tonight." As he spoke, he unfolded himself and enveloped me in a hug. Wukowski is six-foot even to my five-three. I inhaled his chest—mmm, man and soap and clean shirt smell—and wrapped my arms around his back, gently massaging his spine with the knuckles of one hand. He liked that.

"Shoot," I said, "I was anticipating a cholesterol crash at Paul's after we worked out, then maybe a film noir detective movie at my place…or even an early night. Oh, well, guess I'll have to find myself another handsome cop for the night."

"Not funny, short stuff." He ruffled my spiky hair. "Maybe I should hire a PI to keep an eye on you." He pulled back a bit and leaned down to plant a kiss. My insides started to tighten up, little tingles moving southward. Would the sparks eventually smooth into a nice steady hum?

"Work meeting?" I asked him.

"Yeah."

"Want to come over when it ends?" I asked.

"It might be late."

"Well, if it's before midnight, ring my bell. Maybe I'll be up for some nookie, Wookie." The first time Iggy introduced Wukowski to me, I asked him, "Do they call you Wookie?" His response: "Only once," in a Joe Friday, stick-up-the-butt tone of voice. Funny how pairing Wookie with nookie didn't seem to offend. I put my lips to his this time—fair's fair, and a guy doesn't like to do all the chasing! He slowly disengaged from me, climbed into the Wrangler and drove off with a wave.

I grabbed my workout bag from the Miata, put in an hour of sweat and headed home to my Lake Drive high-rise condo. My steam shower with its five pulsating heads beats Rick's communal shower any day. Some folks snidely whispered "middle-aged crazy" when I sold the family home after the divorce and bought the convertible and the condo. They never understood that the tight constraints of the American dream that I forced myself into for twenty-five years of marriage were not the real me. That June Cleaver shirtwaist dress and pearls hid a push-up bra and red thong. My ex's philandering hurt, but it also resulted in the freedom to be the woman I always wanted to be. Don't misunderstand, I loved my life as a wife and mother, but I wanted the rest of life, too.

The lobby mailbox contained the usual junk. My personal mail goes to a rented box at a private service center. It's more secure, and they can sign for packages, so it's also more convenient. I tossed the unopened envelopes on the hall table, planning to shred them later. No paper leaves my home or office unshredded. It's amazing what a dedicated snoop can find out from what seem like innocuous mailings.

I stripped out of my workout clothes as I ambled down the hallway to my bedroom and tossed them into the hamper in the walk-in closet. I admit to being a bit of a sybarite about my clothes, shoes and bags. The closet used to be a small guest bedroom. I converted it so that my stuff would be organized and accessible. No sense buying great clothes and then having them get wrinkled on the hanger. Or letting designer shoes lay in a jumbled heap. I'm a woman who appreciates order and my closet reflects it.

In the shower, I shampooed, soaped, shaved and exfoliated. Then I dried, moussed my hair, applied cream to my face, neck and décolletage, and used three different lotions on my body, feet and hands. Lastly, I pulled on a soft cotton tee and pants, and slid my feet into terry cloth thongs. Body maintenance takes a lot of time and effort.

While I studied the open refrigerator, the phone rang. My papa's deep baritone voice rang out. "*Buona sera*, Angelina." Uh-oh. Use of full first name, not in a sentimental situation. I was in Papa's bad books. At least he hadn't used my middle name, too. Hearing 'Angelina Sofia' makes my heart hitch a beat.

"Hi, Papa. What's up? How's Aunt Terry?"

"What's up?" he parroted. "Let me see. Thanksgiving is three weeks away. Two weeks ago, Aunt Terry invited your police officer friend to join us for the holiday meal. Did you extend the invitation to him?"

Busted. I'd been trying to find the right time and place to talk to Wukowski about it, ever since Aunt Terry told me that she and the rest of the family expected "my new man" to line up, front and center, for inspection. We'd only known each other since early summer, only been a couple since mid-August. I hadn't figured out how to broach the subject yet.

Wukowski is a private man of few words. My Sicilian-American family—Papa, Aunt Terry, my grown children David and Emma and their respective spouses, Elaine and John, David's twins Patrick and Donald and Emma's girl and my namesake, Angela—is pretty darned nosy and noisy. I could picture it now: everyone bombarding him with questions as they passed the turkey and dressing, pasta and salad. Wukowski responding with his deadpan "yes" or "nope." Gary Cooper meets the Corleones. Disaster.

"Papa, I planned to ask him tonight when we went out to dinner. But he got called into work. I'll ask Wukowski this week, I promise."

"Wukowski. You call him by his last name? Doesn't the man have a first name?"

No way could I divulge Wukowski's name. His badge read "W. T. Wukowski" and his buddies called him Ted. When I told him that I wouldn't go to bed with a man whose name I didn't know, he 'fessed up to his very Polish and very embarrassing given names: Wenceslas Tadeusz. Ven-chess-louse Ta-doosh. That's right, his mama named him after the Christmas carol, "Good King Wenceslas." Apparently, it was playing on the radio as his dad barreled up the icy drive to St. Mary's hospital with his laboring wife humming along. And then she threw in an unpronounceable middle name. No wonder the poor guy went by Ted.

Back to my dilemma. "He thinks it's cute that I call him Wukowski, Papa. Kind of a pet name."

"What does he call you?"

"Angie." *Among other things.*

"Hmph. Very strange. What will we call him?"

I could see there was no escaping Thanksgiving, short of death or hospitalization. "His buddies call him Ted. I'm sure it would be fine with him for my family to call him that."

"So his name is Theodore?"

The man was a pit bull, jaws clamped down hard, unwilling to release his victim's leg from his mouth. I had to think hard. What was Tadeusz in English? "No, Papa, it's Thaddeus."

"Ah, Taddeo. Well, then, they should call him Tad, no?"

"Papa, it probably goes back to his childhood or something. Don't pester him about it, okay?"

"Me, pester? Angel, you wound me. Now, you'll call your aunt this week to confirm that Ted will be there." It was not a question.

"Sure, Papa. No later than Friday."

"*Bene*, Angel. I'll see you for Sunday lunch. Maybe you'll go to Mass with Terry this week?"

"Not this week, Papa." He knew full well that I was what Aunt Terry termed a "lapsed Catholic." I term myself a non-Catholic. Non-religious, really. And Papa, for all his jabbing about church, was pretty much the same. Aunt Terry refused to despair, though. My mother died when I was only five, and Aunt Terry left the novitiate of the Sisters of Charity of the Blessed Virgin Mary to raise me. Now in her late sixties, she still did much work for the order and even dressed a bit like the modern nuns I knew: short hair, dowdy clothes, flat sensible shoes. A few months ago, she started to date for the first time ever and we saw signs of femininity surfacing. To be truthful, Aunt Terry has a way to go to even reach average. But she never stops praying, especially for me and Papa. To paraphrase Tennyson's 'kind hearts are more than coronets,' selflessness is worth more than beauty.

I hung up, wrung out from the exchange and the anxiety of introducing Wukowski to my family. Food. I needed food. Somewhere in the fridge was a plastic container of leftover stuffed cabbage rolls that Wukowski cooked for us the previous night. He told me that the Polish name for them meant 'little pigeons' in English. There they were. I slid them onto a microwaveable plate, nuked them, tested the inside for heat, and sank my fork and then my teeth into them. Mmm. Pork and beef, rice and seasonings, all rolled into cooked cabbage leaves, baked in a Dutch oven, served with pan juices and sour cream. Comfort food to the max.

I pictured Wukowski, a folded kitchen towel tucked into his jeans, assembling the meal in my kitchen. When I kidded him about his "man apron," he whipped it off and used it to smack me on my butt. A faithful man, who cooked, could be playful, and was good in bed—make that really good in bed. *Miracoloso*.

Chapter 3

As soon as there is life there is danger.

—Ralph Waldo Emerson

At eight the next morning, I called Adriana to check in.

"Oh, hi, Ms. Bonaparte." Her voice was listless.

Small wonder that she was a bit depressed—her whole world was topsy-turvy. My maternal instincts urged me to make things better for her. "How is the apartment?"

"Really nice. It has cable TV. I stayed up late, watching all the channels."

Obviously, the minor luxuries that many of us take for granted were a surprise to a kid who'd always done without. "Well, Adriana," I counseled, "you can afford some nice things now. Not that you should toss your money away, but a late-model car and a splurge now and then on entertainment is not a bad thing. You might even want to upgrade your wardrobe a bit." When we'd gone to her parents' yesterday to pick up some of her personal things, there was hardly anything in her closet that wasn't beige, tan or black—and all cheaply made. As for makeup, *nada*. The girl needed help!

"I'm not sure yet if the money is really mine. I still have a bad feeling about it. What if it doesn't belong to me? Will I have to pay all this back? I can't afford to, you know."

"I'm meeting with Attorney Petrovitch this morning at nine. I hope to have a better sense of things then. But I believe that if the attorney of record tells you the money is yours, and since you're not spending foolishly, there's no question of eventual repayment. After he and I meet, I'll pick you up and we can talk over lunch." She agreed, but before I rang off, I needed to run a safety check without alarming her. "Adriana, how did you sleep last night? I never sleep very well in a new place."

There was a little pause. "Well, I did wake up a few times. I'm not complaining, Ms. Bonaparte, but I can see why this particular apartment isn't rented, with the overhead door to the parking garage being right below. People go in and out at all hours."

"That would make me wake up, too. I'd probably even peek outside."

She suppressed a little laugh. "I actually did get up, the first few times. But there was nothing to see. And no one approached my rental car."

I was glad she didn't have feelings of uneasiness. That would set off alarms for me. "Did you get any phone calls last night?" I asked.

"No. Of course, no one knows my cell phone number yet."

It was a bit of a struggle to convince her to spend money on the new phone yesterday, but I managed. I'm pretty unstoppable in Mom mode.

We ended the call and, as I assembled my briefcase and purse, I mentally assessed Attorney Petrovitch. I'd run some background checks on him last night. There was very little information available. His name was originally Petrović. He graduated from Belgrade Law School, practiced in Sarajevo and emigrated to the U.S. in July of 1992, three months after the Bosnian War erupted. Because Wisconsin law did not allow graduates of foreign law schools to sit for the bar exam until 2010, he attended Marquette Law School and finished in record time—two years. In the fall of 1994, he became a U.S. citizen, Americanized his surname and opened a solo practice in the far northeast side of Milwaukee. There was no indication of political involvement, nor any information about charities or organizations that he supported. He never married, but Adriana called him "Uncle Herman" and said he was a friend of her parents.

I had other database inquiries pending, but guessed his age to be anywhere from forty-five, if her parents married young and he was their contemporary, to seventy-five, if he was much older than they were. When we spoke yesterday on the phone, he didn't have the reedy voice of a man in his seventies, but he did strike me as a bit pedantic. I guessed he would be about sixty and imagined him as exuding a courtly formality from his Middle European years.

People open up more to others when there is a sense of shared values, so I wore a simple double-breasted coatdress in a deep eggplant color, with nude stockings and black pumps, and small gold Celtic knot earrings as an accent. Very staid, very professional. Of course, the black-lace-and-purple-satin lingerie underneath told another story. Wukowski loved to guess what bra and panties I was wearing under my oh-so-proper business attire.

Petrovitch's office was in a two-story building, no security or reception desk, with ten separate mailboxes in the unlocked lobby. "Law Offices of Herman Petrovitch, S.C." was listed in Suite 203. The adjoining suites, 201 and 205, were either empty or not listed. There was an accountant in 200, an optometrist in 202 and a dentist in 204.

I noticed a small elevator, but decided to walk up.

The building was oddly quiet. The hairs on the back of my neck started to prickle. I adjusted the shoulder strap on my purse, so that the bag sat squarely in the middle of my abdomen, eased my briefcase open and reassured myself that my 9mm was in place in its carry holster. No sense ignoring intuition—or "gut," as Wukowski prefers to call it.

I knocked on the door to Suite 203 and entered the small outer office. Empty. Shades drawn. No lights on. The nameplate on the desk said "Dragana Zupan." The phone handset lay on the desk, one light blinking on the console. I pulled my gun and checked the safety. "Attorney Petrovitch? Ms. Zupan?" I called, and quickly ducked and moved to the side of the desk. Better to feel foolish than to make oneself a target. There was no response.

The door to what I assumed was the lawyer's office stood slightly open. I edged my way along and pushed it hard from the hinge side, slamming it into the wall to let me know that no one was hiding behind the door. The lights were on in the inner office.

A woman's body lay on the floor in front of a massive mahogany desk. The back of her head was blown off. Blood and pieces of what I assumed were skull and brains were splattered across the large front panel of the desk. The copper smell of blood and the acrid smell of gunpowder hit me in the back of the throat. I wanted to retch, but I also wanted out of there. I backed out as quietly as I could in pumps on a wooden floor, moved out into the hallway, and ran downstairs for the street and my car. The 9-1-1 dispatcher instructed me to stay on the line and wait for the police.

It was two minutes before I heard the sirens, two minutes that I spent scanning the street, slumped in the front seat of my little convertible, sure that someone had a gun trained on my head. The black-and-white squad car came to a quick stop and two officers emerged. I holstered the 9mm. It's legal to carry concealed in Wisconsin, but at the scene of an apparent homicide with police approaching, it's only prudent to appear harmless.

"You Ms. Bonaparte?" the male asked. He pronounced it wrong, but I just nodded. His partner, a female who appeared to be in her early thirties, stood behind him, scanning the area.

It took me a couple of minutes to explain why I was there and what I'd seen. I assured them that I was in the outer office, but had not set foot into the inner office, where the body was, nor had I seen or heard anything to indicate who might be responsible. A second squad car pulled up with two more officers, followed by an unmarked sedan. Wukowski got out of the sedan and spoke briefly to the two new patrol officers, who disappeared around the back of the building. Then he came up to my car and bent down to my eye level.

"Angie, you okay?" When I nodded, he turned to the two patrol officers who'd been talking with me. "You two secure the lobby and the second floor. The other team has the back of the building. No one goes in or out. Keep them all in their offices. No one enters the lawyer's suite. Got it?" They nodded and loped off. Wukowski turned back to me. "When I got the call from the dispatcher and she gave me your name, I was the only detective in the bullpen, so I had to respond. We need to keep this professional, Angie."

"Of course. I understand."

He pulled a small digital recorder from his pocket. "Okay if I tape this?"

I nodded.

"Tell me what happened. Nice and slow. No hurry."

By that point, my nerves were under better control. It helped that I wasn't alone and it helped even more that, with Wukowski there, I didn't feel a sense of threat. While I repeated my story yet again, a plain van pulled up. A woman with a medical bag, another carrying photographic equipment, and a man carrying a bulky black bag went into the building. My brain processed them as the crime scene team. I turned my attention back to Wukowski. He was silent, watching me. "Sorry? I missed that," I told him.

"I asked why you were here to see the lawyer."

"I'm working for him on behalf of a client."

"Client's name and address?"

"I'm not sure I can tell you that until I talk with Attorney Petrovitch."

"He wasn't in the office?"

"I didn't see him, if he was there. But once I saw the body, I didn't go further."

"The lawyer may be dead, too." He said it with no emotion whatsoever. Deadpan, pardon the expression.

"Perhaps, but I don't know that yet."

He turned off the recorder and sighed. "Angie, we're treating this as a homicide. That puts limits on personal privacy."

"I'm not trying to obstruct the investigation, Wukowski, but I have a duty to the attorney who hired me. Let me try to get in touch with him."

"Fair enough." His voice softened. "You're sure you're okay?"

"Yes. A bit shaken. I've never seen a dead body outside of a funeral home, let alone someone with her head blown off. It spooked me."

"Yeah. Homicide does that to a person." He raised his shirt cuff and checked his watch, then turned the recorder back on. "It's ten. I'll be here at least another hour. I want to see you and your client at headquarters at twelve-thirty sharp. That should give you time to locate Petrovitch and talk to the client."

"Will do," I agreed.

He turned the recorder off again and placed it in his pocket. Leaning closer, he said, "This homicide may be unrelated to your business with Petrovitch, but be careful, Angie."

By now, a small crowd had gathered on the street. There was nothing to see except the police vehicles, but rubberneckers are a breed apart. I pulled out and edged my way down the block as the TV news van approached.

***

At the office, I ran up the stairs and dropped my stuff on my desk. My hands were shaking so badly that I couldn't unlock my desk drawer. The keys jangled in my hands.

Susan got up and came around her desk. "Angie, what's wrong?"

"Do you have a contact number for Petrovitch, outside of his office number?"

Susan checked her PDA. "Nope. What's up? I thought you had a meeting with him. Did he stand you up?"

"In a manner of speaking. I found his secretary dead on the floor in front of his desk. He wasn't there. No sign of him yet."

"Holy…" Susan covered her mouth with her hand.

"Yeah. And Wukowski got the case."

"Did he blow a gasket?"

"No, he was surprisingly calm." Wukowski has this terrible anxiety about women in dangerous professions. It was understandable, given that his partner, Liz White, was tortured and killed during an undercover drug investigation almost three years ago. They never got the perps. I remembered the news footage of Wukowski, then unknown to me, in dress uniform, ramrod straight, stone-faced, hand to forehead as the rifle salute pierced the air at her funeral. He still has occasional nightmares about it.

We'd barely started to acknowledge our attraction for each other when I was injured in the Belloni case. He never came to the hospital, sent a card, or made a call. I thought it was over before it started, until he showed up at my door five days later. It took him that long, he told me, to decide if he could man up enough to handle my PI work.

There was no sense worrying about how this would affect us. Put one foot in front of the other, Aunt Terry would say. I telephoned Attorney Petrovitch. The call went to voicemail and I left a message that it was extremely urgent that he contact me. Then I went down the hall to the women's bathroom. The mirror confirmed how I felt—pale and a bit shell-shocked. I wasn't kidding when I told Wukowski that I'd never seen a dead body outside of a funeral home. My business is mostly tracking people and information. Even when I worked on the Belloni case, I never saw the victim's body.

I remembered the prayer for the dead that I'd learned as a Catholic schoolgirl. What was the name on her desk? Oh, right, Dragana.

Eternal rest grant unto Dragana, O Lord, and let perpetual light shine upon her. May her soul and all the souls of the faithful departed, through the mercy of God, rest in peace. Amen.

This was the second time I recited that prayer for a murder victim. *May it never happen again*, I thought.

***

When I knocked on the door of Adriana's apartment, it opened quickly and she wrapped her hand around my wrist and dragged me in, then shut and locked the door. Before I could speak, she put her index finger to her lips to shush me and motioned me to follow her into the bedroom. Once there, she shut the bedroom door and grabbed both my hands in hers.

"Angie," she whispered, "there's someone walking up and down the hallway. I heard it and it seemed strange that the same squeaky shoe would be going past. I looked out the peephole in the door. He was across the hall, with something like half of a set of binoculars up to the door. I got scared and ran into the bedroom."

Hmm. A guy with a reverse peephole viewer, a device for seeing into a room from the outside of the door. This couldn't be good. I didn't want to scare Adriana, but she was right to be alarmed. "Do you think he saw you in here?" I asked.

"I don't think so. The first few times I heard him, he didn't stop. Then, when I heard the squeak-stop-squeak-stop pattern, I checked. He was turning toward my door. I ran into the bedroom."

"You did the right thing," I told her. "He might have nothing to do with you. But just in case, I'm calling a police detective I know." This was no time to pussyfoot around attorney-client privilege. I pulled my cell phone out of my purse and extracted the handgun from its briefcase holster.

Adriana's eyes widened and she covered her mouth with one hand, while the other covered her heart. "Omigod," she whispered.

"I'm licensed, Adriana, and I know how to use this. Don't worry, okay?" I called Wukowski on his cell phone. "I'm at my client's apartment. Some guy's patrolling the hallway, using a reverse peephole viewer." I gave him the address and apartment number. "I have no idea if this is related to the murder at the attorney's office, but you should also know that my client's parents were murdered last week."

He sucked in a breath. "You couldn't tell me that earlier?" I heard him yell for an officer to get a couple of squads to the building. Then he came back on the line. "Are you and your client unharmed?"

"We're fine. Holed up in the bedroom for now."

"We're on the way. Stay in the bedroom until you hear me at the door. And be careful." He sounded angry.

Adriana needed to know about the latest development. I took her hand in mine. "Adriana, I have some bad news to tell you. That's why I came over here early. I didn't meet with Attorney Petrovitch after all. When I got to his office this morning, he wasn't there. His secretary was lying in front of his desk, dead from a gunshot to the head."

"Dragana? Dragana is dead?" With a sudden intake of air, she gripped my hand hard and stared at me. "Why?" she whispered.

"I have no idea. I think there must be a connection between your parents' deaths and hers, but I don't know what it is. Without Petrovitch, I'm at an impasse."

"Maybe…maybe I can contact him. There's a number he gave me. He said to never use it unless it was a matter of life and death. I thought he was being dramatic."

I checked my watch. I wanted no record of the call from Adriana's cell, so I handed my phone to her and she punched in the number. We waited, listening to the ringing. *Please*, I thought, *be there*. After six rings, it went to voicemail. I couldn't understand the recording, but Adriana did. She responded in the same language and hung up. "Serbian," she told me. "I left a message for Uncle Herman to call you."

It was a tense half an hour later before Wukowski knocked. "They found no one on the premises," he said in his Joe Friday voice, "but a pried-open basement window was most likely the means of access. They notified the on-site manager, who called a locksmith to secure the window and examine the other basement and first-floor locks."

Wukowski stopped speaking and stared at me. "Your client?" His voice was decidedly cold.

I made the introductions. "Ms. Johnson's parents were found dead last week, at the hardware store they ran. The police put it down to a botched robbery."

"I see."

"No, I don't think so," I said. Adriana's head swiveled between us as she tried to understand the tension in the room. "I couldn't tell you earlier, Wukowski. I needed to talk to Petrovitch, or at least get the green light from Adriana. When I got here and realized the possible danger she was in, I made the call right away."

"It's you who doesn't understand, Angie." At Wukowski's use of my first name, Adriana's eyes opened wide. "By withholding vital information, you impeded the investigation. This isn't a game."

"As I'm well aware. If I thought it was someone playing around in the hallway, I wouldn't have called you."

"Perhaps you and your client have time now to make a statement?" he said in a biting tone.

"Have you located Petrovitch?"

"Not yet. He wasn't at his office or his home. The housekeeper let me in for a quick inspection, once I told her about the murder. No missing clothes or suitcases. No sign of his whereabouts. I put out an APB for him as a person of interest."

"Without legal representation, I must advise Adriana to remain silent. If you give me a few minutes, I can arrange for another attorney for her."

He stepped closer to Adriana, clearly using intimidation. "Any reason you don't want to talk with me, Ms. Johnson?"

Adriana moved back a step, her eyes appealing to me for rescue. "You don't need to answer that," I told her. I turned back to Wukowski. "Of course, I can't stop you from taking her to police headquarters. But my advice to her is to remain silent until another attorney is present."

"You're a pain, Bonapar-TAY," Wukowski muttered.

I snickered. "So I've been told, TED. Listen, we're on the same side here. We all want to find whoever is responsible for these killings. Let me call Bart Matthews and see if he can arrange representation."

Wukowski made a twirling "whatever" motion with his hand. "I'll be in the hallway, waiting." He glared at me and left.

I called Bart's office. Bertha put me right through when I told her there was a homicide investigation in progress and I needed Bart's help. I gave him a rushed account of the Johnson and Zupan murders and asked if he could act on Adriana's behalf.

"Put me on speaker," Bart said. "So, young lady, Attorney Petrovitch was representing your parents' estate. He wanted Angie to work with you regarding the sources of the money, is that right?"

"Yes."

"Did you personally hire Attorney Petrovitch to represent you?"

"No."

"Then, if you like, I can act on your behalf."

"Yes, please," she said. "Attorney Matthews—"

"Let's wait to talk until we meet in person, Ms. Johnson." Bart directed me to bring Adriana to his office, so that we could both make prepared statements for the police. "Wukowski's waiting in the hallway, Bart. I'll let you tell him. I don't think he'll agree, if it comes from me."

I took my phone to Wukowski and stood by as he and Bart spoke. There was some wrangling, but Bart got his way. Wukowski handed my cell phone back to me with a curt, "See you at Homicide," and stalked off.

Chapter 4

*There is no intensity of love or feeling that does not
involve the risk of crippling hurt.*

—William S. Burroughs

Bart's office was located in one of the old ironwork buildings in Milwaukee's Third Ward, populated in the 1880s by Italian immigrants, when the Irish moved up and out. Today, it's a haven for art galleries and cafés, as well as upscale restaurants and clubs. The building was owned by the Family, with a high-tech security system, supplemented by round-the-clock guards. "Ms. Bonaparte," the big woman at the lobby desk greeted me. "Attorney Matthews is in his office. He told me to send you and your client up. Please sign in." She passed a clipboard to me.

"How's school, Mary?" I asked. The security at Bart's building consisted almost entirely of college students from nearby Milwaukee School of Engineering. It's funny when you consider the typical geek profile of an engineer. Not so with Mighty Mary, a former bouncer, who could take an average-sized man. Mary resembled a guy on hormones or a woman on steroids.

She groaned. "Two more weeks until finals. After that, I'll spend some downtime over Christmas with my parents. My boyfriend and I are considering a trip to Florida for some fun and sun." She smiled.

"Sounds great," I told her. "This is Adriana Johnson. Can we leave our stuff with you, Mary? Bart's office reeks of smoke. Last time, I had to have both my coat and my briefcase cleaned. Do you know what they charge to professionally clean leather goods?"

She motioned to a shelf under her desk.

I removed my cell phone and tablet PC. "There's a gun in the briefcase, Mary," I said as I locked it.

"They'll only get it over my cold, dead body," she intoned.

Adriana's eyes widened. I motioned to the stairs and we went up. On the way, I explained Mary's checkered background and her decision to leave the "tavern security profession," as she euphemistically termed her bouncer days, and study engineering at MSOE.

"Wow," Adriana exclaimed, "that's so cool. I mean, she basically reinvented herself."

"Yep. And she's probably ten years older than you are. It's never too late." I hoped it would give Adriana courage for her own future.

Both Bart and Bertha smoke like the proverbial chimney. Even Wisconsin's strict Act 12, which bans smoking almost everywhere, didn't stop them. Although they continued to break the law by smoking in a place of employment, at least Bart had an exhaust system installed, so the fumes didn't penetrate into the hallway. Who would rat him out? Some Mafioso on a health kick?

I knocked and Bertha buzzed us in. We settled in his office, he in his oversized reinforced office chair, Adriana and I in the client chairs. Even those were built for a hulking man, which is what most of Bart's clients are. My feet dangled about two inches above the floor. Talk about undignified!

I introduced Adriana to Bart and filled him in on her parents' deaths and the resulting money situation. Then I explained about finding Petrovitch's secretary that morning.

"*Merda,* Angie. This is bad, very bad. The back of her head blown off? And the brain matter was splattered on the front panel of the desk?" I nodded. "Only way for that to happen is if she was kneeling or bending down when the gun was fired. Sounds like an execution to me."

Adriana covered her mouth with her hands and whispered, "Poor Dragana."

I shook my head. "I missed that, Bart."

"How many executions you seen, Angie?"

"That would be the first."

"I figured."

There was no reason to hide my concerns about Wukowski from Adriana. I took a deep breath. "Bart, I have to 'fess up."

"About what?"

"You know I've been, uh, involved with Detective Wukowski from the MPD, ever since the Belloni case."

"Yeah. Well, everybody has their guilty pleasures, Angie." His smile was insincere.

"That's not what I'm confessing, you idiot."

He laughed.

"Bart," I said, "I have a possible conflict of interest in this case." That elicited a groan. "I'm not sure I can stay on the case."

"Why not?"

"You know Wukowski. He's hardnosed about non-professionals getting involved in police cases."

"You're not a non-pro, Angie. You work for money, right?" I

nodded. "And you get results. Results Wukowski would still be digging for in the Belloni case, if you hadn't been involved."

"You're right, Bart, but he and I weren't, um, seeing each other then. Now, we are."

"So you're gonna play the 'little woman' card and bow out?"

"Dammit, Bart, you know me better than that! This is not a card game and I'm not throwing down with you!" I started to breathe deep, but stopped myself. The air in here was seriously problematic. "I'm simply alerting you to the situation and offering you the chance to remove me from the case."

"Angie, if you don't want to hassle with your man, that's your call. I'll respect it, reluctantly. But I'm not removing you from the case. You're a professional and I trust you to act like one. No need to jump down my throat, okay?"

"Okay. But I'm only being honest when I tell you that I'm uncomfortable knowing information about the Johnsons, which might be related to Dragana Zupan's murder, and not telling the investigating detective…who happens to be my lover."

There. I said it. Lover. Not friend with benefits. Not casual sex partner. Lover, as in, the man I love? Lord Almighty, how did I get in so deep, so fast? And what will happen when I woman up and tell him? If I tell him. Maybe I'll wait for him to man up and tell me. If he feels the same way.

Bart interrupted my reverie. "I can see how that would be difficult, Angie, but it's not an either-or proposition. Adriana is not accused of anything. We're simply acting in her best interests. I see no reason to withhold the information we've discussed from the police. After all, none of it implicates Adriana in the three murders. And she has an interest in seeing her parents' killers brought to justice.

"My concern as her attorney is that Adriana is not put in a position that leads to suspicion of complicity. Before we go to Wukowski, I'll work with both of you on prepared statements. I trust you to know what to share with him, but I don't want Adriana to talk to the police without me being present. And you work for me, which gives you legal standing in the case, so don't let him bully you." He stopped. "As if," he muttered. Then he looked back up at me. "Angie, I see no reason for you to recuse yourself."

He buzzed for Bertha, who came in with her steno pad. Adriana and I settled down to be deposed by a master. Bart knew how to frame a question to elicit the answer he needed. He also impressed me with his skill at putting Adriana at ease. She was able to tell her story with simplicity and sincerity, although when she told about being notified of her parents' deaths and the death of Dragana Zupan, some tears fell. Bart passed her a box of tissues and I patted her hand. Bertha sat to one side, silent, and captured it all in the lost art of stenography.

Chapter 5

I interrogate and examine and cross-examine him...

—Socrates

Wukowski was not a happy detective when we arrived *en masse* at his desk in the Violent Crimes Division common room. His partner, Joe Ignowski, greeted me loudly. "Angie!" he called out, "how ya doin'?"

It seemed as if all eyes were on me. I could almost hear the undercurrent: Angie Bonaparte, Pat Bonaparte's kid, Wukowski's girlfriend. The *b*'s, *p*'s and *k*'s formed a little wave of explosions across the room. I could feel myself getting red. Wukowski wore his poker face.

"This way," he said. He led us to a room whose table and chairs were slightly less scarred and whose atmosphere was slightly less malodorous than an interrogation room. We sat, Bart, Adriana and I on one side, Wukowski and Iggy on the other. "I'd like to record this," Wukowski said.

"Okay, but I reserve the right to rescind that agreement," Bart responded. Then he pulled a small digital recorder from his briefcase. "I find it helps to have my own copy, in case of dispute or faulty memory."

"Fair enough." Wukowski took his digital recorder from his suit coat pocket, pressed a button and set it in the middle of the table.

The *Deliverance* banjos played in my head.

Wukowski stated the date, time, and names of those present, and ended with "Continuing investigation into the homicides of John and Yvonne Johnson and Dragana Zupan."

Wukowski was part of the Johnson investigation, too? I quirked an enquiring eyebrow. He didn't respond.

While Wukowski prepared to record, Bart opened his briefcase and removed the signed statements that Adriana and I made at Bart's office. He handed the originals to Wukowski and copies to Iggy. They took their time reading them.

Wukowski tapped the papers into order and set them aside. "Ms. Johnson," he said, "tell us about the day of your parents' murders."

"They planned to take inventory at the store that night. I would normally help, but I had plans with a friend."

"Your friend's full name, address and phone number."

Adriana was able to give the name and phone, but blanked out on the street address. It upset her that she couldn't remember. "I've been there a thousand times," she said.

I pulled my tablet out of my briefcase and asked permission to do a search. "Was that a cell number or a landline?"

"Landline," she said. "It's her folks' number. She got laid off and had to move back home."

I did a quick reverse lookup on the phone number and showed the results to Adriana for verification.

"That's right." She turned to Wukowski. "Paul and Susan Markov." She read the address to him. Bart wrote the information down as Iggy took his seat again.

"They'll be able to confirm that you were there all night?"

Adriana nodded.

"Please state your agreement out loud, for the recorder," Wukowski said.

"Yes, they will."

Wukowski then opened a folder and perused the contents. "The detective who initially took the case noted that you were home that morning. The police notified you of your parents' deaths at about eight o'clock."

"Yes. Jennifer got a temporary job delivering papers, so we were up early. Then I went home to sleep for a while. But I never made it to bed."

Wukowski ran her through the events of the day: waking up at the Markov home and helping Jennifer on the route; coming back to the family home and finding her parents gone; assuming they worked all night and then went out to breakfast; the police at her door; the woman officer who made a cup of tea and offered comfort; Adriana's call to Uncle Herman, the family lawyer; his rush to the Johnson home, where he went through each room to be sure nothing was disturbed—even though the police assumption at that time was that the killings were a burglary gone bad; Herman Petrovitch's insistence that Adriana leave the family home temporarily and his sorrow that, even as a much older man, he felt it inappropriate for Adriana to come home with him; his request for a house key and the alarm code; Adriana's call to the Markovs, who came immediately to take her to their home and who offered her an indefinite stay with them; their call to St. Sava Serbian Orthodox Church and the subsequent home visit of Father Matthieu, Adriana's priest; a day of tears, prayers, talk with the Markovs about next steps, and eventual exhaustion and an early night.

During the account, Adriana broke down only once—when she spoke of being notified of her parents' deaths. Iggy offered a box of Kleenex. I patted her hand. Bart murmured a low reassurance that "it will be all right." Wukowski merely sat and waited until she was able to continue.

I wanted to damn his cold hard heart. But I knew that his heart was neither cold nor hard. *This is how he gets through his days,* I thought. *This is how he manages the pain and the ugliness. He detaches. Is it only on the job, or does he also deal with his personal life that way? What if we run into trouble? Will he detach from me, too?*

After Iggy and Wukowski left the interrogation room, Bart, Adriana and I took a few minutes to consider options. Adriana looked tired. "Where am I going next, Angie?"

"Well, I have a friend who might be willing to put you up. Bobbie— with an *I-E*—Russell helped me solve the Morano murder. Gorgeous, like a young Rock Hudson. He lives in a great little converted stable on Lake Drive."

"Um…I don't think I could stay with a man."

"I should have explained. Bobbie's gay."

"I've never known a gay man."

"He'll probably try to make you over."

Her chin rose. "Maybe it's time."

The little lion cub roars. Cute.

Bobbie answered on the second ring. "Angie, girlfriend, how are you? Long time, no see. Busy with that studly detective?"

I laughed. "You have no idea. Bobbie, I need a favor. A big favor. I have a client who's in trouble. She needs a place to stay for a few days. Expenses are not an issue."

"Wow. Can I help detect?"

Bobbie loved getting into the role of sleuth. And he was good at it, as I had reason to know. When we were confronted by the real killer in the Belloni case, Bobbie kept his head and surreptitiously used his cell phone to call 9-1-1. Then he held a conversation with the killer that gave the dispatcher enough clues to save our lives. I owed him a lot.

"Right now, there's not much to detect. But I'll fill you in when Adriana and I get there, okay?"

"Adriana. That's an exotic-sounding name. I'll bet she's pretty."

With Adriana right beside me, how could I respond to that observation? "Could be. But she needs help."

"She's come to the right man. I'll get her some fab stuff, at a discount!"

Bobbie's current partner, Stephano Mariscal, was a buyer. His real name was Steve Marshall, but that's too blah for the fashion industry. I once asked Bobbie why they didn't move in together. "We're out of balance," he said. "Steve's got money and connections. All I have are my looks. I want to work on my career before I settle down."

As far as I knew, Steve paid a lot of Bobbie's bills and Bobbie took the occasional local modeling shoot and did a little temping when funds were low. I hated to say it, because Bobbie's a good friend, but he was living the typical too-good-looking-to-bother-with-substance life. But Bobbie was still in his twenties, so there was time for him to grow up.

While I spoke to Bobbie, Bart called to arrange for one of his Mafioso clients to loan a "staff car" to Adriana. It got terrible mileage, but the windows and doors would stop a typical non-armor-piercing bullet. "No sense taking chances when there are alternatives," he told us, before settling Adriana in his own reinforced black Lincoln Town Car for the trip to Bobbie's. I suddenly felt very vulnerable in my little black cherry Miata.

We arrived almost simultaneously at Bobbie's converted carriage house, at the back of a large Lake Drive mansion on Milwaukee's east side. Bart had another commitment and left as soon as Adriana exited the car. "I'll make the withdrawal we discussed for your living expenses," he told her. "One of my people will drop it off at Angie's office."

I introduced Adriana to Bobbie. "Come in," he invited. "Let's see if my place will work for you."

The main house was once the province of a brewery king's son and family. The stone "cottage" that Bobbie rented was originally a stable for eight horses, but now held stalls for three cars and all the grounds keeping paraphernalia that a large estate requires. The upstairs living quarters boasted a totally renovated kitchen, all gleaming stainless and granite; a living room filled with the kind of soft, squishy leather furniture that you sink into and can't get back out of; and two bedrooms, one decidedly sensual, with a large *en suite* bathroom with a double occupancy whirlpool tub.

The guest room was dominated by a teak platform bed with drawers. The bedding was done in neutral grays and silvers, with pops of black in the many decorative pillows. Shoji-style screens covered the tall, narrow window. Serving as bedside tables were black-and-silver boxes on legs. Very sleek, very modern, very Bobbie.

Adriana put her suitcase down. Then she and Bobbie settled in the living room for a chat. Bobbie has that way about him. If he liked you, you knew it and it warmed you from head to toe. I didn't have time for a gossip session, so I broke in. "Sorry to interrupt, but I have to get back to my place and do some more digging on Attorney Petrovitch and your parents, Adriana. I'd also like to visit their hardware store and home. Do you mind giving me keys?"

"Of course not." She opened her purse—Bobbie eyed the vinyl bag and shuddered slightly—and extracted a key ring. "There are two for the store, a deadbolt and a regular. And two for the rental house, same deal. And the key for my parents' car." Adriana shrugged. "Guess I won't be going home anytime soon, right?" Her voice was low, tinged with sorrow. I shook my head. "Then you might as well take the whole thing." She handed it to me. "My parents rented the storefront. The apartment above is empty, so you won't disturb anyone if you go there tonight. Oh, yeah, there's an alarm system, too. At the store, go in the back door and turn left into the bathroom. The panel is behind the bathroom door. At home, it's in the front hall closet. The code is thirteen-nine-eighteen."

"Does the keypad actually go past nine?" I asked.

"Um, no. I guess it's really one-three-nine-one-eight. But my parents made me memorize it the other way. If you count the letters in the alphabet, it's the English spelling of *mir*—Serbian for peace."

"I'll keep my eyes open for anything with that combination of numbers," I said, entering them in my tablet, along with the addresses of the store and the home. "Maybe it's for an account somewhere. Susan will know."

I kissed Bobbie good-bye on the cheek, not one of those kitschy air kisses, but real lips to skin. It seemed silly to shake hands with Adriana after that, but a kiss felt over the top, so I hugged her.

"Thanks for everything, Angie," she leaned down to whisper in my ear. "I don't know what I would do without your help."

"Try not to worry. I'll be in touch tomorrow. Oh, and don't make any personal calls, okay?"

Her face fell. "Can't I call Jennifer? She's the friend I was out with, the night it happened. She'll be worried about me."

"It's best if no one has your location or phone number for now. Why don't you give me Jennifer's number and I'll let her know you're okay and will be in touch." I noted the information and headed downstairs to the Miata. The grounds were quiet and there was no sign of activity. It felt safe. Still, I took a circuitous route to the south side location of Johnson's Neighborhood Hardware Store.

Chapter 6

This is unexpected...like squirt from aggressive grapefruit.
—Earl Derr Biggers

The store was small, situated in what was once a predominately Polish community. The neighborhood opened its arms to former Soviet Union and eastern European immigrants, but was quietly holding out against an influx of Latinos from nearby areas. Serb Hall, a Milwaukee institution for its Friday night fish fries, was only blocks away.

I drove past Johnson's Hardware. Like the other storefronts on the block, it was narrow and mildly shabby. I entered the alley that backed the store, parking the Miata in the loading zone. It was six o'clock on a Thursday—I suddenly remembered my promise to let Papa and Aunt Terry know tomorrow if Wukowski would be there for Thanksgiving—and the alley was empty of life. Not even a stray cat. It felt a bit creepy, but I didn't sense danger. Still, I removed my gun from my briefcase holster, checked the safety, tucked the weapon into the flap of my shoulder bag, and exited and locked the car.

The building was an older brick structure, obviously intended to house the storeowner and family above the business. In the early evening darkness of a Milwaukee November, I saw no lights above or in the store itself. The upper windows sported cheap pull-down roller shades, some with rips and others hanging at crazy angles.

There was no crime scene tape up, the murders having occurred a week ago. I pulled on latex gloves and prepared to go in the back door. After checking the small walkways on either side of the building, which were surprisingly free of debris, I inserted the bigger of two house keys into the bottom lock. It fit. It took two tries for the deadbolt, but I was inside and disarming the alarm within seconds. Leaving the door unlocked, in case I had to make a speedy exit, I pulled my 9mm and disabled the safety. This was a murder site, after all. Better to be prepared.

The bathroom was clean but sparse, with a toilet and sink, and a towel bar holding a threadbare utility cloth. Across the short entry hall was another door. I eased it open and reached in to flip the light switch, sweeping the room with my eyes and my pistol. It was used for storage, with utility shelves all around, mostly filled with stock and unopened boxes. A scarred wooden table sat square in the center, with packing materials on top and flattened boxes underneath. The floor had a layer of undisturbed dust. The police hadn't entered the room. I turned the light off and re-closed the door, deciding to preserve the room for later.

What hit me first when I entered the store area itself were the bloodstains on the wood plank floor and the chalk outlines of two bodies. The deaths occurred a week ago. Why hadn't the attorney arranged for the store to be cleaned?

The reality of the deaths of Adriana's parents almost overwhelmed me. I hardly remembered my own mother, who died when I was barely one, from complications of the flu. But I loved my papa dearly, despite his bossy interference in my life, and I couldn't bear to think of him lying on this floor, cold and dead.

Careful not to disturb evidence, I edged along one wall, noting that the area of blood on the floor was only about the size of a bath mat. Of course, I couldn't tell how much had soaked into the wooden planks.

The Johnsons' blood and brain matter splattered the front wall of the checkout counter. I felt sure I was seeing the results of another execution. I took several slow breaths.

The store seemed typical for a mom-and-pop operation. Shelving around the perimeter, except for the counter area. Paint and painting supplies. Some wallpaper books, but no stock. A large cabinet with many small, neatly labeled plastic drawers, filled with screws and nails. A display of tools: hammers, pliers, screwdrivers, wrenches, even a few handsaws and drills. That's when it struck me: only manual tools were on display.

I quickly reviewed the store contents again. It seemed at first glance as if the store was stocked appropriately, but a second examination revealed that there were no big moneymakers for sale. Where were the electric tools, the carpet shampooers and floor buffers, the high-margin items that contribute to profit?

The checkout counter was a testament to late nineteenth century storekeeping. An ancient manual cash register, its empty cash drawer hanging open. A pad of receipt forms. A metal spindle for holding completed carbons. A small calculator. I located the record books on a shelf below the register. Flipping through, the last day of entries was from the day before the murders. The Johnsons did a good job of bookkeeping, even if they sucked at storekeeping. But everything was paper-and-pen, not a computer in sight.

Something moved outside. I dropped and duck-walked to the end of the counter, and edged around the corner, both hands on the pistol grip.

"Don't move, lady. Set the weapon down on the floor. Slowly."

The voice behind me was deep and male. I remained in my squat and slowly turned my head. A police officer, his revolver drawn and aimed at me, stood in the hallway.

"Okay, Officer," I said, "I'm setting my gun down now." I carefully placed the 9mm on the floor. "There's no need to panic. I work for the owner."

"The owners are dead. Murdered a week ago. Right here."

"I work for their daughter. For her attorney, that is. I'm checking on the place for her. Adriana Johnson." I hoped he would recognize her name and relax a bit. His revolver remained steady.

My thighs were starting to ache and my left calf muscle felt like it would seize up at any moment. My coatdress gaped open, exposing my legs, up to the lacy tops of my thigh-high stockings. "Is it okay if I stand up, Officer?"

"Real slow," he responded. "Up against the wall, ma'am. You know the drill."

I nodded and walked to the wall, where I leaned forward and placed my hands, spreading my legs fairly wide so that I would be off balance if I tried to move. The dress gaped open a bit. I waited for him to approach, but instead I heard him yell, "It's okay, come in the back." A few seconds later, there were more footsteps and murmured voices.

A woman spoke from close behind me. "I'm Officer Opansky. I'm going to check you for weapons." She efficiently patted me down and told me I could turn around.

The man was short, probably only five-six. His dark hair, eyes and complexion, coupled with a slight distinction in his vowels, made me think he might be Mexican-American.

"I'm a private investigator, Officer …?"

"Rodriguez."

"Officer Rodriguez. My name is Angelina Bonaparte. I work for Attorney Bartholomew Matthews, who's been hired by Ms. Johnson to investigate matters related to her parents' deaths and their finances." I nodded toward my purse, lying on the floor. "My PI license and license to carry concealed are in the tan wallet, in the zipper section."

Officer Opansky's head flipped back and forth as she compared my face to the pictures. "Fits," she told Rodriguez. After studying the wallet for a second, she said, "Prada."

"Mother's Day present," I told her.

"You got good kids."

I nodded. "The best."

Rodriguez cleared his throat. "Let's focus, ladies."

"Get over yourself, Julio," Opansky said, as she replaced the wallet in my purse.

"Are you the patrol officers for this area?" I asked. They nodded. "So you got the initial call on the night of the murders?"

"Yes." Rodriguez stopped. There was no hand or head signal, but somehow Opansky let him know he could continue. "A neighbor called in, saying the store lights were still on at two in the morning. We figured it would turn out to be nothing. You know, someone being careless. Or maybe one of the owners working late. I saw them in here at midnight once or twice, for inventory, they said." He took a deep breath. "So when we pulled up, we weren't expecting ..." He gestured to the chalk outlines. "*Malo.* I mean, bad. Very bad."

"Yeah," Opansky affirmed. "I've been a cop for thirteen years, but I never saw a murder. It's not that common. You ever work on a murder case, Julio?"

"No. But I saw a few knife fights, growing up. A couple of guys I knew in high school bought it back then." He paused.

"There wasn't much blood, right, Julio?" She closed her eyes, remembering. "The coroner told me their hearts probably stopped beating real quick, being shot in the head that way. The brain shuts down and the whole system stops, like that." She snapped her fingers. "I guess there are worse ways to go."

"I guess," I said. If Opansky wanted to talk, I would happily try to open her up. "Did you notice the front of the counter, there? It's splattered with blood and brain matter."

"Bullets will do that," Opansky responded.

"What I mean is, it seems odd that it would be so low. Wouldn't you think the Johnsons would be standing when they got shot, and the mess would be on the walls or shelves?"

Seconds ticked by while they stared at each other. "*Maldito*," Rodriguez murmured. "They were sitting on the floor? Or kneeling?"

Opansky turned to me. "What else did you notice, Ms. Bonaparte?"

"Call me Angie. Well, I opened the door to the storage room, across from the bathroom. I didn't go in. There's a fairly deep layer of undisturbed dust on the floor, like the CSI team didn't check that room at all."

"Dammit." Opansky's pale complexion started to redden. "Julio, who got the case in homicide?"

"One of your people. Hard-nose guy, name of Wukowski."

This will make for some interesting pillow talk, I thought.

Chapter 7

The great gift of family life is to be intimately acquainted with people you might never even introduce yourself to, had life not done it for you.
—Kendall Hailey

I gave both Opansky and Rodriguez one of my business cards and asked them to call me with any new developments. It was almost nine o'clock. There was a voicemail from Wukowski, saying that he would be at my place tonight and that I shouldn't worry about supper. It was only a month ago that I gave him a key to my condo, a first since I resumed dating after the divorce. I appreciated his courtesy. We weren't at the stage yet where I wanted him to drop in unannounced.

There were two urgent matters to discuss with Wukowski, and neither could wait. The more pressing was Thanksgiving dinner at Papa's. The more difficult was Wukowski working the same case, albeit from different sides, as me. And why hadn't he mentioned this morning that he was assigned to the Johnson case? Regardless of his responses, another item on my agenda for the evening was to get my guy in the sack. It was almost a week since our last romantic encounter, and I was more than ready.

Even as I eased the front door of my condo open, the delicious aroma hit me. I opted for normalcy and called, "Ricky, I'm home." Wukowski rounded the corner and engulfed me in a hug. "Lucy," he kidded me in a fake Cuban accent, "you're late." He eyeballed me. "Nice dress. Something purple underneath?"

I gave him a Mona Lisa smile. "You can find out yourself…later."

He lifted me up and kissed me, long and slow, while my feet dangled in the air. Then he set me down gently, keeping his hands around my waist.

"Wow," I said, "any special reason for that?"

"Nah. Just…I missed you, you know, and…jeez, Angie, I hate it when we're at odds—even though you deserved some of my anger."

I decided to focus on the semi-apology. "I feel the same way about you." Then I smiled. "I see make-up sex in our future. Our near future." He started to gently suck on my ear lobe. "Not that near, *caro*. I'm starving, and something smells good! What's for supper?"

"*Pierogi*."

Delectable Polish dumplings. I grabbed Wukowski's hand and pulled him into the kitchen, expecting a mess. The kitchen should have been full of dishes, but the counters and sink were clean.

"They're in the warming oven."

"You didn't have to clean up. You know the deal. When one of us cooks, the other has KP."

"Yeah, well, I didn't exactly cook. I warmed. My mom made a big batch and sent some with me. She said a working woman should have a hearty meal at night."

Okay, this was verging on the odd. Wukowski was an only child. I'd never met his mother. He seldom spoke about his family, except to say that his father was dead and his mother lived on the south side, near St. Josaphat's.

"That was very thoughtful of her." I paused. "Maybe I should call her to say thanks."

"Actually, Angie, this is sort of an opening salvo. Mama wants to meet you."

"Really? Must be in the air."

"Huh?"

"Let's sit down and talk while we eat." I loaded up two plates with *pierogi* and cucumbers in sour cream, which Wukowski called '*mizeria.*' He poured us each a shot of Sobieski vodka, a kick-ass distillation made in Poland, forty percent alcohol by volume. I learned the hard way to sip it slowly. The *pierogi* were succulent: a light dough with a hint of sour cream, filled with potatoes and meat, boiled and then pan-fried with onions. The cucumbers were a perfect accompaniment. When Wukowski asked me what I meant by "must be in the air," I set down my fork and sipped the Sobieski cautiously.

"It's like this. Papa called me yesterday to find out if you'd be joining us for Thanksgiving dinner. So when you mentioned your mom, it seemed ironic, given that Papa and Aunty Terry have escalated from hinting about you to outright demanding to meet you." I picked up my fork and took another bite, waiting and watching.

Wukowski gave me his crooked grin, the one that makes my pulse speed up. "Guess it's time to face the music, *moja droga.*"

Moy-ah drow-ga. My dear. Sweet words sound so much more romantic in a foreign language. I mentally shook myself. "The thing is, we've both been so busy, that I put off asking you about Thanksgiving. I promised Papa I'd call him tomorrow with an answer."

"Gee, Angie, I don't know. I can't leave Mama alone on Thanksgiving."

How sweet, that he was worried about his mother. I plunged into the ice cold relationship ocean, hoping not to sink in the 'too soon' undertow. "She'd be welcome to our meal, you know. It's sort of traditional turkey and dressing, with pasta on the side."

He laughed. "Ours is the same—but the side is kielbasa and sauerkraut."

"Pumpkin pie and *zabaglione* for dessert," I offered.

"Ditto the pie, with *budyn*—a pudding—and chocolate icing."

"Well," I said, "the food part sounds like it could work. What about the parents? And others? My kids and grandkids will be there. Too soon?"

"Maybe. I'm not sure about my mom. She might embrace you all, or she might feel out of place and shut down. It's always a crapshoot with her, when you get her away from the familiar."

"We can be pretty boisterous. But I know for sure that my family will welcome her and make her feel comfortable, if she lets them."

"That's the problem. Will she let them?"

"Why wouldn't she?"

He downed his vodka and poured a second shot, but let it sit untouched, like an ex-smoker who needed the reassurance that cigarettes were nearby, just in case. I could almost see the alcohol hit. Then he met my gaze. "Okay. Here's the short version. I had a younger sister, Celestyna. She was a beauty. Abducted and murdered when she was sixteen, walking home from a CYO dance at St. Joe's. It was a revenge thing. Some Polish south side teens insulted a couple of Latin Kings gang members. The Kings wanted to show that they didn't take crap, so they grabbed the first Polish girl they saw—my sister.

"The long and short of it is, Mama never really recovered. She lives in a very small world. Goes to church and shops, volunteers to visit shut-ins, coffee klatches with her neighbors. But when she's in a strange environment, she gets afraid." He paused. "And, in her mind, Sicilians are probably close to Latinos." He raised his hands, palms forward. "I know it's irrational. My sister was killed twenty-five years ago. Mama's been like this ever since."

And what about you? I thought. *First Celestyna, then Liz White, his assassinated partner. Small wonder he has an issue with women in dangerous situations.* "Then why does your mother want to meet me?" I asked.

"I'm sorry to say this, Angie, but I never told her your last name. I figured if you met first, she'd see what a great person you are. Then I could tell her about your family background."

"You mean, being Sicilian-American?"

"Yeah." His silence lasted an uncomfortable second too long. "That, and the Mafia connection. Mama thinks all gangs are the same. I know your dad's legit now, but let's be honest. Back in the day—"

"Papa was a minor figure in the Family, Wukowski. He didn't murder anyone or break any kneecaps."

"Maybe not. But my mom's paranoia might see it that way." He paused. "Let's play it out and see what happens. You tell your papa and aunt that we'll be there for Thanksgiving. Meanwhile, I'll introduce you to Mama. If it works out the way I think it will, no problem. If Mama can't handle it, we'll figure out an alternative. Like eating two Thanksgiving meals, one Polish and one Italian." He shook his head, smiling. "Has it occurred to you how strange this is, to still be worried about what our parents think at our age?"

"I don't see it that way, Wukowski. It's not like I'm going to let my father make decisions about my love life for me. But family is important to both of us, right?"

"Right." He downed his shot of vodka and pushed back from the table. When he came around to my side, I stood and moved into his arms. "Angie, my mom can be difficult. She caused a lot of trouble in my marriage. I don't want to lose you over this."

My heart did a back flip, coming to rest in my throat. Neither of us had spoken the *L* word yet, and I wasn't foolish enough to think that was Wukowski's intent. But it sure came close. I swallowed hard, aiming for a response that would reassure without giving the impression that I read more into his statement than he probably meant. "No worries, Wukowski," I told him. We stood, quietly embracing, his chin resting on the top of my head, my cheek resting on his chest. His heartbeat was strong and steady, like the man himself.

Then it sped up a bit. His hands started to caress my back in circles, moving lower and lower, until he palmed my bum and squeezed. "Thong?" he asked.

"Boy-leg with a low rise waist," I responded, clasping his head in my hands and giving him a come-hither smile. "Black lace over purple satin. Matching demi bra."

Damned if he didn't pick me up and carry me into the bedroom!

Chapter 8

Even if you start with 'Chapter One: I Am Born,' you still have the problem of antecedents, of cause and effect.
　　　　　　　　　　　　　　　—Hillary Jordan, *Mudbound*

Wukowski was still sleeping when I woke at six-thirty. My morning run was a no-go today. Not only did I want to make us both a big breakfast, but we needed to talk about the Johnson case. When I emerged from the bathroom in a short silk robe and fuzzy slip-ons, Wukowski was on his stomach, one arm flung out over my pillow. *Aww, he missed me. How endearing was that?*

I started a pot of coffee. Wukowski appeared in the kitchen doorway soon after. He'd pulled on his boxers, but was otherwise scrumptiously undressed, with his short brown hair sticking up at odd angles and one eyebrow pointing north while the other lay flat. *When did I start finding that appealing?*

I waited until he downed half a mug of java. "Pancakes and bacon?"

"Sounds great, but I need to get to the office. I'll grab a bagel on the way."

"Speaking of work," we said simultaneously. Then we each laughed nervously and Wukowski gestured at me to proceed.

"I was at the Johnsons' hardware store last night, nosing around..." I paused, loathe to disturb the sense of closeness from last night. "And I ran into the beat cops who found the bodies. One of them mentioned that the case had been assigned. To you."

"Yeah, um, I wanted to tell you about that last night, Ange, but I got distracted by your lingerie." He smiled. "Shelly Carlson drew it originally, but the day after the Johnsons' deaths, she gave birth to a little girl. The file got dumped on my desk. I barely had time to read it before..."

"Before you questioned Adriana and me."

"Right. I know I came down hard on you. It felt like you were keeping information from me. I can't let personal feelings get in the way of stopping a murderer."

"I wouldn't put you in that position. I want the killer caught as much as you do."

He cleared his throat. "Adriana stated that her family lived like they were on the edge of poverty."

"She had no clue about the inheritance. I'd swear to that. It wasn't until after the funerals that Petrovitch, their attorney, dropped the bombshell. And Adriana has no idea where the money came from. So not only is she dealing with grief over her parents' deaths, but she also feels betrayed by their living a lie. And she isn't sure she should even accept the bequest. In her eyes, it might be tainted."

I contemplated whether Bart would want the police to know his assessment of Dragana's murder and decided to plunge ahead. "You saw the crime scene at Petrovitch's office. When I described it to Bart, he said it looked like an execution, like Dragana was kneeling when she took the bullet."

He lifted his mug and took a drink. "Funny he would recognize that."

The inference was clear. I didn't respond to it. "I spotted the same pattern at the store last night. The blood spray across the front of the counter. As if the Johnsons were kneeling, too, when they were killed."

His mug clunked onto the counter. "That wasn't in the crime scene report."

"There's something else. The stock room floor had a thick layer of dust over it, like the techs never went in there."

"Damn it. I know they thought it was an opportunistic killing, but there's no excuse for shoddy work. I need to read the report again and get the techs back to the store. Did you go into the stock room?" I shook my head. "Good."

He picked up his mug. "We still need to talk about your working this case."

I waited, silent.

"My parents left Poland after World War II, trying to flee the Soviets. They raised my sister and me to follow the traditional ways. Women took care of the home and the family. Men took care of business and made sure their families were protected and provided for. I know you're a capable person, Angie…in my head. But my heart and my gut say that you're a woman putting yourself in harm's way, and that's hard for me to accept."

I nodded, thinking about what he said. We were both from the generation that had all our early values challenged by the women's movement. I struggled with it in my marriage, wanting not only to please my husband and be a good mother, but also to have something for myself, something I could claim as mine and not as collateral to a relationship. How could I fault Wukowski for his turmoil, when I still dealt with my own?

"Are you asking me to remove myself from the case, Wukowski?"

The silence was painful. It weighed on my chest until I found it hard to take a breath. *Please don't ask me to choose between being me and being with you. Not like my ex. Not again.*

It seemed like forever, before he answered. "I wouldn't try to run your life that way, Angie. Promise me this—don't get into a situation where you're in physical danger. No more stunts like you and Bobbie pulled in the Belloni case. If you learn something or even suspect it, come to me. It's not your job to put yourself on the line. It's mine. Let me do it. Okay?"

"I can't make a blanket promise, Wukowski. There might be a situation that requires immediate action. Or maybe, as a private citizen, I can do something that you officially cannot. But I promise to be vigilant." He started to speak, but I held up my hand. "That's the best I can do. Last night, you said you didn't want to lose me over issues with your mother. Well, I don't want to lose you over issues about my work."

The seconds ticked by. Then he pulled me up and cradled my head in his big hands. His thumbs traced my eyebrows, moved over my cheekbones and feathered across my lips. Neither of us had words, so we simply held each other and kissed, but not with the passion of the previous night. Something else resonated between us. It was, at the same time, both more elusive and more solid.

Chapter 9

A discovery is said to be an accident meeting a prepared mind.
—Albert Szent-Gyorgyi

After Wukowski left, I had a light breakfast of yogurt and fruit. Then I rang Bobbie's number.

"Whoosit?" His voice was scratchy.

"It's Angie. Bad night? Is Adriana okay?"

"It's eight o'clock on a Saturday morning. She's asleep. Like I should be."

"So is this your it's-too-early-for-my-bad-self-to-be-awakened routine? Or is something else in the wind?"

"Hold on." I heard water and the whoosh-thump-thump of Bobbie's coffee brewer. "Ahh. Caffeine. Nothing like it," he said.

"I agree. Now talk. Is Adriana okay?"

"Pretty much. We ordered Chinese last night and watched *Steel Magnolias*. I figured that a little bout of tears followed by an uplifting life-goes-on message would be a good thing. About ten, she went to her room. I watched the news in my bedroom. Letterman's top ten were starting when Steve called from New York. He's working on a new hush-hush project."

I smiled. According to Bobbie, the fashion industry was as plagued by espionage as the NSA.

"We talked until almost midnight. Then I decided to raid the fridge. That's when I heard Adriana crying."

"Oh, jeez," I said.

"Yeah. Sobbing her little heart out. So I knocked on the door and told her to blow her nose and wash her face and come out for some hot chocolate. I slipped a little brandy into the cups."

"Bobbie!"

"A medicinal amount, Angie. Not enough to get her sloshed. It helped her relax and we sat up until three, talking. She's really hurting. Not only over her parents' deaths. It's the betrayal that's hitting her hard. That they lied to her about the money and even worse, about the way they lived."

"Yeah, I got some of that from her, too. So what did you do?"

"Well, I tried to reassure her that her parents really did love her. But she wasn't having it. She was like a whipped puppy, all curled up on the end of my sofa." He sighed. "So I told her the sad tale of how my folks disowned me when I came out. How it hurt. How it made me feel unloved and unlovable."

I thought about how Papa disliked my being a PI. He'd never turn away from me, though. No matter what path I chose, he'd still be my papa. "I never knew, Bobbie. I'm sorry you had to go through that."

"Yeah, well, in a way, it was liberating. I didn't have to pretend any more or try to fit their expectations. That's what I told Adriana. That she could see it as her own personal failure and let it drag her down, or she could see it as their failure and move on, do what she wants to do with her life. I don't know if it helped, but she wasn't crying when she went back to bed. I tiptoed down the hall to check on her about an hour later and all was quiet."

"You're a good man, Bobbie. I'm glad you're my friend."

"Right back at ya, Angie. Not the man part, though!"

We laughed and I disconnected. I tidied the kitchen, took a shower and dressed. Time to visit the Johnson residence. A small note protruded from the phone pocket of my briefcase, reminding me to call Adriana's friend, Jennifer. I left my name and number on her voicemail, with a message that Adriana was fine, but her attorney was keeping her under wraps for the time being. Then I headed out.

Adriana's family home was in an area of Milwaukee's south side known as Polonia, rated "social and gritty" by MapQuest Vibe. Most of the "social" spots were on the north and west, with a local McDonalds the only restaurant in walking distance of the Johnson home. I could see the "gritty" as I drove—big areas of land devoted to railroad usage and I-94. The Johnson home was a small back house on the two-house lot, with a tiny yard and no garage.

The Miata clock showed 9:34. I sat in my car for a quarter hour, watching. All was quiet, almost eerily so. No kids playing outside, no dog walkers, no cars passing by. I extracted Adriana's key ring from my briefcase, leaving it open so that the gun holster was easily accessible, exited and locked the Miata.

The lot was fenced by chain link. I rattled the sidewalk gate, to see if any dogs would come at me. Nothing. I opened the gate and followed the concrete walk to the back house, shivering. Despite my warm winter attire, the wind from nearby Lake Michigan, damp and chilly, penetrated to my bones. Maybe it was time to pull out the silk thermal undies. *Nah, too soon for that. If I give in now, what will keep me warm when it really gets cold?*

I approached the small bungalow. Having already identified the keys for the hardware store, it was only a matter of seconds to unlock the residence's front door and enter. I located the alarm panel inside the coat closet and punched in the code. When it flashed "disabled," I locked the door behind me and pulled my handgun from its holster. I sensed no real danger, but felt edgy. Something was not right here, my intuition told me. I draped my coat, hat and gloves over a chair back as I entered the living room, set my briefcase on the floor, and took out a small, but powerful, flashlight. Then I stood, silent, waiting and listening.

Nothing. Not even the sound of the refrigerator cycling or the furnace kicking in. The house had that singular musty smell of being shut up for days. I walked further into the room, scanning, gun in my right hand, pointing toward the floor.

The furniture was yard sale quality—couch and overstuffed chair in a dreadful blue plaid, tan vinyl-covered recliner, lamps with stiff ruffled shades, a tube-model TV. On the walls were school photos of Adriana, a crucifix, and a yellowed print of Mary and Child. I ached for Adriana, being raised in this environment, when, all along, a better world was readily available. The dining room and kitchen were more of the same—outdated furniture and fittings.

I crossed the short hallway that ran down the middle of the first floor and entered the bathroom. The roller shade on the small window darkened the room. I set the flashlight on 'spot,' to avoid lighting areas that would be seen outside. The room was spectacularly neat, even though there was no counter or cabinet space, just an old porcelain sink, toilet and tub. I opened the mirrored medicine cabinet. Its shelves contained over-the-counter headache and heartburn remedies, an assortment of adhesive bandages and a tube of antibiotic cream.

A small linen closet held bathroom towels and washcloths, and three plastic bins, neatly labeled—Tata, Mama, Adriana. Each bin had a toothbrush and toothpaste, hair care products, combs, brushes, deodorant, and, in Adriana's case, a blow dryer, barrettes and headbands. A bag of sanitary napkins and a box of tampons were pushed far to the back, behind the women's bins. I remembered my daughter's high-school jumble of curling irons and hair straighteners, her collection of eye and lip makeup. This room was sterile in comparison.

Adriana's bedroom was tucked at the back of the house, behind the bathroom. It was a typical room for an older teen—ruffled bedspread and curtains, cheap white twin bed and dresser, stuffed animals, a poster of the Jonas Brothers and another of Ashton Kutcher—but I had to remind myself that she was twenty-four.

The parents' bedroom was small and very dark, due to thick shades and heavy draperies. Setting the flashlight to 'wide,' I scanned the room. It was crammed with oversized furniture. But what furniture! The bed and side tables were mahogany, carved and gilded. The headboard was upholstered in cream-colored silk, in a fanned-out pattern that complemented the arch of the wooden frame. The counterpane—to call it a bedspread would be a desecration—was a hand-embroidered pattern of birds and flowers on a cream linen background. The huge armoire, taller than me, left barely enough room to navigate around the foot of the bed. It would be difficult to change the sheets, given the space constraints. But that wouldn't matter, if one could sleep in that beautiful bed, in that exquisite room—in that ghastly house.

Where did this bedroom suite come from? I wondered. Even if it was the one precious thing they brought from their homeland, it was massive and would be costly to ship. *Did they have the cash in hiding, even then?* I ran my hand lightly over the carved wooden footboard. It was authentic and it was antique. I knew it.

As I turned to leave the room, my eyes fell on a small area in the corner, next to the armoire. There was an exquisitely carved half-moon table, on which rested a framed oil on-wood painting of Mary and the baby Jesus, but not the typical Italian master's Mother and Child scene. In this one, both persons had dark complexions, and the sad-eyed Mother gazed at the baby in her arms, who resembled a diminutive man, with proportions all wrong for a child. Next to it sat a glass votive candleholder and matches. It called to mind Aunt Terry's prayer space, with its kneeler, crucifix, rosary and Thomas Merton's *Book of Hours.* I resisted the urge to cross myself.

Back in the hallway, I heard a clunk and crouched, gun at the ready, scanning with my eyes. Then I felt the heat and heard the sough of air. The furnace had kicked in. I took a breath and waited for my heart to slow back down, before walking through all the rooms again to reassure myself that I was, indeed, still alone.

The hallway ended at a landing, with steps leading down to the basement and up to the attic. I decided to start downstairs. The basement held a washer and dryer, a wooden drying rack, furnace and water heater, and a worktable, on which sat a few hand tools. There were plastic containers in one corner, neatly labeled. Christmas ornaments, Christmas tree, Adriana—grade school, Adriana—high school. I went through the contents. They contained what the labels stated. Time to go up.

The attic was nicely warmed by the sun on its two dormer windows, one facing east and the other, west. The floor was solid, not just floorboards and insulation. I set the gun down and opened an old trunk. It held a mid-century wedding dress carefully folded in linen sheets and smelling of lavender. *Did Yvonne save it for Adriana?* I wondered. A wheeled clothes rack with a heavy plastic protective cover stood next to the trunk. Inside were two men's military uniforms, one camouflage fatigues with combat boots and the other, a dress uniform and shoes. With my phone, I took pictures of each and zipped the cover back up.

I used my height to estimate the size of a heavy-duty storage container that stood beside the rack. It was about five feet high by four feet wide and three feet deep, with a sturdy lock securing the front-opening doors. None of Adriana's keys worked. Perhaps it was on one of her parents' key rings, now in a police evidence locker. But maybe not.

Where would they hide a key to an attic storage unit? Given human nature, they would probably keep it close by. I scoured the attic again, this time lifting the wedding gown from the trunk and shaking it, then examining the trunk itself for a false bottom. I patted down the uniforms. Lastly, I turned the footwear upside down and shook. A smooth river rock, as large as my hand, fell out of one of the boots.

I'd seen such "rocks" in catalogs, touted as outdoor hiding places for a key. I found the seam and twisted the rock apart. Once the face was off, a digital lock guarded the hiding space inside. When I entered the alarm code, the mechanism opened—a reminder that using the same password or passcode is a bad habit. A key lay within the inner compartment. Rising from my squatting position, I tried the key in the storage unit lock. *Yes!* It opened.

Inside the unit were three homemade shelves on a homemade frame, each holding a flat box, and a stash of supplies on the bottom—boxes, paper, plastic sheet protectors, pens, tape and even cotton gloves, labeled "Archival, pH Neutral, Acid Free." I donned a pair of the cotton gloves and eased the box on the top shelf open.

Gold winked at me from a bed of cotton batting, upon which lay bracelets, necklaces and circlets with dangling coins. The style was heavy and ornate, with many curlicues and small drops of gold. Definitely not modern or Western. More Middle Eastern than anything else I was familiar with. I snapped some photos with my phone, replaced the cover and set the box on the floor.

The box on the second shelf held books, none in English. They seemed quite old. I gently opened the largest and gasped at the beautiful frontispiece, a hand-colored page of stylized patterns with what might have been Arabic or Hebrew letters. I took another photo.

The bottom box contained fabric within layers of paper. I took the top item out and let it shimmer open. It was a lovely deep red silk dress, floor length and embroidered in gold thread. I draped it over the garment rack so that I could get a good picture. There were five similar pieces in the box, with little matching pillbox-style hats and soft shoes.

I replaced everything, stripped off the gloves and put them in my pants pocket, and closed and carefully locked the storage unit. The key went on my personal key ring. As Poe demonstrated in *The Purloined Letter*, it's best sometimes to hide things in plain sight.

Downstairs, I replaced my gun, flashlight and cell phone in my briefcase. Then I put on my hat and coat, shoved the latex gloves into my coat pocket, reactivated the alarm and stepped outside, where I locked up and dropped Adriana's key ring into my briefcase.

My watch told me that it was eleven-ten. I was in the house for a little under two hours. Standing on the walkway that led to the street, I now saw signs of activity in the neighborhood—a boy riding a bicycle with training wheels, a man raking leaves. But the front house was still dark and lifeless. I made a mental note to find out who owned the properties and who lived in the front house, as I fired up the Miata and drove to Mickey D's for coffee.

While I waited in the drive-thru line, I called Bart. "I need to show you some pictures. From our client's house."

"I can meet you at my office in thirty minutes," he said.

"I'm at McDonalds. Can I bring you a coffee?"

"Sure. Large, with three creams and six sugars."

I shuddered, but it did no more good to talk to Bart about his weight than about his smoking.

It took about an hour to brief Bart on what I learned at the house. When I showed him the pictures of the uniforms and the storage bin, he asked me to load them on his office computer. Then he said, "Recognize any of this, Angie?"

"No. But I'll find out and get back to you. The uniforms are similar to U.S. issue, but something tells me they're not ours."

"For now, we'll prepare another statement for the police. I want Adriana to come in so she can tell us what she knows about these items. You make the arrangements with her and I'll call Bertha for the statements. I'll messenger those to Wukowski and let him know you have the key to the storage unit." I started to protest, but he interrupted me. "You may need to take another look. Wukowski can always get the key from you, right?" His grin was wicked. I ignored it.

Bertha was there within thirty minutes. "It's too bad that you had to come into the office on a Saturday. My apologies." I kept my voice cheerful, knowing it would irritate her.

"What can't be cured, must be endured." She compressed her lips and frowned. The lines from the corners of her mouth to her chin deepened, giving her a marionette appearance.

Bobbie and Adriana arrived soon after Bertha. "How are you?" I asked Adriana, giving her a real hug.

"I'm good, Angie," she said. "Maybe a little tired. Bobbie's place is great, but it's hard to sleep well when you're not at home."

I decided not to press her. It took a short while to review what I found in the attic.

Adriana knew about the wedding dress. "Never would I wear that on my wedding day," she said. She was ignorant of the contents of the trunk and rolling clothes rack.

Bertha joined us to capture our words in the lost art of stenography, for later transcription. I settled down to be deposed by a master. Bart knew how to frame a question to elicit the response he wanted. So the stash in the attic of the Johnson home, which I suspected was connected to the time before the Johnsons left Yugoslavia, became "personal jewelry, clothing and books of unknown origin." The bedroom furniture, which I presumed to be valuable antiques, was "a high quality bedroom suite and bed linens." I told Bart that I'd shared his suspicions about the killings being executions and he included that in the statement. Adriana's was simpler. She knew of the wedding dress, but not of the other items.

Bobbie and Adriana invited me to join them for a meal downtown and a movie at the Oriental theater. I pleaded work and left. The odor of cigarette smoke was making me feel slightly nauseated. I drove home and showered, ran a small load of wash and bagged my woolen slacks for the cleaners.

Chapter 10

In the spider web of facts, many a truth is strangled.

—Paul Eldridge

Half a ham-and-cheese on rye later, I settled at the kitchen island with my laptop plugged into the Ethernet—Wi-Fi is too easy to tap into, and I would have to provide credit card information to pay the county's fee—and accessed the Milwaukee County web site for property searches. "Serbian Society LLC" owned both houses on the lot where the Johnsons lived. A limited liability company, with the same name as the church group the Johnsons were part of. *Interesting.*

The Wisconsin Department of Financial Institutions is the place where all corporations, companies and partnerships who do business in the state must register. Their web site told me that Serbian Society LLC was formed in 1999, with Attorney Herman Petrovitch listed as the registered agent, organizer and manager. The Society's annual reports were not filed electronically, so I requested a paper copy be mailed to me.

A property search based on "Serbian Society" made my eyebrows rise. Both houses on the two-house lot, the hardware store and the buildings on either side of it were all owned by the company, as were

Petrovitch's home and the premises that housed his office. They were all purchased in 1999, the year that the Johnsons became U.S. citizens.

A new thought occurred and I went back to my case notes. *Aha!* Not only was the front house where the Johnsons lived vacant, but so were the buildings on either side of the Johnsons' hardware store, and the offices that abutted Petrovitch's. *It couldn't be a coincidence. Had someone built a buffer around all the places where the Serbian Society LLC had interests? What about Dragana?* I knew who held the power and had the most knowledge in any organization—the secretary. I needed to know more about Dragana.

Phone listings showed Josif and Dragana Zupan, with an address in Whitefish Bay. The image of her dead body, head blown apart, floated before me. I could smell the gunpowder and blood. My stomach turned and I breathed deeply and slowly. I rose and filled a glass with cold water from the fridge. The clear clean taste of the filtered water helped.

Back at the laptop, I accessed property records for the address from the phone listing. There was a single owner, Josif Zupan. No Dragana. No third party corporation. I had to talk with Josif, but my mind and heart resisted. If he was indeed Dragana's husband, should I tell him the truth about what I saw in the office that morning, or soothe him with lies? Would he know some of it already, from the MPD or even the funeral home? I was sure that her funeral would have to be a closed-coffin affair. I added to my to-do list: interview Josif Zupan. It made me feel more in control, to have it on a list. I could set it aside until the time came to cross it off.

As I reviewed the data, one thing stood out clearly. Herman Petrovitch was the spider in the middle of the web of crisscrossing threads. He was the agent for the Serbian Society, which owned properties involved in the Johnson and Zupan murders. He assisted the

Johnsons in establishing a new home in the United States. He knew the origins of their hidden wealth, according to Adriana. His secretary, Dragana, was assassinated in a manner similar, if not identical, to the Johnsons. Without Petrovitch, or at least more information about him, I was at a standstill.

Perhaps I should approach it from the outside in. Someone at St. Sava's Serbian Orthodox church might connect me to others in the Serbian Society. It was worth a try.

I checked my watch. Seven-oh-two on a Saturday night. The church's web site showed Saturday services at five-thirty. I went back through my notes. In our initial interview, Adriana mentioned Father Matthieu. Maybe someone would still be there to answer the phone.

"St. Sava's, Father Mah-tee-ya," the voice said, sounding harried.

"I'd like to get in touch with Father Matthieu," I responded.

"This is he." I paused, a bit confused, and he continued. "Matthieu is the Americanized version of my name. In Serbian, it's Matija."

"I see. Father, my name is Angie Bonaparte. I'm a private investigator, assisting Adriana Johnson in matters concerning her parents' deaths and her inheritance. Her parents' attorney, Herman Petrovitch, has disappeared. You may have seen on the news that his secretary was murdered."

"Terrible thing, the Johnsons' deaths. I officiated at their funeral. Mr. Petrovitch wasn't a member of St. Sava's, although he did much business within our Serbian community. I knew Dragana Zupan slightly. She sometimes worshiped with us, but she was not a member. May her soul rest in peace." He paused. "How can I help Adriana?"

"There's a group that meets at the church, the Serbian Society. Her parents were active in it, as was Attorney Petrovitch. Can you give me the names of any other members?"

"One moment." I heard the slide of a drawer and papers rustling. "Let's see. They applied to use the church in 2000. They meet on the second Tuesday of the month, in one of our smaller classrooms. The organizer is listed as Josif Zupan, Dragana's husband." I heard a short indrawn breath. "Ironic."

"How so, Father?"

"Well, let's just say that Mr. Zupan is not a believer, and did all he could to discourage his wife from practicing her own religious faith. A few months ago, when Dragana came to confession in preparation for Easter, he caused quite a commotion, shouting at her and trying to grab her arm and drag her out. I told him to leave or I would call the police."

Good grief. "That sounds like abuse to me."

"I thought so, too. After the incident, I offered to help Dragana find a safe place, but she swore that he never hurt her or spoke meanly to her. He exhibits great anger toward religion. That's why I'm surprised that he would meet at the church."

"Maybe it was someone else's idea." I thought for a second. "I hate to call Mr. Zupan so soon after his wife's death. Is there anyone else in the group I could contact?"

"Hmm. No one else is listed on the application to use the church property. Let me think." I heard the distinctive four-note sound of Microsoft Windows starting. "I'm searching for an early church bulletin announcing the group's startup. Ah! There were three initial participants: Adriana's father, John Johnson, Herman Petrovitch and Josif Zupan. I'm sorry, Ms. Bonaparte, but I think it will have to be Josif." He sighed. "You probably shouldn't mention that you got the information from me."

"Right. Um, Father, this is none of my business, but I'm wondering…will Dragana have a funeral service at St. Sava's?"

"I would be happy to conduct such a service, if Josif allows it. But I don't think he will. It grieves me, because she was a woman of faith and because her friends in the Serbian community deserve the chance to mourn her."

We exchanged contact information and I was about to thank him for his help when he said, "Now it's my turn to say this is none of my business, but exactly what does Adriana expect you to do about these murders? Surely that is the province of the police."

"I'm not investigating the murders, Father. Adriana needs help in determining how to handle her parents' bequest to her. If we understand the motives for the killings, it will help Adriana decide what to do about her inheritance."

"Forgive me, but I didn't think they would leave more than personal possessions. Unless there was life insurance. I hope so, for Adriana's sake."

So the Johnsons' lifestyle was no secret. The fact that they never broke cover spoke to me of either great guilt or great fear. "I'm afraid I can't discuss it, Father. But I think it's likely that Adriana will want to talk with you about it in the near future. She feels…uneasy about accepting it."

"Hmm. I will pray for her and for wisdom to counsel her, should she come to me. I will also keep you in my prayers, Ms. Bonaparte. Your life is not the usual one for a woman. May God protect you."

"I certainly hope so, Father." With that, I said good-night and hung up.

It was about quarter to eight. I called Wukowski, but it went to voicemail. I was impatient to know if there were any developments on finding Petrovitch, so I dialed Iggy's home number and got his wife. "Hi, Marianne. It's Angie Bonaparte. How are you and the kids?"

"We're all good, Angie. How's your aunt?" Last year, Aunt Terry sat at the hospital with Marianne while she waited anxiously for Iggy to come through surgery for a ruptured appendix. It was touch and go for a while. Aunt Terry is a comforter *par excellence* in dire situations. A bond formed between the two women, and they'd been active together in several of Aunt Terry's charities and social justice organizations ever since.

"She's great, Marianne. I want to be just like her when I grow up. Listen, I hate to impose, but can I get maybe fifteen minutes with Iggy? I need to ask him a question about a case."

"Sure. Hold on."

Iggy came on the line. "Hi, Angie. What's up?"

"Iggy, I called to ask you about Herman Petrovitch. I caught the department's APB announcement on the TV news. Any results?"

"Couple of false trails. The usual attention grabbers. Nothing real."

"Was his office rifled?"

"No. The files were in order. The computers didn't appear to be tampered with."

"Did he clean out any bank accounts?"

"He withdrew five grand from his savings. Petty cash for a guy like him. And there didn't seem to be anything missing at his home. Clothes, shaving gear, even medications were all where the housekeeper expected them to be. If it weren't for the money, I'd think someone snatched him, or iced him and hid the body. Listen, we're running down every possibility. I can't say much more. *Capisce?*"

"You turning Sicilian on me, Ignowski?"

"I'll be an honorary Sicilian, Angie, any time you invite us for your papa's spaghetti Bolognese." He smacked his lips.

I laughed. "I'll call Marianne to set up a date. And Iggy—thanks for the information."

"It works both ways. Call me if you turn anything up."

By then, it was too late to call Josif Zupan. I decided to catch him in the morning. At least I didn't have to worry about interrupting his Sunday church time.

Chapter 11

With lies you may get ahead in the world—but you can never go back.
—Russian proverb

Sunday morning. I tossed on some sweats and headed for the lakefront to run. It was seven o'clock and the sun was rising above the Lake Michigan horizon. The water was grey, with even swells and no whitecaps showing until the shoreline.

I took off on an easy jog for the first quarter mile, before breaking into my stride. I run about a ten-minute mile—pretty average for a woman, but good for a woman in my age group and size. I concentrated on breath and pace, willing myself to ignore professional and personal issues. Two miles out, I turned and headed for home. Four miles total. Forty-two minutes, including warm-up and cool down. Not bad.

After a shower and attendant body maintenance, I selected a beige bra and panty set and then slid into a smoky blue cashmere dress. The flesh-colored hosiery and dark brown pumps and bag reinforced my professional look. It was eight-thirty by the time I finished a cup of coffee and a small bagel.

I called Josif Zupan's number.

He answered on the third ring. "Yes?"

"Mr. Zupan, my name is Angelina Bonaparte. I was hired by Attorney Herman Petrovitch to assist a client. I was the one who found your wife's body, when I went to his office. Please accept my condolences."

"Why you call me?"

I pondered the possible answers, simultaneously wondering why he didn't ask me about the crime scene. Surely it would be natural to ask what I saw, to want to know if your wife died quickly or slowly, if she suffered or not.

As much as I hate lies in personal affairs, there are times in my work when lies are the best way to get to the truth. Today, the truth seemed best. "I'd like to meet with you. I need to understand why Attorney Petrovitch went missing and what it might mean to my client."

"That no matter to me, Ms....uh." His voice was gravelly, but toneless, the sound of a man without hope or a future.

"Please call me Angie. Mr. Zupan, I don't want to intrude in your time of grief. But my client's parents were murdered last week and she may be in danger, too. She's only twenty-four years old. I think you knew her father, John Johnson. Please, Josif, meet with me and talk. That's all I'm asking."

"Johnson? Jan Jovanović, you mean. Adrijana in trouble?" He sighed. "All right. I meet."

"I can be at your home in thirty minutes. Forty-five if I stop to pick up breakfast. Are you an egg McMuffin kind of guy or do you prefer bagels and cream cheese?" I kept my tone light.

"My doctor say it kill me, but I like the bacon, egg and cheese biscuit. I make coffee."

"Perfect. See you soon." I wanted to foster a sense of comradeship with Josif, so I bought a sausage biscuit with egg for myself. I swore that I would only eat half.

The home was a modest two-story with a detached garage visible at the end of the driveway. There were trees and shrubs, but no flowers. A screened-in porch fronted the residence. I parked in the driveway, juggling the McDonalds bag and my briefcase, with its holstered gun.

Before I got to the front steps, a wiry man with salt-and-pepper hair appeared and held the screen door open. "Ms. Bonaparte?" he asked.

"Yes." I nodded toward my package and briefcase. "Sorry I can't shake your hand."

"No problem. Please to enter my home." He stood about five-seven and probably weighed one-sixty. The tee-shirt he wore showed muscular arms and torso. His baggy sweatpants hid the rest of his build, but I suspected he had strong legs, too. He was a man who did regular physical work.

As we passed through the living room, I noted old-fashioned furniture, heavy and overstuffed, with dark wood trim and matching tables. The dining room was much the same—heavy, dark wood, ornately carved hutch displaying highly decorated china, chairs upholstered with tapestry seats. In all, it was an early twentieth century home, except for the discordant note of a large flat-screen TV.

I smelled coffee as I entered and the aroma improved as we marched through to the kitchen. Aunt Terry calls the kitchen the heart of the home. In the Zupans' case, it was so. The kitchen was the only room that displayed warmth or individuality. In the other rooms, nothing was out of place and there were few personal items on display. Here, it was the opposite, with bright blue and yellow dishtowels, a solid oak round table with captains chairs, a Thomas Kinkade calendar in a wooden frame, and cream and blue gingham curtains, drawn back at the bow window to display the rear lawn and vegetable garden.

Josif motioned to the table and I sat, while he put plates, cups and utensils down. "Coffee?" he asked. It sounded like "kafa." I nodded. He poured milk into a creamer shaped like a cow and set a pig-shaped sugar bowl beside it. I examined his face. It was dour, grim, with deep lines running from the edges of his nose to the edges of his mouth and a groove between his eyebrows. In this bright, happy room, he radiated unhappiness.

I opened the McDonalds bag and put our breakfast sandwiches on the plates. Josif filled our cups and sat across from me. "So, Angie, I know about Jan and Ivana's deaths. Why you are worried about Adrijana?"

Right to the point. No discussion of his wife or his bereavement. He was a man whose wife was killed violently. I wanted to proceed with caution. I bent down to remove a legal pad and pen from my briefcase, which I left slightly open, with my pistol within reach. One never knows.

I couldn't divulge information about the Johnsons' money, so I stayed with the basics. "Someone killed Adriana's parents in a way that suggests an execution. I have no idea why. Adriana may be in danger, if the killer wants revenge on the family for some reason." Then I placed the pad and pen on the table and reached over to gently touch the back of his hand. "I'm sure this kind of talk calls up your own grief. I'm so sorry about your loss."

I felt a small tremor, before he quickly moved his hand from under mine. "Very kind. My thanks." He gulped down some coffee and took a bite of his biscuit.

Okay, I thought, *we won't talk about Dragana*—at least, not right away. "How long did you know the Johnsons, Josif?"

He humphed. "Their name Jovanović"—he pronounced it yo-van-a-vitch—"not Johnson. But Jan—that is, John—he want to be all

American, put old country behind. We work together in Yugoslavia, lay bricks, you know?" I nodded to show I understood. "He come to America in 1999, me in 2000. I get work as laborer, then mason."

"How is it that your wife worked for Attorney Petrovitch?"

"He help get visas and promised work for Dragana so INS let us into country. She keep his papers in good order and work with Serbians here. She speak both Serbian and English well. Not like me." He grimaced.

"Josif, no one seems to know where Attorney Petrovitch might be. Do you have any ideas? Maybe someplace he liked to vacation or friends he might be staying with?"

He thought about it for almost a minute. "No, Angie. He man who keeps secrets, *da*? Even Dragana not know all his ways."

I took a bite of my biscuit. We chewed in silence for a few moments, but it wasn't strained. Josif's tight posture loosened a bit. He got up and refilled our cups.

As he sat back down, I asked, "What can you tell me about the Serbian Society, Josif?"

He stiffened again. "Why you ask?"

"I'm curious about why Adriana's father was so passionate about Serbian culture and heritage, given that he wanted to be 'all American' in other ways. I mean, he didn't even allow Adriana to maintain the language. Don't you think that's odd?"

He shrugged. "Jan like that. He run hot and cold, my Dragana say. He treat me like old friend when I first come to the U.S., then like that—" he snapped his fingers—"he no see me, except at Serbian Society meetings."

I decided to risk his ire. "I know the Society met at St. Sava's."

"Not my choice." Again, he shrugged. "We meet every month, talk about how to recover things stolen in war. Nothing special."

"I see." I paused. "Were you able to facilitate any recoveries?"

He rocked his hand in the gesture for "maybe." "We give information to museum director in Kosovo."

"Are you from Kosovo? You and John, I mean."

"No. Bosnia. But we are Serbs. Artifacts belong to Serbs, they go to Belgrade, in Kosovo, to National Museum there."

There were two potentially explosive topics I wanted to explore, the attic contents and the execution-style killings of the Johnsons and Dragana Zupan. I decided the executions were more critical and I would start with them. If he kicked me out, I could use other resources to research the attic items.

"Josif, I know this is hard to talk about, but I am worried about Adriana. Someone seems to be after something involving your wife, the Johnsons and Petrovitch." His face was closed, stolid. I didn't want to give him information about my findings on the Serbian Society or what I found at the Johnson home. Leading a witness, especially a reluctant witness, is a very good way to be lied to. I plunged ahead. "It seems the Johnsons had money in the bank, money that can't be explained by their small business, money that Adriana didn't know about." I waited a moment. "Did you?"

He leaned slightly to the left and looked down. His lips barely moved as he said, "*Ne*. No."

It was the classic body language of a lie. I forged on. "I'm worried that whoever is responsible for the Johnson killings will come after Adriana for the funds. You have a lovely home here, with nice things. Probably more than a legal secretary and her mason husband could afford on their salaries alone." He scowled at me, but remained silent. "Maybe you should be worried about your safety, too."

"They come for me, they be sorry." He spoke quietly, but it was a quiet filled with dreadful assurance.

"I searched the Johnson home, with Adriana's permission. There were two military uniforms there, one fatigues and one a dress uniform. Did John serve in the military?"

He hesitated. "Maybe. When I go to American embassy for visa, they ask for reference and I remember Jan. So I talk with his mother. But I not in touch with him before then, since six years. Maybe he joined army. Many did."

"Did you, Josif?"

"No. I not fight." He positioned his cup between us on the table and folded his arms across his chest.

I didn't believe him. The deadly aura with which he pronounced that anyone coming for him would be sorry, coupled with his very erect posture and ability to mask expression, made me think he was ex-military or had fought as a civilian.

"Can you tell me anything at all that might keep Adriana safe, or help locate Attorney Petrovitch?"

He shook his head. "*Žao mi.* I sorry. No."

"Josif, although I didn't know your wife, I was the one who found her, when I went to the lawyer's office." I waited for him to question me. His eyebrows rose slightly and his pupils dilated a bit. *Anger,* I wondered, *or surprise and shock?* He said nothing. "Do you know yet when her funeral will be? With your permission, I would like to attend as a sign of respect."

"Not sure. Police have body."

"Since you have ties to St. Sava's, I assume the services will be there."

He gave a sigh of resignation. "*Da.* St. Sava's. I do this for Dragana. Not because I want."

85

"You'd prefer another church?" I knew that wasn't the case, but I wanted to test his answer.

"*Ne*. No church. When I die, burn me and throw ashes. No priest. No church. No lying about love and forgiveness." Every word was clipped, taut with anger and…betrayal?

Let's see how far I can probe, I thought. "I know that churches and churchgoers don't always live up to their beliefs, but surely that doesn't invalidate all religion, Josif."

"You Americans, you know nothing!" His face twisted into an almost beastly mask of rage, but still he spoke quietly. "Your country never invaded. You never kill neighbor, shoot at innocent children. When you live through such things, then you tell me forgive and forget." He leaned forward, challenging me.

Words would probably not penetrate, but I decided to try. "Our country was founded on what we considered invasion by the British, Josif. And in our Civil War, not only did neighbor kill neighbor, but brother killed brother. As for shooting at innocents, children in this country are caught in the crossfire of gang war every day. It's true that Americans are privileged, but we've experienced our own tragedies. I've never been to war, but my work puts me in places where I'm sometimes pitted against bad people. The thing I have to remember is, they're a minority. And I certainly don't blame God for them. It's humans who act that way, not the Almighty."

Josif slowly let his breath out and sat back. "Dragana and you, you would be friends."

"I wish that were possible. I wish she could sit here with us and share coffee and stories."

"Okay." He nodded. "*Da*. I invite you to funeral. You come?"

"Yes. I come." I placed a business card on the table and asked Josif to call me if anything helpful came to mind. I also offered him assistance in protecting himself, but he laughed it off. I wrapped up the remains of my breakfast sandwich and left, calling Bart's voicemail from the car, to tell him I was safely away from the Zupan residence. *Josif,* I thought, *was a man with a terrible past that he had yet to come to terms with. But then, who among us has come to terms with all that is in our past?*

Chapter 12

I always pass on good advice. It is the only thing to do with it.
It is never of any use to oneself.

—Oscar Wilde

I went back to my condo, to change clothes before heading to Papa's and time with my family. Casual was the order of the day, so I selected skinny jeans, a cashmere cowl-neck sweater, classic blazer and brown leather ankle boots.

Sunday afternoons are a family ritual. After church, Aunt Terry goes over to my father's Bay View home, where they begin meal preparations. If I haven't been to church with Aunt Terry—and I probably attend only twice a year, once being Christmas Eve, because I love the carols—I arrive around one o'clock with a bottle of wine and dessert. My son David and his wife Elaine show up about two with their ten-year old twins, Patrick and Donald. My daughter Emma and her husband John arrive soon after David, with my namesake, Angela, now eight going on twenty-eight. Emma sighs when describing how picky little Angie is about clothes. I smile. The child is always quite well turned out. She takes after her *nonna*.

This Sunday was like most, with Papa's spaghetti Bolognese, Aunt

Terry's salad and breadsticks, and a couple glasses of the Montepulciano d'Abruzzo that I brought, its acidity a nice balance to the red sauce. After the meal, I usually go outside with the kids to kick a ball around or play a game.

Because Papa and Aunt Terry made a big deal at the table about my bringing Wukowski and his mother to Thanksgiving dinner, David took me aside after clean-up was over. "Mom, what's up with you and the cop? Is it serious?"

I thought for a moment. "Semi-serious, David. I mean, we're not seeing others, but we haven't made any commitments, either."

"Cops have a rep for being bad matrimonial candidates, Mom. They see too much. They grow emotional shells."

"We're not talking marriage."

"Not now, maybe. But don't you want that, sometime down the line?"

Did I? "I don't know. I'm taking it as it comes."

"So Thanksgiving's not about you two introducing the families and making a big announcement?"

I laughed. "Is that what everyone thinks? I better disabuse them of that idea. We're sharing the holiday because A, your *nonno* nagged me into it and B, Wukowski's mom nagged him into it, and C, he and I wanted to be together for Thanksgiving and we also wanted to be with our families."

I could practically see the flowchart forming in his geek brain. My David does something cutting-edge with computer programming, for which he makes an outstanding living. He also happens to be the proverbial tall, dark and handsome. I plan to advise Angela to set her sights on a geek someday—as long as he's attractive, like her uncle.

"Mom, you know I love Dad, but I'm not blind. I see his faults, especially about women." He blew out a breath. "I decided when I got married to ask myself, 'What would Dad do?'—and then do the opposite."

I grinned. "It seems to be working out well. You're a great husband and father."

David colored at the compliment. "Thanks, that means a lot to me. But here's the thing, Mom. There are lots of good guys in the world. Maybe you should open up to the idea of marriage again. Find a man you respect and enjoy being with."

"David, I happen to enjoy Wukowski." Now it was my turn to blush. "I mean, I enjoy his company. And I certainly respect him. Give him a chance, okay?"

"Okay." He stooped down and kissed me on the cheek. "You're still pretty hot, Mom. If he's not the one, don't wait forever. Move on."

How does a mother respond to her son telling her she's hot and advising her to find a man? "I'll think about it," I mumbled, and made a dash to the kitchen.

Aunt Terry and Emma were enjoying a helping of tiramisu, while Elaine sipped coffee. "Any more dessert?" I asked.

"Plenty." Emma proceeded to fill a small dish for me. "More?"

"No, thanks. I'm saving calories for Thanksgiving." As soon as the words came out, I knew I'd made a tactical error.

"So, Mom," Emma said, "tell us some more about Ted." Aunt Terry and Emma waited, spoons poised over their own dessert cups, as I took a small bite and swallowed.

"Well, he's an MPD detective. Homicide. I met him on the Belloni case."

"We know that, Mom." Emma made a gimme gesture. "What's he look like? How old is he? Is he romantic? Good in bed?"

"Emma Teresa!" They waited. *Okay, here goes,* I thought. "He's six feet tall and well-built, dark hair, reminds me of Dana Andrews in *Laura*." They both sighed and Elaine let out a woo-hoo. We'd watched the movie together several times. "He's a few years younger than I am." Six, to be exact. "He's not much of a romantic—too practical for that, I guess. But he treats me nicely." *Most of the time.*

"And?" Emma waited for a response to her final question.

What the heck! Emma was thirty-two and a mother herself. *"Incredibile,"* I said.

Emma pumped her arm. "Way to go, Mom!"

Aunt Terry's eyes widened and she covered her mouth with her hand. "Oh, my," I heard her whisper.

Elaine simply grinned. "Is it serious?" she asked.

"I just had this talk with your brother."

"You told David that Ted is good in bed?" Emma's brows arched high.

"Of course not! We talked about whether Wukowski and I are serious and I told him that we're seeing each other exclusively, but we're not making long-term plans." I scooped up the last of my tiramisu while they pondered that, and set my dish on the counter. "I have some work to do, so I'll go say my good-byes to everyone and head for home." I hugged Aunt Terry first.

"Be careful, Angelina," she whispered in my ear. She was the only one in the family at eye level with me.

"I will, Aunt Terry."

Emma's advice was the opposite. "Go for it, Mom."

"We'll see, *piccola.*"

Elaine gave me a Mona Lisa smile and said, "It's about time."

And so it went as I bade the men goodbye. With David's hug, came caution. With John's, encouragement. Papa had nothing to say on the subject. He already knew it would be wasted air. I'd proved to him many times over the years that I would make my own decisions, right or wrong.

As I bade Patrick, Donald and Angela goodbye, I promised that on the Friday after Thanksgiving, we'd go to the Betty Brinn children's museum, where they could touch and interact with the exhibits, followed by lunch out with *Nonna*. I'd already cleared it with the parents, who would spend the day either shopping or watching football.

Chapter 13

I have always imagined that Paradise will be a kind of library.

—Jorge Luis Borges

It was only seven o'clock. I could put in some time on the artifacts from the Johnsons' attic. The Milwaukee Public Library was closed, but UW-Milwaukee's Golda Meir Library was open until eleven p.m. My librarian's heart quickened.

Being a Sunday night, there was actually street parking available close by. I never park in ramps. There are too many places where someone can jump out at you and no one likely to be around to help or make a call.

The librarian on duty at the information desk had a scowl on her face, as she rapidly typed on the keyboard. I waited until she deigned to look up. "Yes?" she said.

I didn't think I should appeal to her as a former librarian. She'd probably hate me for getting out. Maybe authority would work. I showed her my PI license and the printed pictures of the Johnson's items and asked if the library had any material that might help me identify the uniforms, clothing or books.

"Hmm. We don't support the general public unless they have

university business or a referral from another library." She paused and glanced around. "But it's pretty quiet tonight and I'm bored to tears. And I've never met a PI in person." She stood up...and up and up. *At least six-two*, I thought, as she peered down at me. "You're pretty small for an investigator."

"You're pretty tall for a librarian." I smiled to indicate I was joking. "And being a PI doesn't take muscle. Most of the time, I outsmart them."

Returning my smile, she said, "I'm Lily March."

"Angie Bonaparte."

She cast her gaze to a table where some students were eating and others slept. Then she put a small sign on the desk: *Librarian will return in 15 minutes*. "Tell me about your case and I'll show you what we've got," she said.

I explained that I found the items at the home of two murder victims, who were killed elsewhere. Her eyes sparkled and she drew in a breath. "Wow, that's exciting." When I mentioned the Serbian connection, she pursed her lips and examined the pictures again. "The uniforms might be Serbian Army, but I can't tell. The women's clothes appear Middle Eastern. Why don't you start with the Serbian War and I'll try tracking down the books—they're my area of expertise. The writing on this cover is odd, a mixture of both Latin and Cyrillic alphabets." She handed the clothing pictures back to me and tapped her lips with her forefinger. "There's a visiting professor on campus from Sarajevo. She and her family lived through the siege." Lily gave a little shudder. "I remember the stories and pictures, after the city was liberated. Terrible. She doesn't say much about it, but she might talk to you."

I nodded. "I recall the awful intensity of the siege, but I'm fuzzy on details. Maybe I'll find a brief article while I'm here."

"Listen, if you need to check anything out, I can arrange it. I'll put in a referral for you now so it'll be ready when you want to leave." She looked at her watch. "We've got two hours and fifteen minutes until closing."

"I'd better get on it." Lily logged me into a computer workstation using a guest ID. While I missed the sensual pleasure of handling catalog cards in their narrow wooden drawers, I appreciated being able to search based on keywords, since I didn't have title or author. There was no material dedicated to Serbian army uniforms or even the Serbian Army itself, but there were hits for books that included or referenced them. I spotted a printer nearby and tried the icon on my monitor. Sure enough, the printer hummed and spit out a piece of paper. *Nice!*

An hour later, I had one very slim pamphlet, titled *Remember Sarajevo,* that I planned to check out and four books with paper tags marking pages with uniform details and pictures. I hauled them down to the main floor and located a pay-as-you-go copier. Two dollars later, I sat at a table and noted the book citations on each copy, then left the books on the table, as directed by signage. Only library personnel were supposed to re-shelve.

Lily was at the information desk, once again clicking away at the computer keyboard. Now, however, her face was intent and animated.

"Lily, I made copies of the pages I wanted, but I would like to check out this pamphlet, for background."

"No problem. Look at this—" she rotated the computer monitor to face me—"I figured out the language on that book. It's probably Bosnian, a language spoken by Bosniaks, the Muslims in Bosnia and Herzegovina. The other official languages are Croatian and Serbian.

No wonder they couldn't get along—different languages, cultures and religions, all forced into one political entity by the Soviets."

"Is that the same book as mine, on the monitor?" I asked.

"I think so, but I'm guessing, based on staring at the letters. It's a work of poetry, probably from the sixteenth century. If that's true, it would be valuable. I'm going to print this for you." She pressed a key and extracted a couple sheets of paper from under the desk. "Were there drawings or illuminations in the book?"

"I only opened it to the frontispiece. I didn't want to damage it."

"Probably wise." She stood and walked around the desk. "This has been the most fun I've had in ages. Listen, if you want, I'll talk to Professor Kolar and explain your findings and that you're trying to understand their significance. Let me make copies of the pictures, if that's okay, so I can show them to her and ask if she'll meet with you."

"Take these. I have them on my computer. But please keep all this confidential, Lily. Don't show the pictures to anyone else. I don't know if they tie into the murders, but in case they do, we need to keep it under wraps." I handed her a small notebook. "Would you give me your full name and how to contact you outside the library? And Professor Kolar's full name, too, please." When she handed it back, I tucked the notebook back into my briefcase and gave her one of my business cards.

"Here's a guest checkout card for you, Angie. It's good for two weeks."

"I'll be sure to have the pamphlet back on time."

She loomed over me, but with no sense of intimidation on her part. "Could I be present if Professor Kolar agrees to meet with you? I'd love to know more about the items and the actual case." There was a sheepish look on her face. "I read a lot of mysteries."

"Let me run that by the attorney I'm working for and I'll get back to you. It might help if you're there, especially if the professor is normally reticent about her experiences in Sarajevo. She might open up more." I extended my hand. "You've been so helpful, Lily, I can't thank you enough."

"My pleasure. Really."

I noted the time as I went through the checkout process for the pamphlet. Ten thirty-five. The family meal was seven hours ago and I suddenly felt hungry and tired and cranky.

The library didn't directly access the street. While I crossed the commons to reach the sidewalk and my car, I pondered whether there was something in the fridge to heat up, or if I'd have to make a food stop. Juggling briefcase and purse to pull out my key ring, I heard a sibilant noise behind me, to the left. Before I could turn, the blow struck on the back of my head. As I fell, I thought, *That's what happens when you let down your guard.*

Chapter 14

A true friend never gets in your way unless you happen to be going down.
—Arnold Glasow

I didn't lose consciousness—at least, I didn't think so. But I heard a piercing whistle and a woman shouting. Then Lily appeared, tall as a building, standing over me. "Angie, are you okay? What a stupid thing to say. Of course you're not okay." She scanned the deserted commons. "Wish I'd brought my cell phone out with me."

As she squatted down, I levered myself up, groaning. With my legs stretched out in front of me, I waited for the pain and vertigo to pass. Then I tentatively probed the back of my head. No blood, but a goose egg was forming and my whole head ached.

"If you think it's okay to move," Lily said, "we should probably go back to the library and call the campus police."

"I can move," I told her. "Nothing's broken. No double vision. Today is Sunday and the president is Barack Obama."

She nodded. "Let me help you up, in case you get dizzy. Then I'll gather your stuff."

I rose slowly, Lily supporting me, and saw that my briefcase was open and the contents were disarranged. *Not a thief. A thief would go for the purse.* I cautioned Lily to tuck the briefcase under her arm so that any fingerprints would not be disturbed.

We made our way to the library entry, where Lily barked at the student behind the checkout desk. "Call the campus police and tell them a woman was assaulted in the commons. Have them come here."

"Yes, ma'am," the young man said, and picked up a desk phone.

Lily assisted me to the information desk. "It's a good thing I came after you. I couldn't believe it when I saw a man standing over your body, rifling through your things."

"What did he look like?" The pain in my head was about a seven on a scale of ten.

"Hmm. Well, you were in the shadowy area between two of the campus lights, so I couldn't see well. But he had gray or white hair. And he wore a nice overcoat—dark, well cut, wool or maybe cashmere. His shoes were shiny leather—they reflected the light. And this will sound odd, but his hands were kind of opaque." Her eyes opened wide. "Gosh, I think he was wearing latex gloves. You know, so there wouldn't be any prints." She took in a deep breath. "There are a lot of muggings in the area these days, which is why I carry a whistle on my keychain. He took off when he heard the whistle and me shouting."

"I'm awfully grateful you were there, Lily. Why were you there?" I asked.

"Right after you left, I thought of someone who might know about the uniforms. UWM's ROTC course is conducted at Marquette University. The colonel who heads it up was part of the U.S. Army deployment to Bosnia. He gave a lecture about building a nightmare bridge there. I thought I'd catch you and give you his name and number."

I asked her to write it down before the campus police showed up.

"Let's not mention my business here tonight, Lily. I don't want an information trail leading back to my client."

The police officer was a young woman, earnest and diligent. She called me *ma'am*, despite my telling her to call me Angie. She checked me for concussion and was insistent that I needed medical care, which I politely, but firmly, declined. I went through my purse and briefcase under her watchful eye. Nothing was missing. She raised an eyebrow over my gun, but the concealed carry permit meant she couldn't object. I let her think that I was there to meet a friend who was finishing work on a paper, but who bowed out at the last minute. We agreed that I would sign a statement in the morning.

The officer was right about one thing. I was in no shape to drive. She assured me that she would tag the Miata so that I wouldn't get a ticket. I didn't want to call anyone in the family. Papa would find out and have a hissy fit. Ditto Wukowski. Lily offered to take me home, but her hours at the library included closing and I didn't want to wait around. I needed a shower, some pain meds and some soothing. I called Bobbie.

"Girlfriend," he said when I gave him the short version, "sit tight and I'll be right there. I'm five minutes away."

"Watch yourself, Bobbie," I said. "Don't be caught unawares like I was."

"I'll be careful."

Lily told him to park in the underground ramp, right next to the outlet door from the library basement. She emptied the paper refuse from her garbage can and used the plastic bag to protect my purse and briefcase from fingerprint contamination. Then she trundled me down and waited with me, quietly watching, but not fussing. I appreciated it.

Bobbie, on the other hand, started to fuss as soon as he got out of the car. "Angie, you're awfully white. Maybe you need a doctor."

"I already had that discussion with the police, Bobbie. All I need is to get into my jammies and take some Tylenol."

"You're coming to my place. You shouldn't be home alone tonight."

I was too exhausted from the post-adrenaline letdown and the pounding in my head to argue. It sounded nice, having someone watch over me. Bobbie knew how to pamper.

When we arrived at the carriage house, Bobbie put one arm around my waist and the other at my elbow and ushered me upstairs to a comfy overstuffed leather chair. Adriana was waiting, her face a picture of distress. She dropped to her knees beside the chair and took my hand. "Oh, Angie," she said. "I'm so sorry this happened to you."

Bobbie could see that her angst was raising my own. "She's fine, Adriana, except for a headache. While I bring her briefcase and purse in, why don't you get her some Tylenol and a big glass of water."

I gulped the pills down and closed my eyes for a minute. When I woke, I heard whispering in the kitchen. "I'm awake," I called, and Bobbie and Adriana appeared.

"How do you feel?" Bobbie asked.

"A lot more human than before," I told him. "I think the pounding has decreased from bass drum to bongo intensity."

"We were thinking that some food might get your blood sugar back to normal."

Suddenly, I realized how hungry I was. "Excellent idea. But nothing heavy."

"There's chicken soup," Adriana said. "My mama thought it was a remedy for everything."

I smiled. "My Aunt Terry thinks the same. Chicken soup sounds perfect." We sat together at the table, where I told them about the library and the attack, between spoons of soup and bites of bread sopped in the broth.

Bobbie drew me a bath in his two-person whirlpool, scented it with lavender bath salts, and placed a cup of chamomile tea within reach. "They'll help you sleep," he told me as he turned me over to Adriana, who assisted me into the bathroom. She giggled and pointed. "One of Bobbie's pajama tops. He told me he never wears the tops! It's black silk." I eyed the panties that lay on top of the shirt. White cotton. Blech. "Those are mine, of course. I thought Bobbie's boxers would be way too big. Now, I'll be right outside the door, so if you need help, call me. Okay?"

I assured her that I would and gently pushed her out the door. After shucking my clothes, which didn't seem any the worse for wear, I gingerly used a new toothbrush that Bobbie provided. Then I sank into the scented water and closed my eyes. There was something I needed to ask Adriana, but for the life of me, I couldn't think what it was.

I was drifting off when Adriana called, "Still okay?" I assured her that I was fine, dried off and put on the makeshift nightclothes. As promised, Adriana perched outside the door. "Point me to the bed," I told her. "I'm about ready to pass out on my feet."

She and Bobbie tucked me in. Bobbie asked me how many fingers he was holding up and checked my pupils and pronounced them even, but warned he'd be waking me every two hours to be sure I didn't succumb to concussion. He interrupted my protests with uncharacteristic firmness. "That's the price for not getting checked by a doctor." I could see there was no arguing with him, so I snuggled down under the covers and went to sleep.

Bobbie did indeed wake me during the night, peering at my eyes with a flashlight and doing the fingers test. I passed and went right back to sleep. When the sun woke me, I was surprised at the time. Ten-twenty. *Good grief!*

Since the Belloni case, I agreed to let Susan know if I would be late to work, so that she could contact Bart Matthews if I didn't show up within twenty-four hours. Sure enough, I had two voicemails from Susan on my cell phone, asking where I was and if I was all right. I called back and left a message that I'd had an encounter with a mugger and was now at Bobbie's, safe and sound.

When I sat up, there was no dizziness. *Good,* I thought. *I'll be okay to drive.* There was considerable tenderness where the assailant clocked me and the headache was certainly still present. I figured that a steady routine of Tylenol would handle both until the effects of the attack wore off naturally.

Bobbie was at the kitchen stove, flipping pancakes, and Adriana sat at the counter on a stool. I could smell coffee and made my way to the cupboard where Bobbie kept the cups. "You—" he pointed at me with the pancake turner "—sit."

"I'm not a dog, Bobbie."

"Sorry." He waggled the pancake turner. "You worried me, girlfriend."

"Thanks for worrying and taking care of me. But I think I'll survive with nothing worse than a headache for a couple of days. And I'm in serious need of coffee."

Adriana popped up, settled me at the counter and brought me a cup of Bobbie's fabulous Joe. Coffee is a sacrament to him—ordering special beans from a grower, freezing them until needed, grinding them fresh every day, brewing them in his French press coffeemaker. I'd heard him talk about it *ad nauseum*—but I sure appreciated the result!

Two cups and some pancakes later, I felt almost human. Bobbie and

I took our mugs into the living room and Adriana joined us with orange juice. I suddenly remembered what I wanted to ask Adriana. "What does Herman Petrovitch look like, Adriana?"

"Uncle Herman? Well, he's older, gray hair, about five-eight, average weight. There's nothing very special about him."

Gray hair, I thought. *Was it was he who bashed me?* "How does he dress? Outside the office, I mean."

"It's funny," she said, "my mama always teased him that he would dress in a suit and tie to fill up the gas tank. Why do you ask?"

"My assailant had gray or white hair and wore an overcoat of wool or cashmere, well-tailored, and shiny leather shoes."

"Oh, no. Not Uncle Herman." One hand lay over her heart, as if it hurt. "He couldn't…he just couldn't kill my parents and Dragana." She shook her head, as if that would negate the reality.

"We don't know if he was the one who hit me, Adriana. And even if he did, we don't know that he was involved in the shootings. It might be more than one person." But as I said it, my mind asked, *What are the odds that more than one person is involved?*

After I redressed in yesterday's clothing, going commando because my panties were no longer fresh and I refused to wear Adriana's granny panties, Bobbie drove me to my car. He was uncharacteristically quiet on the way. When we reached the campus, he double-parked and turned to me. "Ange, this case is a lot bigger than the Belloni case. You know I admire you—hell, I want to *be* you when I grow up—but this is seriously freaking me out. Three deaths and now an attack on you. Maybe it's time to rethink this one."

"I had that discussion with myself already, Bobbie. But while last night was nasty, it didn't cause me any permanent harm. The assailant could have shot me, picked me off right there in front of the library, but he didn't. He was searching for something he thought I had."

His eyes lit up. "Yeah, that makes sense. So what do you have that he wants? And do you really think it was dear Uncle Herman?"

"I'm not sure, on either count. I had copies of the photos from the Johnson house attic with me, but I gave those to Lily for further research. I have the originals loaded on my laptop. As for Petrovitch, either he's behind this or he's a victim, too. I can't decide." We exchanged kisses on the cheek, and I circled the Miata while Bobbie waited. Nothing seemed wrong, so I leaned into his VW Jetta and told him good-bye. He waited while I started the Miata. Guess he thought it might blow and he should be there to pick up the pieces—or join me, since he was parked alongside.

I drove to the campus police headquarters and signed the statement I made the prior night. Then I went home to my condo, where I shucked yesterday's clothing, put on a robe and checked my email. Nothing urgent. I had to let Bart and Wukowski know about the assault. Wukowski's call went to voicemail—again. *Where was the man?* I called Iggy.

After confirming that I wasn't seriously hurt, he chastised me for not contacting him the night before.

"The campus isn't your jurisdiction, remember?" I said.

"Maybe not, but if this is tied into the Johnson and Zupan murders, it's MPD business. Besides, you can always call a friend who happens to be a police detective, Angie."

Now I felt bad. I made my apologies and told him that a copy of the UW police report was available, if he wanted to request it. "Wukowski's been out of touch," I said, hoping Iggy would provide an explanation. He simply said that Wukowski was on a special task force that took a lot of his time.

Bart, similarly angry that I hadn't called him earlier, expressed it in a more lawyerly fashion. "Perhaps we need to rethink our goals and our client's needs, Angie," he said. "I can get some personal protection set up for both of you."

I snorted. "Won't that look good, a PI with her own bodyguard."

"Better than a dead PI. Or a PI with brain damage."

That was sobering, but I repeated my supposition that the attacker was looking for something and didn't intend to hurt me badly or kill me.

"Maybe. Or maybe he got interrupted and didn't want a witness."

"Bart, I'm making headway on the things I found in the Johnson attic. And I connected with Dragana Zupan's husband and the priest at her church. Let me do my job." I waited, holding my breath.

After an extended pause, he said, "I want you on the case, Angie. Be careful. And check in with Bertha so we can trace you."

I hated calling in to Bertha. She always made me feel so incompetent in the face of her own personal mastery. But Bart had a point, so I agreed and hung up.

Before I could set the phone down, it rang. Caller ID showed 'unknown caller." I decided to answer anyway. It could be connected to the case.

"Hello."

"Angie, it's Wukowski." He didn't give me a chance to speak. "Iggy left me a message that you were attacked, but you're okay. Listen, *droga*, I've only got about three minutes before the meeting resumes. I'm sorry I've been out of touch. We got a lead on the gang that killed Liz, but my captain wanted it turned over to Narcotics. No way am I letting them take this over. So I got sucked into this infernal team. Forgiven?"

"Of course."

"You really are okay?"

"Just a residual headache. Bobbie took care of me last night."

"Hell. I have to get off the phone."

I heard the click of his disconnect and set my phone down with shaking hands. Liz White had been tortured and killed by really bad guys. And now Wukowski was part of a team to find them and bring them to justice. This was what it would be like if we made a commitment to each other—me worrying about his safety, wondering if he would come home in one piece, dreading the department chaplain and Wukowski's captain at the door. By the same token, I knew he would worry about me every time I went on a job.

I sighed. It went with the territory. I didn't want to give up on this relationship. So I'd woman up.

My head was aching something fierce. I finally gave in, put on my oldest and softest flannel PJs, downed a couple more pills and climbed into bed. Before I fell asleep, I prayed that God would keep Wukowski safe. After all, Aunt Terry likes to quote, 'ask and it shall be given unto you.' I didn't know if God would grant my petition—it seemed like I only prayed in times of duress, and who wants to be a cosmic vending machine for favors?—but I figured it couldn't hurt.

Chapter 15

...life is but an endless series of little details, actions, speeches, and thoughts. And the consequences whether good or bad of even the least of them are far-reaching.

—Sivananda

It was two-thirty when I awoke. I sat up slowly. No dizziness, and the headache was background noise. Nothing in the fridge appealed, so I brewed some tea and toasted an English muffin. I settled in the living room with my snack, enjoying the view of Lake Michigan from the wall of windows. Today was sunny and the lake was a brilliant blue, with small breakers creaming the shoreline. I sipped and munched, and let the rhythm of the water soothe me.

Twenty minutes later, I levered myself off the couch and showered. Paperwork awaited me at the office and I needed to check the briefcase for prints. Lily might have been mistaken in thinking the attacker wore gloves.

I had no clients scheduled and didn't plan to interview anyone, so I dressed simply in French blue wool slacks, a stone-colored turtleneck and a navy wool blazer with a small herringbone check in fuchsia. Black ankle boots were the final touch. I left a message for Bertha and headed out, briefcase in a garbage bag under my arm.

My office building was quiet. When Susan and I decided to start up our separate but conjoined enterprises, I deliberately selected a building with no security guard or cameras. There are people who don't want the fact that they're doing business with a private investigator on film or even noted in a guard's log.

However, during the Belloni investigation, a threatening letter was delivered to my desk when the office was supposedly locked. That's when Susan and I had intruder-resistant doors and an upgraded alarm system installed. If someone really wants to break in, it's possible, but it's a lot of trouble and the police don't respond like they do to a 9-1-1 call. False intruder alarms are so common that they don't get a high priority.

The office door was locked, so I assumed that Susan was either with a client or in the ladies' room. We were careful to keep the door locked when neither one of us was there. No signs of someone trying to jimmy it, so I unlocked it and stepped inside, where I reset the alarm and relocked the door behind me.

I settled at my desk and plugged in my laptop. There were invoices to be sent for work completed—a runaway teen found in Rhinelander, where her boyfriend attended UW, and some background checks for a local landlord who'd been burned once too often by deadbeats or felons. Lastly, I updated my Quicken books.

I pay Susan to do my taxes. She would have my hide if the books didn't balance when I forwarded them to her in early January. I got a reduced rate because I did the initial data entry myself. Folks who show up with a shoebox full of receipts were both the bane of her accountant's heart and money in the bank—cha-ching for every hour spent on their disorderly little financial lives.

With the routine work out of the way, I took the bagged briefcase and my small fingerprint detection kit into the conference room. Donning latex gloves, I removed the briefcase from the garbage bag and set it on the table, atop the spread-out bag.

Since reading about the nasty germs that linger on the bottom of women's purses, I developed the habit of wiping down my briefcase and purse once a week. Any prints on either should be mine or the assailant's. Since I always carry the briefcase by its handles, I thought it doubtful that my prints would be on the sides, so I started there, dusting powder from the kit over the leather surfaces. As I suspected, no latent prints appeared. Next, I dusted the handles, which were rolled leather. I'd chosen the briefcase partially for the comfort of the handles. However, this style meant prints were unlikely. As I suspected, there were some blurry palm prints, but nothing more.

I checked the zipper tab, removed the contents and dusted the inside surfaces. Smudged prints were all that appeared. That wasn't surprising, since one doesn't need to put one's fingers or palm against the inner surfaces when placing or removing items. The gun holster did show prints on the flap, where one would unsnap it, but they were mine.

The next job was to dust the contents. Fortunately, I'd only had my gun, my concealed carry permit, a steno pad and my tablet PC with me. I no longer hauled a lot of paper around, thanks to my nifty new toy, the tablet. I didn't want to contaminate it with the dusty powder and I didn't have chemical reagents in the office. I thought it was probably a moot point, anyway, since I believed Lily's assessment. Furthermore, the assailant only had seconds to search before Lily appeared.

So much for technology.

After cleaning off the case and contents, I carefully turned the garbage bag inside out, to keep the fingerprint dust from settling everywhere. Then I tied it, exited the conference room and tossed it into the garbage can beside my desk. Placing the briefcase next to me, I extracted the steno pad and sat down to make a list of my next steps:

- Find out if Susan or Bart uncovered anything about the Johnson finances
- Call Colonel Lewis at Marquette University
- Find out about Dragana's funeral
- Observe the Zupan residence
- Talk to Aunt Terry about what I should bring to the Thanksgiving meal

It seemed like I was forgetting something, but darned if I knew what. I rubbed my temples. The back of my head ached, but I couldn't rub there. The goose egg was too tender.

As I stared at the list, I heard Susan's voice coming down the hallway. *Was that Bobbie's voice, too?* The door opened and Susan stepped in, disarming the alarm.

"Angie's here, Bobbie," she spoke into the hallway.

He marched in. "I expected you to stay home today, Angie." Hands on his hips, he glared at me.

"Time and tide wait for no woman."

"Don't give me your librarian quotes, girlfriend. What are you doing here?"

"There were things I needed to get done today, if I want to be paid by the end of the month. And I also dusted the briefcase and contents for prints."

He sat in my side chair and leaned forward, eyes sparkling. "Anything?" he asked.

"Nope. I'm afraid Lily was right. The perp wore gloves."

He sighed. "Too bad." He saw the notes on my desk. "Making a list?"

"You know me too well."

"There must be something there I can do. Please."

"You're already helping by watching over Adriana." I straightened up abruptly and regretted it when a small wave of pain moved down my neck and up my skull. A breath later and it was gone. "Where is she?" I asked.

"Well, we had a little talk after we put you to bed last night. See, Adriana's always felt like the ugly duckling. But I can see there's a swan under that Plain Jane exterior. So I took her over to Kevin's salon for a makeover." He raised his right hand, palm facing me. "Now, don't fuss, Angie. I told them to keep her out of the front of the salon and that the makeover needed to be subtle. She's as safe there as she would be at my place. After all, if a guy comes at her with a gun, all I can do is call 9-1-1, and they can do that at the salon, too."

"I suppose," I conceded. "And I would love to see her a bit more stylish, like a modern young woman and not someone who recently emigrated from the old country with two dresses to her name."

"So, Angie, what's on your list that I can help with?"

Bobbie, like Lily, is fascinated by the idea of private investigation. He has no idea how routine it can be. I checked the list. Observation on the Zupan residence jumped out.

"What time will Adriana's appointment end?" I asked.

He checked his watch. "It's four thirty-five. I'd say she'll be there until six."

"Okay. Here's what I need." After telling him I would pick up Adriana, I gave him the Zupan address and instructed him to park on the main street that intersected the cul-de-sac the Zupans lived on and log every vehicle that entered or left—license plates, make, model, color, distinguishing characteristics—and to also log any occupants. I ran a quick query on Herman Petrovitch's car, a year old Mercedes-Benz E-class, and printed the particulars for Bobbie. If he saw the vehicle, I wanted a call ASAP. If he simply spotted a gray-haired man, I told him to unobtrusively get a picture with his cell phone.

"Wow! I get to do surveillance!"

I hated to deflate his enthusiasm. "Take a book or something to do. It can get boring. And be sure to pee before you get there. Don't drink anything while you're in the car, unless you're willing to use the container as a waste receptacle later. If you do, be discreet. A guy I know was arrested for indecent exposure when he had to urinate in his car. And if anyone seems to be watching you, drive away. Your safety is worth more than the information. Got it?"

"Got it, Angie. I won't let you down." He jumped up from the chair and softly kissed my cheek. "And you be careful, too. Don't overdo, okay?"

"I promise. I'm going to pick Susan's brain about the Johnsons' bank accounts, get Adriana, take her to my condo, and call for some Chinese."

"Chinese *food*," Susan corrected me. "Unless you plan to have an orgy with some Chinese men."

"Nope," I said, laughing. "My body's not up to it tonight. Not to mention that Adriana is most likely a virgin."

Bobbie gave me the naughty-naughty finger shake that Aunt Terry perfected during my childhood, and left.

I turned to Susan, who sat at her own desk across from mine. "Have you uncovered anything about the Johnsons' finances? How the heck they got all that money? By the way, exactly how much is there?"

She handed me a one-page printout. The spreadsheet showed fifteen accounts, five local, in New York, Chicago, LA, Miami and Milwaukee; the rest offshore in Toronto, Switzerland, London, the Caymans, Singapore and Sydney. I closed my eyes and visualized a map. "Someone wanted the money to be geographically available in all areas of the globe. And at points of entry, like ports or major airports." I perused the sheet again. The bottom line was impressive—close to six-hundred million dollars. *Good grief,* I thought. *How could they sit on that all those years and live the way they did?* "Which is the account Adriana can draw on?"

Susan indicated a local Milwaukee bank, with an account balance of two hundred and sixty-six thousand. The spreadsheet showed it as 0.0044% of the current total balance. I had to reach back to my grade school math to interpret it. Forty-four ten-thousandths of one percent.

"Let's take this in the conference room," I said. Susan locked the office door and we sat, side by side, with the spreadsheet on the table in front of us. "Susan, how much can you disclose to me? Were you hired by Petrovitch?"

"Not exactly," she said. "He sent Adriana to me for financial advice, with this overview of her assets. But before he could ask me to work for him, he disappeared. Adriana's the one who authorized me to act for her. She's my client and I want to protect her interests, so I'm willing to disclose what I know, since you're working for her attorney."

"Fair enough." I gestured at the printout. "Where did the funds originate? Are more funds coming into the accounts? Are there disbursements? Who has control?"

"All the accounts except for the one Adriana can draw on—let's call it her account, for simplicity—were set up in 1999, with the Johnsons as the principals and Serbian Society LLC as cosigners."

I went back to my desk and grabbed my tablet, where I found the initial interview with Adriana. "That was the year the Johnsons became citizens. It was also the year the Serbian Society was formed." I glanced at Susan. "There's got to be a connection. Especially since Petrovitch was named as their registered agent."

"I agree," she said, "but unless we can prove fraud or crime, the banks aren't going to open up to me about how the money was deposited or what activity the accounts have. Adriana will have to approach them."

"Or her attorney. Bart can sic Bertha on them." A little sense of glee lit up my sore head. Better them than me.

"True." She paused. "Adriana's account is different. It was opened in 2010, the year Adriana turned twenty-one. She and her parents were signatories. I wonder if her parents wanted to be sure she'd have something to fall back on, in case they…" Her voice trailed off.

"In case they died," I finished for her. "We need details." I checked my watch. Six-fifteen. Time to pick Adriana up at the salon. "Can I keep this copy of the sheet?" Susan nodded. "I'll get Adriana's permission to share it with Bart. Tomorrow, we'll go to his office to sign papers for the various banks, so they'll disclose account information to him."

As I drove to Kevin's, I pondered the financial trail. Someone put a lot of money into banks throughout the U.S. and the world in 1999. They set the Johnsons up as account signatories. Judging by how they lived, the Johnsons never took a dime. *Loyal, or scared?* I wondered. Suddenly, the meager measures we'd taken to protect Adriana seemed hugely inadequate. I gave the Miata a little more gas, wanting to see for myself that she was safe and sound.

Chapter 16

It's a new challenge to see how people can change your look. I like words like transformation, reinvention, and chameleon.

—Naomi Campbell

Kevin's salon was a very high-end place, one of the most recognized—and expensive—in Milwaukee and environs. I pulled into a curbside parking space, thankful that I didn't have to fight the daytime crowds. The chic young man at the front desk greeted me with, "Love the hair, but it can use a trim and some new styling products."

"Not today, thanks, but I'll think about it. I'm here to pick up a friend. Bobbie Russell brought her in for a makeover. Adriana?"

The receptionist's eyes glazed over. "Ahhh. Bobbie."

"Right," I said briskly, to snap him out of his reverie.

"This way." He stood and indicated a curtained-off area.

I swear, without his guidance, I wouldn't have known it was Adriana, except that her clothes hadn't changed. But the hair, the face, even the nails! Understated sophistication and devastatingly different from her "before" look.

When she noticed me, Adriana turned away from the mirror and ran to me, hugging me and causing my head to pound. I sucked it up.

She deserved to celebrate.

She pushed back, still with her hands on my shoulders, and, sounding very unsure of herself, asked, "Like it?"

"No," I told her. "I LOVE it. Wow! Just wow."

Her mousy brown hair, normally in a ponytail, was now a glowing russet mass of swingy layers that flattered her face to no end. And the face was no longer young teen, but young woman. Subtle foundation evened out her olive complexion. Equally subtle blush and highlighter defined her cheekbones. And for the first time, the girl had eyelashes— long, lovely, curled, and mascaraed. Bronze eye shadow and natural pink lip gloss finished the look.

As I stared, Adriana began to blush. "It's not too much, is it?"

"It's perfect," I assured her.

A man came into view, his hand held out. "I'm Kevin," he said.

The man himself. I silently calculated how much this would cost. It was worth every cent. "Angie," I told him my name, as we shook hands. "This is…I mean, she's…" I sighed. "Fabulous."

Kevin smiled and gestured toward a very large salon bag. "Those are to make sure she stays that way. Instructions included." He turned to Adriana. "Remember, you'll need a trim and touch-up every six weeks, more if your hair grows fast."

She nodded. "I will, I promise." Her eyes sparkled with unshed tears.

Kevin embraced her in a gentle hug, flipped her hair slightly and said, "So lovely." Then he ambled out, opening the curtains on his way.

"Tip?" Adriana mouthed.

"Not for the owner," I whispered, "but for the persons who shampooed and polished and so forth. They all get a tip. I usually split twenty percent among them."

Adriana paid the damages at the front desk. She then asked the receptionist for an envelope, wrote a note on the outside, added a short list of names, and inserted her tip money. *Nice touch*, I thought.

Outside, I settled her in the Miata, with the salon's bag between her feet. As I started the car, I glanced over. Honestly, it was hard not to stare at the transformation. "How about we head to my condo and order in? I was thinking Chinese, but if you don't like that, we can order pizza." I chastised myself for not remembering Susan's comments about the difference between Chinese and Chinese food.

"Chinese is great," Adriana told me.

I showed Adriana how to use my tablet—another technology that she never learned—and asked her to order while I drove. When we arrived at my condo, she wandered around the living room, taking in the view of Lake Michigan and checking out the family pictures, framed and nestled among the books in my custom bookshelves.

I called from the kitchen area. "Something to drink?"

"Mmm—maybe a diet soda?"

"Coming up," I told her. I carried her glass and my water into the living room and sank onto the sofa, glad to be off my feet. She turned from the bookshelves in time to see me chug some Tylenol.

"Oh, Angie. I've been so caught up in my makeover, I never asked how you were feeling."

Points to her for recognizing the lapse. At her age, after a major makeover, I would have been caught up in myself, too. "Not bad," I told her. "Just a bit of a headache."

She took a seat in the chair at right angles to the sofa, shucked her shoes and tucked her feet up underneath her. "Where's Bobbie?" she asked.

"On a surveillance job, watching the Zupan home to see if Petrovitch shows up."

"Surveillance, huh? I bet Bobbie was thrilled."

I laughed. "He was. But one'll get you ten that he won't be as thrilled when he gets done. Surveillance is plain boring. All you do is sit and watch. You can't even get too involved in a book, in case you might miss something. I usually spend the time making up stories about the personal lives of people I see going by."

"Boy, I bet you could write a book."

"Not me. I love to read, but I don't have the author gene myself. A woman's gotta know her limitations." The intercom rang and I excused myself to go downstairs for the food. I never buzz people into the building unless I know them personally. There's more safety in meeting a stranger in the lobby, and fewer opportunities for someone to drop off the order and then wander around, looking for a chance to do harm.

When I came back with the bag in hand, Adriana had plates and flatware out on the dining table. "I hope you don't mind that I was in your cupboards," she told me.

"Not at all. Thanks for taking care of it." I asked Adriana to open the little white cartons while I made tea. I took a couple of linen napkins from a drawer and placed them on the table. "Tea will be ready in a few minutes. Dig in," I told Adriana. "Let's not stand on ceremony."

The egg rolls were scrumptious, with a hint of peanut sauce in the fry batter. I dipped mine in a combo of sweet and sour mixed with hot mustard sauce, but Adriana smothered hers in the sweet and sour. We each enjoyed some beef and broccoli and chicken fried rice. Adriana found the kung pao chicken too spicy, so I ate the majority of it. Our small cups of tea were replenished several times from my majolica teapot.

Of course, the meal had to end with fortune cookies. I motioned to Adriana to choose first. She tore open the wrapper, split the crunchy shell and extracted the slip of paper. Laughing, she read aloud: *If you don't have time to live your life now, when will you?* She handed it to me. "That is so true, Angie." Her face sobered. "I hate to admit this, but since my parents died, I feel a real sense of freedom, of possibilities. It's not that I didn't love them, or that I don't miss them. But I feel like I never really knew them." She sat back, quiet.

How could they hold back their own daughter like they had? I reached across the table and placed the fortune in her hand, squeezing it gently. "Adriana, I understand your conflicted feelings about your parents. Even at my age, I have those conflicts, too. There's a part of my papa's life that isn't hidden, like your parents', but which he's never let me into, probably for my own good. Even so, I feel a little alienated from him at times."

"Really?"

"Really." I sensed that she needed more from me, but didn't want to ask. "Like your folks, Papa was an immigrant—from Sicily. Some men on the east coast got him work in Chicago. He ended up in the fruit and vegetable business here in Milwaukee. It was a legit business, but with ties to the Mafia. He only talked about it once with me. Nowadays, he's retired from both."

Her chin wobbled a bit, but she didn't cry. "Thanks for telling me that, Angie. It helps." She set the fortune on the table. "Your turn."

Mine was a doozy: *You are going to get new clothes.* "Oh, wow, this is a great fortune for a clothes freak like me," I read out loud. She was dressed in yet another fade-into-the-background outfit. "How about we do some shopping?"

"That would be so great!" she said. "I really want to look put together, like you do."

"Well, I appreciate the compliment. But you need to dress a little younger than I do. Maybe some clothes for campus, if you're going to enroll in nursing school." Her eyes widened. "And something nice for a dinner date or church. And some bumming around clothes. And lingerie." I inwardly shuddered, remembering her granny panties.

While I packaged leftovers and put them into the fridge, Adriana rinsed the dishes. Then my phone rang. I barely said hello when I heard Bobbie's breathless voice. "Angie, I found him!"

"Petrovitch?"

"Yeah. He drove by the Zupan house twice—kinda circled at the dead end. He didn't go in."

"Did you get the make and model of his car?"

"I did better than that, Angie. I got the license plate, too."

I could almost sense him wriggling with excitement. "Excellent! Are you still on the street outside the residence?"

"Well…um…actually, no. I tried to follow Petrovitch."

"Bobbie!" I was aghast and let my voice show it. "The man may be a murderer!" I glanced over at Adriana, who was listening intently. She didn't seem scared, but mouthed, "Is he okay?" I nodded.

"I was careful, Ange. I stayed three cars behind him, like it says in all the mystery novels." He paused. "Problem is, I lost him."

"At a light?"

"Um…no. He may have spotted me. I mean, he took a lot of turns. Some even brought him back to an earlier position."

"I see. Well, it's possible that he's very cautious and always drives like that. Anyway, come on over to my condo. We have leftover Chinese food and you can give me the details on the car." I gave him the code for the parking garage entrance and my space. "Pull inside and double park behind the Miata, in case Petrovitch did spot you and decided to tail you."

"I should have thought of that, Angie. I don't want to lead him to your place."

"He already knows I'm working for Adriana. He can find me if he tries hard enough. And it's probably overkill on my part." After we hung up, I filled Adriana in on the conversation and asked, "Are you okay?"

"Yes. I am. In a way, I'm glad to know that Uncle Herman is still alive. I can't picture him as a murderer, Angie."

"He's obviously involved in some way, but let's hope it's not that." I grabbed my keys and told her I'd be back in a moment with Bobbie.

Adriana was loading the dishwasher when we walked in from the underground garage.

Bobbie didn't say a word. He took her by the hands and gently pulled her into the living room, where he circled her quietly, pausing, nodding, making little mm-hmm sounds, flipping her hair behind her ears and then forward again.

I felt like a teacher whose prize pupil was one word away from winning the National Spelling Bee. *C'mon, Bobbie*, I silently urged, *say something*.

He did. Standing in front of Adriana, he took a deep breath, flung out his arms and said, "You're beautiful, girl!"

She blushed and released the fists she made during his examination. "Oh, Bobbie, I really love it! I can't thank you enough for taking me to Kevin's. I'd never have gone there myself." Tears welled up in her eyes and she reached for Bobbie. They hugged, then opened their arms and welcomed me in. We were all weepy.

After we settled down, Adriana asked him, "Are you hungry?"

"Ravenous."

She filled a plate and put the tea kettle back on the burner. I smiled as I plugged my laptop into the internet connection, logged in, and sat down at the peninsula that separated the kitchen from the dining room. Adriana seemed like a natural caregiver—a good trait for a nurse.

Bobbie sat beside me at the counter.

"Give me the make, model and plate of the car you think Petrovitch was driving," I told him.

He pulled a small notebook from the inner pocket of his narrow wale corduroy jacket, flipped it open, and placed it on the counter.

I was impressed. He must've recorded information about every car that turned onto Zupan's dead end street. Not only that, he included the time. "Nice work, Bobbie."

He gave me a big smile. "Really?"

"Really," I affirmed. I scanned the entries. Only one car was there more than once. I pointed to it. "Is this the car you followed?"

"Yep."

It was an Illinois plate. I brought up the website I use to get DMV records. You have to be authorized and pay an annual fee to use it. "Look away, please," I told Bobbie and Adriana, who'd circled to stand behind me. I hated to let them think I didn't trust them, but time and circumstances can alter trust. Explanations would only make it worse, so I simply logged in and said, "Okay. I'm in."

I entered the plate number. The record that came back was for a 2002 Buick Park Avenue, black, four-door. I checked Bobbie's notebook. It tallied. The owner was listed as Oliver Wendell Peterson, with an address in Glenview, Illinois.

Behind me, Adriana spoke. "Peterson—that is the American form of Petrovitch."

"Interesting," I said. "Oliver Wendell Holmes was a prominent lawyer who served on the U.S. Supreme Court." I swiveled so I could speak to both of them. "Maybe this is an alias for Petrovitch."

I expected Bobbie to be bouncing up and down, but he sat quietly, with a serious expression on his face. Finally, he spoke. "That would be a real break in the case, right?"

"Absolutely."

"What's next? I could do surveillance on the Illinois address." He looked me in the eyes, chin up, shoulders set. "PI work is something I'm good at."

I didn't want to discourage his interest in a real career, but that was something I needed to consider carefully. Meanwhile, we had a clue and I was on the hunt.

"You may be right, Bobbie. For now, let's concentrate on the case at hand."

He nodded. "Right. Absolutely. Can I do obbo again?"

"Obbo?" I turned to Adriana. "British police slang for observation. Bobbie, you've been watching too many BBC mysteries. Let's start with the computer." I Googled Glenview. It was on the Amtrak route from Milwaukee to Chicago and had a Metra stop, making it easy to get to the Chicago bank where the Johnsons had an account. The satellite view of the address showed three blocks of townhouses. Peterson's was about a mile from the shared Amtrak/Metra station. If it was Petrovitch who attacked me and fled, I'd say he was vigorous enough to make that walk. I shared my conclusions with Adriana and Bobbie.

"So," Bobbie jumped in, "if someone wanted to have a nice little getaway location ready, Glenview would be a good choice."

"Right. And a large townhouse complex can be very impersonal. People can come and go without attracting much notice."

"How do we find out if it's Petrovitch who lives there under the Peterson name?" Bobbie asked.

Bobbie lit up like a Times Square sign when I said it required 'obbo,' and he pleaded to be part of the surveillance. Even Adriana volunteered.

"I'm sorry," I told her. "I can't put you in harm's way. The Serbian Society is a signatory on all the bank accounts except for your personal drawing account, Adriana. And Petrovitch is the principal of the Society. He may be desperate to eliminate anyone who has knowledge of the funds."

Bobbie shook his head. "If he can access the money in the accounts, why hasn't he done it and left the country? It's certainly enough to live on for the rest of his life."

"Maybe it's not the money itself," Adriana said. "Maybe it's where it came from or who had it before the accounts were opened."

"Could be," I said. "Lots of people would kill to keep that much cash secret, if there was anything fishy about it." We sat in silence for a few moments. "I'll talk to Bart and see what kind of connections he has in Illinois. Maybe he can get MPD input about the original deposit that opened the accounts, at least the ones in the U.S. With three murders and a missing attorney, I'm sure they can show probable cause for a financial search warrant."

It was almost ten o'clock and my headache had retreated to a holding position. I suddenly felt exhausted. Shutting down my laptop, I told Bobbie and Adriana that I really needed to sleep. "I think Adriana would be safer here for tonight. My building is pretty secure and I do have a gun."

Bobbie blinked, the wheels turning in his head. I could see him on the shooting range before long.

"Bobbie, we don't know if Petrovitch saw you or not. If he is behind all this, he can probably get your address from your license plates. Why don't you bunk on my couch?"

"Got sweats that will fit me?"

I laughed. "Mine will be Bermuda shorts on you, and Wukowski's will drag on the ground. But I can give you some clean boxers and the usual toiletries."

"Needs must," he said.

I turned to Adriana. "My guest suite has the basics." When I handed her a gown-and-robe set, ivory charmeuse trimmed with black lace, her eyes went wide. One way or another, I was determined to introduce Adriana to nice lingerie. Tonight, the gown and robe. Tomorrow, maybe some lacy panties. *Who knew what could happen after that?*

Chapter 17

Power is standing strongly in your own center and living from your heart.
—Susan Ariel Rainbow Kennedy (pen name SARK)

The next morning, I found a pair of satin low-rise boy-cut panties, beige with a lacy café-au-lait overlay, still with tags on them. Feminine, but not too sexy. There was nothing I could do about her bra, since my cup size was larger than hers.

Bobbie had coffee brewing when Adriana and I appeared in the kitchen doorway. She clutched the borrowed robe tightly closed.

"I'll grab a quick shower and shave," Bobbie said, looking away from Adriana. What a gentleman!

"I hope you slept well, Adriana."

"I did." Her hand moved slightly over the robe. "I never had anything this nice to sleep in, Angie."

"Glad you liked it. During the lean years, when my ex established his legal practice, I learned to make do. I'm still not extravagant, but I do treat myself a bit. I save, of course, but there's no sense living in misery when a few small luxuries are within reach." I wanted her to understand that she didn't need to perpetuate her parents' lifestyle. The lingerie was a chink in their Scrooge armor.

She considered my words while doctoring her coffee. I put a slug of cream into my mug and settled at the table. "So, here's my plan for the day. First, I'll call Bart to check in and find out what he knows about the bank account transactions. Next, I'll call a PI who owes me a favor and ask him to canvass the area, to see if anyone is keeping this building under surveillance. If Mack spots anyone, I'll get in touch with Tony. His people will clear the area. Then we'll get dressed and go out for breakfast."

"Why can't your PI friend ask them to leave?"

She was so innocent! "Tony's guys are not constrained by legalities the way my PI acquaintance would be, but I trust Mack to find anyone who's out there. Tony's muscle is just that—muscle. Not noted for their high IQs."

"I see. I suppose if someone followed Bobbie here and waited outside all night, he doesn't have good intentions."

"Exactly."

I left a message for Bart, asking if the "account information was available." Then I placed the call to Mack and we finished our coffee. "I know you didn't come prepared to stay overnight, Adriana. I can offer you some new underwear, but I'm afraid none of my clothes will fit. My pants would be high-waters and my skirts would be scandalously mini on you."

I brought the panties into the guest bedroom and laid them on the comforter.

"Ooh," she said on a long exhale. "Those are so pretty." She blushed as she ran a single finger across the lace. "My friend Jennifer kids me about my ugly underwear. Mama always told me that a lady doesn't wear sexy things."

I snorted. "These aren't that sexy, Adriana. But even if they were, what's wrong with a woman dressing to please herself and her man? After all, nobody else would see them." I decided to go a step further. "It's kind of fun to know that under your sedate clothing, you're wearing a cute bra and panties set."

After a moment, she smiled. "I can see that. It's not like I'm flashing the world, right?"

"Right. Feel free to use the shower. There are toiletries in the bathroom vanity."

The phone rang as I stepped out of my shower. No ID. I wrapped a towel around myself and answered.

"Angie." Mack's deep baritone voice bordered on bass. "I found a guy sleeping in his car, half a block from the front door of your building. Another one, awake, at the garage entrance." I walked into my bedroom and grabbed a pen and notepad from my night table as he rattled off the plates, makes and models of their cars. "I didn't spot anything else in a three-block radius. Want me to roust 'em?"

"Thanks, Mack, but I think I'll call some muscle for that. I want them to think twice before they put me under surveillance again."

"Muscle. Nice for you to have contacts like that."

Mack was a dour Scotsman who worked solo and, as far as I knew, lived solo. "Sometimes yes, sometimes no," I responded.

"So, we even?"

"You bet. In fact, you're a bit ahead. If you ever need a favor—some muscle, for example—let me know."

"Will do."

He hung up without a goodbye. A man of few words, Mack.

I called Tony Belloni and asked for an inconspicuous car and some help with the guys who were staking out my building. "Nothing extreme, Tony. I mean…well, I need them out of the way, but still breathing."

"*Capisco*, Angie. Nothing major. My guys will say they're security for the building and got a call about suspicious lingerers. We'll rough them up a little and send them on their way. And I'll have a nice Family sedan at your building in thirty minutes. No worries."

I gulped. But it had to be done, for my team's safety. *Wait a minute! When did I start thinking of Bobbie as part of my team?* I never had a team before, although I had resources to call on. I felt the heaviness of taking responsibility for another person's safety, but also the lightness that comes from sharing a load. *Hmm, maybe an apprenticeship would be a good thing.*

I finished my morning routine, wiped down the bathroom surfaces and made the bed. When I approached the open door to the guest suite, I could hear Adriana talking to herself. "No, that's not right. Darn it, why can't I do this? It looked easy yesterday."

Uh-oh, I thought. *Morning-after-makeover meltdown.* I knocked on the doorframe.

Adriana appeared, mascara wand in hand. Her unoccupied hand took my wrist and propelled me into the guest bath. Products were spread across one side of the large vanity. A small mirror, blow dryer and curling iron occupied the other half. Several papers with application instructions and drawings lay next to the sink. Adriana was almost in tears.

"Nothing works the way they showed me," she wailed. She capped the mascara and set it on the counter. "I can't do this."

I remembered my Emma experimenting with makeup in the sixth grade. A mother's touch was definitely needed here. Age-wise, Adriana might be in her early twenties, but style-wise, she was years behind even that young Emma. "It's okay," I reassured her. "It just takes practice. Let's look at the instructions they gave you at the salon."

Adriana gave a tremulous smile when I said that her hair looked good—smooth and swingy and curled in at the ends. The makeup, however—well, let's just say we started over. I showed her how to apply foundation using a slightly wet makeup sponge. I directed her in the use of blush, cautioning her to use a light hand when dipping the fluffy brush into the loose powder and then to tap off any excess in the sink. She looked alarmed, as if a few grains of waste were too much for her to contemplate, but I assured her that was the way to avoid clown cheeks. She smiled at that. As we worked through the eye and lip products, referring to the makeup stylist's instructions, Adriana settled into the process. By the time we finished, she was lovely again.

I gestured at the mirror. "See? You can do it!"

"Maybe." She turned to me. "But you're here today, Angie. What if I can't do it on my own?"

"I'm only a phone call away," I said.

"Okay. Thanks." As she replaced the products in the salon bag, she muttered, "I can do it. I can."

I smiled and walked out. Best to let her finish convincing herself.

Tony called to give me the all-clear and I went down to get the keys to the Mafia-mobile and park it behind the dumpster for a few minutes. When I came back upstairs, Bobbie and Adriana sat on the couch, watching the morning news on TV. "Breakfast at Ma's, my treat," I said.

Ma Fisher's is a Milwaukee institution, originally two booths and a counter with stools, that morphed into a decent-sized East Side restaurant, by serving good basic food and staying open late for weekend revelers on their way home from the bars. In addition to that, George, the owner, was known to help out the needy with a meal.

"Before we go, let's check on the plates for the two surveillance cars."

It took five minutes to find out they were both registered to the Serbian Society LLC. I was frustrated. That blasted Society was at the hub of what began to look like a vast conspiracy. I had to dig further, find more connections. But not now.

"Let's head out," I told Bobbie and Adriana. "We can talk over plans at Ma's."

I couldn't be one-hundred percent sure that Mack spotted all the surveillance people, so I covered my signature white spiky hair with a scarf and told Adriana and Bobbie to duck down in the car until we were several blocks from my building. They were excited about being on a covert operation. I didn't want to deflate their balloons and I figured I could start to train Bobbie a bit, so I explained to the tune of London Bridges (it's fairly easy to spot talking vs. singing and I wanted any watchers to dismiss me as just another woman alone, singing along to the radio) about misdirection by the use of hats, glasses, wigs, outer clothing and quick changes in hair or makeup.

"You can change your hat or coat, hat or coat, hat or coat; you can wipe your makeup off, my fair lady." Bent over nearly double in the passenger front seat, Bobbie's eyes were bright with interest. When I gave Bobbie and Adriana the all-clear, Bobbie sat up, pulled his little notebook out and started writing. I was glad to see he took me seriously, despite my less than stellar alto voice and the silly rhyming. Adriana grinned.

At the restaurant, George greeted us and showed us to a booth. We perused the menu and ordered. Bobbie ate very healthy—egg whites, unbuttered toast, turkey sausage. Adriana got a Belgian waffle with cherry compote and whipped cream on top, looking guilty as she ordered it. I gave her an encouraging nod and asked for a gyros omelet with sourdough toast. When in a Greek-owned restaurant, eat Greek food.

As I raised my cup to my lips, my cell phone delivered a twangy country classic, *Will Your Lawyer Talk to God for You?* Bart had the "account information" I asked for earlier. I told him I'd meet him at the office and I would be bringing "our client" along because we needed to talk about her safety. I also promised to fill him in on the latest developments since Sunday night.

We finished our meals and headed for Bart's office. On the way there, my young friends chattered away like BFFs.

***

Parking is at a premium in the old Third Ward, where Bart's office is located. Wanting Bobbie and Adriana to keep a low profile, I dropped them off in front of the building, parked on the street and fed the meter— figuratively. The coin models are obsolete, replaced by a credit card machine at the end of the block. *Yet another way to track a person's movements,* I thought. But I didn't want to use a ramp and take the chance of getting blocked in. For now, paranoia took a back seat to safety.

As I stepped into the lobby, I heard Adriana talking with Mighty Mary about college applications and the SAT versus the ACT. I unbundled and left my outerwear at the desk. *I hope they connect,* I thought. *Mary's had a rough life, too, and she could help Adriana find confidence in moving ahead.*

We climbed the stairs to Bart's office on the third floor. Bobbie and Adriana took a settee along the wall opposite Bart's desk. Although neither Bart nor Bertha was smoking, their rooms stank. I took a guest chair near a window and cracked it open for some fresh air, despite the temps outside.

Bart noticed, but didn't comment. He settled back into his oversized desk chair.

First things first. "Bart, it seems to me that Adriana's a natural target for whoever wants to get at the money in the bank accounts. Even with our precautions, I'm concerned."

"I agree. Especially after your attack on Sunday night. It isn't safe for her or Bobbie."

"That's the other thing. Bobbie was helping me with surveillance on the Zupan residence, and thought he spotted Petrovitch circling the cul-de-sac. He tailed him for a couple miles, but Petrovitch took precautionary measures and Bobbie lost him. Bobbie and Adriana stayed at my place last night and this morning, I called Tony Belloni to roust two guys who were keeping my building under surveillance. It's a pretty sure bet that Petrovitch was already aware of my involvement in the case, based on Adriana's hiring me to investigate the money angle, but last night, he either followed Bobbie to my condo or decided I was worth keeping tabs on." I gestured to the settee. "I'm a pro and I'm willing to take some chances. But I don't want them in the line of fire."

"We can set them up in a safe house until this is resolved," Bart said.

"Wait a minute," Bobbie piped up. "I can't hide away somewhere if I'm going to be Angie's intern. I need to be with her, learning stuff."

"Intern?" Bart turned to me.

"It's not defined yet, but I agreed on a trial. So far, he's done quite well at small assignments." Bobbie sat up taller. "But Bobbie," I continued, "you're a beginner. I don't think you're ready to go up against killers. Neither am I, for that matter."

Adriana spoke up. "I can't go into hiding while others put themselves in danger for my sake. Plus, I have a life to live." Her chin went up. "I want to register for UWM's nursing program, but there's a very small window for me to get all the paperwork done before the next semester starts."

Bart and I exchanged glances. What now?

"Here's what I propose …" A puzzled look crossed Bart's face. "You look different, Adriana. Really different." He nodded in approval. "Very nice."

Adriana blushed, but met his gaze with a smile. "Thanks."

"So, that's an advantage—that you've changed your look—but we can't count on that outfoxing anyone." He buzzed Bertha on the office intercom and she whooshed in, steno book in hand and pencil poised. "Bertha, Adriana needs personal security, 24/7. See if Mighty Mary can cover nights."

I relaxed a bit, knowing that having a female bodyguard at night would be more palatable to Adriana.

"Alert her security team to the situation and see that they have good photos of Petrovitch, Zupan…" He looked at me. "Anyone else?" I shook my head and he continued. "And she needs a different safe location every night." Bertha nodded and made a note. "Who do we know at UWM?" he continued. "Someone in the registration office, who could help Adriana get started with classes next January."

Bertha stood for several seconds, pencil tapping her rather prominent chin. "Do you have any college coursework?" she asked Adriana.

"No. Only a high school diploma from South Division."

"And your intended field of study?"

"Nursing."

Bertha pondered for a moment. "I'll check into it." She pivoted and left the room.

Bart gave me a wry grin. "She might get on your last nerve, but she's good at her job."

"I believe you," I said, "on both counts."

"Now, Bobbie, Angie's right about this case being over your head. That doesn't mean you can't be working on skills, though. You can start with some basic self-defense and move on to counteroffensive tactics. Ever shoot a gun?"

"No, but I really want to learn."

Bobbie's calm amazed me. For that matter, so did Adriana's. My little chicks were hatching out well.

"Okay, here's what I can do," Bart said. "I'll set you up with a guy I know, retired military, but not an old geezer. He blew his knee out on a hush-hush mission. He can teach you and you can maybe get him out of the pity pit he's been in since he was forced to take disability. Name's Abraham York, but he goes by Bram."

"Bart, is he Family?" I wanted to keep Bobbie away from Mafia connections.

"Nah. I met him through a guy who does building security. He and Bram were in the same unit, although neither of them will talk specifics, not even what branch they served in." Bart looked back at Bobbie. "You in?"

"Absolutely." He planted his feet firmly on the floor.

"It's not all physical action, Bobbie," I said. "A lot of it's done on the computer. We can talk about that later, though."

Bart placed a call to Bram York and left a message. Then he asked Bobbie, "The reinforced car is still at your place?" Bobbie nodded. "So, you'll take my car there, collect Adriana's stuff and bring it here to my office. Leave the keys to the other car under the driver's seat and lock the doors. Come back here and we'll get you to safer lodgings. There are ways out of this building that don't involve going back outside."

That was news to me.

Bart continued. "We'll make it easy for anyone watching your cottage to conclude that Adriana is no longer in residence. Still, you need to take precautions. They might try to use you or Angie to learn Adriana's whereabouts."

"Oh, no," Adriana whispered, her face stricken with regret. Bobbie put his arm around her.

"You're not responsible for what they did or what they might do." Bart's voice was firm and steady. I'd seen him work a scared witness or defendant that way, preventing panic or retreat. He glanced at each of us in turn. "Our charge is to mitigate risks while we pursue the bastards. Right?"

Of course, we all agreed. The only other option was to live our lives in hiding.

I thought I'd escaped his planning session, but now his gaze was intently on me. "Angelina," he said.

Uh-oh. Use of full first name. Definitely a Papa moment.

"It is my duty to let Pasquale know about the possible threat to you." He held up a hand to stop my impending disagreement. "Your papa may be retired, but he is still a powerful force in our organization. I cannot keep him in the dark. But I will assure him that you have matters well in hand, and that I am providing personal protection for you, also."

He had me between a rock and a hard place, and he knew it. I didn't want to raise Papa's hackles. Besides, there was some logic to the idea. I'd been attacked, after all, and the surveillance last night made me wary. *What had they planned to do this morning if they'd caught me unawares?* It might be time to go on the offensive. Scared people and worried people make mistakes.

"Okay, Bart, I'll accept personal protection, but under one condition. Nobody obvious. No Jimmy the Arms." Jimmy was one of

Tony's guys. His biceps measured larger than his IQ. I didn't want to be with goons all day, and I also had to be sure that my bodyguards would be discreet and confidential. PIs have a code much like priests. We don't reveal a client's business.

Bart arranged for a car and personal protection to take Adriana and Bobbie back to the cottage, with the expectation that anyone who followed us to Bart's office would see Adriana leave Bobbie's with her stuff and realize that she was no longer in residence. He told Bobbie to pack a bag and arranged a temporary residence in Brookfield, an upscale western suburb of Milwaukee. "It's closer to Bram York and easier access to the shooting range he uses."

After they left, I filled Bart in on the information we'd gathered on Herman Petrovitch.

"Is this bigger than a single person, Angie? Is there an organization behind this? Or is it the work of Petrovitch alone? We need to get to the heart of this, ASAP."

"I agree," I told him, "but every corner I turn leads me right back to that same dead end—the Serbian Society and Herman Petrovitch. I can't find the man behind the organization or the organization behind the man."

"Maybe that's because they're one and the same. He could be hiding behind a dummy non-profit."

"Then why name the Johnsons on the bank accounts? Why not use the Serbian Society?"

"That much money in the hands of a non-profit would raise a big red flag to the IRS."

"So you got the banks to send the info on the accounts?"

"Only the U.S. banks, so far. International banking isn't very interested in local murders. We'd have to prove something illegal about the deposits to get them to open up. That's another good reason for individuals to own the accounts. If the Society is shady, setting the accounts up with the Johnsons as the signatories makes sense." Bart retrieved a folder from his desk and handed it to me. "Here are the account statements."

Except for the small (by comparison) Milwaukee account, all the other U.S. accounts were opened in 1999 with identical deposits of eighty million dollars. The Chicago account showed no activity other than interest accruals. Monthly withdrawals from the New York, Chicago, LA and Miami accounts varied from 100K to 300K. The withdrawals were made almost daily.

"What does this tell you?" I asked.

He began to count on his fingers. "One: the deposits are well over the FDIC insurable limit of 250K for an individual. With the Johnsons as the owners, only half a million was insured. So there was no interest in having the government insure the accounts. Two: the daily withdrawals never reach 10K, so there's no requirement to file a Currency Transaction Report with the IRS under the Bank Secrecy Act of 1970. They're skating under the limit. Three: U.S. citizens must file an FBAR Report of Foreign Bank and Financial Accounts—with the IRS if they have interest in or authority over foreign accounts." He stopped. "I wonder if the Johnsons filed or not. And how did they explain those transactions? It isn't like any money laundering scheme I ever heard of, with no money coming in other than the initial deposits. Any ideas?"

"Hmm, a one-time windfall and then lots of relatively small payments. Did any of it go to Petrovitch personally?"

"No way to know. I got the statements from the U.S. banks because Adriana signed papers for my access and she now owns the accounts.

But the payments were all made via check to Cash. I have no legal standing to get at Petrovitch's accounts."

"Bart, we need police help. They have probable cause for a warrant, right?"

"I believe so," he said.

"And we need to give them our information." Bart's eyes narrowed. It was against his principles to get in bed with the cops. They were natural adversaries. Persuasion was called for. "The way I see it, we each have information that the other doesn't. But if the police get a warrant for the accounts, that leaves us on the outside. If we want Petrovitch's finances, we need the cops."

Bart's Cheshire cat grin was wide and insincere. "Angie, we got the account totals directly from Petrovitch via Susan Neh. What are the odds that information is still in his office? Or that the cops know to talk to your office mate?"

He was probably right. I doubted that Petrovitch left any information behind about the Serbian Society or the money. I did tell Wukowski how I got involved in the case, but I inadvertently never mentioned Susan to him. He must have thought that Adriana came to me directly from Petrovitch.

Suddenly, an even more basic fact jumped out at me. "Bart, the lawyer sent Adriana to Susan with a list of the accounts and their balances. Why? Why alert her to that? The Serbian Society was a signatory on all but the Milwaukee account. He could have closed the rest and taken off. Why tell her about them?"

"Two reasons that I can think of. One, only an owner can close an account. He could leave a small amount in and take the rest, but the banks would report a large transaction to the IRS and they'd likely make it hard for him to leave the country, if that was his plan. Two, he couldn't hide the accounts from Adriana forever. Assuming her parents filed an FBAR, sooner or later, the IRS would come looking for the yearly report on the offshore accounts. If they never filed, they might still have records at their home or even in a safe deposit box. We haven't located one, but that doesn't mean it doesn't exist. If Petrovitch wanted to stay stateside for any length of time, he had to make her aware of the accounts without revealing too much about how the money got there."

I thought about the day I went to Petrovitch's office to review the financials, and his secretary's dead body on the floor in front of his desk. "Three," I continued Bart's list, "Dragana Zupan was Petrovitch's secretary. I bet you don't keep secrets from Bertha. What if Dragana knew about the money and made a stink? According to her husband and her priest, Dragana was a kind woman and a good Christian. So maybe she didn't want to see Adriana shorted. Or maybe she didn't want to see Adriana involved in dirty business. Whatever the case, I think it's possible that Dragana backed Petrovitch into a corner, so he told Adriana about the money, but gave her as little information as possible. Dragana wasn't happy about how he handled things, so Petrovitch offed her. He didn't have a chance to get the funds and hop a flight to Singapore or the Caymans. Now he's on the run."

"It fits," he said. "There's only one way to stop this. Get Petrovitch."

Get, as in put hands on him? Or get, as in permanently remove him? I would not be a party to murder, even of a murderer. "Bart, he must be turned over to the police. I can't be a party to vigilante justice."

"Of course not, Angelina. I am hurt that you would think such a thing of me."

Bart's eyes were a little too wide, his hand on his heart a little too rehearsed, his language a little too formal. I knew when I was being schmoozed. "My apologies for offending you, Bart. I wanted to make my position clear." *Might as well go the whole way,* I thought. "Also, I'm concerned that if we don't cooperate with the police, we'll feel the repercussions later."

"Maybe you will, Angie, with your boyfriend. They can't touch me."

He spoke with such assurance that I knew he'd been down this road before, with few consequences. I'd have to try a gentle threat. "Bart, if it comes out later that we knew facts that would lead to Petrovitch's arrest and we didn't share them with the police, they could charge you with obstructing justice, right? I'd probably earn some bad will, but you're an officer of the court. Not only that, we'd look like schmucks— or worse—in the media. You may have a steady income from the Family, but I need other clientele to keep afloat." I paused, hand to chin, and sighed. "Maybe I should withdraw from this case," I said in a small voice.

Bart came around the desk to me. "Angie, *cara amica,* there is no need for us to discuss such drastic measures. I see that you are convinced that informing the police is the right action. So let us sit down together and decide what we will tell them."

Since when was I Bart's dear friend? I asked myself. His stylized language signaled that he'd moved into Family mode and I was about to enter into a formal agreement with a Mafia lawyer. *Watch yourself, Angie!* Matching wits with Bart would take all my concentration.

"I will be happy to discuss this and come to common ground with you." My formal reply acknowledged that I understood the upcoming discussion. "But first—" I rose, causing Bart to take a step back—"I need coffee. You?"

"Good idea. You know how I like it."

Indeed I did. "I'll go to the café next door. Be back in a flash."

Bertha sniffed as I passed her desk. "Leaving, Ms. Bonaparte?"

"We're not quite done. I'm going on a coffee run. Can I bring you some, Mrs. Conti? And maybe a pastry?"

"Perhaps a jelly donut." She opened a desk drawer and withdrew her purse.

I would kill her with kindness. "Oh, please, this is my treat," I told her as I breezed out. She'd hate to owe me even a small debt.

I contemplated strategy while I waited to place an order. Where would I draw a line in the sand? First, if we got our hands on Petrovitch, he would be turned in to stand trial. No compromise on that. Second, the police needed to know what we knew about his probable whereabouts. Third, since we needed their help with Petrovitch's banking records, it seemed only fair to give them the information Susan had. It didn't have to come from Bart. I could let Wukowski or Iggy know to talk with Susan. Fourth, the police needed to know how tightly the Serbian Society was tied to Petrovitch. I suddenly realized that I was using Bart's listing methodology and smiled. Two could play that game.

After an hour of haggling, Bart and I reached agreement on all my major points. He made copies of the financial records. "Be sure that the police—" he smirked and I knew he wanted to say Wukowski—"know that this came from my office in a spirit of full cooperation, with the expectation that they would reciprocate," he said. He also insisted that Adriana stay under his protection and not the police's. "They're too hampered by budgets and legalities. I can do more to keep her safe." Since he was probably right, I agreed. "And there's no need to bring Bobbie into the discussion," he said. "Everything he knows is second- or third-hand." Again, I had to agree with his assessment. Besides, while there was a delicate acceptance between Bobbie and Wukowski, I knew

143

that homophobia ran rampant in the MPD, as in most police departments across the country. I didn't want Bobbie to face that prejudice so soon in his PI career.

Chapter 18

Data is not information, information is not knowledge, knowledge is not understanding, understanding is not wisdom.

—Clifford Stoll

On the way to the office, I stopped at the service center where I have my mail delivered. Lobby boxes, even locked ones, are easily jimmied or broken into.

All was quiet when I arrived. Susan left a note on my desk. "Out on an audit. Back Thursday." Today was Tuesday. A two-day audit boded well for Susan's finances and indicated that she was taking on bigger clients. *Good for you*, I thought.

I shredded all the junk mail, put my personal mail into my briefcase to review when I got home, and then opened the envelopes addressed to "AB Investigations." There were two checks from clients whose cases closed in October. I filled out a deposit slip for the bank and put the envelope into my briefcase. There was one new email in my business inbox, a request for a background check on a job applicant for a local after-school tutoring center. They'd been burned once by a felon—thankfully, not a predator—and now they came to me to vet their applicants. That would be a good training assignment for Bobbie, I decided. I responded that I'd get back to them by Monday.

My bank was on Prospect, close to the office and my condo. I never set up internet access to my accounts, preferring to make in-person deposits and withdrawals. Hackers are everywhere, and while it's impossible to totally guarantee the security of one's information, I wouldn't make it easy. Besides, I liked the personal touch. The tellers knew me by now and I'd even solved the case of the missing Ragdoll—a cat—for teller Cynthia.

I headed back to the condo, where I sifted through my personal mail. There was an 8½ x 11 envelope from my daughter Emma.

Odd, I thought, *I saw her on Sunday.* I slit it open and retrieved a picture of a turkey, carefully drawn and painted, with "Happy Thanksgiving" in pretty cursive script at the top. It was signed by my granddaughter Angela: "I love you, *Nonna*." *Aww.* Emma included a note: "Angela couldn't wait for Sunday and she informed me that it's always more fun to get mail."

She was right. With a big smile on my face, I promptly fastened the picture to the fridge door with magnets.

The rest was junk mail, which I shredded. I checked my watch. Three o'clock. *Too early to call Wukowski?* I asked myself. *Not for business reasons*, I responded, so I dialed his desk number at the MPD. If he wasn't there, I'd call his cell phone.

"Detective Wukowski."

His deep baritone caught me off guard. I hadn't expected him to answer. "Hi. It's Angie."

"*Anielica*, I'm up to my eyeballs in paperwork for the task force. Everything that no one else wanted to tackle got dumped on me."

It was another *aww* moment. *Anielica*—pronounced ahn-yell-eet-sa—means 'angel' in Polish. "*Caro*," I said, "I hate to put more on your plate, but there's some information concerning the Johnson and Zupan murders that I want to share with you and Iggy."

There was a small intake of breath. "Can you meet us at five-thirty?" he asked.

"Sure. At headquarters?" Homicide, a part of the MPD Violent Crimes Division, had its offices at police headquarters on Seventh and State. The courthouse was nearby and it was a nightmare to park.

"No." He thought for a moment. "There's a neighborhood tavern on 60th and Forest Home—Jacko's. They serve a good burger and Iggy likes the onion rings. Will that work for you?"

"Are the rings thick or shredded?"

"Shredded."

"Mmm. I'll be there."

He hung up without saying good-bye. *Distracted*, I thought, *or he didn't want anyone to know who was calling*. I didn't care. He'd called me by a pet name—while he was at work. Sigh.

It would take thirty minutes to get to the tavern in rush hour. That left slightly more than an hour to organize my notes and change clothes. It wasn't a date, but I wanted to look good. Flirty. Okay, sexy without being skanky. I wanted Wukowski to stay with me tonight.

As I headed for the walk-in closet, Bart's ringtones sounded on my cell. "Hello, Bart."

"Angie, the people I wanted you to meet, they're available tonight. I'll send them over to your place, okay?"

It took me a moment to realize he was talking about personal protection. "Not needed tonight, Bart. I've made other arrangements."

I heard him draw on his cigarette and exhale. "Other arrangements, as in official arrangements?"

"That's right."

"Well, far be it from me to interfere. Will you discuss the matter we talked about earlier?"

"Yes, we're meeting for a meal, for that reason."

Puff. Exhale. "Okay. Keep me posted. And when he leaves in the morning, call me. I want you to meet the team."

"Will do."

It would be a cryptic exchange to anyone who overheard it. Cell phone transmissions are quite easy to intercept, since they use public airwaves—witness the Camillagate and Squidgygate conversations that embarrassed Prince Charles and Princess Diana.

***

The tavern had a long bar, where the serious drinkers sat on stools. Bart and Iggy were at the corner table, farthest from the bar, their backs to the walls. With no other patrons nearby, we would have privacy.

When I reached the table, Wukowski pulled out a chair and gave me a kiss on the cheek, then whispered, "Missed you." Holy PDA—and in front of his partner! Iggy grinned.

I wore a deep emerald green wrap dress made of clingy silk jersey. The overlapping neckline revealed a bit more cleavage than the average dress and the fabric clung to my curves. Wukowski got an eyeful as he helped me off with my coat. His hands briefly caressed my shoulders as the coat sleeves fell away. I couldn't wait to get home.

A tall iced glass of beer sat in front of each man. *Must be off-duty*, I mused. The server came over to get my order. "Any chance you have a Riesling?"

"No. We got red, white and rosé." She pronounced the last "rosy."

"Make it a whisky sour," I said.

"Cocktail?"

"On the rocks."

"Gotcha." She walked away.

Wukowski handed me a laminated menu card. Burgers, brats, hot dogs and pizza, with sides of fries, onion stacks, deep-fried cheese curds and cole slaw. Iggy leaned toward me. "Ix-nay on the pizza, Angie. It's frozen. And the last time Marianne ordered a salad, Barb—the waitress—just laughed. This is no low-cal joint. But the burgers are good and the onion stack—mm-mm."

Until we got Petrovitch, Bart's security guys probably would "ix-nay" my morning run. I'd pay for this meal with time on the treadmill in the condo exercise room.

Barb came back with my drink and took our orders: cheeseburgers and onion stacks all around.

While we waited for the food, Wukowski cut to the chase. "That attack on you was too close for comfort."

"I agree," I said. "Bart Matthews is setting up personal security for Adriana, Bobbie and me." He started to object, but I interrupted him. "He has pros, Wukowski, former government special ops guys. I'll be fine, really."

"You're not going to walk away from this, are you?"

"No." I shook my head. "Not with Adriana in jeopardy. Let's move on. Bart has given me permission to share some information on the case with you."

"Nice of him," Wukowski responded sarcastically. There was no love lost between them.

Iggy jumped in. "Whatcha got, Ange?"

"Three things: property ties to Petrovitch, financial information from the Johnsons' U.S. bank accounts and a possible second home for Petrovitch. It comes with a price tag," I told them. "We need to see records on Petrovitch's bank accounts and any other financial information you can garner."

They perked up immediately and Wukowski extracted a small notebook and pen from his inner suit coat pocket. "Fair enough. What've you got?"

I pulled out the copies of the bank records from my briefcase and handed them over, keeping one set for myself. I gave them several minutes to glance over the pages.

"What's your take on this?" Wukowski asked.

"Bart is pretty savvy financially and here's how he sees it. The accounts were all set up at the same time, with identical deposits of eighty million. The Johnsons owned the accounts, but the Serbian Society is a signatory on all but the small one for Adriana. The only officer of the Serbian Society is Herman Petrovitch. There were no withdrawals from the Chicago account, ever. The others all have regular withdrawals via checks made out to Cash, but no individual withdrawal is big enough to trigger a report to the IRS. It can't be money laundering because there's no money coming in, except for interest accrual." I paused. "We don't have information yet from the offshore accounts."

"So what's the scheme?"

"Damned if Bart or I know."

Iggy jumped in. "Big deposit, lots of payments, all to Cash, right?" I nodded. "He's paying somebody off."

"But it's been going on since 1999," I objected. "A blackmailer wouldn't be that patient."

"Naw," Iggy said. "But a partner would. Somebody who has as much to lose as the guy who owns the accounts."

As Barb approached the table with our food, we set the papers aside and switched to innocuous conversation about Iggy's kids and the Packers.

The burger was big and juicy. The onion stack was a mini-loaf of deep-fried onion shreds, delicious but greasy. There was a small mountain of used paper napkins next to my plate when I finished. "There must be two thousand calories in this meal."

"Mine was a double burger. Add another five hundred," Wukowski responded. "I'll need a good workout later."

It sounded innocuous, but I read him and met his gaze. "You bet."

He smiled, a relatively rare occurrence, but one that transformed his usual grim expression. Anticipation was killing me.

Barb cleared the table and we ordered coffee, mulling over the figures until she came back with the cups and left us alone again. "A partner," I said, picking up the conversation from before our meals. "It's funny you say that. Bart thinks there's some kind of conspiracy, too, but I haven't found any evidence that supports it. Petrovitch is the sole officer of the Serbian Society. He runs a solo legal practice, and his secretary is now dead. He isn't married, no steady woman—or man— in his life. No children. His only friends, if you can call them that, were the Zupans and the Johnsons, and Josif is the only one still alive. Petrovitch is a loner."

I pulled out more printouts. "I ran a property search on 'Serbian Society.' The Johnsons' rental house and the front house on the lot, the empty apartment above their hardware store, Petrovitch's legal offices and the offices on each side," I said, "were bought by the Society in ninety-nine, the year the Johnsons emigrated from Serbia, and are all vacant. It's like the Society—Petrovitch—wanted to build a buffer zone."

"Nice catch, Angie," Iggy told me.

Wukowski nodded. "Real nice. But it doesn't help us understand what's going on."

"There's more." I put my papers aside. "You know my friend Bobbie, who helped in the Morano case? Well, he's pretty hyped about becoming a detective."

"Police detective?" Wukowski asked, his face carefully neutral.

"No, private. He's been after me to let him help on the case. I wanted to see if he could stand the boredom, so I sent him to observe the Zupan residence on Monday night." I took a breath. "He thought he spotted Petrovitch in a black Park Avenue with Illinois plates. The car circled the cul-de-sac twice, but didn't stop. Bobbie, against my instructions, followed it the second time, but he lost it. However, he did get the plates, so I ran a search. It's registered to Oliver Wendell Peterson." I explained about the name coincidence. "It could be an alias for Attorney Petrovitch. My plate search didn't provide a DMV picture for Peterson. The address for the plates was a townhouse in Glenview, Illinois."

"With easy access to the Chicago bank account and every form of transportation short of a space launch," Wukowski added.

I nodded and we all sat in silence for a few moments.

Iggy piped up. "This is real helpful, Angie."

"Payback time," I told him.

Wukowski and Iggy exchanged glances. Wukowski nodded and Iggy spoke. "I can apply for a warrant for Petrovitch's bank records, with this as probable cause. He's not officially a suspect, but the evidence, while circumstantial, is pretty damning. I'll go back to the office tonight and start the process. I'll also request the Illinois DMV picture and ask the Glenview PD for information on the address and on Peterson. But it's a small village, Angie, and I imagine the PD there doesn't have a large investigative unit. I'll ask for surveillance on the place, but it's not likely I'll get it."

Wukowski joined in. "We need a way to contact Adriana and Bobbie without Bart's interference." I gave him the cell phone numbers and he wrote them in his little notebook. "We got the autopsy reports yesterday," he said. "The bullets that killed the Johnsons and Dragana Zupan were 9mm NATO. They're used by NATO forces and some military forces around the world. Private gun enthusiasts use them, too."

"Not police?"

"Nope."

"Is it easy to buy those bullets?"

"You can get them online and at a few local dealers. Some Walmarts sell them. It doesn't tell us much, without the gun." He checked with Iggy. "Have I forgotten anything?"

Iggy shook his head and rose. "Good to see you again, Angie. Marianne sends her regards and says to call her when you have time."

"I will." We hugged briefly and he headed outside.

Wukowski and I remained seated. He looked mighty fine to me. By the dilation of his pupils and his fast breathing, I surmised that I looked good to him, too.

"Who's providing protection for you tonight?" he asked.

"You are."

It didn't take long to get our coats on and drive to my condo. Once inside the front door, I was grateful that my dress was stretchy and had no buttons. Let the workout begin!

Chapter 19

I am prepared for the worst, but hope for the best.
—Benjamin Disraeli

I felt very relaxed and clear-headed when Wukowski left the next morning. There was a message on my answering machine from Bart Matthews, recorded at seven-oh-eight last night. "It's Bart. I was able to find accommodations for your out-of-town friends." Translation: Bobbie and Adriana were tucked away safely.

People who want to leave secure messages don't use voicemail. There are companies that sell fake caller ID equipment that lets you mimic another number from your phone. Then you can call the number and check or even delete their voicemail—unless they've established a password, which many people don't do. Of course, my message box was password-protected, but it's only a matter of time before some hacker figures out how to get past that, too.

I returned Bart's message. "It's Angie. Thanks for getting rooms for my friends. Is this a good time for your consultants to come over?" Translation: Send the personal security team to my place.

After showering, I wiggled into skinny dress jeans and a soft raspberry-colored boat-neck sweater, settled on the couch with a cup

154

of java and dialed Bobbie's cell. He picked up on the second ring. "Angie—"

I interrupted. "Remember this isn't a secure call, *amico*. Don't give me any information that could help someone locate you. And no names."

"Uh. Well, I'm fine."

"Good to hear."

"This is crazy, Angie."

"It is," I agreed. "But necessary. Call my home number from a landline." I figured no one could tap a hotel phone that quickly and I have a detector on my line that alerts me to anything short of a government tap.

Bobbie called back within a few seconds. He blurted out, "Angie, sometimes you scare me."

"A private investigator has to be vigilant, Bobbie. If you prepare for the worst, you are often pleasantly surprised, and if the worst comes to pass, you're glad you were ready for it."

"Gotcha." After a moment of silence, during which I bet he was making a note, he said, "You'll never believe what happened after Adriana and I left Bart's office yesterday."

"You're both okay, aren't you?"

"Oh, sure. Nothing bad went down. I got her stuff from my place, packed a small bag for myself and took them out to the car, which I deliberately parked outside, where anyone could see it. Then I drove back to Bart's office, parked on the street, and hauled the suitcases in. This is where it gets good."

I could almost hear him squirming with delight through the phone line. "Tell me."

"Remember Bart said there were ways out of the building that didn't involve going outside? Well, there are underground tunnels, Angie! We freakin' went through a tunnel, into the basement of another building, up to the roof and across to a third building, via a metal grate. From there, we separated. Bart went with me and Mighty Mary went with Adriana, each of us in anonymous black sedans with smoked glass windows. I felt like Will Smith in *Enemy of the People*."

"Man, Bobbie, I had no idea about this. How did Adriana take it? Was she scared?"

"Maybe at first. I don't think she liked the tunnel. But Mary talked to her, which helped. Once we were aboveground again, Adriana was okay. I have to hand it to her, she's got courage."

"As do you, my friend."

"Thanks, Angie. That means a lot, coming from you."

I had to defuse this before it got maudlin. "So how'd you spend the night? Don't tell me where you are. I'll ask Bart in person."

"I thought your phone was secure."

"I believe it is."

"Hmm. Prepare for the worst. Well, after Adriana and I were…relocated to different hotels, Bart's security guy came over and swept the room for bugs. His name is Spider. I bet he has an interesting background, with that name." Bobbie paused. "Maybe I should get a nickname that's more suitable for a PI. What do you think?"

"You're asking a woman named Angelina Sofia Bonaparte?"

Bobbie laughed. "At least you have a woman's name. I don't know why my parents named me Bobbie with an I-E. It's not even short for Robert. You'd think two people who were so horrified by my being gay would pick a masculine name for a baby boy."

"Well, I see no problem with your name or your sexual orientation. But if you want to use a macho name for your life as a PI, fine with me.

Just let me know what to call you when we're in the office or on a case."

"Yeah. I'll think about that. To continue, while Spider checked out the room, Bram showed up. You know, the guy Bart said could teach me defensive moves and how to shoot. Bram and Spider are friends from…I don't know what branch of the military they served in. But Bram checked out the hotel and grounds—he called it 'securing the perimeter'—and then spent part of the night reading while I tried to sleep. That man is restless. I swear he got up to look out the windows and walk the hallway every half hour."

"Sounds like a pro," I said.

"He's very intense. A bit scary, to be honest. And he uses a cane. I guess his knee isn't healed yet, but I have no doubt he can handle himself. That cane would be a deadly weapon in his hands."

"Is he still there?"

"No, the day shift is outside, getting ready to tail me. I'm allowed to go about my business during the day, according to Bart, as long as I have personal security."

"Good. I have an assignment for you."

"Already? That's…that's great! Will I be watching, you know, the place in…uh, south of us?"

"Nothing so exciting. I'll meet you at the office at one and show you how to run a basic background check."

"Okay." He still sounded pumped. "See you then."

Before I could place a call to Adriana, my cell phone rang. "Angie," said a gravely male voice, "this Josif Zupan. Service for Dragana is on Saturday at ten. At St. Sava. You be there?"

"Of course, Josif. Thank you for letting me know."

"Meal after, in the church hall. You come?"

"I'd be honored." I wondered how to phrase my request. "Josif, I have an intern. His name is Bobbie Russell. With your permission, I'd like to bring him to the service and meal. He can be another set of eyes for me."

"You think killer be there?"

"There's no way to tell, but Bobbie is good at reading people. He might pick up on something I've missed." I wasn't sure if Josif was involved in the murders or the money, but if he wasn't complicit, he needed to know. "I have something unsettling to tell you, Josif. I assigned Bobbie to watch your house on Monday evening, on the off chance that Petrovitch would show up."

"You mean, on the off chance we are—what is word?—in cahoots."

"Yes. In my line of work, I can't take things for granted. That night, Bobbie thought he spotted Petrovitch go past your home, twice. The car didn't stop, just drove through the cul-de-sac. If Petrovitch is involved, he's a danger to you and Adriana. You need to take precautions. I can set you up with personal security, Josif. I wish you'd consider it."

"He no hurt me." His laugh was like a bark. "I hope he try."

"There's no proof he's involved. It's all circumstantial, for now."

"I know him, from Yugoslavia and Bosnia. Bad man. Very bad. Like cowboys say, I shoot first, ask questions later."

"Vigilante justice can land you in prison." I took a breath. "Would you meet with me again, Josif, and tell me about Petrovitch? About the old days in Bosnia? I can't shake the feeling that all this is connected to that time."

"*Ne*. I no talk about those days. *Nikada nije*—never."

"Please consider it. It could lead to his arrest, if he was involved."

After a long silence, he spoke. "I no promise. Understand?"

"Yes, I understand. And is it okay for Bobbie to be there?"

"*Da,* is okay."

"Do you need any help getting ready?"

"*Ne,* Father Matthieu, he handle everything."

"Then I'll see you on Saturday morning."

I needed to get some food into me, despite last night's pig-out, so I toasted half an English muffin and opened a small yogurt. Just as I prepared to eat, the kitchen phone gave three short rings, the signal for the building intercom in the lobby.

I lifted the handset and a man spoke. "Ms. Bonaparte, I'm Spider Mulcahey. Bart Matthews sent me."

"I'll be down in a minute, Mr. Mulcahey."

When the elevator doors opened, I spotted a thirty-something man waiting near the front of the lobby. Points to him for not cornering me as soon as I exited. He moved toward me, hand extended. "Spider Mulcahey."

"Angie Bonaparte," I responded. His untamed black hair and busy eyebrows were amusing. I struggled to hide a smile. "Can I see some ID?"

"Smart," he told me. "Lots of folks assume you're legit because you mention the name of someone they know." He produced a Wisconsin driver's license and a business card that read, "Secure Windows and Doors." "I've got a picture of my wife and son in here, too."

I laughed as we moved toward the elevator. "This'll do. Come on up. I was just having breakfast. Care to join me?"

"I ate at home with Joey while Magdalena got some shut-eye. We're expecting twins in a few months. She gets pretty tired and Joey is a three-year old whirlwind."

By now, we were at my unit. "I do want to see a picture," I told him as I ushered him inside.

We settled at the breakfast bar and I poured coffee for us both. Spider showed me the family photo: him on a big John Deere riding mower, a miniature version of himself alongside on a toy John Deere, and a dark-haired beauty, gazing at them with an indulgent smile.

"Lovely family," I told him. "I'll show you my son and daughter and my grandkids later." I finished the yoghurt—by now, the muffin was cold—and we took our mugs into the living room, where I pointed out my family.

"Nice," he said. "Very nice. I can see me and Magdalena a few years down the road, with grandsons who all have unruly hair and twitchy eyebrows, and granddaughters who are beautiful and serene."

"May it be," I told him. Then we got down to business.

Spider would be my "day man," because Family bodyguards were conspicuous, like rougher versions of the Secret Service. He walked the condo, approved my internal security, and told me to call when I planned to leave the building. He'd be outside in his company van and would follow me unobtrusively until the night team showed up around six. They would be Family, unless I had plans that precluded having bulky guys with attitude at my side. We exchanged cell phone numbers and he left.

Time to touch bases with Adriana. She picked up on the first ring, breathless. "Are you okay?" I asked, after identifying myself.

"Yes, I was just running for the phone. I'm at the hotel pool."

"Don't say anything that might tell someone where you are. Even knowing there's a pool eliminates a lot of places."

"Oh. I never thought of that."

"Why don't you call me back from a landline? Say, in the next hour?"

"I'll just take a quick shower to wash off the pool chemicals and call you right back."

It was about twenty minutes later when my kitchen phone rang. "Angie, it's Adriana." She still sounded breathless. "Did you talk to Bobbie? Did he tell you about Bart's building?"

"He did. Were you scared?"

"A little, at first. But Mary made a lot of jokes and pretty soon, I was more amazed than afraid. Imagine, tunnels under the street!"

"I knew there were some downtown, but I didn't know that about the Third Ward. How did you sleep last night?"

"Not all that great. Mary kept leaving the room to patrol and that woke me up. I'm not complaining, though. I was glad she was there. The last time I remember hearing her, it was around three. After that, I crashed."

"Is she still there?"

"No. She went home around eight. Bram York is here now, but I only notify him when I'm leaving the room." She giggled. "He was sitting in a lounge chair at the pool when you called—in khakis and a polo shirt. Talk about out of place!"

"Well, he could hardly wear swim trunks. Where would he hide his gun?" A twist on the old risqué joke popped into my head—is that a gun in your swimsuit, or are you happy to see me? *So wrong*, I chided myself, especially with Adriana. She laughed again, sounding young and carefree. "What are your plans for the day?" I asked.

"I suppose I can't call my friend Jennifer?"

"Probably not a good idea. Anyone who wanted to find you would have her followed."

She hesitated. "We talked about shopping for clothes, but I'm sure you're too busy."

"Let's see. I'm meeting Bobbie at one for a training session on background checks. Why don't I call you when we finish? We should be done by two-thirty at the latest. I don't want to overload him."

"Great. I'll be waiting. This will be so much fun, Angie!"

"It will." I meant it. I love to shop and I really wanted to see Adriana in flattering clothes.

I called Lily at the UWM library, to see if she had any updates on the book of Bosniak poetry or Professor Kolar.

"Angie, I was planning to call you this morning. Can you come down here in person? I have something to show you."

"I'm on my way." I notified Spider and left the building in the Miata. Knowing about his special ops background, I felt confident that he would have my back. If the bad guys wanted me, they'd be in for a surprise.

There were no empty spaces on the street that fronted the library. I drove a couple blocks and saw a residential home with a sign offering parking in their driveway for four bucks an hour—a bit more than the U's parking ramps, but I don't park in ramps. The Secure Windows and Doors van pulled into the same driveway, as I walked down the block toward the library. Spider got out with a flyer in hand and started to talk to the homeowner. Nice cover.

Lily was waiting for me at the information desk. She asked a student worker to cover for her while she helped a 'visiting scholar' with a project. We went into a workroom and closed the door.

"Angie, I think I'm onto something," she said as she sat at the room's computer. A few keystrokes, and she had an image on the screen. "Look—this is the same book in the photo, the one from the victims' home. But here's what's really interesting." She tapped and a web page headed "INTERPOL—CRIME AREAS—WORKS OF ART" appeared. When she entered the name of the book (using the Latin alphabet), up popped a listing:

Type: DOCUMENT/BOOK/PRINTED MATTER/BOOK
Period: Circa 1582
Artist(s): Mulhid Vahdeti
Height: 18.5 cm
Width: 14.5 cm
Materials: CARDBOARD, PAPER
Case happened in: Bosnia
Date: 1994

"So the book is on Interpol's stolen art works database. Great job, Lily." I pulled my tablet computer from my briefcase and accessed the notes on the case. "The theft occurred a year before the victims left Bosnia and came to the States."

"Then they might be the thieves."

"Or receivers of stolen property. Or the book in the attic might be a fake. But I don't think so."

"I'll print this and give it to you so you can file it with the picture of the book."

"The photo?"

"No, the picture. The one I gave you on your first visit."

Suddenly, I realized what it was I'd forgotten after the attack. The perp took the printout from my briefcase. Just that, nothing else. "I need another copy, Lily. The guy who hit me took the original picture. I didn't think anything was missing until you mentioned it. Bad call on my part." *There were so many rabbit trails in this investigation!* Nonetheless, I was chagrined about my lapse.

As she typed, Lily said, "You had a head injury. It's understandable if you overlooked it. After all, it wasn't something you'd normally have in your possession. Hang on." She left and returned with a printed image of the book. "Here you go."

I placed it in my briefcase. "Why would he want the picture?"

"Is it possible he didn't know the victims had it? Or maybe he did know, but he didn't have details. Or maybe he didn't want you to have it. Of course, if you printed it once, you could do so again."

"I'm pretty sure he and the Johnsons were involved together."

The air swooshed out of her mouth. "You know who it is?"

"There's a lot of circumstantial evidence pointing toward the victims' lawyer."

"So, what are the next steps? Are you ready to talk to Professor Kolar? She told me she would make up her mind about how deep the conversation would go, once she met you."

"That's fair. Should I contact her?"

"It might be better if I accompany you to the meeting. She's very reserved, but we often work together on her research and she's comfortable with me. That could help."

"Good idea. Go ahead and set it up. I'll make myself available."

"And Colonel Lewis, the ROTC officer who served in Bosnia? Have you talked with him?"

I sighed. "Not yet. It probably seems like I've been slacking off, but believe me, that's not the case. I think I'll handle that one on my own, but I'll be sure to keep you informed. Without you, this would be so much harder. Thanks, Lily."

"My pleasure. Really."

We parted company and I walked back to my car. Spider's van was no longer there, but I felt confident that he was nearby. I paid my eight dollars, checked my watch, and decided to stop for a falafel platter.

Chapter 20

This change to a higher phase of alert is a signal…that certain actions now should be undertaken with increased urgency and at an accelerated pace.

—Dr. Margaret Chan

I called Spider to tell him I was getting takeout from Abu's Restaurant of the Gold and then going to my office to eat. Did he want anything? I asked. He declined, stating that Abu's was great, but his wife Magdalena's leftovers were better.

While eating falafel at my desk, I checked my to-do list. The two items remaining were to contact the ROTC leader, Col. Lewis, and talk to my aunt about Thanksgiving, which was two weeks from today. Yikes! I knew Aunt Terry would probe me for more details on Wukowski, so I pushed that down the list and called the colonel's number, expecting to leave a message.

Instead, a smooth tenor voice said, "ROTC office, Colonel Lewis."

"Colonel, my name is Angelina Bonaparte. Lily March at the UWM library gave me your number. I was hoping I could meet with you."

"Concerning the UWM program?"

"No. Colonel, I'm a private investigator. Some uniforms that may be from the Bosnian War era are part of a case I'm working. Would you be willing to look at photos and help me identify them?"

"Are they U.S.?"

"I think they're either Bosnian or Serbian."

"I'm no expert on the variety of forces or uniforms in that region, Ms. Bonaparte. And I can't do anything that would violate Army rules. I would need to know more about your case."

"Fair enough. Could we meet so I can show you the pictures and explain about the investigation?"

"I'm heading out of town tomorrow and will be away until after Thanksgiving. If you can be at my office on the Marquette campus by twelve forty-five, I can give you thirty minutes."

I didn't want to miss this opportunity and wait two weeks to get an opinion on the uniforms. "I'll be there." He gave me the location of his office and the closest visitor parking.

I texted Bobbie to cancel our meeting. I asked him to get in touch with A (no use of full name on texts) and tell her that our plans were postponed, too. Then I called Spider to alert him.

Marquette University is situated just west of downtown Milwaukee. Parking is impossible in the area, so I was forced to use the parking ramp that Col. Lewis mentioned. With Spider as a backup, I felt secure, both with parking and with walking two blocks to the ROTC office.

I knocked on the colonel's door and heard a melodious "Come." When I entered, the man seated behind the desk stood. "Ma'am," he said. "I'm Colonel Lewis."

"Angie Bonaparte," I said, extending my hand. "We spoke on the phone."

He was about five-ten, but muscular, and he held himself in that upright military posture that appears such a strain to civilians. His short-cropped salt-and-pepper hair was also military issue. He came around the desk to shake my hand, then helped me off with my jacket and hung it on an old-fashioned coat tree. *Very courtly manners*, I thought.

He pulled a visitor chair up and returned to his desk. "My time is limited, Ms. Bonaparte. It would be best if I looked at the photos first. If I don't recognize anything, there's no need for you to tell me your story. If I do, we can go from there. That work for you?"

"It does," I told him. I took my tablet out of my briefcase and went to the folder that contained the downloaded pictures from my phone. They were much easier to see on the larger display. "Here's the first one. Just scroll through. There are two uniforms and two sets of footwear."

He took his time, gazing intently at each photo, holding the tablet upright and then laying it flat on his desk to change visual perspective. There were six pictures, two of each uniform—front and back—and one each of the boots and dress shoes.

I forced myself to sit still while he studied them. There would be no fidgeting in the colonel's office!

He swiped one time too many and the lovely deep red of the embroidered dress appeared on the screen. "These are all part of the same investigation?"

"Yes. I found the clothing, the jewelry and book in an attic, along with the uniforms. Scroll through the rest. Maybe there's something there that you'll be able to help with."

He studied all the photos in the folder. Then he set the tablet down and held my gaze. "I need to hear the story," he said.

I cautioned him about confidentiality before explaining about the murders and my subsequent work for the victims' daughter. When I told him that the family emigrated from Bosnia in the late nineties, his already erect posture straightened just a fraction more, but his face remained impassive. "Colonel, the family was Serbian. Their attorney also claims Serbian roots. That's why I wanted you to see the uniforms."

He nodded, then leaned forward, eyes down, and rested his forearms on the desk, hands clasped. After an intake of breath, he spoke. "I can't be absolutely sure about the uniforms because there's no insignia on them, not even a belt for the dress uniform. The hangers obscure the inside necks, where size and issue tags would be sewn. A lot of the uniforms in that area are alike in design, especially the camos. They could be Serbian, though."

Then he picked up the tablet and scrolled back to the photo of the red dress. "This is a Bosniak woman's wedding dress. I'd bet my retirement on it. I was invited to a family wedding during my tour there and I'll never forget the elaborate bridal gown, the little hat, the embroidered shoes." He handed the tablet back to me. "Can I see these things in person?"

"I'll need to contact my client, but I'm positive she'll say yes."

He said nothing.

"Uh, you mean now?" I asked.

"Yes. It's important."

It was obvious that he knew something, but would not share it until he was certain. I called Adriana's cell and got voicemail. Crap! She was supposed to be lying low. I left a message that I was taking an expert to see the items in the attic and asked her to call me within the next fifteen minutes if she objected. Then I put my tablet and phone in my briefcase. "Before we leave, Colonel, I have to call my personal protection guy. I don't want him to think I'm leaving here under duress. And I want to know if my client, who didn't answer her phone, is okay. He can contact her guy."

His right eyebrow rose slightly. "You have a bodyguard?"

"Yes."

"Glad to hear it. We'll take my vehicle. I'm rated for counter-terrorist driving. I'll call my wife and tell her I'll be later than planned."

Counter-terrorist? I swallowed hard. "While you make your call, I'll let Spider—my bodyguard—know."

"Spider Mulcahey?"

I nodded.

A small smile, barely more than a twitch of the lips, lightened his sober features. "Tell that...tell him I'm waiting for an invite to his farm."

Spider texted Bram and reassured me that Adriana was fine, so I breathed a bit easier. I explained our mission—I felt like a secret agent at this point—and he chuckled when I conveyed the colonel's message. "Well, old whiskey tenor'll have to sing for his supper." A red blush crept up the colonel's neck when I told him.

Rank has its privileges. Lewis's Chevy Suburban was parked in a reserved space outside the building. I directed him to the Johnsons' south side home, noting that his eyes were in constant motion as he drove. Right mirror, left mirror, windshield, rear view mirror. He made several unexpected turns and parked in a supermarket lot, engine idling, watching for anyone who mimicked our route. When we arrived at the residence, he motioned for me to stay in the SUV and walked once around the property.

I used the time to look up the alarm code on my tablet, feeling spooked and expecting an attack at any moment.

Lewis returned to the Suburban and motioned for me to join him. "Nothing odd on the property," he said. Some of my tension must have communicated itself to the colonel—he gently placed his hand under my elbow to walk me up to the home's front door. "I'll go in first."

Had anyone been in there since my initial visit? Were the attic's contents still intact? I extracted the 9mm from my briefcase and held it in my left hand, pointing down. Feeling like an insubordinate lieutenant, I said, "No, sir. I need to disarm the alarm panel."

His eyebrows rose. "I assume you're rated for that." His chin dipped at the gun.

I nodded and opened the door with Adriana's keys, then dropped them into my briefcase and transferred the Beretta to my right hand. Inside, I stood for a moment—waiting, listening, smelling. It was musty, like before. I didn't think anyone had been there to introduce fresh air into the house. I quickly handled the alarm system and allowed Lewis in.

We walked the entire first floor and basement. Nothing had changed since my initial visit, five days ago. It seemed like a lifetime, with all that happened since then. When we reached the master bedroom, Colonel Lewis stood in the door, then entered to examine the bedding and the furniture. He paid special attention to the corner where the religious objects were displayed, but said nothing.

We proceeded to the attic, where I stopped on the top step and bent to peer at eye level across the wooden floor. There was a slight layer of undisturbed dust. It appeared that no one had been there after me. Behind me, Lewis made a slight hum. I took it as a sign of approval for my caution. "The uniforms are in the wheeled clothes rack," I told him.

He removed each one, turned the sleeves and pants legs inside out, and examined the collars and cuffs. Then he unlaced the boots and found the river rock inside one. Setting it aside, he carefully probed each boot with a keychain flashlight and his hands, repeating the process for the dress shoes. After he placed everything back into the protective cover of the rack, he turned to me. "Someone did an excellent job of removing tags, buttons, markings—anything that would provide a conclusive identification." Placing his hands on his hips, he said, "What's with the rock?"

"It's a safe, of sorts," I told him. "I found the trunk key inside." I twisted the outer part of the rock open and showed him the little keypad.

"You know the code?"

"Same as the door code."

"Clever of you."

At his praise, I felt like a prize cadet. "However," I said, "I kept the key, on the off chance that the house might be searched." After slipping the rock back into the boot's toe, I located the key on my key ring and opened the trunk. Taking out two pairs of the cotton gloves that were inside the trunk, I handed one set to him. When we were both ready, I started from the top shelf and showed him the contents—gold jewelry, books, women's garments.

The whisper of silk broke our almost breathless silence when he removed the deep red dress from the bottom box and held it up. "Yes," he said, "I've seen this type of clothes before. And the jewelry." He carefully refolded the dress and replaced it in the trunk, then turned to me. There was a moment of silence, in which I feared he would not share what he knew.

"Ms. Bonaparte, do you know what a Bosniak is?"

"A citizen of Bosnia?"

"A Muslim citizen." He gestured toward the trunk. "Why does a Serbian Christian have personal items from a Bosnian Muslim?" He waited, expecting me to answer.

"Although I didn't know exactly what they were, I've been speculating all along that these things were stolen."

"Stolen!" He barked it at me. "More like plundered." He paced a few steps away, then turned back. "Armed conflict is not pretty. I've seen terrible things in my lifetime, Ms. Bonaparte. But I've never seen anything like the atrocities that were visited on the Bosnians by the Serbs. Muslim women captured and put in holding cells, raped over and over, for days and weeks and months. When they fell pregnant, the Serbs kept them until the pregnancy was too advanced to be terminated, then sent them back in disgrace to their families and villages. And Sarajevo! That was a killing field. The longest siege of a country's capital in modern warfare. Systemized slaughter. There is no limit to the depths humans will sink." He ran his hands through his short hair. "I'm sorry. I get angry all over again, every time I remember."

"There's no need to apologize. I've never been where you have, Colonel, or seen the things you've seen. But just hearing what you've told me about it makes me feel sick." I promised myself that, tonight, I would read the pamphlet from the UWM library. "Do you think the items in the trunk were looted by whoever wore those uniforms?"

"Yes, I do. Of course, there's nothing conclusive here. But that's what I think." He pressed his lips together, then spoke. "I need pictures of your client's parents, the attorney and the woman who worked for the attorney. Also the husband. I want to run a search of the Bosnian War Criminals database. There are facial recognition programs that use biometrics to match persons to known terrorist or war criminal groups."

War criminals. That caused a lurch in my gut, as I pictured the courtroom scenes from *Judgment at Nuremburg*. If her parents were indeed war criminals, how would Adriana, sweet and gentle as she was, get over it? Still, the truth had to come out. The sick game of execution and threat had to end. Even if innocents were hurt.

"There are Johnson family pictures downstairs. As for Petrovitch, I may be able to find something from the *Journal-Sentinel* or the *Wisconsin Law Review*. There might even be one from his law school days at Marquette." I flipped through my tablet notes. "He graduated in '94. As a last resort, I'll ask the police if there's a picture from his home we can copy. Getting one of the Zupans will be more problematic. Josif Zupan is not cooperative. But maybe we can take a clandestine shot at his wife's funeral this Saturday. I feel bad about using such circumstances—"

"Don't." His voice was clipped, the mellow tenor harsh. "We have to know. Use any means necessary to get me the pictures." He stopped. "Of course, I mean any legal means, Ms. Bonaparte."

"Of course." I knew he was willing to go outside the law for the pictures. At this point, so was I. The less said about this to Wukowski, the better.

I secured the trunk and we made our way downstairs, where I took a framed family photo down from the wall, snapped a picture of it with my phone, and gave the original to the colonel. Then I alarmed the house and holstered my gun.

Spider Mulcahey waited on the Johnsons' small front stoop. "Colonel Lewis," he said, as he turned from surveying the yard.

"Mulcahey," Lewis responded, "I thought we got past rank the night I passed out on your couch."

"Guess so, sir," Spider said. "That was a real fine lullaby you sang Joey to sleep with before the drinking got too far along."

Whiskey tenor indeed, I thought.

Lewis checked his watch and grimaced. "I'm later than I thought. Deb will chew my…tail." He looked at Spider. "I assume you'll escort Ms. Bonaparte back to her car?"

"Sure thing, Colonel. I mean, sir, uh, Baddon."

"Bad one?" I asked.

"Baddon. It's a Welsh name, ma'am," the colonel said. He turned to Spider. "Keep a close watch on her. DEFCON 2."

Spider snapped to attention. "Yes, sir."

Colonel Lewis and I exchanged business cards. He wrote his cell phone number on his and said to call as soon as I had pictures. With an exchange of handshakes all round, he departed.

"Time to get off the streets, Angie," Spider said. "And I'm waiting to hear why the colonel thinks this is a DEFCON 2 situation." He hustled me to his van.

"DEFCON?" I asked him as I buckled in.

"Defense Readiness Condition. It's an Armed Forces graduating alert status. Five is situation normal. One is nuclear war. We're at two—ready to deploy and engage the enemy. And I need to know why." He started the engine and pulled away from the curb.

Chapter 21

He who fears dangers will not perish by them.

—Leonardo Da Vinci

Spider took a circuitous route to Marquette, doubling back and getting on and off the freeway several times, all the while checking his mirrors like the colonel had.

"Are we being followed?" I asked.

"Not to my knowledge. And believe me, I'd know."

I relaxed a bit. "Good."

"So tell me why the colonel upped our alert status."

"I'd rather wait until Bart is available and only tell the story once."

"Okay. I'll call Bram York and let him know the situation is more tense than we thought. I want him in on the discussion with Matthews."

"Spider, my call to Adriana from the ROTC office went to voicemail. She wasn't supposed to go out."

"No worries. She's with Bram. If anything went down, he'd call me."

"What if they both are in trouble?"

He motioned toward his phone, lying on the console between us. "We have an emergency signal. I'd know if there was a problem."

I didn't feel totally satisfied with that, but there was probably no way I would be totally satisfied with any of us being safe until we had the killers in custody. I suddenly realized that York was with Adriana and Spider was with me. "Who's covering Bobbie Russell?" I asked Spider.

"A buddy from Army days who lives near Chicago. I called him and he drove up last night. Name of Eugene Malone, but they call him Mad Man Malone." He glanced over at me. "You don't want to know. But Bobbie is safe with him."

"Does Bram have a nickname, too?"

"Nah. He's just the captain."

"Did you both serve with Colonel Lewis?"

"Nope."

Silence. Clearly, I asked too many questions.

"So, here's the plan," Spider said. "I'll take you to your car. I'll check it out before you get in. Then I'll deliver you to your office, check it out and take up a surveillance position outside. You call Matthews and set up a meeting, then let me know. I'll contact York."

His tone was matter-of-fact, but it didn't escape me that DEFCON 2 apparently meant someone else was running my life. Yes, it was for my own safety, but I still felt a bit smothered. Smothered was better than dead, though.

We got to Marquette without incident. Spider used a mirror attached to a long handle to check under my car. Then he took my keys and asked me to park the van on the street and wait.

"For what?" I asked.

"For the sound of no explosion," he told me.

Good God! "I can't let you take that chance, Spider. You're a family man."

"I'll stand way back, behind a concrete pillar, when I press the door release button, Angie. I don't want my van torn up by shrapnel again."

Again? I moved the van and waited.

Five minutes later, he jogged out of the parking structure and grinned at me. "All clear. I'll be right behind you. No sense in stealth at this point. Let the bastards sweat."

He did a similarly thorough job in my office, even though I assured him that new door locks and a motion detection alarm system were installed only a few months ago. When he was done, he pointed to the floor in front of the door. "I'll install a door sweep later."

"It's not drafty, Spider."

"It's too easy to blow a chemical agent into the office through that space."

Holy …! Spider was full of frightening ideas, but I could see the point. I nodded, too shaken to speak.

With Susan out on an audit, the office was quiet after Spider left. I booted my laptop and started to scan my inbox, when Spider unlocked the office door and came in.

I hadn't given him a key. "Spider, you are one scary dude."

He nodded. "Yeah, Magda says that, too. I checked the building. Security's okay, considering all the offices, but the owner needs to install a lock on the roof door. Anybody can get in from the roof."

"How would they get to the roof in the first place?"

"This is an older area of downtown, Angie. The buildings are close. It would be easy to jump across from one roof to the other."

I made a note to call the supe.

"I'll be parked out front in a silver Dodge Ram when it's time to meet Bart."

I didn't ask how the truck would get here. Spider had unlimited resources, it seemed. I placed the call to Bart's cell.

"What's up, Angie?"

"I need to meet with you and your two security consultants today. The situation has reached a higher alert level."

"Yeah? You okay?"

"I am. My guy is very…thorough."

"That he is. Hold on." He came back on the line in a few seconds. "It's three-thirty. How does five o'clock work for you?"

"I'll make it work. And Bart, do *you* have personal security?"

"Always." He paused. "It's that bad?"

"DEFCON 2, Bart. Ready to deploy and engage the enemy."

"Huh. Spider's assessment?"

"Nope. Colonel Lewis, who runs the ROTC program at Marquette and UWM. He was in the Bosnian War. I had him check the uniforms. I'll fill you in when I get there."

I called Spider. Then I finished scanning my emails and checked my office phone for messages. There were none.

Ninety minutes with nothing pressing to do. Ninety long minutes to think about all that I learned this afternoon. My head ached and my stomach felt queasy. I started to shake. I took my phone into the conference room and set the alarm for four-twenty. Then I lay down on the love seat and covered myself with the crocheted throw. A picture of Adriana, lying here the first day we met, came unbidden to mind.

Maybe Wukowski was right. Maybe I wasn't cut out for this kind of investigation. I wiggled against the back of the loveseat, somehow feeling more secure with its cushions against me. I wished it were Wukowski behind me, spooning me, wrapping his arms around me. *Dear God, keep us all safe*, I prayed.

The cell phone alarm sounded. I was surprised to have dozed off on the office love seat. *My mind needed to escape the harsh reality of the situation*, I decided. After folding and replacing the afghan, I went down the hall to the ladies' bathroom, used the facilities, and freshened my makeup and breath. Then I gathered my briefcase and purse, secured the office and waited at the door to the building lobby.

It was almost full dark. It would be March before Milwaukee saw twelve hours of daylight again. I missed the sun waking me in the morning and keeping me up and alert in the evening. The cold murky night made me shiver. Spider pulled up and I exited the building.

The bottom of the Ram door was at knee height to me. Even with slacks on, it would be ungainly to boost myself into the truck. I needn't have worried. When Spider reached over and opened the door, a bar with LED lights lowered from underneath the carriage. "Use the granny handle on the door," he told me.

I climbed in and slammed the door. *It's true, I was a grandmother, but I was no granny!* "Granny handle?" I challenged him.

"Don't get your undies in a bunch, Angie," he said, smiling. "It's a joke between me and my wife. She's height-challenged, too. Nothing personal."

Hmph. Height-challenged! I decided to ignore it. "Do you push a button to raise and lower the step?" I was curious.

"It's wired to come down when a door opens and retract when it closes. And it's called a nerf bar." He pulled out onto Farwell Avenue, driving south toward the Third Ward and Bart's office. "I spoke to Bram while I was on surveillance. Seems that Bobbie and Adriana met up for some shopping this afternoon." He laughed and shook his head. "York and Malone must've felt like a couple of pit bulls at a poodle grooming salon. Neither one of them is domesticated yet."

I was a bit ticked off that Bobbie pre-empted my plans to outfit Adriana. Then I reasoned that he was probably more in tune with what a twenty-something woman would wear than I was. I worried, though, about the expedition. "After what I heard this afternoon, their being out in public was a bad idea, Spider."

"They didn't go out. Bobbie's, um, friend, Stephano, set up a private session for Adriana in a meeting room at her hotel. Mad Man said that Bobbie called Stephano with the size specs, including cup size." He laughed. "I could almost hear Malone blushing over the phone. He's not used to women. He joined up at eighteen."

We arrived at Bart's building and a Family guy stepped out to raise the security gate to the building occupant underground parking. There were about thirty spaces. "Bart cleared it for us," Spider said as he drove around a row and put the truck into Park, facing the gate and still running. "Stay put while I run recon."

I cut my eyes toward the beefy guard.

Spider replied to my unspoken question. "I don't trust someone else's work until they prove themselves to me. There's too much at stake here. Scoot over and get behind the wheel. If you hear any commotion or if I'm not back in three minutes, take off. Drive through the gate if necessary." He tapped his watch and pointed at me.

Irritating alpha male! I checked my watch and nodded agreement, but there was no way I'd leave if he wasn't back in three minutes. I did lever myself over the gigantic console and into the driver's seat, though, glad that the guard watched the street and not my butt in the air.

Spider was back in two minutes, eighteen seconds. I lowered the window.

"Pull it over next to the stairs and park facing out," he said, then hesitated and reached for the door handle. "Maybe I should …"

I raised the window and deftly slipped the Ram into the spot closest to the stairway. Just because you're small, it doesn't mean you can't park with the big boys. Spider trotted over and waited. I grabbed my purse and briefcase from the passenger side and handed them to him, then took hold of the granny handle (there must be a better name!) and stepped down onto the nerf bar and then the pavement. At this point, I didn't care if my backside was toward him. It was spooky underground and I wanted out of there.

There were Family soldiers at every landing. Spider told each of them "*massima allerta*" as we passed. High alert. Apparently DEFCON 2 didn't translate into Italian. My already jangled nerves did another little dance. Bart had a man outside his office, too. I hesitated, but decided not to leave my briefcase or purse in care of the guard. I did, however, fold my jacket and place it on the hallway floor, next to the door. The guard gave me a "whaddya, crazy?" perusal, but said nothing. The same password gained us access.

From her desk, Bertha gave me a steely stare and nodded toward Bart's door. "He's waiting for you."

Spider walked over and offered his hand. "Evening, Mrs. Conti. I'm sorry we're keeping you so late."

How did he know to call her "Missus"? He oozed charm, but I was sure Bertha would cut him off at the knees.

To my shock, she gave a little simpering smile and responded, "It's part of the job, Len. Can I bring you a coffee?"

Good grief! Who was this woman and where was the real Bertha Conti being held? I breezed by and went into Bart's office. Spider followed after about a minute. "Len?" I asked him.

He doffed an imaginary hat and swept me a bow. "Leonard Aloysius Mulcahey, at your service."

"I take it you know Bertha."

Bart smiled. "He's been charming her for about a year now, since he first set up new office security for us."

Bertha entered with a tray holding a carafe, three mugs, and sugar and creamer. All she'd ever done for me was allow me to pour my own. I was pretty sure that Bart never got this treatment, either. The old Bing Crosby song started to play in my head. *When Irish eyes are smiling, sure, they steal your heart away.*

We doctored our coffees and sat down. Bart checked his watch. "I'm expecting Bram and Malone any time now."

"Are they bringing Bobbie and Adriana?" I asked.

Bart nodded.

If the suspicions that her parents were war criminals were confirmed, Adriana would have to face the ugly truth. For now, I wanted to protect her. Before I could explain Colonel Lewis' theory, the rest of the team arrived.

Bram York was tall, trim and muscular, with brown eyes and dark hair, graying at the temples. His mouth was set in a grim line. He used a cane, but didn't lean on it. *Must help his balance*, I thought.

Mad Man Malone did *not* fit his nickname. He was so darned normal. Average height, average weight, nondescript brown hair, unremarkable hazel eyes. He dressed in khakis and a blue short-sleeved knit shirt, worn rather loose. The polo hid his impressive biceps and his pants were cut to accommodate very muscular thighs. I decided not to underestimate either man.

Adriana wore a figure-flattering pants-and-jacket outfit in a lovely deep saffron color that avoided being mustardy. A neutral shell with a lacy band peeked out under the blazer and ankle boots in an orangey tan leather completed the look. So sleek, so current, so in tune with the new Adriana. I hugged her and whispered, "That's so cute! I have to see all your new clothes—later, once we get away from these alpha men."

She smiled and whispered back. "I told Stephano I wanted to shop with you for lingerie."

"Deal," I said, happy that I could be part of the makeover.

After introductions to Malone and another tray of coffee from Bertha, we all took seats. The security team's positions covered the window and door. I made sure to sit next to Adriana on the couch. Bobbie was in a chair on her other side. I didn't know if that was coincidence. Bobbie probably wanted to be close, in case Adriana fell apart at whatever bad news I had to impart.

Bart nodded at me and I started to tell the afternoon's story. I didn't sugarcoat it. The only way we would be safe was if the whole team knew the danger and was prepared to react. I took Adriana's hand when I reached the part where Colonel Lewis gave his opinion about the hidden attic finds. "He thinks they may be items that were looted from Bosniaks—Muslim citizens of Bosnia." Adriana gave a quick indrawn breath. "An associate of mine at UWM already identified one of the books as being on Interpol's art crimes list. Lewis is going to do some checking with Interpol."

Adriana spoke, her voice quiet, but resolute. "Angie, my parents had Bosniak friends when we lived there. I played with a Muslim girl, Reema. Mama gave her family many of the things we couldn't bring with us when we left for the United States. My parents didn't hate the Muslims. And there is no way they would steal from neighbors. No way." Her eyes challenged me to refute her.

"How do you explain these things being locked away in the trunk in their attic, Adriana?"

"Perhaps someone gave them the trunk to keep it safe and they didn't know what was in it. I don't know how it got there." She took her hand from mine and placed it in her lap. "My parents were the ones who were killed. Someone—maybe Petrovitch—took vengeance on *them*, not the other way round."

"Uncle Herman" had now become "Petrovitch" in her mind. That was probably good. She needed to distance herself from him. But I couldn't ease her fear or anger at the expense of the truth.

"Adriana," I said, "there are millions of dollars in the bank accounts, with your parents' names on them. There are these Bosniak artifacts. And someone killed your parents and Dragana Zupan. We don't know why, not exactly, and we certainly aren't sure who. We need a plan to expose the truth and none of us can afford to take any chances with these killers on the loose."

Bobbie reached over to pat Adriana's shoulder and she grasped his hand and held on. After an uncomfortable silence, Bram York said, "Bart, I believe the time has come to terminate your protection of Adriana, Bobbie and Angie. It would be best if I arrange for their personal security, until the guilty party or parties are brought to justice."

I expected Bart to object, but he nodded. "I think you're right. This calls for brains and specialists, not brawn. My primary concern is for their safety. How can I help?"

"First, step up your own personal security. Don't be predictable. Same for Mrs. Conti. Next, transfer 50k to my bank account. I'll use it to hire a trained force. The three of us"—he nodded at Spider and Mad Man—"aren't enough. We need more manpower to guarantee the safety of your team. Last, with your permission, I'll get in touch with Colonel Lewis and work with him and his contacts." He spoke with authority, the natural leader in the room.

"Adriana," Bart said, "do I have your authority to transfer the money from your drawing account?" She nodded. "Give Bertha the banking particulars," he told Bram. "You'll have the funds tonight." He paused. "I assume you don't want to disclose where they'll be?"

"It's better that way."

"Hold on, guys," I said. "I'm not willing to be put into some sort of security cage. Outside of the financials, almost everything we know about this case came from my digging. I can't let it go now. And there are people involved who won't speak to anyone else."

"Who would that be?" York asked.

"One, Josif Zupan, Dragana's husband. Two, a survivor of Sarajevo who teaches at UWM. I believe they have important information. I can connect with them. I don't think you can." I challenged him with my eyes.

To his credit, he considered what I said and didn't play the "little woman" card. "Very well. You'll be guarded 24/7, though." He looked at Adriana. "You're in the most danger. I want you in a secure location. Agreed?"

"Angie?" she asked, her voice wavering.

"I think it's wise to do as Bram suggests." I gently leaned toward her and offered my hand. She took it. "It won't be for long. I think we're close." *True?* I wasn't sure, but it felt like there would be an important break in the case soon.

Bobbie broke in. "I need to be with Angie. It's the best way for me to learn the ropes."

"You're not ready, Bobbie," Bram said. "You're not out of boot camp yet, and this is a high-level mission." His voice was firm, but quiet. "You need time to learn the basics before you can be effective. Self-defense, driving techniques, firearms, hand-to-hand combat." He turned to me. "I'm sure you've mastered those, Angie."

Was this a Wukowski-style snipe at my skills? I checked his posture and facial expression and decided it was genuine. Problem was, my basics were more along the lines of computer searches and interviewing techniques. "I can handle a gun and I know enough self-defense to disable the bad guy and run. My PI work doesn't usually require more than that."

Bram assessed me. "Smart. You're too small to take on most men." He turned back to Bobbie. "I won't waste my time trying to keep you in line. Are you in with the plan?"

Bobbie sagged a little, then straightened his spine and nodded. "I'm in."

"Good man. Spider will make some contacts and set you up with instructors. You'll know your stuff when they're done, I guarantee that."

This time, I wasn't so sure about Bram's sincerity. But if Bram was pumping Bobbie up, it worked. The light came back to his eyes. I wondered if the intern would soon outpace the mentor in the physical aspects of the job. That would be okay with me. A woman's gotta know her limitations.

The security team went into a small huddle to discuss tonight's logistics. I turned to Bart. "We need to let the MPD know what's happened."

"Not yet. It's all conjecture."

"Bart, now we have a paper trail on the book in the attic. I don't want to take a chance that someone will break into the Johnson house and steal our only hard evidence. And I won't let the police walk into this blind. They need to know." I made up my mind as I spoke. If Bart wouldn't back me, I'd tell Wukowski anyway and resign from the case. There was no way that I'd let Wukowski, Iggy or any other police office take that risk.

He sighed and leaned back in his reinforced office chair. "You're a hard woman, Angelina."

"Damn straight, I am." I puffed myself up like a little bantam rooster.

That broke the tension and we laughed. "Okay, you have my permission to tell Wukowski what's up. They'll want evidentiary custody of the items in the attic. That should ease your worries about burglars."

We split up as we left Bart's office. Once again, Bobbie and Adriana made for the tunnel route out of the building, Bobbie explaining it to Bram and Malone in a serious voice. Spider and I left the same way we entered, from the parking garage in his Ram truck. As he pulled out, he told me, "There's little sense in spiriting you away, if you're determined to stay on the hunt. Sooner or later, you'll be tagged. Your condo is fairly secure. We might as well take advantage of that."

"I plan to call the homicide detective on the case, Ted Wukowski, and set up a meeting at my place tonight. He needs to know about today's developments."

"Bart told me a little about him. Uh…he staying the night?"

"Maybe. It's his call."

"Ask him, Angie. I'll feel better outside, knowing you've got backup inside. Once Bram gets a few more guys on the team, it won't be an issue."

"I can handle myself, you know."

"Yeah, I got that. But we always work in pairs on a mission. Safer that way."

I felt better, knowing that Spider thought of me as another team member and that he wasn't applying special rules to me simply because I'm a woman. "Okay, I'll ask him and I'll let you know."

When we got to my building, Spider escorted me upstairs and ran a check of the condo. "Be sure to let me know if Wukowski is staying tonight. I'd hate to get rousted for assaulting a cop," he said as he headed out the door for an uncomfortable night in his truck. As far as I could tell, the only sleep he got in the last two days was in catnaps at Adriana's hotel or on the street outside my unit. He didn't look or act tired, though. *Must be the training*, I thought.

Chapter 22

I know there is strength in the differences between us. I know there is comfort where we overlap.

—Ani DiFranco

I called Wukowski and told him there were developments I needed to share. Then I asked, "Are you available to stay here tonight?" I usually flirted to entice him to my bed.

He picked up on my serious tone right away. "Is there a problem?"

"Yes. I don't want to say more until you get here."

"It'll take me twenty minutes, Angie, but I can call the local station and have an officer there in five."

"It's not that urgent or serious, *caro*."

"Okay, I'm on the way. Stay safe."

I gave Spider a description of Wukowski and the particulars on his Jeep. Then I sank down on the couch, feeling the aftereffects of post-adrenaline rush—dead tired, but jittery. I wanted Wukowski here, right now. I wanted food, but felt too anxious to concentrate on cooking.

My phone rang. "Angie, I'm on the way, but I missed lunch and I'm starving. Is everything under control? I'm thinking about stopping at Cousins."

My man! I reassured him that all was well and ordered a meatball sub with provolone on half a crusty wheat loaf. With broccoli cheese soup. I needed it.

I met him at the door, took the Cousins bag and set it on the hall table, wrapping my arms around Wukowski and shoving the door closed with one hand. Then I squeezed him. Hard.

"Whoa, *droja*," he said as he enfolded me in a gentle embrace. "You okay?"

"I am now," I told him. I released my fierce hold and backed up a bit. "Come on, let's eat and then I'll tell you about my day."

While I got plates and silverware out, Wukowski hung up his overcoat, removed his shoes and padded into the kitchen in his stocking feet. I found it endearing to see the little boy side of such a large and otherwise grim man. I quickly cut the subs—mine six inches, his a full foot—and assembled the plates. "Decaf?" I asked. The last thing I needed was to put my body chemistry into overdrive again.

"Fine with me." He pulled mugs out of the cupboard and set them on the table, then removed his suit coat and hung it on the back of the chair. He didn't remove his shoulder holster as he usually would. We sat down to tuck into the meal. "I assume this isn't about Thanksgiving," he said.

Thanksgiving—another sword of Damocles hanging over my head! "Nope, it's not. But I'd rather wait until we're done eating to bring you up to date."

"Fine with me, *Anielica*." The coffee maker gasped and Wukowski stood, filled our mugs and replaced the carafe. When he passed behind me on his way his seat, he bent down and kissed my neck. "You scared me, Angie. No secrets, promise?"

I reached up and brought his head down a bit so I could kiss his cheek. "No secrets, Wukowski."

We finished the meal in record time. The soup was warm, thick and comforting, but the meatball sub sat heavy in my gut as we moved into the living room and settled on the couch. Normally, I would snuggle up against Wukowski, but he still wore the gun holster. "You planning to sleep with that on?" I asked him, gesturing with my chin at the offending item.

"Only if you think it's sexy," he said. "Course, I'd have to duct tape the safety. Just to be sure." He grinned, trying to embarrass me into blushing about our rather active bedroom fun.

I didn't bite. "Take it off, Wukowski, so we can cuddle."

"Cuddle, huh?" He shrugged out of the holster and set it on the table, loosened his tie and put it next to the gun holster. After he unbuttoned his shirt collar, he put his arms out and gathered me into his side. "Better?"

"Much."

He stroked my face and my free arm, not in a sexual way, but as a means of comfort. Then he kissed me, set me upright on the couch and said, "Be right back." He went into the kitchen and returned, carrying the carafe and a small notebook. After refilling our cups, he set the carafe down on a coaster and took a digital recorder from his shirt pocket. "Okay with you?" he asked.

Bart wouldn't like it, but I nodded. Wukowski turned the device on and gave the official police description of the interview: name, place, date, time.

He listened in silence, making an occasional note, while I gave him the rundown: meeting with Lily; the Interpol report on the stolen book; my trip to the ROTC office and then to the Johnsons' with Colonel Lewis; his suppositions about the trunk contents; Spider, Bram and Mad Man; the team meeting at Bart's office. What a day! It made me tired just recounting it. I released the tension in my neck and shoulders.

"Ms. Bonaparte, for the record, would your fingerprints or those of Colonel Lewis be on any of the items in the attic?"

"On the uniforms and footwear, yes. We didn't use gloves when we handled them. I touched the trunk key without gloves and may have left prints on the faceplate, but the Colonel didn't touch either. We handled the contents while wearing gloves, so they should be uncontaminated. One moment." I went to the hall closet and returned with my key ring. "Here," I said, handing three keys to Wukowski. "Also for the record, these are the Johnsons' house keys, this is the trunk key, and this is the key to their hardware store. There's a security alarm at the store. The code is one-three-nine-one-eight."

"So noted," he said. "Where are Mr. Russell and Ms. Johnson now?"

"I don't know. The security team thought it was better that way. But their cell phone numbers haven't changed."

"Is there anything else you wish to add?"

"No. Nothing else."

He turned off the recorder and shut his notebook. His face was still the impassive face of the interviewer. I wasn't sure what to do next. Everything felt so disconnected. *Who was he now—lover or homicide detective?*

Then he sighed, leaned back into the couch and rubbed his eyes with the heels of his hands. "That's over. I'll get an evidence team to the Johnsons' in the morning." He looked at me and smiled the endearing smile that transformed him. "Where were we?"

Suddenly, my energy level rose. I climbed on his lap, straddling him, and unfastened the rest of the buttons on his dress shirt. He returned the favor by easing my arms out of the sweater I wore and pulling it over my head. He groaned when he saw the shell pink demi-bra.

My couch was comfortable and wide, but I wouldn't want to change locations afterward. I stood and took Wukowski's hand to lead him into the bedroom. He picked up the gun holster and brought it along. I decided to ignore the aura of danger. Just this once.

Chapter 23

The people must be the ones to win, not the war, because war has nothing to do with humanity. War is something inhuman.

—Zlata Filipovitch

I woke to Wukowski spooning me. It was reassuring to feel so safe. When his breathing and his body told me he was awake, I turned in his arms and snuggled.

He kissed the top of my head and said, "Nothing I'd like better than to stay in bed with you, Angie, but my plate is overflowing at work. I need to be in the office by seven-thirty. Coffee?"

Darn. I filled my coffee cup and retrieved the *Journal-Sentinel* from the hallway while Wukowski took a shower and dressed. He emerged from the bedroom, looking all professional.

"Wukowski, I got a family photo of the Johnsons yesterday, but I might need some help with pictures of Herman Petrovitch and Josif Zupan."

"I can get their DMV photos, but you know how good they usually are."

"Better than nothing. Can you send them in an email, with the DMV stats, too? Colonel Lewis is out of town, but he wants me to deliver them ASAP so he can start a search on the Interpol and Bosnian war criminals databases."

"Provided he sends me the search results as soon as they come in, even if they're negative."

"Of course. I don't want you in the dark about any of this." I didn't say that I understood how dangerous this game was. Wukowski had enough angst about me already.

"When the meeting is over, I'll get on it." He hugged me close and spoke quietly into my ear. "Be careful."

"Don't worry. I have no intentions of engaging these guys. And Spider has my back." I raised my head and kissed him. "Go. I'll be fine."

"I'll call later. Okay if I spend the night?"

It was rare that we were together on two consecutive nights. We both liked to have a little break. To be honest, we were probably afraid of moving any faster. But I sensed his request was more about needing to keep me safe than it was about sex. "Absolutely okay," I said.

It was too early to call Lily about meeting with Professor Kolar. I perused the newspaper and came across the obituary for Dragana Zupan. Her parents, brothers and a sister were listed as deceased. Josif was her only survivor. She was born in Sarajevo. Her maiden name was Osmanović. Based on the Jovanović-Johnson and Petrovitch-Peterson paradigm, her English name would be Osmanovitch, translated to 'son of Osman.'

I pulled out my tablet and did a search. 'Osman' came from the Arabic boy's name Uthman. Several Ottoman rulers were named Osman. So before her marriage, Dragana was either a Muslim woman or a woman whose family had a Muslim heritage. She married a Serbian and practiced the Serbian Orthodox faith. How did that connect to the contents of the attic?

I marked my calendar for the funeral and added to my to-do list to ask Bram if it was safe for Bobbie to attend with me.

The weather forecast predicted cloudy skies with temps in the mid-40s, but no precipitation. I wandered into my walk-in closet. I could get by with my short Burberry trench coat, as long as I kept the lining in and wore layers underneath.

Assuming Lily set up a meeting with Professor Kolar today, I wanted to look professional, but approachable. I sorted through the winter side of my work garb and settled on a soft teal blouse, gray shawl-collar sweater that ended just above the waist and skinny leg gray wool pants. I'd wear deep eggplant pumps for a flash of fun. I laid the clothes on the bed.

My cell phone rang. "Angie, it's Lily. I'm sorry to call so early, but Professor Kolar is leaving for a conference on the west coast tomorrow. Can you meet us at the library at ten-thirty?"

"That's perfect, Lily. Should I just come to your desk?"

"Yes. I'll arrange a private room. And, Angie, she seemed sort of...I don't know, maybe withdrawn or worried, when I asked her."

"Hmm. Why don't you make the introductions and then say something to lighten things up?"

"Like what?"

"Well, talk about how much you love mysteries and how excited you were to meet a real private investigator. Then I'll tell how we met while I was trying to identify the stuff I found in the attic. It's liable to get tense from there, so do whatever you can to put her at ease."

"I guess that makes me the good cop, right?"

I smiled at her enthusiasm. "It does. I really appreciate your help in setting this up, Lily."

"My pleasure. See you later."

I dialed Spider.

"Yo," he said.

"Spider, when do you sleep?"

"York sent a retired Feeb over last night so I could get a couple hours. I figured you'd be fine, with police protection right there at your side."

I blushed a bit. "A Feeb, eh?"

"Yeah, FBI. But don't ever say "feeb" to their face. What's up?"

I filled him in on the meeting. He wanted to be in the room, but I explained how nervous the professor seemed and he agreed to wait nearby. He had the code to my building's underground parking and would pick me up at the elevator in a reinforced sedan, on loan from Bart. Thank goodness I wouldn't have to navigate the Ram again.

I checked the bedside clock. It was a few minutes after eight. I'd start getting ready to leave around nine-ten. I ran a quick check of Professor Kolar's curriculum vitae. She earned a B.S. in biological science at Oxford (1986), a master's in chemistry at Princeton (1988) and a Ph.D. in biochemical engineering at Stanford (1991). They were all top-rated schools in those majors. Based on the years when her degrees were awarded, she went lockstep through the higher education process. She then returned to the former Yugoslavia and taught at the University of Belgrade, another school that was in the top world ratings. I flipped back to my notes. Petrovitch was a graduate of the Belgrade Law School. Interesting, but it was a large university and there was every chance they'd never met.

There was still plenty of time until meeting with Lily and Kolar. It made no sense to keep putting it off, so I called Aunt Terry.

"Angelina, how nice that you called," she said.

Huh? Aunt Terry had caller ID? Since when? "Hi, Aunt Terry. Last time I checked, you still had an old rotary dial phone. How'd you know it was me?"

"Well, um, Fausto convinced me to get a smartphone. For safety. And it has a lot of features. I like the GPS thingie a lot. He transferred my regular phone to this one. I'll probably get rid of the old number, as soon as I notify everyone."

It appeared that Fausto convinced Aunt Terry that it was all right to spend money on herself. This made me think more kindly of him. "Did he show you how to set up a ringtone, so you know who the call is from without looking?"

She giggled. "Yes."

"Okay, give. What's mine?"

"'Private Eyes Are Watching You.'"

I laughed. "Good one. What about Papa?"

"'I'll Get Even with You.' But it's not what you think. It's a really nice song about paying back someone who's done a lot for you."

"Aw, Aunt Terry, that's sweet." I took a deep breath. "I called to ask about Thanksgiving. What can I bring?"

"Besides your guy and his mother?"

Uh-oh. She wasted no time. "I'm talking about food!" Maybe if I turned the interrogation tables on her, I might escape. "And by the way, is Fausto joining us?"

"Yes." There was a slight hesitation. "He doesn't have family. Of course I asked him to join us."

"Out of pity?"

"Well…no. I like him, Angie. He seems to like me. We're just playing it by ear, you know?"

I knew only too well. "That's all any of us can do. You can talk to me anytime you have concerns or just want to vent."

"Same for you, *la mia nipotina*."

My little niece. How many times had Aunt Terry consoled me or encouraged me or expressed her pride in me with those words? "*La mia dolce zia*"—my sweet aunt—"there must be something else I can contribute for the meal. *Vino*? Dessert? Appetizers?"

"Wine would be good. You know I'm hopeless with wine. And an appetizer. But don't go overboard, okay?"

Aunt Terry never wanted anyone else to go to any trouble, despite the fact that she went to great lengths to care for others. "I'll keep it simple. And don't be surprised if Wukowski's mother brings a Polish dish. She's a great cook—I've tasted her *pierogi*."

"Oh, I hope she likes Italian food. Maybe I can find a recipe for something Polish…"

"Don't you dare! Just make what you always do. If she's not fond of pasta, there's still the turkey and dressing, cranberries, rolls, green bean casserole—all the things that every other American household will serve on Thanksgiving. There'll be plenty for her to choose from." Thanksgiving was a week away. I promised to phone Aunt Terry on Monday and we ended the call.

After that, I printed the pictures of the attic items and the Interpol listing for the stolen book. I hoped Professor Kolar would divulge any information she had at the meeting, but she might need time to think about what Lily and I would tell her. She could take the pictures with her. I tucked them away in my briefcase.

Barring an epiphany or a sudden break, it looked like my Friday afternoon and evening would be free until Wukowski joined me. The background check was still pending and I couldn't afford to lose a good client by delay. I could manage it from home, but I wanted Bobbie to get his feet wet on the computer side of the job, so I called and arranged to meet him at my office at one-thirty. I wished we could have lunch together, but being in a public place was no guarantee of safety when dealing with an evil conspiracy.

The thought stopped me in my tracks. I wasn't up to the challenge of dealing with that caliber of criminal, but having Bram's team on our side gave me some reassurance. I wasn't a quitter. I'd take extra precautions, follow all the security rules and do my best. *Chin up*, I told myself. I started to dress for the meeting.

Spider waited for me at the elevator, as planned. When I opened the front passenger door, he said, "Better if you sit in back, Angie. The tinted glass will conceal who's in the car. I called the library and spoke to Lily. She'll be waiting at the loading dock so we can pull right in."

"Does she know the password?"

He laughed. "I forgot to give that to her."

It broke the tension a bit, but I was still on edge and didn't want to communicate that to Professor Kolar. I relaxed back into the seat, closed my eyes and did some yoga breathing, not opening my eyes until Spider said, "We're here."

Lily greeted me with a brief hug and looked at me closely. "You're recovered from the bash on the head?"

"I'm fine—no headache since Tuesday. Lily, this is Spider Mulcahey. Spider, Lily March."

Lily made no bones about giving Spider the once-over as they shook hands. "Well, you look like you can handle yourself."

"Yes, ma'am."

She nodded once. "Good. Let's get to the meeting room. Professor Kolar seems spooked enough to leave if we're not there when she arrives." She turned to Spider. "There's a student study carrel a few feet from the room. You can camp there and still keep a lookout. She won't be able to see you if you're sitting."

He nodded and showed me a small silver button. "It's a transmitter. I'll be wearing the receiver. Let me attach it to the inside of your briefcase. All you have to do is put the case on the floor and leave it open, but not so open that the prof is likely to see it. Test it when you get in. I'll cough real loud to let you know it's working. If you don't hear me, bring it out to the carrel."

It was on the shady side of legal, but, like the colonel, I was willing to cut a corner on legalities if it meant we could roll up this case. I handed Spider my briefcase. Lily watched the process with an avid gleam in her eye.

We settled in the meeting room. It was far from opulent, just a long fake-wood table and chairs, and a credenza with a computer monitor and phone. I unlocked my briefcase and set it down next to the chair at the far head of the table, where I could watch the door. "How long a break do you get for Thanksgiving, Lily?"

A hacking cough sounded from outside the room. I sat and smiled at her to continue.

"I'll be off starting next Thursday—Thanksgiving—and the following week."

"Nice."

Lily rose and walked to the door. "We're in here, Professor," she called.

Kolar was medium height and a little overweight. She wore a black skirted suit with a plain white blouse and black pumps. She carried no purse. Her briefcase was also black. The only color relief was a headscarf of light blue, worn like a Westerner, with her dark brown hair visible at the temples and top of her head. She entered and closed the door, then frowned. "Lily, may I ask to exchange seats, please?"

Lily was seated on my left, with her back to the wall, facing the doorway. She rose and walked around the table, where her back was now to the windows that looked out onto the open space and stacks.

The professor nodded and silently walked to Lily's former position. She extended her hand to me and said, "Dr. Rua Kolar."

Keeping her back to the wall indicated her deep-seated desire for safety. I rose and took her hand, saying, "Angelina Bonaparte, but call me Angie." Perhaps being on a first-name basis would relieve her obvious tension and establish a sense of trust.

She didn't reciprocate with her first name. "Master's in library science from UW-Madison," she said. "Good school."

She'd done her homework on me, too. *Was that more a sign of her intelligence or her wariness?*

As she sat, Lily jumped in. "Professor, you'll never believe how Angie and I met. So funny." She paused and slowed her speech. "I was on duty last Sunday night, staffing the desk, bored out of my mind. It didn't seem like there were any serious scholars on the floor, just a lot of goofing off. It made me grouchy."

Kolar nodded. "I see."

I worried that the whole interview would consist of two or three word responses from her. Maybe I could provide a little comic relief. "Lily is pretty scary in mean librarian mode, and she's about a foot taller than I am. I hated to even ask her a question."

"I was intrigued," Lily continued, "by this put-together woman in clothes to die for, that looked absolutely perfect on her. And here's me, all gangly and grumpy, wishing I could look that good." She tugged at her long sleeves, which ended about two inches above her wrist bones. "They just don't make clothes for women my height."

Kolar smiled slightly. Her full lips curved into a lovely cupid's bow and her stern look softened. "We all have our gifts, Dr. March. I'm sure you never worry about weight." She sighed and patted her slightly round tummy.

"Please, call me Lily."

Kolar had little choice but to reciprocate, unless she wanted to be rude. "Rua," she said.

We all shifted a bit and Lily continued her story. "When Angie showed me her private investigator's license, I got pretty excited. You see, I love mysteries. Devour them. I've been that way since I read my first Nancy Drew." Kolar lifted an eyebrow and Lily explained. "Nancy Drew was a series for grade-school kids about a girl detective." She sighed. "I so wanted to be Nancy and I guess that wish has continued into my adulthood. Kinsey Milhone, Bertha Cool, Amelia Peabody, Stephanie Plum, Sigrid Harald, Eve Dallas—I've read them all and then some. And here was a real live female detective asking for my help. She showed me some pictures that were part of a current case and asked if I could help identify them. Of course, I shut down the desk and went upstairs into the stacks with her."

It was my turn. I needed to move slowly. The book was probably the least threatening item. "I had pictures of an old book. Lily examined the alphabet used in the book and saw that it contained both Latin and Cyrillic characters. She did some preliminary digging and decided that it could be written in old Bosnian." I handed her the pictures of the book. "Would you agree?"

Kolar removed a black case from her briefcase and settled narrow black-framed glasses on her face.

Why all the black? I wondered.

She studied the paper prints carefully, while Lily and I waited. When Lily opened her mouth a bit, I caught her eye and gave a subtle shake of the head, indicating that she should stay quiet.

After several long minutes, Kolar stacked the papers and set them on the table, then folded her hands and looked at Lily. "You're right. The language is Bosnian. The book looks old, but one can never be sure in these days of forgery. If it is real, it is an important work by an important Bosnian poet of the sixteenth century." She handed the papers back to me. "Angie"—she pronounced it *On-gee*, which I found charming—"how did you come across this book?"

"It was among some other items in an attic trunk, in the home of a client whose parents are recently deceased. She hired me to look into her parents' assets."

"Were her parents Bosnians?"

If she caught me in a lie, there was no way she'd trust me again. I had to tell the truth and hope it didn't spook her. "Serbian. They emigrated to the U.S. in 1995 and became citizens in 1999."

"Their names?"

I watched her closely, looking for a reaction as I spoke. "Originally, Jan, Ivona and Adrijana Jovanović. They Americanized to John, Yvonne and Adriana Johnson. John and Yvonne were the parents. Adriana is my client." If she knew of the Johnsons, there was no sign of it.

"Why would she hire a private investigator to look into assets? Wouldn't an attorney or an accountant be more suitable for that?"

She was far too insightful. I couldn't gloss over this. "Her attorney sent her to the accountant who shares office space with me. Susan brought me into the equation when she found out that Adriana inherited a large amount of money and had no idea where it came from. Her family always lived simply. Her parents led her to believe that they were among the working poor. Adriana didn't want a bequest that might be tainted."

"You said that both her parents are recently deceased. Did they die in an accident? Or were they old and one gave up when the other passed?"

"There's no easy way to say this, Rua. They were murdered while working at their little South Side hardware store."

She gave a sharp intake of breath. "Murdered! How?"

"Shot in the back of the head."

She stared out at the common area on the other side of the windows. The large wall clock ticked mechanically as its second hand snapped from point to point. Then she spoke. "I cannot determine with certainty what this book is, even if you bring it to me. You need to seek an expert." She reached for her briefcase and began to rise.

"Rua, there is more," I said. "Would you look at pictures of some female clothing and jewels that were also in the attic?"

"Why?"

"If you can identify them as belonging to a particular cultural group, perhaps it will help us understand where the money came from and why the Johnsons were killed." I offered her the pictures. My outstretched arm waited. She took them and resumed her seat.

When she viewed the first picture, her body hunched over, taking shallow breaths. Her hands shook. She stacked these pictures, too, and placed them before her on the table. Then she crossed her arms, with her palms on her forearms, as if hugging herself. It was a classic anxiety reaction.

"The dress, hat and shoes are for a Bosniak woman's wedding. A Bosnian Muslim, you understand?" Her voice was steady, but she didn't look up as she spoke. I sensed her struggle to remain calm. "The jewelry, too, especially the headdress. It would be worn at a wedding. It was often a woman's only financial security, the headdress." She looked at me. "No Bosniak woman would surrender these items willingly. Are you sure the Johnsons were not Muslim?"

"They attended St. Sava Serbian Church and were active in a group that wanted to locate and restore looted Serbian artifacts after the war ended."

"This makes no sense. Why would they have these items?"

"We're not sure. Adriana says they were friends with Muslim families in Bosnia. Maybe someone gave them as a gift?"

"So unlikely as to be impossible. A Bosniak would have to be *in extremis* to give up these things."

"Many were, I understand." I was teetering on the brink. She would either withdraw completely or finally open up. I waited, my body tense and my back aching, not daring to move.

Finally, she broke the silence. "You have no idea, Angie. Lily has heard some little part of the story of my family's existence in Sarajevo during the siege. It was four years of hell. Snipers, shelling, no water, no electricity, no schools, no civilization. My husband went out to get water one day and was killed by the Serbian snipers who sat on the hills outside the city, shooting at anything that moved. When we took his body to the cemetery, they shot at the mourners. Our three-year old son died at his father's graveside. We had to leave their bodies until nightfall. Then my uncle pried open the coffin and we put the little one into his father's arms and buried them both. We were fortunate. Eventually all the wood was used for fires to stay warm and no more coffins could be made." Tears rolled down her cheeks as she spoke, but her face remained stoic. It was like watching a statue cry.

I choked back my own tears and rose to sit beside her, taking one of her hands in mine. Across the table, Lily wiped her eyes and blew her nose. "Rua, I'm so sorry for your loss. There are no words for what you endured."

"No," she said. "None." Then she turned to me and covered our clasped hands with her free hand. "There was much looting, much death. The Johnsons had these things, and much money, from what you say, and they wanted to conceal it. My heart tells me they were involved in the destruction of my people. How can I help your investigation?"

"There are other pictures. Uniforms that were in the attic. A local American, Colonel Lewis, looked at them, but could not identify them for sure. I know this will be hard, but would you see if they mean something to you?"

She nodded. "He is a good man, Angie. He was part of the team that built a bridge over the Sava River so that U.S. troops could enter the country. The conditions were extremely harsh. He spoke about it to a symposium of engineering students from several colleges here in Milwaukee and the area. I attended because it was part of my history. I honor him and his engineers."

She took a tissue from her briefcase, wiped her face and straightened up. "*Da*, I will look."

I set the pictures on the table in front of her and sat beside her again, ready to reassure or comfort.

After a short interval, she handed them back to me. "I cannot be sure about the camouflage uniform. Many troops in the area wore those and they all looked alike to me. But I believe the dress uniform is from a Serbian officer. There was no insignia?"

"None. All identification, even clothing tags, was removed when I found them."

"Colonel Lewis couldn't be sure?"

"No. Rua, the colonel is investigating the possibility that the Johnsons and a man who helped them get to the States might be on the war criminals database."

"If they are, may they live forever in the nightmare they imposed on my country and my people. May there be no respite from their pain, no end to their misery." Her gaze was steady.

I placed my hand on her shoulder and gently squeezed.

"So," she said, "enough!" She slapped her palms on the table and rose. "You will keep me informed about the progress?"

"As much as I can, Rua. Whoever is behind this is not aware of you, as far as I know. But be careful."

She stood and tipped her open briefcase toward me. I glimpsed a revolver in a holster. She took a couple of business cards out, wrote on them and handed them to me and Lily. "My cell phone number and personal email are on those. Call me any time, day or night. I will help however I can. These monsters must not go free." Then she closed and fastened the briefcase and, turning, put her hands on my arms. "Allah protect and guide you, Angie."

I clasped her arms. "God grant you comfort and peace, Rua."

She repeated the farewell with Lily. "Allah watch over you."

"And you, Rua," said Lily.

Then she left the room, quietly closing the door behind her. Lily and I stood in silence. I don't know what was passing through Lily's head, but I prayed without words. I had none. I trusted that God would know.

***

Spider entered the room quietly, pausing in the doorway to assess Lily and me. "That was intense. You two okay?"

Lily said, "I'll probably have bad dreams. But they'll only be dreams. Rua has the reality."

"Come in and close the door, Spider," I said. We all sat again. "I'd like to do something to help her. She's probably dealing with PTSD. She gave a few indications—needing to protect herself by facing the door, difficulty with social interaction, wearing black as a sign of mourning, stress reaction from the pictures." I stopped. "Although she did wear the blue scarf. That might be a sign that she's recovering."

"She always wears it, Angie," Lily said. "I complimented it once and she told me it was her mother's. I think it's part of her mourning garb, to be honest."

"Yeah, PTSD is a given," Spider said. "Anyone who lived through what she described would need counseling." He pinched the bridge of his nose, took a deep breath and exhaled slowly. "So—next steps."

I recognized his need to move away from emotion and toward action, a classic male response. Wukowski does it, too.

"I'll have DMV pictures of Petrovitch and Josif Zupan later today," I said. "They may not be the best images. Lily, can you help us find other photos? Petrovitch got a law degree from Marquette. I have no idea about Zupan. He's a mason."

"A Freemason?"

"No, a bricklayer."

"I'll get in touch with Marquette and the local bricklayer's union and see what they can do."

"You're a godsend, Lily." I meant it. I could do the legwork myself, but I wanted to read the pamphlet on Sarajevo and spend time with Bobbie on background searches. Lily's offer would give me some precious alone time to process Rua's story before Wukowski came over tonight.

"I want to do anything I can to help. For Rua and all the victims."

"Me, too." I turned to Spider. "Bobbie and I plan to meet at one-thirty at my office. I have a pending background check to run for a client that I'll use for training. Then I'm going home to rest and recover. Wukowski will be over for supper." I didn't want to make a statement about his staying overnight in front of Lily. "Will you be on duty tonight?"

"Nah. Once Wukowski arrives, the Feeb can take over until morning."

"That's slang for an FBI agent," I told Lily.

"He's retired. Don't say Feeb in front of him," Spider cautioned.

Lily's eyes lit up a bit. I could see she was temporarily enjoying detection again.

"Spider, I want Bobbie Russell to attend the funeral for Dragana Zupan with me tomorrow. Another set of eyes will be helpful. I haven't checked with Bram York yet. I know he said that Bobbie could go about normal business, but Zupan is still a suspect in my mind."

"One sec." He pulled out his cell phone and called. "Bram, Angie wants Bobbie Russell to accompany her to the Zupan funeral tomorrow morning. Whaddya think?" He listened, then said, "Yeah, well, sometimes you gotta shake the tree and see what falls. Remember Dakar?" More listening. "We can keep them safe, sir." Rumble. "Sorry—Bram. Old habits…Okay…Right…Hang on." He turned to me. "He'll have some men in place. Looks like it's a go for Bobbie, but Adriana wants to be there, too." He handed the phone to me.

"Angie," she said, "I feel so bad about Dragana. Can't I attend the funeral? I want to pay my respects and tell her husband how sorry I am. She was a nice lady."

She was focused on her emotions, while the rest of us concentrated on the logic of protecting her and discovering the killer. "It wouldn't be safe for you," I said. "After this mess is cleared up, perhaps you could send an offering to the church for prayers for her soul's rest. I'm sure that would comfort Josif." With his attitude toward religion, I doubted my words, but they appeased Adriana and we disconnected. I handed the phone back to Spider.

Then Lily piped up. "Could I go? I'm pretty observant."

"I'd love to have you there, Lily. I know you'd pick up on anything that was happening. But Zupan is borderline paranoid. Not without reason, but still…I managed to get permission for Bobbie to be there, but I don't think Josif will agree to another person and I don't want to spook him." I leaned over the table toward her. "Not only that, but you're an unknown resource to the bad guys. I don't want them to find out about your involvement. It's too dangerous and we can barely keep the security team afloat as it is."

"I see." She was clearly disappointed. "Well, as long as I'm helping in some way."

"Believe me, you are."

She escorted us back to the loading dock, where we made our farewells. In the car, I asked Spider about lunch plans.

"Better if you're not in public, Angie. I'll take you to the office and call for a delivery. What would you like?"

Culver's didn't deliver, but they did have a drive-through. "Let's get something to go at the Culver's on east Capitol Drive. I'd love a chicken salad."

"Mmm. A pumpkin spice shake for me. I'll work it off later."

Which reminded me that some gym time was overdue, but what the heck. "A small one for me," I told him.

After the food run, Spider drove to the office and inspected the premises before leaving me to eat healthy and drink naughty.

Bobbie arrived right on schedule, perky and oh-so-handsome. "Hi, Angie," he said, kissing my cheek. Then he held me away. "You look a bit peaked. What's up?"

I recounted Rua's story, trying for an unemotional tone, but failing.

Bobbie seemed less affected than I imagined he would be. "Let's be honest, Angie. Human nature is not all that kind or altruistic. We distrust anyone who isn't like us. Take it from me. I know." He paused for a moment. "I'm not comparing the subtle and not-so-subtle ways that gays are treated badly in this country to what the Bosniaks experienced. But I am saying that, without the protection of law, who knows? If we were in an armed conflict on our soil, would we band together or break apart, faction by faction? The current political situation doesn't give me much hope for the former."

Those were not the observations of a shallow person. Bobbie's thinking had more depth than I'd given him credit for. I couldn't disagree with his assessment, but I did have hope that individuals could transcend factionalism. *Was one-by-one action enough?* I didn't know. "Still want to go to the funeral with me tomorrow?" I asked.

"Yes. I want to find these…guys. Badly. Bram says he'll have undercover men there to keep us safe. Actually, he said to "ensure our safety in the event of offensive action," but same diff. He'll send me in a car to your condo and we'll go from there. Work for you?"

I nodded. "Okay, let's put in some real PI work, shall we?"

It was fun showing Bobbie the ropes. I ran through the background check process. The potential employee was squeaky clean. I created a report for the tutoring center and printed it. Then I had Bobbie take over and run a check on himself. Doing is better than watching.

There was one arrest, a misdemeanor for possession of pot. He was barely twenty-one at the time. Two months earlier and it would have been a juvenile offense. "Still using, Bobbie?"

"Nah. I grew up. I admit to a few beers, a glass of wine, maybe a shot now and then—and caffeine, of course." He said it with a cheeky smile.

It was a serious matter to me as his potential employer. "Caffeine won't harm your record, unless you get wired and do something crazy. Alcohol—beer, wine, booze, it doesn't matter—can get you into serious trouble. I can't have an associate who is impaired on the job or gets into a situation on his own time. And any kind of drug, even pot, can result in an arrest. One felony conviction and your license is revoked. Period. End of PI career."

"No problem, Angie. Honest." His hands went up, palms forward. "I will not drink unless I'm off duty and if I do drink, I will not put myself in a position to be arrested. I am totally drug-free and will stay that way."

"I'm counting on you to make good on that, Bobbie. I don't want my business compromised."

"Absolutely clear. I swear it will not be a problem."

"Good." I took the client's report off the printer and set it on my desk. "Let's make an invoice for the work. Never forget that this is a business. If we don't take care of that side of things, tedious as it can be, we'll fail. Keeping accurate billing records and getting the invoices out is essential."

"Got it."

"So, how many minutes did I spend on the client's background check?"

"Uh, maybe thirty?"

"Fifty-three. We had to check more than one database because of her out-of-state schooling. What about creating the report?"

"Fifteen?"

"Twenty-two." I ran Susan's invoice program. "We spent seventy-five minutes so far. I still have to put it in the mail. I don't use the lobby box—it's too easy to jimmy open. So that makes it over ninety minutes for time and I always round up to the next quarter hour, which also covers the few minutes to print and read the paper copy. I tend to make mistakes when reading on the computer." I put an hour and thirty minutes in the space provided on the online document and the program calculated the total cost based on my hourly rate. "Last thing—expenses. First postage; second, eight-tenths of a mile to the post office. Don't be careless about those little expenses. They add up."

I printed the invoice, read it and the report, and put both into an envelope. Then I weighed the envelope and affixed postage.

"I'm just trying to make you see the necessity of careful record-keeping. Same goes for car mileage. Keep a steno pad in your glove box. Don't use it for anything else. Write down the odometer reading before you start the ignition and when you switch it off. Then enter every detail of the ride: client; date, time, purpose and address at start; date, time and address at end. No shortcuts. The IRS likes to audit those who deduct mileage and they'll eat us up and spit us out if the records are bad."

"Okay. I'll get right on that, as soon as I can drive myself again."

I set the envelope on top of my briefcase and turned back to Bobbie. "Not too thrilling, right?"

"Well, I guess if you do it a lot, it would seem routine. But isn't it interesting to find out about people? I mean, the tutoring center's applicant—it's fascinating that she spent time as a church missionary in Cambodia. Especially since her DMV photo is for a pretty blonde woman. I bet she stuck out there like a sore thumb. Not just the hair, either. Cambodia's population is short and she's five-ten."

That impressed me. He retained information, he was interested in the person under investigation and he made inferences about her. "You're going to do well, Bobbie."

His cheeky smile reappeared. "I will. Thanks for giving me the chance."

Bobbie left, brimming with enthusiasm. Even though he was a friend, I would have to terminate the agreement if he didn't work out, so I was happy that he was a good fit.

Spider swung by the post office and I shot the envelope into the curbside box. Then we headed for condo, sweet condo. At the door of my place, he gave me a business card. "The Feeb's cell phone number, for tonight."

The name on the card was Andrew du Pont. "If I call him Feeb, I'm blaming it on you, Spider."

"Take the heat for me, Angie. He won't kill *you*." He kissed my cheek—a first—and headed down the hallway to the stairs. It was more than twenty floors to the garage.

Good grief! I really had to get to the building's gym.

Inside the condo, I hung up my outerwear, slipped off my pumps and put the tea kettle on. I settled in the living room with a cuppa and the Sarajevo pamphlet—seventy pages of images and text, from a journalist who was in the city during the shelling and saw the terror and loss of human dignity. I read it and set it down, shocked by the photos of the children, in particular. Many were missing limbs. Their faces were blank, unfocused, emotionless. I sipped my tea and sat quietly, returning to the account several times. I didn't want to, but I had to. Because of the change to daylight savings time, the sun set about four-thirty. I sat in the gloom for a while.

Wukowski's call startled me out of my reverie. "Angie, I'm leaving the office early. Okay if I come over now?"

"Yes. Please. Come now."

"You okay?"

"I'm not hurt or in danger, but, no, I'm not okay. I'll explain when you get here."

"I'm on my way."

I called Du Pont and let him know to expect Wukowski and his red Jeep Wrangler. Then I changed into a tank top and sweatpants, washed the makeup off my face (except for lipstick and mascara), turned on lights in the living room and waited.

Wukowski rapped at the door around five-thirty and let himself in. After hanging up his coat, he came to the couch, scooped me up in his arms and sat down with me on his lap.

I snuggled my face into the crook of his neck and wrapped myself around him.

"Tell me," he said.

I couldn't. The words were stuck somewhere deep in my chest. I pointed to the pamphlet, still on the coffee table, and he picked it up and began to read. Neither of us spoke. I had no idea how much time passed, but eventually, he set it down. He kissed my cheek and ran his hand up and down my back. "Pretty awful," he whispered.

"I met a survivor today," I whispered back, my voice low and mournful. Then the dam of words broke and I told him about Rua, about her husband and little boy, about the pain. He listened without saying anything, but continued moving his hand along my back and keeping me close. I was glad for the solace of his body, glad that he didn't try to redirect me, glad that he just let me tell the story. I didn't cry. It was too deep a hurt for tears.

Once it was out, I felt a renewed strength. Edmund Burke said that the only thing necessary for evil to triumph is for good men—and women—to do nothing. I would not allow this evil to triumph. I sat up and caressed Wukowski's cheek. "Thanks for being here, *caro*. You know what I need now?"

He shook his head.

"A workout. I've been a lazy pig too long."

He changed into sweats and asked me for a gym bag, into which he tucked his cell phone and police-issue revolver. That would normally unnerve me, but today, it was reassuring. I placed a quick call to update Du Pont on our whereabouts and we headed for the basement gym.

An hour later, after punishing myself on the treadmill, elliptical and various resistance machines, I was ready to call it quits. I cleaned the equipment with an antibacterial wipe. Wukowski did the same. Then we headed upstairs, using the elevator. I didn't think even Spider would climb up that many flights.

We enjoyed the multiple heads in my steam shower. I needed to know that I was still able to savor life. Wukowski certainly didn't mind that I used him to prove a point to myself.

Afterward, we wandered into the kitchen to forage, both wearing flannel sleep pants and tee shirts. No sexy for me. I needed comfort.

The larder was almost bare. I seriously had to shop. I pulled out frozen vegetables, pasta and the ingredients for Alfredo sauce. Wukowski uncorked a bottle of Pinot Blanco, just right to cut the richness of the sauce. I sipped as I cooked. It wasn't long before we settled on the couch with big bowls of rich pasta and veggies. *So much for the workout!* I dug in.

After supper, Wukowski went to the closet and brought me a flash drive. "Here are the DMV pictures of Petrovitch and Zupan. They're not bad. The stats are on the disk, too. Iggy got the Illinois DMV picture of Peterson. Could be Petrovitch, but it's not an obvious match. We're still waiting for the banks to respond to our request for information."

I took the portable drive. "I thought you were going to email this."

"I didn't want MPD security to pick it up."

"Is this a problem for you, sharing information with me?"

"Nah, short stuff. But the bureaucracy makes me a little nuts. It's easier to just circumvent it."

I loaded the data onto my laptop and did a stare-and-compare of the Petrovitch-Peterson photos. The hair color was different, but anyone can buy a bottle of hair dye. The noses were close. Peterson's appeared more bulbous. His hair was long and shaggy, covering his ears, and a full beard obscured his chin. The stats showed him as two inches shorter than Petrovitch and twenty pounds lighter. Of course, they don't actually measure or weigh you at the DMV. This wouldn't resolve the question of whether the two men were indeed one person, but Lewis' facial recognition software might think otherwise.

"Did you already send it to Colonel Lewis, or should I?"

"No. You send it."

That was odd. How long does it take to write an email saying, 'Here is the information I promised you,' attach three files and press 'Send'? I pulled out my laptop and the Colonel's business card and did the deed in less than a minute, including adding Bram York as a recipient. Hmph. Wukowski had that closed-in look on his face. I decided to worm the truth out of him later. For tonight, I just wanted to relax with my guy.

Chapter 24

Out of this nettle, danger, we pluck this flower, safety.
                                                    —William Shakespeare

I reminded myself when I awoke that this was the day of Dragana's funeral. Wukowski would attend in his official capacity. "That old saw about the killer wanting to revisit the scene of the crime? It happens," he said. "They sometimes show up at the funeral, too."

"Why?" I asked, as I perused my dark-colored dresses.

"Not sure. Some get a power kick out of knowing they were the cause of the mourners' grief. Others need to be sure the deed was really done. I've known a couple who did it to throw off suspicion. Regardless, if the case is open, we have someone at the funeral." He removed his dark blue suit from the rod in my closet and ambled into the guest bathroom to get ready.

I decided on a deep cinnamon long-sleeved wool challis dress with a boat neckline and flared skirt. A dark amber smooth cup bra with wide-set straps and matching thong panties would present no lines to mar the soft drape of the fabric. Neutral hose, metallic bronze stacked-heel pumps and bronze button ear clips completed the look.

When Wukowski and I sat down to coffee, he asked, "Will you be carrying?"

"In my purse." I wrinkled my nose. "Although it means I'll have to use my concealed carry bag." It was hand-sewn leather, with a pocket for a hand gun, but too bulky to be attractive. The upside to its size meant I could tuck my tablet in, too.

He shook his head and smiled. "Safety over fashion, *draga moja.*"

"I strive for both. But today, it's safety first."

"Good choice."

The intercom buzzed. Bobbie and Bram were downstairs. I took the Burberry from the hall closet, but Wukowski shook his head. "High in the upper twenties today. Wear the heavy wool one." He reached over my head and took a knit scarf and lined leather gloves down. "You'll need these at the cemetery."

"That wasn't part of my plan. Will you be there?"

"Yeah. Iggy and I will stay back and watch."

In the basement parking area, Bobbie and Wukowski greeted each other and shook hands. After introductions between Bram and Wukowski, Bram said, "Retired FBI agent Andrew du Pont is with Ms. Johnson. I'll relieve him after the funeral." He handed Wukowski a set of photos. "Spider Mulcahey, Eugene Malone and I will be inside the church." He pointed to each photo as he spoke the name. "Bart Matthews has some goo…uh, guys watching outside."

"Josif Zupan is suspicious of everyone," I said. "It might be better if your team waits in the church foyer."

"No worries," Bram said. "Zupan is a real loner. There are no friends or acquaintances to act as pallbearers and ushers. We'll be members of the congregation who volunteered to assist."

"Good plan." Wukowski tucked the photos into the breast pocket of his suit coat. "I'll hang onto these to show my partner, Joe Ignowski. He goes by Iggy. Five-ten, skinny, thinning red hair. We're not undercover. Zupan knows we're there to watch for suspicious persons or activity."

"Let's head out," Bram said.

Wukowski surprised me with a small kiss. "Be careful, Angie," he said.

"You, too."

He left in his Jeep. Bobbie and I got into the back seat of Bram's PT Cruiser. It took Bram a few extra seconds to swing his bad leg into the car. "My knee isn't a hundred percent yet, but it's getting there," he said. "The Cruiser is easier to get in and out of than my truck."

Another truck guy. Was it macho or utility? As we exited the garage, I said, "It's really gloomy today."

"It's the window tinting," Bram said. "The doc who treated my injuries certified me for fifty percent instead of the usual thirty-five. I like my privacy."

Hmm. He didn't seem paranoid. I decided to reserve judgment and enjoy the relative anonymity that the tinting provided. Turning to Bobbie, I ran down a brief list of instructions. "It's fine to let people know we're together. I don't want to call you my associate, though. I don't want anyone to try to track you."

"I can be your boy toy. Acting straight is no problem."

The reflection in the rearview mirror showed Bram's eyebrows rising. "Okay, but no PDA. Wukowski wouldn't like it." Besides, Bobbie and I were just buddies. Physical affection would be too weird. "Next, don't hover over me. We'll split up before the actual service begins and observe anyone who comes into the sanctuary. When it starts, we'll sit together, toward the back. Watch for signs of anything out of the ordinary. I honestly don't know what that might be. Let your intuition be your guide. Don't be obvious, though."

"Me? Obvious?" He grinned. "I'll be your slightly disinterested boyfriend who's only there because you dragged me along. That'll give me leeway to rubberneck. Don't worry, Angie. I can do this."

"Good." I faced ahead and asked Bram, "What about your team?"

"We'll be in the last pew once everyone's seated, observing, but also for security. It's unlikely that the perps will try anything, but I didn't live through…missions by being careless."

Bobbie and I left Bram in the church parking lot and entered the sanctuary. The church was ornate, with glass mosaics covering almost every inch of the walls, ceiling and dome. A long, deep red carpet led to the front of the church and the closed casket, which was flanked by lit candles in tall candlesticks, and was covered in a blanket of white daisies and yellow gerberas. I thought of the bright kitchen of her home and knew that Dragana would appreciate the pretty, cheery flowers. Josif Zupan stood at the head of the casket, wearing a dark blue suit and an impassive expression.

In a side aisle, a man in a cassock headed toward the altar. "I think that's Father Matthieu," I told Bobbie. "I'm going to introduce myself."

"No worries," he said. "I'll do some gazing upward. The mosaics are spectacular, even if I don't get the subject matter."

I scurried after the priest, my heels echoing in the large enclosure. "Father Matthieu?" I whispered.

The tall man turned and approached me. He had kind eyes and a smile that was almost hidden by his beard and mustache.

"I'm Angie Bonaparte, Father. We spoke on the phone about the Serbian Society."

"Yes, I remember. This is a sad day for Josif and those who knew Dragana, although I believe she had few friends. That is a shame. She was a lovely woman. It's kind of you to pay your respects."

"My...friend and I want to stay for the funeral. Is that allowed?"

"Most certainly. It's not a full funeral service, you understand. Dragana was not a member of our church or any church. But I am happy to celebrate the Trisagion for her and for Josif's sake."

"Tree-sigh-on?" I asked.

He handed me a printed bulletin and pointed to the word. "It's normally conducted at the funeral home, with a full service at the church on the following day. Because Dragana was not formally affiliated with St. Sava's, I'll hold the Trisagion here today. It is brief, but meaningful. I hope Josif will benefit from it." He ruffled the small stack of papers. "Please excuse me while I robe and vest myself. My assistant is not here to greet the mourners and hand out the bulletins." He had a harried look.

"I can place the bulletins on the table at the sanctuary door, if you'd like."

"Thank you." He handed me the stack and turned to walk quickly up the aisle.

I went back to the foyer, where Wukowski and Iggy were entering the church. We ignored each other. I put the bulletins down, keeping the one which Father Matthieu gave me and taking another for Bobbie. Then I moved away and walked around the sanctuary, admiring the wall mosaics and waiting to scope out other arrivals. Bobbie sat in the fourth pew from the front. So far, no one else was there.

I approached Bobbie and handed him a bulletin. "Here's the order of service," I whispered. "Why don't we leave these here and greet Josif together? I'll introduce you."

Bobbie nodded and rose. "I sat closer than you said, Angie. I thought her husband might want the sense of someone at his back."

"That was insightful of you," I said.

"Angie," Josif said when we reached the front, "most kind of you to come."

His voice was a monotone, his body stiffly erect. His arms hung at his sides and his face was a mask. Only his left eyelid betrayed emotion. It twitched rhythmically.

When he extended his arm for a handshake, I made an instant decision. He needed the warmth of a human touch. I grasped his upper arms, afraid that a full-on hug would be too much for him, and kissed his cheek. "Josif, you have my deep sympathy," I said in a low voice.

I heard a sharp intake of breath and his biceps flexed under my hands. Then he gripped my shoulders and said, "Many thanks." There was a small catch in his voice. He released me and backed away.

"Josif Zupan, this is my friend, Bobbie Russell."

Bobbie stepped forward and they shook hands. Then Bobbie covered Josif's hand and said, "I'm so sorry for your loss. Although I didn't know your wife, many people have said how caring a woman she was."

Josif's face crumpled for a moment, before the mask was back in place. "*Da*, she wonderful woman. I miss." He turned back to me. "You and Mr. Russell"—he pronounced it Roo-sell—"stay for the service and the meal?"

"We'd be honored," I said.

"And you come to burial?"

I could see that, without us, it was likely Josif would be at the gravesite with only Father Matthieu, the funeral directors and the police. "Of course," I said.

I stood before the coffin, remembering the day I found Dragana's body. I thought of John Donne's poem, *Death Be Not Proud*, which ends with this assurance:

One short sleep past, we wake eternally,
And Death shall be no more: Death, thou shalt die!

I prayed that it was so. Then Bobbie and I returned to the pew.

Footsteps sounded at the back of the church and five women with covered heads entered together, bowed in front of the altar, and sat in the second pew. Bram, Spider and Mad Man Malone were in the last pew on the left side. On the right side, three unknown men also occupied the final pew. Father Matthieu must have recruited some pallbearers from the congregation.

About five minutes before the service was set to begin, a woman in a UPS uniform came in and greeted Josif. The church was so empty and silent that I could hear her speak. "I'm afraid I can't stay," she told him, "but I wanted you to know that Dragana was one of my favorite regulars. She always had something fresh-baked to offer me when I stopped at the law offices."

He smiled. "My Dragana, she very good cook."

The woman moved forward to hug Josif, but he blocked her by turning sideways and extended his arm for a handshake.

After she left, an older couple and a young mother with a preschool girl approached Josif. I heard "good neighbor" and "Stephie loved her cookies." I hoped they would stay, that there would be someone here who actually knew and missed Dragana, that it wouldn't just be Josif who mourned her. The neighbors sat in the third pew, behind the church ladies and in front of Bobbie and me. *Thank you, Lord.*

Nineteen people to remember and celebrate a life. Probably only six knew Dragana. Deep sadness settled on my heart. No one should leave this life with so little sorrow, so few to remember. If Petrovitch was indeed responsible, I would find him.

A small bell rang and Josif seated himself, alone, in the front pew. Father Matthieu entered the chancel, bowed toward the altar and turned to the gathering. "Holy God, Holy Mighty, Holy Immortal, have mercy on us," he intoned three times. There were prayers, chanted hymns and a litany, in which the congregation and the priest alternated reading lines from the bulletin. We recited the Lord's Prayer together and Father Matthieu ended the service with "May your memory be eternal, dear sister, worthy of blessedness and everlasting memory." As we responded with "Amen," I saw Josif surreptitiously wipe his eyes with a white handkerchief and return it to the breast pocket of his suit coat. One of the church women leaned forward and patted his shoulder. He remained ramrod straight.

Father Matthieu invited everyone present to stay for a luncheon and motioned the pallbearers forward. The six men approached the casket. Bram and Spider rotated it on its rolling bier so that it faced down the central aisle of the church. The pallbearers took hold of the casket handles and lifted it, while Father Matthieu waited in the aisle. Then he turned and led the way out of the church, with Josif following the coffin and the rest of us falling in behind. The hearse waited outside. Once the pallbearers slid the coffin inside, we trooped back into the church and assembled in the basement for food. As I surmised, the five ladies with headscarves were the food servers.

There was none of the usual camaraderie of a funeral meal. No stories, no laughter as someone recounted something the deceased had done, no celebration of a life well lived, only a prayer before the meal and desultory conversation as we ate. I tried to engage Josif, but he didn't respond. Wukowski and Iggy were not at the table. I was sure the meal was delicious, but the only thing I tasted was the coffee, strong, hot and sweet.

Toward the end of the meal, I asked Father Matthieu about the cemetery. Bram picked up on the fact that Bobbie and I intended to be there and dipped his chin slightly.

The funeral director came into the room and handed out flyers to those who would be at the graveside service. The burial site was fifty miles away, at the Most Holy Mother of God Monastery in Third Lake, Illinois. I didn't want to spend the afternoon going back and forth to the cemetery, but I felt cornered, having already told Josif I'd be there.

Would Bram drive us and blow his cover as a member of the congregation? I needn't have worried. When Bobbie helped me on with my coat, I found a set of keys in the right pocket. "Are you okay with this trip, Bobbie?"

"Sure," he said. "It's all experience, right?"

I handed the car keys to Bobbie. "Bram left these in my coat. Would you mind driving?"

"That Bram's something," he whispered in my ear as he pocketed the keys.

The funeral director made a brief announcement to the "bereaved" concerning directions and explained that there wouldn't be a car procession, because we'd need to take I-94 to get to the monastery. It was twelve-thirty. We were told that the drive should take about an hour and we would meet at the site at two o'clock.

Josif's neighbors said their good-byes in the church hall, with appropriate expressions of sorrow and requests that Josif should let them know if he needed anything. The members of the congregation stayed behind to clean up the kitchen and fellowship area. Father

Matthieu told us that he would see to the sanctuary and be along in time for the graveside service. That left Bobbie and me, with Josif and the funeral director in the hearse. I had no idea where Wukowski and Iggy would be, nor did I spot Bram's security team, but I trusted that they were close by.

Bobbie and I exited the church and made our way to the parking lot. There was a folded note on the Cruiser's passenger seat, with "Angie" lettered on the outside. I opened it and read, "This car has some non-standard engine features. Take it easy on the gas pedal or you'll get pulled over."

I handed it to Bobbie, who grinned. "Fun," was all he said.

On the drive south via I-94, I pulled out my tablet PC. It was a fifty-mile straight shot down the interstate to the monastery, which was situated on several acres of rural land. I scanned the traffic around us as we drove, using the side and rearview mirrors. Bobbie noticed, so I gave him a quick lesson in the use of mirrors and how to spot unlikely or suspicious cars. We amused ourselves by speculating about the occupants and drivers around us.

About one-twenty, we exited I-94 and drove to the monastery. Two large wrought iron gates, each topped with a single cross, blocked access. "Turn around," I told Bobbie. "I'd like to circle the grounds."

Bobbie drove along the Rowlins Savannah Forest Preserve, which bordered the monastery property before dead-ending at Third Lake, a public lake fed by Fourth Lake—go figure! Cottages, homes, taverns and bait shops were built along the water. There was no access to the church grounds from the lake side, short of using an ATV.

"Let's wait in the forest reserve area, just before it intersects with the monastery road. We can watch for the hearse from there," I told Bobbie. Even though the day was sunny, my tablet app showed the temperature was thirty degrees and the wind chill was twenty-five. It was too cold to stand outside and I didn't want to wait on the grounds, even assuming they'd let us in without Father Matthieu or the funeral director to vouch for us. That forbidding gated entrance made me think that unexpected visitors were not welcome.

"Good thing it's not gloomy," Bobbie said. "I hate gloomy days for a funeral."

"Me, too. It seems to add oppression to grief."

We sat in silence for a few minutes. The dashboard digital clock read 1:40. I saw a black vehicle ahead and motioned to Bobbie. "Is that the hearse?"

Bobbie stiffened. "I think that's the Park Avenue I saw circling Zupan's house."

My heart rate sped up. "You think it's Petrovitch?"

Bobbie leaned forward, his hands gripping the steering wheel so hard that his fingers turned white. "There's no front plate and I can't see the driver. I'm not sure."

Fear and a sense of foolishness gripped me. "Wukowski warned me that the perp might show up at the funeral. I never thought about the burial."

The car turned onto Grant Avenue, which fronted the church grounds. I took my gun from my purse, safety on. "I'm going to scout it out. You stay put." He started to argue, but I pointed at my weapon. "I'm armed. You're not. Don't worry, I'll stay in the tree line and try to get the license plate number."

I exited the Cruiser, but left the door open for easy access. Scuttling forward, I stood behind a large tree trunk and peeked out. The rear of the Park Avenue displayed the plate issued to Oliver Wendell Peterson, Petrovitch's supposed alter ego. I backtracked to the car and told Bobbie. Then I dialed Wukowski.

Before he could say 'hello,' I asked, "Where are you?"

"We'll be there in ten. The service doesn't start until two."

"Bobbie and I are at the grounds. There's a Park Avenue up ahead, same plates as the one Bobbie spotted at Josif's house. I think it's Petrovitch." Bobbie poked me and pointed. "He's leaving," I told Wukowski. "We're going to follow him."

There was a tense silence. I waited for Wukowski to protest or, even worse, give me orders to stay put. It surprised me when he simply said, "Don't do anything crazy, Angie. I'm calling the Illinois state patrol now. What's the license plate on Bram's car?"

"I have no idea. Hold on." I rummaged in the glove box. "No registration in the glove box."

"Okay. I'll call him." He paused. "You're armed?"

"Yep. I'm packin'."

"Not funny. I'm giving this phone to Iggy while I make the calls. Keep talking to him. We need to know where you're at."

I released the safety on my weapon. Bobbie's eyes cut to me. "Stay back," I said, "but don't lose him, Bobbie. Wukowski and Iggy are ten minutes behind us and we should have a state trooper on our tails PDQ."

He took a deep breath. "Got it." Then he glanced at me. "Angie, he's never seen this car. For all he knows, we're just locals leaving the lake area. But your hair is pretty distinctive, girlfriend."

I fished the scarf out of my coat pocket and wrapped it around my head and neck, pulling it low enough to obscure my hair. "Good call."

"He's turning around. Headed our way. I'm backing up." Bobbie threw the Cruiser into reverse and hit the gas. When the Buick passed us, Bobbie gently edged ahead. "Okay, he's heading north on US 45."

I relayed the information to Iggy, who said, "Don't be a hero. There's always another day."

"Like hell," I said. "This has to stop."

I could hear part of Wukowski's conversation, as he first called Bram and got the plates on the Cruiser, then relayed it to the Illinois authorities. His voice was filled with tension, but controlled.

Iggy came back on the line. "Where are you now?"

"On US 45, coming up to the traffic lights at Illinois 31. We're still heading north. There's a pizza joint on the right, Malnati's." I turned to Bobbie. "Try to keep a car or two between us, but don't lose him."

As we approached the lights, a box truck made a right turn from 31 onto 45, obscuring our view of the Buick. Bobbie checked the driver side mirror and pulled out into the left lane, just as the truck signaled the same move.

"Watch out," I said. "The truck's moving into our lane. I don't think he sees us." Bobbie gunned the Cruiser and we shot ahead, directly adjacent to the Park Avenue. It was, indeed, Petrovitch driving. He glanced over, did a double take and pointed a finger pistol at me. "He spotted us. Drop back, Bobbie. It'll be harder for him to get a shot off."

There was barely a car length between us and the truck behind us. Bobbie set his jaw, tapped the brakes and flipped the right turn signal on. The truck driver blared his horn and gave us half a peace sign as he passed us. We were now directly behind Petrovitch and going seventy-five in a forty-five zone. "Iggy," I said, "he saw us and made a threatening gesture. We're still behind him on 45, just passed 132. That was the exit we took off of I-94 on the way here, so I assume he's not heading directly for the interstate."

"One minute, Angie." After some mumbling—I assumed Iggy covered the phone—he said, "We're exiting I-94 now on 132. You and Bobbie pull over. We'll take it from here."

I paused a moment, thinking. "If you can't see him, that's not an option. There are too many places for him to exit 45 and be lost in traffic. We're staying with him until I can see you."

"Damn straight, we are," Bobbie mumbled.

The chase continued up 45, past County Road 74. I considered taking a shot at Petrovitch's tires, but I wasn't that accurate at high speeds, and if I did manage to blow one of his tires, he could lose control and hit another vehicle. Instead, I continued relaying our status, while Iggy continued to tell me to pull over. I heard Wukowski cussing in the background. We kept driving.

At County Road 14, Petrovitch briefly tapped his brakes and made a wide screeching right turn. Bobbie swore, slowed down and turned, then hit the gas. We were on Petrovitch's tail within moments. Bram wasn't kidding about the Cruiser's engine.

This road was sparsely populated. The Buick pulled ahead and the Cruiser leaped up to eighty-five. We passed a cemetery on the right side of the road. I thought about Dragana's burial and hoped Josif wouldn't be upset that we weren't there. Then I realized how ridiculous it was to worry about propriety, when we were hot on the fender of her murderer.

Petrovitch turned left onto County 29 and took a right through a traffic circle onto Wadsworth. I frantically checked the map on my tablet. Where in blazes was he headed? I-94 was coming up, but there was no on-ramp. He zoomed under the interstate overpass, turned left into a truck stop plaza and drove into the area where the big rigs were parked. I couldn't see the Buick anymore. I let Iggy know our location. Bobbie put the Cruiser into park and we idled, waiting at the fork where cars turned one way and semis another.

"I can't tell if there's another way out of here," I said. "Can you circle around behind the trucks? Carefully. He can take a shot at us pretty easily here. I won't think less of you, if you want to get out and wait at the convenience store."

He stared at me. "You think I'd let you go out there on your own?" He shifted into drive and we turned toward the big trucks. We were close to the first row of parked semis when we heard a bang and our front driver's side tire blew.

"Duck and park, Bobbie," I said. "Iggy, we're near the semis. Petrovitch just shot out a tire on Bram's car."

"Are you hurt?" It was Wukowski back on the line.

"No, we're both okay." I peeked over Bobbie, bent down in the driver's seat. "You must be kidding me," I said.

"What's happening?" Wukowski's voice was a growl.

The Buick sped toward us. "He's driving straight at us. Bobbie, lower the window. I don't want to misfire because of glare." Bobbie pushed the button for the electric window.

I raised my Beretta and sighted on the Buick. The car swerved and I missed. It was a matter of seconds before he'd be right on us. I continued firing until the gun was empty.

A semi hauling a load of huge pipes pulled out of the line, apparently unaware of the drama in front of him. "There's a semi coming toward us, with a long load of pipes. See it, Bobbie?"

"Yes."

"We're making a run for it. Use the semi for cover. There's got to be a trucker over there with a gun."

I opened the passenger door and slid out into a crouch. Bobbie followed and we broke into a run. The semi was moving excruciatingly slow. I glanced back and saw Petrovitch's vehicle cut in front of it and round on us. We wouldn't make it to the parked trucks.

The back end of the trailer was just ahead of us. I was too short, but Bobbie had a chance. "Hoist yourself up into the truck," I yelled. He nodded, made a running leap, and somehow managed to lever up and into one of the pipes.

"C'mon, Angie," he shouted, dangling an arm. "You can make it."

I sprinted to the trailer bed, but I couldn't reach Bobbie's hand. Petrovitch stopped just yards away and I could see his pistol pointed at me as he leaned out the window.

"Throw the scarf," Bobbie called. "The scarf."

Still running, I unwound the scarf from my head, made a knot, and tossed the knotted end to Bobbie. He caught it and waited for me to get as close as I could, before he started hauling me up. I hung on for dear life, literally. The truck put on a small bit of speed and I dangled for a moment, my abdomen banging against the trailer bed, as I struggled to keep hold of the scarf while Bobbie reeled me in. With a sudden jerk, I was lying face down next to him. He dragged me further inside our concrete haven and lay on top of me, shielding me. We heard the ping of bullets hitting the sides of the pipe, as the semi exited the truck stop and pulled onto the I-94 ramp, heading north for Wisconsin.

Bobbie and I lay there for several minutes, just breathing and holding each other. Then I squirmed and told him to move off me. The pipe was gigantic. I crawled forward, past Bobbie, and turned myself around so I could see out the back end of the pipe and the truck. There was no sign of a Park Avenue on our tail. "I think we lost him."

Bobbie's laugh was quiet at first, then built to a full belly laugh, bordering on hysteria. "Lost him, huh?" he said, as he finally settled into a chuckle. "You think he doesn't know where we are?"

I was laughing along with him, the release of tension so sharp that it was either laugh or cry. "Not in this inconspicuous vehicle."

Our merriment ended when the semi picked up highway speed. The cold air whooshed through the pipe and, with every slight adjustment in steering, the load of pipes shifted in their chains and we bounced from one concrete side to the other. Bobbie grabbed me and lay back, spread-eagled, with me on top of him, as he tried to shelter me from the worst of it. Even so, our shoulders, elbows and lower bodies took a beating. I shoved my scarf under Bobbie's head to protect his skull.

"I lost my cell phone back at the truck stop," I told him. "Do you have yours?"

He released me long enough to feel inside his overcoat. "Thank God, I do." He dialed 9-1-1 and tried to convince the dispatcher that we really were rolling along I-94 in a load of concrete pipes being hauled by a semi, with a madman on our trail. As the dispatcher questioned him further and Bobbie's exasperation grew, I said, "Tell them to call the state patrol and ask for Wukowski."

It seemed like an hour, but it was probably only ten minutes before flashing lights and sirens approached. The truck pulled over and the trooper exited the squad car and headed for the cab. Wukowski and Iggy were right behind in their unmarked police-issue vehicle. Wukowski ran for the pipes, yelling, "Angie? Bobbie?"

We crept up to the end of the pipe and I waved the scarf. "We're in here."

Wukowski found a step of some sort and pulled himself up, face to face with me and Bobbie. "You okay?"

"Battered as all get-out, but we're okay," Bobbie said. "Angie took the worst of it, being so small. I think we need a hospital."

"No!" I insisted. "Nothing's broken, no bleeding, I'm breathing fine." I looked at Bobbie. "You?"

"Same here. But there isn't a part of me that doesn't hurt."

"Did you get Petrovitch?" I asked Wukowski.

"We did." His voice was solemn and his expression was stern.

"Alive?"

He nodded.

"Then, please, take me home."

I won't describe the process of emerging from the pipe. It took the driver—who kept repeating, "Honest, officer, I had no idea they were in there,"—the trooper, Wukowski and Iggy to ease me out and lower me down. Bobbie only needed two sets of strong arms.

The trooper went back into the pipe, once Bobbie and I were out, and emerged with his Smokey Bear hat in hand, shaking his head. "Darnedest thing I ever saw," he said. "Ma'am, I think you both need to be checked. You could have internal injuries or concussion. It's ninety minutes to Milwaukee. Anything can happen in that amount of time."

Wukowski agreed and Iggy refused to listen to my pleas, so we got into their car and headed for the nearest ER. Diagnosis: severe bruising. An hour and some pain pills later, we were released.

Wukowski was very solicitous, helping me into the back seat and sitting with me, feeding me sips of highly sugared hot tea. Bobbie and Iggy sat up front. I saw Bobbie pop a pill and lean back. Wukowski handed me one and I swallowed it with my tea. Then I twisted around, despite the seat belt, and put my head in his lap. I was grateful that he didn't harangue me about the danger I put myself in. That would probably come later. "Home?" I asked.

"Not yet. Next stop is Illinois State Police Headquarters."

The troopers were considerate. They took a short verbal statement from Bobbie and me and told us they would fax it to Wukowski after it was typed up. We could sign at MPD headquarters. Petrovitch's story was that we fired the first shots, but the truck stop surveillance cameras proved him a liar. Although there was no warrant for his arrest in Wisconsin, they agreed to have him transported back to Milwaukee, as a person of interest in the murders of Dragana Zupan and the Johnsons. Probable homicide trumped discharge of weapons.

By the time we left the station, the pain pill kicked in and I was barely awake. Wukowski tucked me up in the rear seat again and the car started to move. He stroked my hair, leaned down, and whispered, "You okay, *moja miłość?*"

I nodded, vaguely registering the words. *Moja* meant 'my.' But I had no idea about 'me-washed.' I decided to ask him later. Much later.

Chapter 25

Hey, Cochise, circle up. The wagons are gonna attack.
—Cheech and Chong's Next Movie

I awoke when we reached my condo building. Wukowski had an access card for the garage, so we pulled into my parking space and he helped me upstairs, while Iggy kept a hand on Bobbie's elbow. Aunt Terry waited at the door. I glared at Iggy, who shrugged.

Aunt Terry gently extracted me from Wukowski's hold, guided me to the couch, lowered me down and covered me with a cozy pashmina throw. Bobbie hobbled in and she assisted him to the other side of my sectional. Once we each had a cup of hot chocolate—I was out of herbal tea and Aunt Terry declared anything with caffeine off limits for the time being—she gave Wukowski her fiercest glare, the one that used to make little Angie shake in her shoes.

"Detective Wukowski, how could you let this happen to my niece?"

He looked abashed, all six feet of him. "Uh…well, ma'am, I didn't exactly *let* it happen. Angie's not easy to hold back, you know." He glanced at me, asking for understanding as he sought to escape the wrath of Aunt Terry.

She turned on me. "So, young lady, you disregarded police advice?"

I lay back against the couch pillows and put my hand over my forehead.

Aunt Terry immediately went into Mom mode. "Does your head hurt? Are you sure there's no concussion? I should call Dr. Palmieri. Two concussions in such a short time could be very bad. Just look at all those NFL players."

"I'm fine, Aunt Terry. So is Bobbie. The ER ran tests. It's just bruising from the pounding we took."

"Pounding? Who put his hands on you?" Again, she glared at Wukowski.

He raised his hands, palms up. "Not me, ma'am. Not Iggy, either."

"Nobody touched us, Aunt Terry," I interrupted before Wukowski was forced to cry 'mercy.' "It was pipes—really big pipes. Why don't you offer Iggy and Wukowski something to drink and I'll tell you the story." She bustled into the kitchen.

It took a while to recount our adventures in Illinois. Aunt Terry *tsk'd* and *oh-my'd.* Several times, she whispered, 'Angelina!' in a horrified voice. When I got to the end, I took a big slurp of my now lukewarm hot chocolate. "Your turn," I told Wukowski and Iggy. "What happened with Petrovitch?"

"Illinois has him in custody," Iggy said. "They'll hold him until the MPD sends a squad to bring him back to Milwaukee."

"I want details. What happened at the truck stop?"

"Yeah," Bobbie chimed in. "Did he just surrender when the cops showed up?"

Wukowski ran his hand over his hair. "It was the damnedest thing I ever saw." He glanced at Aunt Terry. "Sorry. Darnedest thing." Then he returned to me. "We pulled into the truck stop, following the Illinois cops, with their sirens and lights on. We saw the Cruiser and its shot-

239

out tire. There was no sign of Petrovitch. Iggy was driving—"

"But not fast enough for Wukowski," Iggy interrupted. "He told me to get my, um, butt over there, PDQ. There were maybe eight semis circled up, like a wagon train. So I stopped at the Cruiser, the troopers behind us. Three truckers walked over from the circle, all with firearms."

Wukowski took over. "They set them on the pavement and one of them—Al—told us that they saw a man and a woman make a run for it, after the guy in the Buick fired on them. The Buick tried to follow, but they penned him in with their semis. They shot off a few rounds from various directions, to warn him. He put his weapon down and locked the car doors. One of them called 9-1-1 and then they all sat there, engines idling. They saw Petrovitch make a call on his cell phone, but didn't approach him. When the State Police arrived, he cooperated. What else was he going to do, penned in by semis and with plenty of weapons trained on him, both civilian and police?"

Iggy laughed. "First thing I had to do when we caught up with you and Bobbie was call Al and tell him you were okay, so he could let the rest of the guys know. They couldn't believe you two made it into those pipes. 'Especially the grandma,' one of them said."

I decided not to take offense. "Well, I am a grandmother, and proud of it. Although *nonna* sounds better than grandma."

"Oh, Al said to tell you that he made arrangements to have the tire repaired."

I groaned. "Was there other damage from the gunfire?"

"I'm not sure," Wukowski said. "Once we heard what happened, we took off after the truck. But Iggy called Bram about the car. He said not to worry about it. He can use his truck. He and Spider will drive down to pick up the Cruiser later."

"Later? Where are they now?" Bobbie asked.

Wukowski glanced over at Aunt Terry, perched on the edge of a chair, cup halfway to her mouth, where I think it stopped as soon as Wukowski and Iggy began their account. "They're outside, on guard duty. Spider told us that Petrovitch had someone watching your condo, Angie. We need to be sure the threat is over before Bram's team disbands."

Aunt Terry set the cup and saucer down hard on my side table. "Angelina, you will come home and stay with your papa and me." She frowned, daring me to disagree.

I sighed. "Bram's security is better than anything Papa could organize. Bram had a top-secret special ops government job. It's safer if I stay here and let him work out the details." I turned to Bobbie. "Adriana's still under guard. I think you need to take up residence in my guest room, Bobbie. At least for a little while."

Bobbie nodded and closed his eyes. "I know they said we don't have concussion, but my head is about to burst open and I can't wait until it does."

"Small wonder," I said. "You took the worst of it, trying to shelter me. Your head was on the concrete pipe. Mine was on your chest."

"Bobbie," Aunt Terry said, "there's nothing so important being discussed here that you can't hear about it later. Come. You need to take your pain medication and lie down." She shepherded him into the guest room, emerging in a few minutes and closing the door carefully. Then she marched back into the living room and stood in the center, hands on hips. "Iggy, Detective Wukowski—" her head swiveled to each one as she named them—"do you believe Angie is safe with Bram and this Spider person?"

"Safe as can be." Wukowski's answer could be taken two ways, but it satisfied Aunt Terry, who sat back down in the chair.

"So, what's next?" I asked Wukowski.

"We bring Petrovitch in, book him with assault with a deadly weapon and interrogate him. So far, all we have is circumstantial evidence connecting him to the Zupan and Johnson murders. We're still tracking the money and the connections to the Bosnian War."

"Will you come back tonight and give us an update?"

"If I can." He stood and walked over to the couch. Settling down on his haunches, he gently put a hand to my cheek. "*Moja droga*—"Iggy's eyebrows rose—"we'll talk about your recklessness once you've recovered. Iggy and I need to get back to the unit and report." Before I could protest being termed reckless, he placed a butterfly kiss on my forehead, rose and turned to Aunt Terry. "Ma'am, Angie and Bobbie have the best protection available. Try not to stress. I hope to see you on Thanksgiving."

As they made their way to the door, I closed my eyes and thought about the talk Wukowski said we would have. I'd worry about that later.

Chapter 26

What's to come is still unsure: In delay there lies no plenty.
—William Shakespeare

It was just after eight that night when I got a call from a clerk in homicide. Detectives Ignowski and Wukowski were tied up and would get back to me as soon as they could. Bobbie and I were directed to appear at headquarters in the morning to sign the statements for the Illinois state troopers and make new statements for the MPD. I knew it was unreasonable—after all, Wukowski had bigger things to worry about than updating me, but I resented not knowing the current status of the investigation.

Aunt Terry wanted to stay overnight, but I convinced her that, with Bobbie in the guest suite, she'd have to share my bed, and I'd sleep better if she went home. When she left, I knocked softly on Bobbie's door. A "sup?" gave me permission to stick my head in and tell him that we wouldn't get any news tonight. I made a quick call to Spider, asking him to let Adriana know that Bobbie and I were okay and I'd call in the morning. Then I took a pill and fell into a restless sleep.

In the morning, I made a half-cut pot of coffee before calling Bart Matthews. A morning with no caffeine is simply not worth living.

After hellos, Bart chided me. "Bram called me last night to fill me in. Angie, you took a big chance, following Petrovitch."

Another man telling me I was reckless! "It was a calculated risk, Bart. I couldn't take the chance that Petrovitch would disappear again."

"Yeah, I get that. Still, I hate to think about having to face Pasquale if anything happened to you."

"To be honest, I hate to think about facing Papa, too." That got a laugh. "I called to tell you that the MPD wants Bobbie and me to come downtown for statements. We also have to sign the statements we gave the Illinois state police yesterday."

"Why don't I pick you up at, say, ten? I'll drive. That way, I can look over the paperwork before you sign."

"Sounds good. I haven't been in touch with Bram or the team. Is Adriana safe?"

"They moved her again. Bram won't disclose the location. He says that no one short of Special Forces can get to her. I'll tell him about today's plans."

"Let me call him. I want to apologize for the damage to his car."

We ended the call and I took a long hot shower, relaxing in the steam and spray. I was still plenty sore, so I popped a couple of ibuprofen and wrapped myself in a luxuriously soft terry-and-microfiber robe.

When I emerged from the master suite, Bobbie sat at the kitchen peninsula, sipping coffee. "It's half-cut," I said. "In case Aunt Terry interrogates me, I can honestly say I drank decaf this morning. I don't have to tell her it wasn't all decaf."

He grinned. "You are a master—um, mistress—of the strategic evasion."

"It comes from years of living in a Sicilian family." I ran down the scheduled events of the day.

"I'll need some clean clothes. Mine got pretty ripped up yesterday. I don't think Wukowski's stuff will fit. We're close in height, but he's built huskier."

"It's all muscle," I said in defense of my man. "And he doesn't keep clothes here."

Bobbie raised one eyebrow.

"Well, maybe a clean shirt or two and some boxers and socks. I'll call Bram and see what he can organize. Okay if he or one of the team goes into your drawers and closet? Or medicine chest?"

"Yeah. But they'll need to stop by for my key."

"I doubt that not having a key will keep one of that bunch out."

We ate toast and jam, neither of us having much appetite. I didn't even have a second cup of half-cut. Aunt Terry was probably right about the combination of head trauma and caffeine. I told Bobbie to use the toiletries in the guest bath. Then I went to my closet.

What does one wear to homicide headquarters to make a statement, especially when one's sweetheart is there in a professional capacity and is slightly ticked off at one? *Sheesh—does the queen of England talk to herself that way?*

My body protested the thought of any pressure on the red and purple bruises on my shoulders, hips and legs. My tummy was also purple, where I banged it climbing into the pipe. I settled on a figure-skimming knit tunic in dark amethyst, paired with gray leggings and dark gray ballet flats. A bright floral scarf, tied very loosely around my neck, finished the look. I groaned over wearing a bra, but I could hardly bounce into Wukowski's domain. A stretchy sports bra and panties would suffice. I gingerly dressed, moaning with every arm raise and bend. Thank God, my feet didn't hurt!

At nine o'clock, Spider arrived with a satchel. "Hope Bobbie's okay with my choices. He had some pretty strange colors in his closet. I have no idea what goes with what, so I stuck with browns and blacks." He smirked a bit. "And boxers." Then he carefully enclosed me in a hug. "You're really okay?"

"Really. Just sore all over."

"I can't believe you pulled that stunt." His voice rose. "You could have been killed."

"Would you or Bram let Petrovitch take off and not follow him?" I challenged.

"Course not. I don't mean that. But Iggy told us you kept on Petrovitch's tail even after he spotted you." He shook his head. "Not smart, Angie."

The hair on my head would have stood up straight, if I hadn't already gelled and spiked it. "We took a calculated risk, Spider. There was no way we were letting him get away. I bet you would've done the same. And don't give me any crap about being a woman." I yanked the small suitcase from his grasp, walked down the hall and set it outside the guest room door. "Bobbie, your clothes are here," I called as I knocked.

Bobbie opened the door, covered only by a towel slung low on his hips. "Uh...thanks."

I stood there, breathing deeply.

"Angie?" he said.

"Sorry. I'm trying to regain my composure."

"Huh?" He put a hand on the knot of his towel.

I suddenly realized that he thought I was overcome by his physique and laughed, holding onto the door jamb for support. My ribs hurt, but it felt good to release the tension. "Sorry," I sputtered. "It's not you, it's Spider."

"Really? Does Wukowski know?"

"Idiot! I was taking deep breaths because Spider hacked me off. Or rather, because he, Bart and Wukowski hacked me off. He was just the last one in the line."

"For a minute there, I saw a little silver dragon, breathing fire." Bobbie picked up the suitcase and disappeared into the bedroom.

I went back to the hall and "made nice" with Spider, who assured me that he meant nothing condescending in his remarks and was just worried about me. I, in turn, apologized for overreacting. We parted on friendly terms.

Dialing Bram, I sent up a prayer that he, too, wouldn't come down on me. "Hey, Bram," I said when he answered. "It's Angie. I'm so sorry about your car. Please let me repay you for the tire repair and any other damages. Have you seen it yet?" It all came out in a rush. *Slow down*, I told myself.

"A friend is going to drive it up for me today. Don't worry about the damages. It'll go on the bill I submit to Bart Matthews." He sounded very nonchalant.

"And Bart will put it on the bill for Adriana."

"Yeah, you're right. Let's do this. If Adriana gets the money from her parents' bequest, we'll let her cover the costs. After all, it's legit. We *are* working on her case. But if she doesn't come out of this okay, I'll eat it. And don't tell me otherwise, Ms. Bonaparte!"

I huffed a bit, but agreed. If it gave Bram a good feeling to do something benevolent, who was I to deny him? It was a relief that he didn't mention my part in the chase.

Bart showed up promptly at ten and we set out for police headquarters. Iggy and Wukowski were nowhere in sight when we arrived. A moment of stillness interrupted the usual conversations in the bullpen, until a gray-haired man grinned at me and gave me a two-fingered salute as he walked over. "Matthews." He nodded to Bart. "How are ya?"

"Good, Penske. You?"

"Good." He turned to me. "You Ms. Bonaparte?" He got the pronunciation right.

"Yes." I extended my hand. "Call me Angie."

"Art," he said as we shook. "You?" he asked Bobbie. They completed the introduction routine. "Wukowski and Iggy're tied up." He shook his head. "This one's a doozy, all right." He looked me up and down, then did the same to Bobbie. A gravelly laugh burst out. "I saw the video from the surveillance cameras. Gotta hand it to ya both. Didn't think you'd make it onto the truck. You did good, bothaya." He laughed again. "So, I get to take your statements. Let's go to a room."

The process was the usual. Penske asked us questions, Bart vetted them and we responded when he gave us the nod. He only objected when Penske asked us to surmise. While our statements were being typed, we read over the faxed copies from Illinois and signed them. When Penske came back in the room with the MPD statements, we read and signed them, too. "Thanks for comin' in," Penske said. He gathered all the copies and turned to leave.

"Wait a minute." I was determined to get a status. "What's happening with Petrovitch?"

Penske rubbed the back of his neck and twisted to look over his shoulder at me, grimacing slightly. "I can't tell ya. Sorry."

I felt my body tighten and I stood, but before I could protest, Bart spoke. "Officer, our client, Ms. Johnson, is still under our protection. I think we deserve to know more about the progress of this investigation in order to assure her safety." He remained at the table, hands folded, waiting.

Penske turned back to us. "Yeah. I get that. So here's what I can say. We're still investigatin' Petrovitch's contacts in relation to the money. Obviously, we're also tryin' to tie him to the murders. We got a coupla cooperative witnesses and we're hopin' it breaks soon. Fellow from ROTC—Colonel Lewis—he brought in some interestin' info. So, bottom line, stuff should hit the fan pretty soon. Meanwhile, I'd keep a close watch on yer client." He paused. "Wukowski would have my butt if he thought I said anythin' ta set ya off, Angie."

I could only imagine. "Don't worry. I'm lying low and nursing my bruises. So is my associate." I nodded at Bobbie.

Bart handed Penske a card. "Let the officers in charge know that I'm waiting for a status."

"Will do," Penske said.

***

Once in Bart's car, I put my head back and closed my eyes. The events of the past nine days—*was it really only nine days?*—ran through my brain. Adriana's story. Dragana's murder. Petrovitch's disappearance. The attic. Lily. Josif Zupan. The Serbian Society. Spider, Bram and the security team. Bobbie deciding to pursue a PI career. Colonel Lewis. Rua Kolar. Sarajevo. The funeral. The chase. The pipes. I felt as if I were still rolling around in one of those huge concrete cylinders, tossed and battered, at the mercy of events. And in the background, Thanksgiving loomed, only five days away. My hands clenched and I exhaled loudly.

Then I felt Bobbie's hand gently soothe the top of mine.

Suck it up, I told myself, opening my eyes and smiling as I patted his hand.

"Okay?" he asked.

I nodded.

Bart drove us to the Milwaukee Athletic Club for lunch. It was far more than just a gym, with its luxurious guest rooms, two restaurants and a bar. Best of all, it was a members-only venue, so there was little worry about any of Petrovitch's associates. Bart asked the maître d' for a secluded table. Once we were seated, I ordered a brandy old-fashioned. Bobbie raised an eyebrow, to which I responded, "It's five o'clock somewhere." Our beverages arrived quickly. I took a swallow of the old-fashioned and let it hit. Then I sat back and perused the menu, suddenly ravenous. I went for the chicken capellini and a Mediterranean salad. Bobbie and Bart decided on sandwiches.

"What's next?" Bobbie asked.

Bart shrugged. "It appears that we're at the mercy of the MPD—not a situation I care to be in. However, they hold all the cards, at present." He ticked off his points on his fingers. "One, they have Petrovitch. Two, they seemingly have 'cooperative witnesses'—probably co-conspirators, who are looking for a plea bargain. Three, they have Colonel Lewis' findings." He doctored his coffee and took a sip. "Much as it galls me, all we can do is wait."

"Is there any reason we can't talk to Lewis?" I wanted to know. "I mean, would that compromise the case?"

Bart thought before answering. "I think it's best if we simply assure our safety and wait. I know that's not the answer you want, but I'm concerned that whatever the colonel has discovered will involve a number of people. We can't take a chance on information leaking, or possibly planting ideas that will invalidate a witness's testimony in court."

I sighed. "Okay, I get that. But it galls me, too. I was in on this at the beginning and I hate feeling like a bystander now."

The meals arrived and we made small talk while we ate—the Milwaukee Symphony's concert schedule, Adriana's new look, Bobbie's uncertainty about Steve's Thanksgiving plans, my own plans with Wukowski and his mother. Bart didn't offer his own Thanksgiving agenda, so I casually invited him to the Bonaparte meal. "Thanks. I'll get back to you," was all he said. We didn't linger after finishing, since Bobbie and I were due for pain meds. Bart delivered us to my condo, where we downed our pills.

Bobbie retreated to the guest room and I settled on the couch. Today, the lake was gray, with no whitecaps to relieve the dullness. It felt like a reflection of my inner self. Just as I decided that inaction was worse than the pain of movement and I would go into the office for a couple of hours, my cell phone rang. Lily March, read caller ID.

"Lily," I answered, "I'm so glad you called. You won't believe what happened after the funeral."

"Let's see. Did it have anything to do with a shoot-out at an Illinois truck stop and subsequent escape in a load of pipes?"

I groaned. "It was on the news already?"

"Oh, yeah. It got a lot of play this morning. Are you and Bobbie okay?"

"Mostly. There were no major injuries, but we're both black and blue and hurting."

"What can I do to help? Do you need groceries? Medicine?"

"I'm sure that my Aunt Terry will take care of that. Why don't you come over? You've been such a big part of this. I want to tell you the story in person." When she agreed, I notified Spider.

The news reports meant that there were calls I had to make. I reassured my kids that I was fine. I left a message for Professor Kolar that I was banged up, but okay, and that Petrovitch was in police custody and there was nothing more I could say.

Then I listened to my voicemail. Gracie Belloni, Tony's wife, left a message that meals were on the way. "I'd come myself, but with three preschool kids, you'd just end up with a bigger headache than the one you probably already have," she said. Marianne Ignowski was brief. "I'm so glad you're okay, Angie. I'm sure Terry has things organized, but call me if you need anything, even if it's just to talk." Susan assured me that things at the office were quiet and she would call later. Then Aunt Terry arrived, loaded with shopping bags from Sciortino's Bakery and Glorioso's Italian Market, and proceeded to stock my cupboards and fridge.

We were settled on the couch with herbal tea, courtesy of Aunt Terry's shopping, when Lily arrived. Aunt Terry answered the door. "Come in," she said. "I'm Angelina's Aunt Terry." She ushered Lily into the living room, where I made more extensive introductions and Lily agreed that a cup of tea sounded lovely. "Don't talk about the case until I'm back in the room," Aunt Terry ordered.

"Angelina," Aunt Terry said, as she handed Lily her tea cup and placed a small plate of Sciortino's lemon sandwich cookies—my favorite—on the coffee table, "I should warn you that your papa is not pleased that you once again are injured. He is ranting about your job and that you need to find a husband and settle down."

"Been there, done that. Turned out badly."

Aunt Terry grinned. "That's what I told him. But he's worried about you, so he takes the Sicilian attitude. I told him you needed to rest today. You have a respite, but expect him at your door tomorrow."

I shuddered in mock horror, which only made me grimace in pain. "Thanks for holding him back. Maybe I'll be up to hearing 'Angelina Sofia' by then."

"Today, he even used your confirmation name."

Oh, Lord. Angelina Sofia Margherita. If he threw in Bonaparte, I might as well run away. I turned to Lily. "Thanks for coming."

"My pleasure. I actually wanted to talk with you about Josif Zupan. Remember that I promised to check him out with the bricklayer's union? He's a member in good standing of the local, but they wouldn't tell me more. However, the UWM maintenance chief put me in touch with a guy who does a lot of tile and brick work in Milwaukee County. This Dave told me that he knew Zupan, but not well. 'Keeps to himself,' he said, 'but there's a couple of other Serbians in the union you could talk to.' So I called their homes." She leaned forward, tense with excitement. "Angie, they're both at police headquarters! So is Josif. What do you think that means? Maybe they're part of a bigger conspiracy, with Petrovitch at the center."

"It could be. It seems the MPD has some 'cooperative witnesses.' That's all they'll tell me at present."

Bobbie's bedroom door opened and he emerged in sweats, yawning and scratching his chest with one hand. He stopped when he realized we weren't alone. "Um, hi, Terry, Lily."

Aunt Terry bustled over, asking him how he felt and offering tea and cookies. It wasn't too long before the intercom rang to announce Meal Mobile. Aunt Terry went down to the lobby and brought back a huge shopping bag of prepared meals from various Milwaukee restaurants, courtesy of the Bellonis. I wouldn't need to worry about cooking for at least a week.

I couldn't hold back my yawns. Once Aunt Terry and Lily left, I lay down for a nap. I dreamed about a trio of masons bricking me up inside a big concrete pipe, while Edgar Allen Poe offered me a glass of Amontillado. I awoke in a sweat.

Chapter 27

Friendship…has no survival value;
rather it is one of those things that give value to survival.

—C. S. Lewis

That evening, after Bobbie and I shared a Thai meal from the Bellonis' largesse, my landline phone rang. Caller ID showed it was Wukowski. *Finally, news!* "I've been waiting all day," I said. "What gives?"

"Uh, Ms. Bonaparte? This is Lena Wukowski, Ted's mother."

Good grief! Wukowski's mom. I needed to tread carefully. "Mrs. Wukowski, I'm so sorry. When I saw the caller ID, I assumed it was your son."

"He hasn't called you? Tsk. I will speak to him. That is not the way to treat a lady."

"Well, in his defense, I understand that he and his partner are tied up at headquarters on a really big case."

"Yes. I saw it on the morning news and again tonight. I was worried, so I called Marianne Ignowski and asked for your number. You are all right?" Her voice was soft and gentle, with a slight accent. I found it charming.

"Yes, I'm fine. My partner and I are a bit banged up from the unexpected truck ride, but no real damage was done."

"*Bogu niech będą dzięki.* I mean, thanks be to God." She paused. "So, my son tells me that we are invited to your family home for Thanksgiving dinner."

"Yes, we'd love to have you. I should warn you that it's a big family and we can get a bit boisterous."

"That's nice, to have a big family. I always wanted more children, but it was not to be."

I thought of Celestyna and the grief of her death. *Would Lena be able to handle us, or would she withdraw, as Wukowski worried she would?* "I have two grown children and three beautiful grade-school age grandchildren. Plus, my papa and my aunt, who raised me when my mother died young. Oh, and my aunt's, um, beau, will be there." I didn't mention Bart, since he hadn't confirmed.

"Lovely. I will enjoy. So, what can I bring to the celebration?"

This was going almost too well. *Was Wukowski mistaken about his mother's mental state? Or was she hiding her fears?* Best to find out now. "We have the traditional meal—turkey, dressing, cranberry sauce, green bean casserole, rolls, pumpkin pie. But we're Sicilian-American, so we also include pasta, Italian bread and *zabaglione*—that's sort of like mousse. Maybe you could bring a traditional Polish dish for us to share."

After a moment of silence, she spoke. "Sicilian-American?"

"Yes, that's right. Papa immigrated as a young man. Times were tough in Sicily and he sought a better life in the U.S. Eventually, he moved to Milwaukee and opened up a fruit-and-vegetable business."

"I see." I heard a deep intake of breath. "Well, perhaps I could bring kielbasa and sauerkraut, if you think your family would enjoy it."

She didn't plan to back out. That was a small victory. And now she had time to adjust to the idea of our being Sicilian-American. "I've had your *pierogi* and *mizeria*, Mrs. Wukowski. They were delicious. I know my family would love anything you bring."

"I am so glad you liked the meal, Angie. I may call you Angie?"

"Please."

"And you must call me Lena." She pronounced it leh-na. "Now, tomorrow, I plan to bring you *gulasz*—stew flavored with paprika, like Hungarian, but better—and *kopytka*—potato dumplings. We will meet and talk."

I quickly ran down options. "That would be lovely, but I'm concerned for your safety, Lena. My friend and partner, Bobbie Russell, is staying here temporarily. We're under a twenty-four hour security watch until the Petrovitch case is closed. I don't think Wu…Ted would approve of your being in the path of danger, however small."

"Hmm. Yes, you are probably right. He is very protective of me. Well, that is too bad, that we cannot meet before Thanksgiving. You will take care? Be cautious?"

"I will, I promise. I've had all the excitement I need for quite a while."

"I imagine so. I am very glad to talk with you, Angie. My Ted is much happier since he met you. That pleases a mother."

Her words touched me and I got a little choked up. "Thank you for saying that, Lena. He is a wonderful man and you and your husband did a great job raising him. I look forward to Thanksgiving." My hands were sweaty when I replaced the phone in its cradle. If Wukowski was right, that call was not easy for his mother to make. I was glad we connected before the holiday meal and thankful that she didn't sound as fragile as he made out.

After the call, Bobbie opened a bottle of Riesling and brought up the WISN news report on my smart TV. "Time to see us in action," he said. He accessed the internet and scrolled to the morning news. We sipped our wine as we watched two idiots trying to outrace a madman by jumping into a truckload of pipes. On the first go-round, we said nothing.

The second time, we commented on the action. "Bobbie, I can't believe you made that leap so easily. Were you a hurdler in school?" "Good thing it wasn't windy, Angie, or your assets would have been on film." "I will never again tuck Aunt Terry's knitting in the back of the closet. Her scarf saved my neck in more ways than one."

The third time, we laughed, able to distance ourselves and see it as farce.

Bobbie paused the TV and turned to me. "So, that was Wukowski's mother on the phone?" I nodded. "What gives?" he asked.

"It's complicated," I said.

He waited, silent.

I filled him in. "I'm really surprised that she called tonight. That took courage. And get this, Bobbie—she told me that she hadn't seen Wukowski so happy in a long time."

He nodded. "He's loosened up a lot, since I first met him this summer. And it's obvious that he cares about you."

"Cares?"

"Ahh. Nobody's said the L word yet?"

I shook my head.

"Do you want him to? Do you love him?"

"Lord, Bobbie, I don't know." I took a deep breath. "I mean, I know I love him. No question. But do I want him to say it? I'm not sure. Because, if he loves *me* and I love *him*, things will change. I don't know if I want things to change."

He handed me my glass of wine. "It's not like you have to go from saying 'I love you' to moving in together. Just take it one step at a time. And listen, girlfriend," he said as he took my free hand, "don't let fear ruin a good thing." The gold flecks in his deep brown eyes seemed to glisten for a moment.

"You're right." I took a deep breath and smiled. "That's pretty much the advice I gave my Aunt Terry when she started seeing Fausto. To take it slow, that he had to respect her wishes." I shook my head. "Who would think that Aunt Terry and I would have the same issues—in totally different circumstances, of course. I'm sure she's still the oldest living virgin outside the convent." I set down the wine and reached out to hug Bobbie. "Thanks, friend."

He retreated. "My back's a mess. Consider yourself hugged." Then he pressed Play on the remote. "I have to see that again. We were awesome."

Chapter 28

Ah Love! could you and I with Fate conspire
To grasp this sorry Scheme of Things entire,
Would not we shatter it to bits—and then
Re-mould it nearer to the Heart's Desire!

—Omar Khayyam

I waited all day Sunday to hear from Wukowski. Around five that evening, the phone rang. Caller ID said "Milwaukee Police Department." *Odd*, I thought, *that he didn't call from his cell phone.* "Hello. Wukowski?" I asked.

A raspy voice responded, "Nah, sorry. It's Art Penske, from Homicide. Wukowski asked me ta call ya. So, the thing is, there's still nothin' we can tell ya, but Ted wants ya ta know that as soon as the DA issues charges, he'll be in touch."

"I'm dying here, Art."

He chuckled. "Yeah, I can tell. If it helps, we expect the charges on Monday morning. It's a helluva case, Angie. Probl'y bigger than ya expect. That's all I can tell ya. So just sit tight. Ted'll get to ya as soon as possible." He took a breath. "I gotta say, I never seen him this tied up in knots. He's itchin' ta talk to ya."

That, at least, was gratifying. "Okay. Thanks, Art. I appreciate the call. Tell Wukowski I'll be waiting to hear from him."

"I'll pass it on. Take care, ya hear?"

Bobbie and I spent the day playing Scrabble (I whipped his butt), Parcheesi (the dice were incredibly kind to him) and cribbage, which I taught him (just beginner's luck that he fought me to a tie over the course of several games). We foraged from the stocked refrigerator, when the spirit moved us. Since we were off the prescription meds and using Tylenol for pain relief, Bobbie mixed a couple of Tom and Jerries that evening. "Close enough to the holidays for me," he said, as he handed me the foamy drink.

I inhaled the scents of cinnamon, nutmeg, brandy and rum. "Me, too." My first sip tasted like heaven, smooth and strong. "Bobbie, have you and Steve finalized your Thanksgiving plans?"

"Not yet. Steve's got some big New Yawk City thing." His eyes twinkled as he mauled the pronunciation. "He thinks he'll be back in time for us to go out for a meal."

"Ew. Thanksgiving in a restaurant. You should come to Papa's. If you can stand the family, that is. Steve's welcome, too."

Bobbie stared down into his mug for a few seconds. "I haven't had a family Thanksgiving since I came out." He took a drink. "I'd really like that, Angie, as long as it won't cause problems."

I read between the lines. "I'd be shocked if it did. Besides, you're my friend, Bobbie, and now we'll be partners, so even if someone does have a problem, they'll have to deal with it." I lifted my T&J and we clinked mugs.

***

Monday morning at nine o'clock, the landline rang. It was Wukowski. "Angie, how are you?"

"Turning green and yellow in the less bruised spots. Still black, blue and red in most places. Enough chit-chat. What is going on with Petrovitch?"

He laughed. "It'll hit the noon news. It was a lot bigger than we thought. Here's the short version. In the late 1980s, when it seemed obvious that Yugoslavia was going to break up, Petrovitch decided to take advantage of the coming turmoil and ethnic factionalism. He recruited a bunch of Serbian families with Muslim ties, promising that he'd get them out if war broke out. In return, they were to watch for opportunities to loot both Serbian and Bosnian national treasures, like the book from the attic, and any personal items worth money, like the jewels and wedding clothes. If they didn't agree, he not-so-subtly wondered out loud what would happen if their Serbian neighbors found out they had Muslim associations. We got that from two informants, and, no, Zupan wasn't one of them. He refused to speak at all.

"By the time the Bosnian War was well underway, Petrovitch was already a U.S. citizen. As each family reached its quota of booty, or if things got hot enough that they might be caught, he arranged for them to emigrate and promised them sponsors and jobs. They didn't all come to the States. Some of them went to Germany or places in the Caribbean. A couple even ended up in Singapore and Australia."

"His connections were that good?" I asked.

"Yeah. He pretty much ran the organization from Milwaukee and Glenview. We confirmed that the Oliver Wendell Peterson identity was his. We're not sure if there are others.

"Unknown to Adriana, her maternal grandmother was a Muslim who converted when she married the grandfather. Ditto with Dragana Zupan, whose parents were Muslim. We think Josif and Adriana's father agreed to the scheme so their wives wouldn't be in danger from Serbian fanatics.

"Dragana met the Johnsons through the law practice. We don't know the whole story—and we probably never will unless Petrovitch opens up—but we think that she and Mrs. Johnson were in the dark until recently. When they found out how Petrovitch forced their husbands into illegal trafficking in stolen artifacts and money, they objected. We also think Petrovitch either hired or extorted someone from among those he recruited in Bosnia to kill them.

"Two of the men he extorted into working for him were more than happy to sing, in exchange for immunity or diminished charges. Colonel Lewis and the International Criminal Tribunal for the former Yugoslavia used them to track the money and some of the stolen artifacts. U.S. immigration charged Petrovitch with failing to disclose the crimes on his application for residency and citizenship, and the Tribunal issued a request for extradition today. He'll probably be turned over to the war crimes court in weeks. He'll do hard time, Angie."

I sighed. "I guess that's better than getting away with it. And, in the larger scheme of things, war crimes trump murder. But it burns me to think of what he did to those families. Speaking of which, what happens to Adriana and her parents' bequest?"

"Not sure. All the accounts are frozen, pending investigation by the ICTY. It'll probably be months, if not years, before the money trail is tracked and the original owners get their property—or recompense for property that can't be found. Adriana won't see it, that's for sure."

"It's a shame that her parents didn't use some of it to give her a better start. She wouldn't have to pay it back and she could have her nursing degree by now."

"Yeah, well, there's a reason for Lady Justice's blindfold and her two-edged sword. Sometimes impartiality hurts innocents."

I was shocked at that admission. I knew how important the law was to him.

"But without the rule of law, there's no justice for anyone," he continued.

My heart was heavy for Adriana and all she'd go through when this news broke. But I had to agree with Wukowski. Law was an imperfect instrument, but a necessary one. Petrovitch's actions proved that.

"What happens next?" I asked.

"Petrovitch will be arraigned in the U.S. district court in Chicago. The Milwaukee DA plans to issue conspiracy to commit murder charges against him, in case the extradition to the ICTY falls through. The IRS is also investigating his tax statements. If nothing else, he'll do time for tax evasion."

"Shades of Al Capone," I said, recalling the mobster who ultimately went to Alcatraz, not for murder or racketeering, but because he cheated on his taxes. "Don't mess with the IRS." Wukowski snorted. "Who else knows the story?" I asked. "Bart? Adriana?"

"Don't rip me a new one, but we had to bring Adriana in for questioning. Bart was with her."

"You thought she was involved in this?" My tone was cold and hard enough to crack iron.

"Honest to God, I didn't," he said. "Nobody did. But we had to follow procedure."

Procedure be damned. "Where is she now?"

"Spider and Bart took her away when we finished. I think any threat is over, but they weren't convinced." He took a breath. "I was just doing what I had to, Angie. You wouldn't want Petrovitch to get off on a technicality, would you?"

"No. And I wouldn't want Adriana to be terrorized by the very people who are sworn to protect her."

"Now just a minute. That's way out of line."

It was my turn to breathe. It was several seconds before I could respond. "You're right. I'm sorry."

His sigh came across the line, loud and clear. "Okay, apology accepted. Jeez, Ange, you have to know I wouldn't…"

"I do. I'm really sorry. I can get a little overprotective." I paused. "So, I assume there's no need for secrecy after the news comes out. I mean, I can get in touch with all the people who helped me on the case and let them know the outcome?"

"Sure. And believe me when I say, the MPD owes you a big thanks. Without you, this would still be an open case and Petrovitch would probably have fled the country in another week or so. He was making arrangements to close down his network and consolidate funds. You, Bobbie, Lily, Bart—you made it happen."

That was sweet vindication, from a man who didn't think women investigators had a place outside an office. Maybe Wukowski was rethinking that aspect of my life. "I'm glad to know that," I told him. "But don't forget the one who really started everything. Adriana could have taken the money without asking any questions. She put everything in motion, because she didn't want a tainted inheritance. And now, her innate honesty and sense of rightness have cost her."

"I hate to say it, but I see it all the time. Someone does the right thing and it comes back to bite them. While lowlifes get away with…murder."

I could hear the exasperation and frustration in his voice. "Remember what you said during the Morano case? 'Do not be deceived, God cannot be mocked. A man reaps what he sows,'" I reminded him.

"Yeah. And I believe that. It's just that, sometimes, the payback isn't fast enough or drastic enough to suit me. I guess it's a good thing I'm not the judge or jury."

"I'd have to agree on that for myself, too. But, *caro*, you're probably the most decent man I know."

Wukowski said it would be best if we didn't see each other until Petrovitch's arraignment. He didn't want our relationship to be the cause of issues with the case.

Our relationship? I wondered exactly what that relationship was. But there would be time for us to work that out later. Right now, I had calls to make and people to see, starting with Adriana.

Chapter 29

It only takes bad leadership for a country to go up in flames, for people of different ethnicity, color, or religion to kill each other as if they had nothing in common whatsoever.

—Savo Heleta

I called Bart first, to find out what went down at police headquarters. He assured me that they treated Adriana gently, as a witness for the prosecution. Her only cause for upset was the reality of "Uncle Herman's" heinous crimes and the revelation of her parents' involvement. He gave me the green light to call Bram and set up a meeting with Adriana. "But Angie, the news vultures are all over this. You and Bobbie are already targets, because of the film at the truck stop. It'll be worse now."

"I'll deal," I told him. "They'll give up once they realize I'm not making statements or giving interviews. I'll just refer them to you," I said with a lilt in my voice.

"Thanks," he rasped back. There was no missing the irony in his.

After we hung up, I called Bram.

"Miss A is with Spider and his family," he said. "I'm on guard duty at your condo. I agree with Bart that there should be no problem with a meeting, now that the…stuff has hit the fan. There's no reason to muzzle anyone now. In fact, Adriana can probably come out of hiding, although I still think she needs personal protection, just to keep the news hounds at bay."

"So it's okay if I leave the building without supervision?"

"Yes. Unless you want some help with the reporters."

I thought about it and decided that the sooner I started the "no comment" process, the sooner they'd tire of it and leave me alone. Bram and I agreed to meet at the UWM library at one o'clock, for a trip to Adriana's safe place.

Before the news broke, I had to talk with Rua Kolar. Petrovitch's perfidy was just a story to us, albeit an awful story. It was Rua's life. I couldn't let her hear it on the news.

I spoke with Lily next. She, too, was taken aback when she heard the scope of Petrovitch's crimes. When I asked if she'd arrange a meeting with Rua, she said, "Yes. She needs to hear this in person. I'll call her and get back to you." She paused. "I think Colonel Lewis should sit in, too. Rua knows him and respects him for his service in Bosnia. He'll be able to reassure her about the Tribunal process." In fifteen minutes, she had the meeting set up at the library for eleven-thirty. Bobbie planned to get a ride home from Bram and would then meet me at the library after my talk with Rua.

It was now ten-fifteen. I set out my clothes, took a quick shower and completed the usual rituals. I was sore, but much better than yesterday. Once dressed, my full length mirror reflected a woman ready for a funeral, in a black Anne Klein pantsuit with a lacy black camisole underneath. Rather than adding to the heaviness, I wanted my clothes to reflect the hope of justice delivered, even if deferred. I switched out the black cami for a cream-colored blouse with satin piping around the crew neck. A chunky turquoise choker and black Ferragamo pumps with a grosgrain ribbon finished the look.

It felt good to ease into the Miata and drive. So far, there was no snow on the ground, nor was any forecasted. I savored the freedom of cruising down Lake Drive, with the sun shining and Lake Michigan a rich blue. It was good to be free of constant protection and the stalking danger of the last week.

I met Lily in the same conference room we used to interview Rua the first time, only last Thursday. So much had happened since then. How would I tell her about Petrovitch and his scheme without adding to her trauma? I finally decided that there was no way to make this easy. I would have to tell the truth and just be there if she needed help. Presence, Aunt Terry once told me when I asked her what she said to the many people she comforted, is sometimes all we can offer and is sometimes all that is needed. I hoped that Rua would allow Lily and me to give her the gift of presence.

"You want to tell her?" I asked Lily as we sat down.

"No. I think you need to do it. I'm just a bystander."

I snorted. "Not so, Lily. Your work identifying the artifacts helped bust this case open."

"That's nice of you to say, but you're the one who put your butt on the line. I learned something about myself, Angie. I learned that reading mysteries and trying to figure out who committed the crime is a lot different from being involved in a real-life mystery. After I watched that video of you and Bobbie scrambling to get into those pipes, I knew that being a detective is not something I could ever do. I'll stick with being a librarian and trying to knock these kids into shape." She smiled. "But anytime you need a researcher, I'm your woman."

"That's a deal," I told her. We shook on it.

Colonel Lewis and Professor Kolar arrived, silent as they entered the room. "We ran into each other on the stairs," Rua said. She took a seat across the table from Lily and cattycorner to me. Lewis pushed the chair next to hers to the wall and sat beside her, with plenty of space between them. *Very insightful of him to not crowd her,* I thought.

Time to woman up. "Rua," I said, "there have been a lot of developments in the case. I need to bring you up to speed, because it's going to hit the news this afternoon and I don't want you to be surprised."

"Thank you," was all she said.

I told myself I could act like this was doomsday, or I could present it as a hopeful ending to a terrible situation. I fingered the turquoise choker at my neck, a gift from a dear friend with New Age leanings. The little handout that came with it attributed healing and protective force to the stone. The Native Americans believed that if the turquoise was ever cracked, "the stone took it," meaning the stone took the blow for the wearer. *Please,* I prayed, *take this blow for Rua.*

I began to speak. She sat, unmoving and stoic, until I told of Petrovitch forcing Serbians with Muslim ties into securing loot for him. Then she covered her face with her hands and murmured, "How long? How long?" When I spoke about his arranging for the murders, she lowered her hands and her eyes flashed. "Evil, evil man," she said. "May he suffer the eternal torment of the damned."

Colonel Lewis edged a mite closer to her. "Professor, because of you, Lily and Angie, Petrovitch is behind bars and we've identified some of the persons he dragged into this scheme. We also have frozen the bank accounts that started the investigation and we're looking for others."

"That is all to the good," Rua said, her voice hard, "but it does not repay the debt he owes."

Lewis nodded. "Nothing can bring the dead back to life, but we can close down his operation and send him to trial."

"And how many years will that take?" she protested.

"I think the International Criminal Tribunal for the former Yugoslavia—"he gave each word great weight—"will act decisively and with all due speed."

"The ICTY? He will be tried at The Hague?" Lewis nodded. "Then there is hope for justice."

"I believe that, with all my heart," Lewis said. He rose and took a card from the inside pocket of his uniform jacket. "Please call me with any questions you might have. Or if you want to talk."

She stood and took the card, her hand extended. "Thank you, Colonel Lewis. You are a good man."

Lewis moved a half step closer to Rua and placed her hand between his, saying, "*Fi Amanillah*." To my surprise, as she repeated the words, Rua lightly kissed him on each cheek. He smiled very slightly and left the room.

Neither Lily nor I spoke. Rua reseated herself, her expression serious.

"Rua," I said, "help me understand. Why is it that this intense hatred of Serbs for Bosniaks erupted after Yugoslavia was divided?"

"Ahh," she sighed, "there is much history behind it. In 1389, the Ottomans conquered the Serbs. The roots are that deep. In 1918, after centuries of Ottoman rule, the Serbians took control of Yugoslavia. Back and forth it went, like the Arabs and Jews. We grew up learning to distrust and disparage each other. Under Communist rule, there was enforced peace. But when the Soviet Union broke apart, the factions rose against each other once more. No restraints then, just open power struggles. War gave both sides the excuse to hurt, rape, starve, kill.

Muslims were not entirely innocent, but we did not have the same means as the Serbs, so our misdeeds were less. It is sad, no?"

"Very sad," I said. "Thank you for speaking so honestly." I paused. "Will you be all right?"

"Yes. I have learned to survive."

***

After Rua left, Lily said, "That went better than I thought it would."

I nodded. "It must be healing to know that at least one bad guy will get his comeuppance."

As I rose to put on my coat, Lily said, "Enjoy your Thanksgiving, Angie."

When I thought about the family interactions and the not-so-subtle assessments Wukowski and I would undergo, not to mention concern for his mother, I felt caterpillars crawling on my skin—not dangerous, but slightly creepy. "Thanks, Lily. What are your plans?"

"Mmm, well, it'll be a quiet day for me. I'm originally from North Dakota, but my family's scattered all over the States. The guy I was seeing finished his Ph.D. work and took a job in Seattle last summer. I'll probably just get a supermarket turkey meal and curl up with a book. It'll be a nice change from herding students." Her smile didn't reach her eyes.

"Listen, I'd love to have you share the meal with us, if you can stand my Sicilian family and the attendant noise and nosiness." I grimaced. "I've been dating the homicide detective who coincidentally got assigned to this case. His name is Ted Wukowski. He and his mother are going to be there and will meet my family for the first time. I've spoken with his mom on the phone, but this is our first face-to-face. I'm feeling the tension."

"You won't want a stranger in the middle of that," she said.

"The way I see it, you'll be a buffer. I already invited some others—Bobbie and maybe his partner, Steve, if Steve makes it back to town in time. The attorney on this case, Bart Matthews. How about it?"

She hesitated for a moment, but then agreed with a smile.

After I gave her the details for Thursday, she returned to her desk. I met Bobbie at the library entrance. "Bram just called me," he said. "He's waiting on Hartford Avenue. He said to leave the Miata here. The news broke and the hounds are on our trail."

I sighed. "I guess that shouldn't surprise me."

We crossed the commons and saw Bram's truck idling at the curb. As we approached, he reached over and opened the passenger side door. "I'm smaller. I'll sit in the middle," I told Bobbie. I didn't see a granny handle, but there was a running board. I set my purse and briefcase on the floor and used the side of the truck for purchase as I stepped up. Bobbie gave me a boost that was mostly goose, while Bram offered me a hand and pretty much hauled me inside. *Oh, the indignities visited upon the short people of the world!*

"I'm sorry about the Cruiser," I said as I buckled up. Soft jazz played on the radio. "I know it's harder for you to use the truck."

"No big deal. Really. I'm pleased to find out that it isn't as hard to climb in as it was. Guess the therapy's working." He headed south, turning the radio volume down. "Adriana's been staying at Spider's place since the funeral. It's not procedure, but he has the highest tech security outside the Pentagon." He grimaced. "The way things are these days, maybe it beats the Pentagon. The Mulcaheys live in Delafield, about thirty miles from here."

"Mulcaheys, plural? His wife and son are there, too? I hate to think of them in harm's way, if someone tries to get at Adriana."

"Spider wanted to send Magda and Joey away for a couple of days," Bram said, "but she refused. She told Spider that no one would threaten her family and live to tell the story. She's in Mama Bear mode, now that they're expecting again. Twins."

"Spider showed me a snapshot. How old is their little boy?"

"Joey's four. Great kid. They asked me to be one of the godfathers for the twins." His voice was soft and contained just a hint of bemusement.

"How wonderful. Do they know the babies' genders?"

"Not yet, but I know they hope for at least one girl, even though Spider says it scares him a lot more than parenting a boy."

"It's nice that he cares that way," Bobbie said. "Not every father does." He cleared his throat. "Will they have a problem with me being there?"

"Why should they?" Bram asked.

"Some people have this crazy notion that all gays are pedophiles."

Bram glanced over. "Yeah? Well, that's stupid thinking."

"No doubt, but it's their home we're going to."

"Uh, Bobbie," Bram said, "Spider and I already knew...well, guessed...that you're gay. He knows that you're coming with Angie and he didn't object, so no worries."

As we traveled west from Milwaukee, city gave way to suburbia and then to farmland, punctuated by small towns. Bram took the Delafield exit, turned off Main Street and drove past St. John's Northwestern Military Academy, a boarding school for boys. The fall colors had morphed into bare tree branches. Winter was hard on our heels.

The mellow music on the radio was suddenly interrupted midstream by a jarring voice. "Breaking news," the announcer said. Bram turned the volume up. "Herman Petrovitch, a local attorney accused of immigration violations and conspiracy to commit murder, was shot and killed as he exited the county jail under police escort this afternoon. He was being transported to Chicago for arraignment in the immigration violations. The shooter then turned the gun on himself. The apparent murder-suicide happened about fifteen minutes ago. Police are not releasing information on the shooter yet. We'll update you as events transpire."

Bram pulled the truck over and put it into park. We sat in silence for a few seconds, stunned. Bobbie put an arm around my shoulders and squeezed gently. Then Bram's phone rang. He checked the display and answered. "Du Pont, what the hell is happening?" He listened. "Yeah, I know. If you don't mind dying yourself, there's not a lot that can stop you. I'm with our two investigators, on our way to…the girl." More listening. "Okay. Keep me updated." He set the phone on the dash, silenced the radio, rested his hands on the steering wheel and stared straight ahead.

After a long silence, he spoke. "That was Du Pont. He got a call from one of the U.S. Marshals on the case, a buddy of his who knew he was involved." Bram sighed and turned to us. "Josif Zupan showed up at the jail with a sawed-off shotgun and blew Petrovitch's head off. Before they could get to him, Zupan put the barrel into his own mouth and pulled the trigger."

Bobbie gasped.

"God almighty," I whispered, half curse and half prayer.

"There'll undoubtedly be a big investigation and lots of accusations of improper conduct on the part of the police. Bottom line, though, a killer on a suicide mission is nearly impossible to stop." He put the truck into drive and made a U-turn. "The cops are on their way to pick up Adriana."

"Don't turn back," I protested. "She needs someone with her. There's no way she was involved in this."

"They know that, Angie." He glanced at me. "Zupan had a note in his coat pocket. Part of it is addressed to Adriana."

"Bram, she needs someone with her, a friend, when she reads that."

"Yeah." He thought for a moment. "Call Spider and tell him what just went down. Have him make sure Adriana asks for legal representation at the station. Then call Bart. He can maybe get you in as part of his legal team."

Spider's response to the news was to shift into planning mode, just as Bram had. If I ever needed someone to get me out of a bad situation—worse than the one I'd been in for the last week—it would be them. "I don't want the police on my property," Spider said. I'll call Wukowski and tell him I'll escort her to Homicide. You call Bart and we'll meet up there. And Angie, don't worry—I won't let them talk to her until you arrive." He sighed. "She's still in a bit of shock over Petrovitch's betrayal. This'll hit her hard."

As I called Bart, I wondered out loud why Spider didn't want the police at his house. "Too much high-tech security," Bram said. "They might start wondering why a door-and-window guy would have that."

Bart answered my call. "Angie, I just got the news about Petrovitch. Helluva situation. But maybe it'll work better for Adriana. She won't have to testify against him."

How cold, I thought, but then I reminded myself that Bart was charged with protecting his client's best interests. "The police haven't revealed the shooter's identity yet, but Bram found out via Du Pont, that it was Josif Zupan." Bart inhaled. "He left a letter, partly for Adriana. Spider's taking her to headquarters. Can you meet us there? She'll need someone with her whom she can lean on, not just a couple of police detectives watching her for a reaction." *Wukowski and Iggy weren't cold-hearted men, but they had their jobs to do.* "Bart, I need to be with her when they show her the letter and you're my only hope to make that happen."

"I'm on it. See you there."

Chapter 30

*It is impossible to suffer without making someone pay for it;
every complaint already contains revenge.*

—Friedrich Nietzsche

The Homicide bullpen was chock-a-block with officers when we arrived—MPD, U.S. Marshals, courthouse security. Testosterone—or maybe it was just adrenaline—laced the air. Wukowski strode over to us. "You know?" was all he said.

I nodded. "Bart Matthews is on his way. Adriana needs someone besides police with her." I stuck my chin up, ready to do battle.

He ran a hand through his hair and motioned for our little group to follow him to his Lieutenant's empty office, where he closed the door and spoke softly. "The U.S. Marshals are shouting for jurisdiction, the FBI is doing the same. MPD is hanging on by the skin of our teeth. We hadn't completed the transfer when Petrovitch was shot, so we're claiming Zupan as our case. At least, for now."

Bart Matthews knocked lightly and opened the door. "Detective Wukowski," he said, offering his hand, "I'm here on behalf of my client, Adriana Johnson. She's asking for legal representation in the proceedings."

Wukowski said, "We're not charging her with anything, Matthews. The contents of Zupan's suicide note pertain to her future, not to her involvement in the Petrovitch case."

"Nevertheless, she wants representation. Her legal team—Ms. Bonaparte and I—are entitled to be present."

Wukowski's eyes shifted to me. I shrugged and he turned back to Bart. "I think that will be acceptable." A low buzz reached us through the glass of the office door. Spider and Adriana had arrived. "I'll set up a private room," Wukowski said. He opened the door and marched over to the cluster of uniforms and suits that congregated at the opposite corner of the open space. There, he waited on the fringes, as fingers pointed and fists slapped on palms. To my surprise, Colonel Lewis was in the thick of it, standing at what I believe is called "parade rest," feet apart, elbows out and hands behind his back.

Adriana saw me and rushed over. I turned from the tableau to envelop her in a hug, ignoring the pain from her hold on my bruised body. She didn't cry, but little tremors rippled through her. I patted her back and comforted her with a mother's stock phrases: *there, there; it's okay; it'll be all right; shh.* When the shaking stopped, she stepped back and grabbed my hands. "Please, Angie, stay with me."

"I'll do all I can, Adriana. Bart's working on getting me access."

Iggy walked over and stood, shifting awkwardly from foot to foot. "Uh, Adriana, we're gonna put you and your legal team"—he looked at me and Bart—"in an interrogation room. We're still trying to work out the logistics." He ran a hand across his mouth, clearly unsure of how to proceed. "For now, we just want you to wait."

Bart turned to Bobbie, Bram and Spider. "I don't think we can push the boundaries enough to get you in, too."

"No problem for me," Bobbie said. "I'll just observe. This is better than 'NYPD Blue.'" He took a small notebook and pen from his coat and sat in a row of chairs along the wall. Spider and Bram joined him.

In the interrogation room, Bart said, "Detective Ignowski, I want your assurance of no surveillance, visual or audio, in this room."

"Course not, Counselor."

When Iggy left, we sat, Bart facing the door and Adriana next to me on the other side of the table, our backs to the glass upper wall. Bart opened his briefcase and extracted a legal pad and pen. "Adriana," he said, leaning forward, "I understand that the police found a note on Mr. Zupan's body that mentions you. Were you acquainted with him?"

"Not really. I knew his wife, Dragana. My parents would sometimes take me with them to the law office, when I was younger. She often had homemade cookies, and would give me paper and crayons and look after me while they were in Petrovitch's office. She was very kind, very gentle."

Tears welled up in her eyes. I took her hand and held it.

"I did meet Josif Zupan, once or twice, when my parents went to Serbian Society meetings and couldn't find a babysitter. Again, I was much younger. I would sit in the hallway outside the meeting room at the church and do homework or read a book."

She paused. "The only time Josif did more than greet me was right before Christmas, one year. He asked me what I wanted from Santa. I told him I didn't believe in Santa and that my parents were too poor to buy me toys. He just patted my shoulder and went into the room. Honestly, he was a scary man. I didn't want him to notice me." She looked at Bart and her hand trembled. "Why would he mention me in his…last words?"

"There's no sense speculating," Bart told her. "We'll know soon enough."

In an effort to distract her a bit, I said, "I've been thinking about where you might stay. Bram thinks the threat to you is over, but…well, do you want to go back to your family home?"

"No." It was an adamant refusal. "I need to get my personal belongings and clean out the place. I could never stay there overnight."

"You're welcome to use my guest room."

"Thank you, Angie." She took a deep breath and relaxed her shoulders. "Spider and Magda—his wife—invited me to stay with them for a few weeks. They have a guest suite and Magda insists it would be no trouble. I've been helping take care of their little boy, Joey. He's a good boy, but very active. Magda is expecting twins and she needs to rest. So we can help each other, you know?"

The Mulcaheys would provide her with protection from the press, but, more important, she'd be with a loving family and learn from their interactions. It was a good solution.

Wukowski and Iggy entered, followed by three men whom Wukowski introduced as his Lieutenant, a U.S. Marshal and an FBI agent. Bart rose and moved to sit on Adriana's other side. The official contingent took seats across from us.

Wukowski took out his digital recorder and quirked a brow at Bart, who nodded and set his own on the table. Both men pressed the start buttons. "Ms. Johnson," Wukowski began, "this is not an interrogation and you are not suspected of any crime. We asked you here to view the contents of a letter found in the coat pocket of Mr. Josif Zupan after his death. You're aware of the circumstances of his demise?"

Adriana nodded and took a ragged breath. Wukowski put on latex gloves and extracted an envelope from a glassine folder. He took a sheet of paper from the envelope, unfolded it, and placed it on the table, facing us. He spoke in a quiet voice. "Please don't touch it. It's evidence." He held it open with a thumb and index finger on each side.

Adriana turned to me. "I don't know if I want to read this."

"I think you need to, Adriana."

"Read it out loud for me. Please, Angie." She closed her eyes and sat back.

Wukowski shifted the paper slightly, to rest before me. I leaned forward and began to speak Josif Zupan's last words.

November 2 (transcribed by Dragana Zupan from a verbal statement by Josif Zupan)

Herman Petrović—

I looked up. "He uses the Serbian spelling."

—forced me and many others to work for him in looting and robbery during the Bosnian War. I agreed because he threatened my wife, whose family was Muslim and who would be in danger from Serb fanatics if that became known. I sent him goods by way of contacts in Greece and money deposits made to various banks in Europe. In exchange, he secured U.S. visas for my wife and me, when it was too dangerous for us to stay in Serbia. He employed my wife as a legal secretary in the United States.

My wife was ignorant of this until she overheard an argument between Petrović and Jan and Ivona Jovanović, at the office. They wanted Petrović to provide financial support for their daughter, Adrijana, and threatened him with exposure for war crimes if he refused.

Adriana gasped. I gave her a moment before I continued.

When Dragana asked me, I told her the truth and begged her not to involve herself. I suspected that Petrović was responsible for the Jovanović deaths. I told Dragana that we would quietly sell all that we could and disappear.

The typewritten statement changed at that point, to cramped printing, each line of text angling downward on the page. "This part is handwritten," I said. "I assume Zupan added this after Dragana's death.

Dragana very angry. She tell Petrović no more work for him. Petrović kill my Dragana. I no want to live. I kill him—evil man. Then I be with her, if her God forgive me. I hurt many people. Jovanović, too. Adrijana know nothing of this. Dragana put work money into bank. This not bad money. This money for Adrijana. Is not much. I sorry.

Yesterday's date and his signature were written in script at the bottom of the page, even smaller than the packed lines of writing, as if he wanted to be as invisible as possible.

I turned to Adriana. She sat motionless, hands in her lap, stiffly upright, with her eyes cast down. "Adriana," I said, keeping my voice pitched low and even.

She didn't move.

I carefully placed a hand on her upper back and gently rubbed. "Baby, it's over now."

She covered her face with her hands, folded herself almost double and broke into wrenching sobs. I rubbed her back and waited, knowing that my presence was all I could offer at that moment.

Bart spoke. "Gentlemen, my client is too distraught to continue. You can contact her via my office if there is a need for more discussion." He paused. "But I certainly hope there is not. She's been through enough." He turned off his recorder and placed it in his briefcase, along with his papers.

They trooped out quietly, Wukowski at the end of the column. As he passed us, he said, "Angie, I'll call you tonight." I nodded and he left.

Bart stared at the wall while I continued to soothe Adriana. Her sobs subsided into tears and then hiccups. She sat up and wrapped her arms around herself. I took some tissues from my purse and put them on her lap. She wiped her eyes and face, blew her nose loudly and resumed the self-hug.

"Better?" I asked.

She nodded. After a long silence, she said, "I always thought my parents didn't love me. Now I think they just wanted to protect me, to shield me from the ugliness of their lives. And Josif, living with that secret all those years." She looked up at me, her eyes blazing. "He was right. Petrovitch was an evil man."

From the corner of my eye, I saw Wukowski through the half window in the door. He knocked softly and eased it open. "The reporters are downstairs. We can arrange for you to exit another way."

"Much appreciated," Bart said as he rose. "Adriana, do you still plan to stay with the Mulcaheys?" She nodded. "Good. Let's get Spider. You two can probably leave without incident. There's nothing public to tie you to the case at present." He looked at me. "You and I, on the other hand, are chum for the sharks."

I grimaced and took Adriana's hands. "You'll be fine, Adriana. I know you'll come out of this okay. I'll call you tomorrow, but if you need to talk before then, call me. Any time." We hugged and she and Spider left.

Bart and I walked over to Bram and Bobbie. "The Miata's still on the street at UWM," I said, "undoubtedly with a parking ticket affixed to the windshield. Bram, can you give us a ride there?" Bram left to move his truck to the secure lot.

Bobbie, Bart and I ambled to the elevators, reluctant to leave the police cocoon that, however disturbing, was safe. As we waited, Bart muttered, "Craziest thing I've ever been part of."

"You've got that right," I said. "Instructions, Counselor?"

"You and Bobbie need to lie low. Recuperate. Stay out of the public eye. I'll make a statement when the time is right."

"It's okay for me to go back to my place?" Bobbie asked.

"Should be fine," Bart said. "They'll have to trespass to get to you at the back of the property. Screen your calls, though. There'll be a boatload, until the press tires of leaving messages."

We parted downstairs, Bart exiting the front of the building as a sacrificial offering to the gods of journalism. I blessed him for that.

In the lot where the cops parked, we climbed into Bram's truck and ducked down behind the dash until we were several blocks away. "I'll take Bobbie home first. It's unlikely that the press is there yet. They're probably lying in wait for you, Angie." There was no activity at the manor that fronted Bobbie's carriage house. We hugged good-bye and promised to be in touch the next day.

As anticipated, the Miata sported a parking ticket. I plucked it from under the wiper blade and waved it at Bram. He followed me back to my condo, where about a dozen reporters waited at the garage entrance.

The rest must still be at headquarters, I thought. The hellhounds blocked access to the card reader and thrust their mics and recorders at me, shouting questions and blinding me with videocam lights.

Bram, close on my tail, got out of his truck and stalked toward them. "Back off," he said. "Let the lady in. She's not the only person who lives here. I wanna get home to my wife and supper." He moved forward, body puffed up and threatening, and those closest to the reader stepped back. I slapped my card up, the garage door opened and I drove in. Bram followed me and waited until the big door closed behind him, assuring that no one snuck inside behind us.

He pulled up beside me. "I'll head out now."

"You told them you were coming home. You can't leave right away. They'll suspect something and try to find out who you are."

"Nah, I'll just shout at them to get out of my way, that I forgot to pick up milk on the way home." He waved and headed back to the overhead door.

No one waited at the elevator. I gave thanks for small favors as I rode up. I was in no frame of mind to exchange small talk with neighbors. Inside my condo, I kicked off my shoes, hung up my coat and put my briefcase in the hall closet. Sagging in relief, I headed for the kitchen and a glass of wine. On the way into the living room, I passed the shelves that held books and family photos.

Home and family. Sometimes a source of joy, sometimes a wellspring of sorrow. I settled on the couch and looked out over the darkness, punctuated by the city lights. I sipped the wine and thought of Josif. My Catholic upbringing taught me the prayer for the "faithful departed." What does one pray for a nonbeliever?

"Because I could not stop for death," wrote Emily Dickinson, "he kindly stopped for me. The carriage held but just ourselves and immortality." I liked to think that Josif was riding in Death's carriage, heading for the eternity that Emily imagined in her poem. *God*, I prayed, *grant him the forgiveness he asked for. Reunite him with his Dragana*. I raised my glass. "Josif," I said aloud, and took a sip.

Chapter 31

The only gift is a portion of thyself.
—Ralph Waldo Emerson

I roused myself around seven, turned on lights in the living room and kitchen, and looked in the fridge. It was still full of food from the "Pipe Incident" offerings, but nothing appealed, so I heated a can of soup. *How can something be too salty and too blah at the same time?* I finished half a bowl anyway. The rest went down the disposal.

There were no messages on my landline or cell phone, no texts, no emails. *Wukowski, where are you?* I stewed, despite knowing that it was unreasonable to expect him to call me in the midst of what was undoubtedly turmoil at Homicide.

After brewing a cup of green tea, I settled back in the living room and turned on TV, searching for something to distract me. *Antiques Roadshow* was a nice mixture of information, personalities and surprises. When it ended at eight, I rose to take my empty teacup to the kitchen. The landline rang and I jumped for it, causing the cup to rattle in its saucer.

"Angie," Wukowski said, "it's a freakin' mess here. The higher-ups are still angling for position. Iggy and I have been dismissed for the night." His voice held traces of both anger and relief.

"Come over," I said without hesitation. I suddenly felt hungry. "I've got a fridge full of food."

"And I've got the heartburn from hell."

"Well, I can scramble eggs and make toast. That shouldn't upset your digestion."

"Yeah. That sounds good. See you soon."

Twenty minutes later, my phone rang again. "Ange, there are reporters at the front of your building and the garage entry. I drove past and parked a block away. I don't see how I can make it into the building without their spotting me."

"Oh. I guess that would be bad, for you to be associated with me outside the job." I was disappointed and my voice reflected it.

"I'm not worried about that, *moja miłość.* I don't want to put you on the spot, though."

"If that's all that's stopping you, come on in. And I've been meaning to ask you what *moja miłość* means."

"I'll tell you after supper." His voice rumbled, a bit lower than his usual baritone.

This might be the perfect end to a horrible day.

When the intercom rang, I answered and buzzed Wukowski in, waiting at the door to hug him. He smelled fresh and frosty, like the winter wind off the lake. We embraced for several long seconds, until he kissed me and said, "Let me get out of this coat."

I waited as he hung it in the closet and took off his shoes. "C'mere." He opened his arms and enveloped me in another hug, rubbing my back with one hand while he pulled me close with the other.

"You okay?" I spoke into his chest.

"Yeah. Long day, though. Long, bad day." He loosened his hold.

"You mentioned eggs and toast? 'Cause all I've had today is coffee and more coffee, punctuated by a Danish and several loads of crap."

I laughed. "No wonder you have heartburn." Taking him by the hand, I led him into the kitchen and gave him a little push toward the stools at the peninsula. "Sit," I said in a mock-stern voice. I boiled some water and steeped peppermint tea. "Drink that, *caro*. It should help." As I scrambled eggs and toasted bread, he swallowed the tea and his shoulders slowly descended from his ears. I didn't want to see him tighten up again, but I had to ask. "How'd it go with the reporters downstairs?"

He shrugged. "They were shouting questions to anyone who headed toward the building. 'Do you know Angelina Bonaparte? What kind of neighbor is she? Do you ever see Mafia goons hanging around the building?' Everybody ignored them. I thought I'd get in unnoticed, but that female investigative reporter from WITI spotted me and shoved a mike in my face. 'Are you here to arrest Ms. Bonaparte?'" He laughed. "I wanted to say, 'No, I'm here to make love to Ms. Bonaparte.'"

I almost dropped the egg carton I was putting back into the fridge.

"But I thought better of it," he added with a big grin.

"Thank you. I don't think my papa or Aunt Terry would appreciate that announcement on TV."

While we ate, he gave me the rundown on the afternoon and evening developments. MPD still had tentative jurisdiction, but he was sure that would end tomorrow when the Feds took it to court. "We searched the Zupan residence and found Josif's paystubs in the file cabinets," Wukowski said. "He only worked twelve weeks this year, and none of them a full forty hours."

"Doesn't surprise me. Lily talked to one of the guys in the union, who told her that Josif was standoffish. Small wonder they didn't offer him jobs."

"Dragana made good money working for Petrovitch, though. The average salary for a legal secretary in Milwaukee is about twenty-five thousand. For a paralegal, it's thirty-one. She pulled in fifty-two grand last year, according to their tax returns."

"Hush money?" I wondered.

He set his fork down on his empty plate, wiped his mouth with the napkin and pushed back a bit from the table. "Thanks, Angie. I needed real food."

"Any time," I said, and was surprised to find I meant it. There was a time in our relationship when I wanted—no, needed—space. Right now, I wanted and needed to be close.

He resumed the conversation. "Iggy and I wondered about that, too—if Petrovitch was paying for her silence." He shook his head. "It doesn't feel like that to me. Josif's letter stated that she found out the truth because of an argument between Petrovitch and the Johnsons. And if she lied to Josif and was complicit in Petrovitch's dirty dealings, why would she confront him?" He rubbed the back of his neck. "With Petrovitch, the Zupans and the Johnsons all dead, this is shaping up to be one of those cases where we never understand all the motives or even all the outcomes. I hate that."

"Me, too, *caro*. I like all the loose ends to be tied up in a pretty bow, like a Poirot story, but real life isn't like that." I rose to clear the table.

As I loaded the dishwasher, Wukowski came up behind me and put his hands on my waist. "You asked me what *moja miłość* means." His tone was low and somewhat apprehensive. "It means, 'my love.' *Kocham Cię*, Angie. I love you."

I turned in his arms, fear and caution tossed away like clothes that were too tight. "*Ti amo*. I love you, too, Wukowski. I don't know where it's going, but I love you."

"I know where it's going." His kiss was tender, as his hands caressed my head, back, hips.

The dishes would wait until morning.

Chapter 32

The course of true love never did run smooth.
—William Shakespeare

Wukowski's cell alarm woke me at six a.m. My pique vanished when he leaned over me and kissed me in the *uber*-sensitive area just underneath my ear. "Sleep," he said. "I've got to get to Homicide early."

"I'll make breakfast," I told him.

"No time. I'll grab a shower here. I can stop for something on the way downtown." He feathered kisses across my shoulder. "Sorry to rush out like this."

I brewed coffee and left a mug for him on the bathroom sink. It looked like snow outside. I turned on the early TV news to catch the forecast. "In an emergency hearing at the federal courthouse here in Milwaukee last night, a judge ruled that the case involving Herman Petrovitch, a local attorney who was shot and killed yesterday afternoon prior to being transported to Chicago, is now under FBI control. The Milwaukee Police Department issued a statement saying they would do all that is necessary to aid the FBI in their investigation." Pictures of Petrovitch, Dragana Zupan and Josif Zupan flashed on the screen as the reporter speculated about motives.

Behind me, Wukowski snorted. "FBI didn't waste any time." He walked up to me, mug in hand. "I don't know if this will lighten the load at work or make it worse." He bent to kiss me. "I'll call you later."

As he turned to walk to the hall, the video from the truck stop played and the announcer continued. "Related to this story, our investigative reporter learned that Homicide Detective Ted Wukowski, who led the MPD investigation into the case, entered the building where Private Investigator Angelina Bonaparte lives at about eight last night and was not seen leaving the building before our reporter left at midnight."

"Holy…" I sputtered, aghast at the display of pictures and the newscaster's words.

Wukowski came back and stood beside me.

The reporter continued. "Ms. Bonaparte was one of two persons who escaped Attorney Petrovitch's alleged attack at an Illinois truck stop, by leaping into a moving semi's load of giant pipes. The video of those events has gone viral. It is unclear if Ms. Bonaparte, who was instrumental in the exoneration of alleged mobster Anthony Belloni last year, is in police custody. The police have issued a 'no comment' response to our request for information regarding Ms. Bonaparte." He smirked directly into the camera and my cup jumped in its saucer. "Reliable informants tell us that Detective Wukowski and Ms. Bonaparte have a personal relationship."

"That sonofa…" I was so angry that my muscles contracted in shivers.

Wukowski squeezed my shoulder, took my cup and steered me to the couch, where he sat down next to me. 'Angie, if I'd thought for a moment that this could happen—"

"Don't you dare tell me you would've turned around last night, Wukowski!"

"Settle down, little tiger. I'm only trying to say that I'm sorry for the news account, not for anything between us."

I huffed a sigh of relief, then stiffened. "Omigod, Papa will explode when he hears this. And he's an early riser."

"Yeah, Mama won't like it either," Wukowski said. "Aw, hell, Angie, we're not fifteen-year old virgins. We don't need to hide from our parents."

"True, but this is Milwaukee, not Hollywood. People don't flaunt their..."

"Relationships? Lovers?" He shook his head. "Look, this isn't casual to me. I don't exactly know what to call this."

"It's not casual to me, either, *caro*." I took his hands in mine. "Maybe we should just refuse to answer questions and let it die down."

"You think that'll work with your family?"

I groaned. "Not a chance."

His cell phone rang. It was his turn to groan. "It's Iggy, probably wondering where I am. We agreed to meet at six-thirty."

"Go, go." I shooed at him with my hands. "Call me later."

I sat on the couch, stared at the TV and double-dog-dared them to make suggestive statements. I knew lawyers! Okay, I knew one lawyer, but *he* knew people. I'd sic Bart on them!

Papa called five minutes later. "Angelina, were you in jail? Why didn't you call me?"

He thought Wukowski'd been here to arrest me. How could I explain the truth to my straight-laced papa, who still treated me as if I were a girl living under his roof? "Um, no, Papa, there was no arrest."

"Thank God." There was a moment of silence. "So, I conclude that this man cares so little for your reputation that he spent the night at your home while reporters lurked outside?"

"Honestly, Papa, we didn't know they'd hang around half the night."

"I see. Then as long as no one knew, it was all right with you?"

I had to stop for a moment and consider. If it had been my Emma caught in this situation, I'd be upset *for* her, but not *with* her. Papa was a different generation, though. To him, a woman's virtue was paramount—although the men of his generation fooled around just as much as men did today, so where'd they find those "unvirtuous" women to dally with? His response would be: the women of my family behave as ladies, regardless of what other women do. I'd never make him see any different. I decided to address the effect rather than the cause.

"It's very embarrassing to have that on the news, Papa. I'm sorry. I didn't mean to bring shame on the family." I waited, hoping the code words would work.

"Hmph. Well, I suppose you will lead your life as you see fit, Angelina."

Thank God, use of only my first name.

"But I expect this man to make amends."

Huh? "I don't understand, Papa. Do you want Wukowski to call and apologize to you?" I couldn't imagine asking him to do that.

"No, Angelina, he must repair the damage. He must offer marriage to you."

He couldn't be serious! "This is the twenty-first century, Papa. People have love affairs. That doesn't necessarily mean marriage is in the offing. I'm not sure I'd marry Wukowski if he asked me."

"*Madre di Dio.* You are intimate with men you do not love?"

I was, in the past. Not often, though. But now, at least, I could give Papa the answer he wanted to hear. "I love Wukowski and he loves

295

me." I suppressed a sudden urge to giggle at the still-new words, before sobering. "But we're not at the stage to talk marriage. Maybe we will be, someday, but not yet. You wouldn't want me to rush into anything, would you?"

"No, of course not." His voice softened. "I want what is best for you, Angelina. I want you to be happy."

"I know that, Papa. And I'm sorry about the news. I hope you won't let this make our Thanksgiving meal uncomfortable for Wukowski or his mother."

"I would not dishonor my home by behaving that way to a guest."

We each said "I love you" and the call ended. I still had to phone my kids and warn them. First, I needed a shower and a hot cup of coffee. I turned off the blasted TV.

***

Neither of my children was shocked or dismayed by the "news" that Wukowski and I spent the night together. David just gave me a "No duh, Mom," and told me to be happy. He also offered to beat Wukowski up if he hurt me. Sons!

Emma, on the other hand, wanted details of where the relationship was headed. "I don't really know," I told her.

"Has the *L* word been spoken?"

I smiled. "Quite recently, as a matter of fact."

"Was he the first to say it?"

"He was, although I had it on the tip of my tongue."

She whooped. "Good sign, Mom, when the guy says 'I love you' first. If you say it first and he gives you the 'Me, too' routine, you can't be sure if it was even in his head. Hang on." I heard a muffled, "Just a sec, sweetie. I'm on the phone with *Nonna*." Then she said, "Mom, I'm sorry, but I need to get Angela's breakfast. The school bus will be here in twenty minutes."

"Give her a hug from me. I'll see you on Thursday."

One more to go. *Why, oh why, did I wait to let Aunt Terry know about the extra people I invited to our Thanksgiving meal?* I had to call her and she was sure to bombard me with questions and advice, if not outright admonishment.

"Hi, Terry," I said. Maybe I could do an end run around the issue. "I hope you have a big turkey. I invited some friends who didn't have anyone to celebrate with. You know Bobbie Russell. His partner, Steve, is out of town on business. He might be back on Thanksgiving Day, but we're not sure. And Bart Matthews, Papa's attorney, but he's waffling. And Lily Marsh, the UWM librarian who helped me with research on the Petrovitch case. Did I overstep?" As soon as the question left my mouth, I told myself, *Idiot. That opened the door!*

Aunt Terry walked right through it. "Your friends are always welcome, Angelina. There is plenty to eat. And speaking of overstepping, what is this on the news about you and Wukowski?"

"Aunt Terry, Papa already took me to task. I'm sorry for embarrassing the family, but I'm a divorced woman with grown children and grandkids. Is it so terrible that I have a boyfriend?"

"That's not why I asked, *la mia nipotina*. I'm not chastising you. I'm just curious about how serious you and Wukowski are. Is it more than…sex?"

Hearing her stumble over the word made me smile. I remembered when we had the birds-and-bees talk. She was red and stammering, but she told me the facts and bravely answered all my questions, assuring me that I could come to her with anything. All these years later, she was still that young woman, struggling with her niece's sexuality.

"We love each other, Aunt Terry, and we're not seeing others. I'm not sure if it's heading toward a more serious commitment yet."

"I will pray for your wisdom and guidance, Angelina."

I thanked her and sighed with relief when I hung up, wondering if Wukowski made the same kind of call this morning to his mother. At least he didn't have to run the gauntlet of father, aunt and children, though I felt a bit sad that he was so alone in the world. If all went well, he might come to enjoy my big crazy family. Or not. It was too soon to know.

I checked in with Bobbie and Adriana. There was no news—and no reporters—on their fronts. I decided to pick up my mail and go into the office for a few hours. I needed to type up my notes on the Petrovitch case and update my expense report for Bart.

The Miata was well known to the press. I didn't want them following me. It was time to put my taxes to use. I called the police.

"Milwaukee Police District One. Officer Franks."

"Officer, this is Angelina Bonaparte. I wonder if you're aware of the news regarding my involvement in the Petrovitch case." It would be more honest to say "my involvement with Homicide Detective Wukowski," since it was our relationship that the news sharks were circling, but that would be inappropriate.

"Uh…we're aware of it, Ms. Bonaparte."

"Well, I have a problem I hope you can help me with. The news reporters are camping out at my condo building and my neighbors have complained to me about being harassed and having access to the garage area blocked." It wasn't true yet, but it was a matter of time before folks in the building got fed up. I thought the police would have more compassion for the innocent bystanders than they would for me. "I know the press has a job to do, but I don't want my neighbors to suffer for it."

"One minute."

A few clicks later, I heard, "Lieutenant Reynolds here. So the newshounds gotcha pinned down, Ms. Bonaparte?"

"That's right, Lieutenant. Is there something you can do to help?"

"If they're on building property or blocking the driveway to the garage, it's trespassing. They can stand on the sidewalk, though. You want I should send a squad over to remind them of the rules?"

I smiled at his Milwaukee-ese. "Please. Moving them back to the sidewalk would at least let the residents get into the garage a little easier." And also make it easier for me to leave. "Thanks so much. I'm sorry to put you to the extra work."

"Not a problem, ma'am. We got a kick outta that video of you and Mr. Russell." His laugh was a deep rumble. Then his voice got serious. "Wukowski and I were buddies at the Academy. Haven't seen him in a while. He dropped out of social occasions after his partner was killed." He cleared his throat. "You be good to him, hear?"

Now that was a role reversal! Papa gave that same advice, backed by the unspoken consequences of his displeasure, to every boy I ever dated. I suspected he'd do the same with Wukowski on Thursday. I assured Reynolds that I would treat Wukowski with the utmost care.

Chapter 33

If I had my choice I would kill every reporter in the world, but I am sure we would be getting reports from Hell before breakfast.

—William Tecumseh Sherman

The newshounds were congregated on the sidewalk when I drove past in the Miata. Thanking my lucky stars for a one-way street with no traffic, I rolled past and drove to the private mail center, where I emptied the contents of my box into my briefcase and hustled out. I drove past my building, parked four blocks west, and walked to the small dry cleaning establishment I patronized on Farwell. Their shop backed onto my office parking lot.

The Vietnamese couple that ran the cleaners had sufficient English to communicate with customers, but it took some time for them to understand that I wanted to walk out their back door. Mr. Phan stood beside me as I did a quick surveillance of the alley that led to my parking area and the entry to my building. I saw no one resembling the press, so I thanked him and headed out, while he stood on the outside stoop and watched me. I waved to him as I went inside my building. It was nice to know that he had my back.

The back hallway from the parking area was plain—beige walls,

300

scuffed from tenants moving in and out; a freight elevator; a door marked "Maintenance—No Admittance." I knocked, on the off chance that the elusive maintenance man was in. No response. I wrote a note—"Please call the police station if news reporters are a nuisance. They are not legally allowed to block any entrances and they should not enter the building. My apologies. I hope their interest will die down soon. Angie Bonaparte." I slipped it under the door and walked upstairs.

The office was empty, which was just fine with me. Susan loves a good romance and I didn't want to answer questions about Wukowski. It was too new. I wanted to hold it close, to savor it, to have time to examine it without having to explain it. *Those stinking reporters outed us at the most vulnerable time in a newly-professed love relationship!*

I checked the mail. It was all junk, which I shredded. There were twenty-seven emails from news organizations and forty-two voicemails from reporters. I deleted them without reading more than the heading or listening to more than the initial greeting. Then I called Bart.

Thankfully, the call went right to him. I didn't feel like dealing with Bertha's reaction to the news report. "Angie, you're quite the media sensation," Bart said.

"That's why I'm calling, Bart. The reporters are camped outside my condo building and in front of the office building. I had to sneak into work via the dry cleaners on Farwell. Can we get them off my back?"

"Doubtful. Unless they print or broadcast something slanderous or untrue." He took a drag. "*Did* Wukowski stay at your place last night?"

"Yes." I refused to offer more information.

"I know it seems like an invasion of privacy for them to make that connection public, but you two are involved in a big case. That makes you fair game. You can refer them to my office, though, if they want a comment. Bertha will be glad to handle them."

I conjured a mental image of a shark with Bertha's head, biting and swallowing the detestable investigative reporter who exposed Wukowski and me. "Thanks, I'll take you up on that. Be sure to let Bertha know you gave the green light."

"Will do."

"I'm wondering about Adriana. How do we keep them from devouring her?"

"I just prepared a press release. I'll send a copy to Spider for Adriana, and another to your email. There's nothing in it that's confidential. Let me know what you think. Especially the part where I ask the press to respect her in this period of grieving." He gave a snarky laugh. "They'll look bad if they hound a poor little orphan whose parents were brutally murdered barely three weeks ago."

Bart's statement glossed over the Johnsons' participation in Petrovitch's scheme and made them appear to be victims. Adriana came across as altruistic and heroic in her refusal to take money that wasn't hers. I was mentioned tangentially as "the investigator hired by the legal team to uncover the truth about the funds." Fine with me. I didn't want any more attention than I already had. Bart wrapped it all up nicely by stating that the case was "under the control of the Milwaukee Police Department, the Federal Bureau of Investigation and the United States Marshals. Any requests for further information should be referred to them. This office, my client and anyone else connected with the case are not at liberty to provide any information related to the case or their involvement in it. We ask that you respect Ms. Johnson's privacy in this difficult time, as she grieves the loss of both her parents in this terrible tragedy."

I replied to the email, "Nicely done."

I checked my personal email next and was relieved that there were no messages from the press. I was judicious in giving the address out, but people can be bribed with money and attention. There was one message from Wukowski:

Hope your day is going well. Want to come to my place tonight?
I'll pick you up at 6:00. Pack an overnight bag.
W

I sat back in my chair. I'd never been to Wukowski's home. His asking me was a sign of his willingness to be vulnerable. I felt both scared and elated. Before I could chicken out, I responded: I'll be waiting.

Today was Tuesday. I still needed to buy wine and prepare an appetizer for the Thanksgiving meal. It was almost a mile to Glorioso's market. I locked up the office and made my way downstairs, through the Phan's store and to my car with no reporters in sight. Maybe the story was a one-night wonder.

The air was noticeably warmer than last week, but the skies were overcast. Snow was on the way. I popped on a knit hat with a brim and headed toward Brady Street and the market.

Glorioso's was jammed with shoppers. Keeping my head down, I selected fresh vegetables, homemade *giardinieria*, sausage, cheese and wine. I managed to get outside without being recognized.

Sciortino's Bakery, just across the street, boasted the best bread in the city and their cookies were to die for. I bought three loaves of Italian bread and assorted cookies. Snow started to fall as I drove home. The heavy wet flakes slid down my windshield and accumulated in a little slushy barrier under the wiper blades.

Reporters stood on the sidewalk, on either side of the driveway. So much for my optimism about their losing interest. They shouted at me as I put my card up to the garage door reader. "Any comment on the Petrovitch case?" "Are you and Detective Wukowski involved?" "Where's the girl hiding?" I ignored them and pulled into the garage.

After hauling the bags up and divesting myself of boots and outerwear, I put the groceries away and investigated the refrigerator. There were still lots of goodies that were dropped off after what I mentally referred to as the "Pipe Incident." I heated meatballs, grated cheese and sliced a loaf of Sciortino's bread. It made a delicious sub sandwich. As I sat at the counter, my mind traveled back to yesterday, when nothing appealed to my appetite. Love was a superb seasoning.

After finishing the meal, I packed an overnight bag and spent an hour preparing my final report for Bart. The last three weeks were almost entirely devoted to the Johnson case and the bill was in the five figures. I hoped Adriana got some money out of the inheritance from her parents or from the Zupans. If not, I'd have to write off the charges. There was no way I'd hound her for the money.

Wukowski arrived at five-thirty. We kissed at my front door, at the end of the hallway...heck, we pretty much kissed all the way to the couch, where we kissed some more. I pulled back a bit and said, "Is the plan still to stay at your place? Because if it is, we should stop now."

He gave me an unrepentant bad-boy grin. "You're right. Let's get your things and go."

He took the small suitcase and hoisted my garment bag over his shoulder. "Of course, you're welcome to stay the week," he said, with a cheeky grin.

I swatted his arm. "I'm not the kind of gal who wears the same clothes two days in a row. No 'walk of shame' for me."

At the doorway, as I started to put my coat on, he said, "Uh, Ange, about my house." I waited. "Well, it's a lot different from the condo."

"Don't tell me it's full of pizza boxes and beer bottles."

"No. It's presentable, but it's not really…decorated."

I reached up and put my hands on his cheeks. "It's clean?" He nodded. "There's a bed?" Another nod. "And you'll be there. So I'm happy."

Wukowski's Jeep was double-parked in the garage, behind my Miata. He carefully placed the suitcase and garment bag in the back seat, out of sight of the reporters, should they take pictures of us leaving. "Ready to face the media, *moja droga?*"

"You don't think they'll stake out your place, do you?"

"They'd have to follow me there. If they do, I'll call the lieutenant. He'll send a couple of squads. We don't take kindly to civilians stalking an officer."

"If they have your license, they can find the address."

"Nope. It's not public record, for our protection."

"Good." I settled back into the seat and waited for the garage door to rise. Sure enough, the newshounds pounced, but the windows were up and we ignored them. I stared straight ahead, refusing to cover my face or otherwise present a guilty front.

We listened to *All Things Considered* on WUWM as we drove south on I-94. Wukowski took the Howard Avenue exit and continued east. He pulled into the driveway of a red brick Cape Cod home. As the door to the detached garage rose, I saw a small fenced back yard.

"We're here," he said.

I leaned over and kissed him lightly. "So I see. C'mon, show me your bachelor pad."

Wukowski took the overnight case and garment bag and joined me in the driveway, where he punched a fob on his key ring to close the garage door. Then he ushered me to the back door of the dark house.

Once inside, I was surprised by the modern kitchen, with concrete countertops stained a swirly brown, creamy maple cabinets and top-of-the-line stainless appliances. It was small, but functional and appealing. "Wow," I said as I turned in a circle to take it in. "This is really nice."

He set the case down and hung the garment bag inside a coat closet. Then he helped me off with my coat and turned to hang it up. "It was pretty much a 1950s kitchen when I moved in after the divorce. I had it remodeled two years ago."

"I like it, a lot." His face relaxed. I found it endearing that he wanted my approval.

The small dining room came next, unremarkable except for the hickory flooring with its strong variations in color and grain. It continued into the living room, which was pretty much what I expected. Brown leather couch and recliner, dark wood coffee table and side tables, big square ottoman with several days of newspapers still rolled for delivery and the obligatory huge flat screen TV, mounted above a brick fireplace. A tall glass curio cabinet stood in one corner. I walked over to it.

On the top shelf was a picture of a man in a suit and homburg, a woman in a full-skirted dark dress with polka dots, a dark-haired boy and a beautiful little girl. The shelf below it held a framed photo of a young Wukowski, dressed in a beat cop's uniform and peaked hat with visor. There were two medals of valor and accompanying plaques—a lifesaving medal, for resuscitating a woman who collapsed with no pulse, and a rescue medal, for leading a group of senior citizens from a fire in an assisted living center.

Behind me, Wukowski said, "Those aren't there to make me feel like a hero. They're there to remind me that my world isn't all about catching bad guys."

I turned and walked into his somewhat stiff body. "You are a hero, though," I told him.

His arms came around me and held me loosely. "Let me show you the rest of the house."

I got it. He didn't want to talk about the cabinet's contents. I gave him a squeeze and backed away. He went back to the kitchen, gathered my bags and led me down the hallway.

A king-size bed dominated the rather small bedroom, a four-poster made of gray metal uprights connected at the top with crosspieces to form a large rectangular box. The bedding was also unrelieved gray. A small wooden nightstand held a clock and lamp. In the corner was a tall dresser and on one wall was a door, probably for a closet. The room was spare, almost sterile. I imagined that Wukowski liked to retreat to it at the end of a tough day.

He set the overnighter on the bed, opened the closet door and hung the garment bag on the rod. "Move stuff around if you need more space, Angie. I wouldn't want your clothes to be wrinkled." There was a twinkle in his eye.

"I only brought enough for tomorrow," I protested.

He decided to ignore that. "Bathroom's across the hall. It's small, but serviceable. There's no room downstairs for an en suite. I've been thinking about converting the unfinished upstairs space into a master suite."

"Big project," I said, as I picked up my bag and headed for the bathroom. Like the kitchen, the room was updated, but small. "Will it bother you if I leave stuff in here?"

"I emptied a drawer for you. Make yourself at home, Angie." Wukowski stood in the doorway, bouncing slightly from foot to foot. We eyed each other, both a bit wary. *Might as well name it*, I thought.

"*Caro*, I think we both feel a little strange with this. I'll just leave the bag here for now."

We ambled into the living room. I curled up on the couch—leather is decidedly cold and there was no afghan—while Wukowski lit a wood fire. He shifted me over and sat down, taking me into his arms. "Chilly?" he asked.

"A bit. You need an afghan."

"Lord, don't say that to my mother. She's the queen of knitting and crocheting. She'd have every surface in here covered with a doily, antimacassar or throw, if I let her."

"One neutral-colored afghan wouldn't hurt."

"It would be a beachhead. Within a week, the place would explode with yarn. Trust me." He rested his chin on my head. "So, our options for supper are limited. The only places that deliver are pizza joints or Jimmy Johns."

"It just so happens that inside my overnight bag is another bag, which contains a serving dish of Mama Mia's lasagna. It was part of the "Pipe Incident" food."

"Garlic bread?"

"Sciortino's."

"Woman, you are amazing!"

I retrieved the food, put my nightie across the foot of the bed, and left the undies and toiletries in the bag. In the kitchen, I set the oven for 350. "I'll need butter and garlic powder or salt," I told Wukowski. "And a sweater. This place is chilly."

"Sorry, short stuff. I got distracted and forgot to reset the temp on the thermostat when I came in." He headed for the hallway and returned with a Packers sweatshirt. "I'm not exactly a sweater kind of guy."

It reached almost to my knees, but it was warm. The oven beeped and I put the lasagna dish inside. Wukowski set a cookie sheet out for the bread, uncorked a bottle of Chianti and started to make a salad. The tension melted away as we worked side by side.

We ate, cleared away the dishes and went to bed, where we made love and then snuggled under the covers. "Are you working tomorrow?" I asked.

"Yeah. I couldn't wriggle out of it."

"What time are we getting up?"

"Six. I need to drop you off and get to headquarters by eight. Traffic's a bear during rush hour."

Uh-oh. We'd have to run the news gauntlet again. I could imagine their insinuations about our leaving tonight and not returning until the morning. *Let them*, I thought. *This is worth it.*

After a minute of silence, I heard a gentle snuffling sound. I fell asleep in Wukowski's arms, in Wukowski's bed, in Wukowski's house. It didn't seem strange any longer.

Chapter 34

When I started counting my blessings, my whole life turned around.
—Willie Nelson

Wukowski drove me home, past a small group of reporters. They yelled their questions as we rolled by: "Where's Adriana Johnson?" and "Is Adriana keeping the cash?" and "Are you two an item?" *Two-thirds actual news requests—not bad.*

We kissed in the parking garage, agreeing that we wouldn't get together until tomorrow for Thanksgiving. There was an unspoken acknowledgement that we both could use some time to decompress.

Bart called to thank me for inviting him to Thanksgiving at Papa's, but he decided to spend the day with his brother and family.

"I didn't know you had a brother, Bart."

"Yeah, well, we're not close. I haven't seen him for a couple of years. But he called, so I said yes."

Christmas and Thanksgiving—the holidays that shine a light on all the hidden corners of family dysfunction! I thought about the opposing forces at our own table tomorrow. A man with Mafia ties sitting down with a police officer; a scared woman confronted with a large noisy group; a gay man among what, I assumed, was a convocation of straights; a woman alone, surrounded by family and lovers; a father and his daughter's lover. There were so many ways that our meal could turn into a verbal brawl or an icy silence. I couldn't control any of it, so I decided to soak in the tub with my face slathered in a pumpkin mask—how seasonal!—that my stylist assured me was appropriate for "older skin."

Adriana called to update me on Thanksgiving at the Mulcahey residence. She proudly informed me that she helped Magdalena make the dressing and even stuffed the bird, but wore gloves because it was yucky to put her bare hands into a turkey. "Angie," she said in a quietly tense voice, "Mrs. Conti called me to let me know that I can take the admission tests for UWM in December and start classes in January. I can live in the dorms at first, but I'll be older than most of the students and I'd love to find someone to share an apartment near campus. Josif left me twenty-five thousand in the account he mentioned in his…letter." She swallowed. "I'm going to accept it, if it's legal. I want to finally start on a nursing degree and bring some good out of all this horror. Do you think that's okay, to use the money that way?"

"I think that is absolutely okay, Adriana. I'm so proud of you." We set a date to meet after the holiday and wished each other Happy Thanksgiving.

Afterward, I started on Christmas cards. It kept me from dwelling on the *what-ifs* of my relationship with Wukowski. As I signed cards and addressed and stamped envelopes, a sense of wellbeing wrapped around me like a comfy old shawl. Each of those cards represented a friend or family member.

For a moment, I stopped and thought about all the new people who'd come into my life this year. Those I met on the Belloni case—Bobbie, Anthony and Gracie Belloni and their brood, Iggy and his wife,

Marianne, Mrs. Lembke. Those I met during this investigation—
Adriana, Spider, Bram and Mad Man Malone, Lily, Professor Kolar,
Colonel Lewis. I didn't know if they would stay in my life, but they
were people I was glad to know for even a short time.

And of course, Wukowski. When we met this summer, I had no
idea that, by November, I'd again be saying "I love you" to a man or
hearing him say it to me. Perhaps he wouldn't stay, either. It scared me,
but not enough to back away. He was worth the risk. *We* were worth
the risk.

***

Thanksgiving morning dawned sunny and cold, with the likelihood of
clouds and snow later in the afternoon. Papa's house would be warm
with cooking and people, so I chose a muted orange silk turtleneck and
almost-khaki wool blend pants. I could toss a rust-colored pashmina
over my shoulders if I got chilled. I didn't forget Angela's Thanksgiving
gift to me last year, a hand-painted macaroni broach intended to
resemble a turkey. I'd wear it for the joy of her smile. My underwear
drawers did not contain anything as tacky as holiday-themed panties.
A peach silk charmeuse bra with smooth cups that wouldn't show
under the turtleneck and matching French-cut panties would be
comfortable while working in the kitchen or playing with my
grandchildren. I took a quick shower—the bruises were mostly yellow
and fading—and dressed.

There was no need to eat. Aunt Terry would have food out all day,
including breakfast munchies for the early birds. I packed my offerings
into a bag, suited up for the cold, and headed outside.

Amazingly, there were no reporters waiting. Apparently, even
newshounds celebrate Thanksgiving. I drove to Papa's house and

parked the Miata on the cement pad next to the detached garage. Aunt Terry met me at the back door and divested me of the bag. Papa kissed me on the cheek and wished me a Happy Thanksgiving. Then he headed for the living room and the *Journal-Sentinel's* holiday edition. The Packers-Lions game started at twelve-thirty. Until then, the big screen TV would remain off. The meal was planned for four, but family and guests were invited to watch the game, too. With munchies and hors d'oeuvres, no one would go hungry waiting for the turkey.

"So, Angelina," Aunt Terry said, after we put my food away and settled at the kitchen table with coffee and Danish, "what is new with you and Detective Wukowski?"

I collected my thoughts. Was it too soon to tell the family that I was in love? The phrase rankled a bit. "In love" was for those in the throes of infatuation. I loved and was loved, but there didn't seem to be a word for that.

"We're taking it a step at a time." I didn't mention love. It was too new.

"And the case? Very disturbing, what Mr. Zupan felt compelled to do. May God forgive him."

"Petrovitch terrorized him for years with threats of disclosure and then had his wife murdered. I think God will take that into account."

"May it be," she said.

Soon we heard the sounds of cars pulling into the driveway. Emma and John arrived with Angela, who rushed over to me. "*Nonna*, you're wearing my pin."

"Of course, *cara*. It's so pretty, I'll always wear it on Thanksgiving." I meant it. Her gift glowed with love and that made it beautiful.

They hardly had their coats hung up when David, Elaine and the twins came in. "Happy Thanksgiving, Mom," David said as he hugged me. "You ready for this?"

I knew he meant introducing Wukowski to the family, but I pretended ignorance. "Don't worry, the meal will be on the table, on time and delicious. Aunt Terry will see to it."

He laughed and herded the boys into Papa's study to play Mario Brothers. Then he and John got themselves beers and settled in the living room, where they and Papa began a friendly argument about the odds being offered on today's game. Fausto arrived, placed a chaste kiss on Aunt Terry's cheek, and joined the men. I smiled at her.

"We're taking it slow, like you said."

"Good," I told her. "You'll know if you want to speed things up a bit."

Angela sat with the women in the kitchen, carefully eating a jelly-filled donut that was dusted with powdered sugar. I smiled at her dainty manners.

Emma cut to the chase. "So, Mom," she grinned, "what's the latest on you and that good-looking police detective?"

Angela's head shot up. "Do you have a boyfriend, *Nonna*?"

"Well, there's someone I'm dating, Angela. His name is Ted Wukowski. He and his mother will be here later."

Her big brown eyes assessed me. "Are you in love?"

An expectant hush fell over the kitchen and living room. I couldn't lie to my granddaughter! "I love him, *piccola*." Angela clapped and Emma hugged me. Elaine lifted her cup in a toast. Aunt Terry mumbled, "One step at a time?" and there was a low buzz from the living room. I felt a sudden release of tension from saying it to the world and broke into a huge grin.

Wukowski and his mother arrived at eleven-thirty. Papa went to the front door and ushered them in. "Detective, Mrs. Wukowski, welcome to my home."

Wukowski said, "Thank you for inviting us, Mr. Bonaparte."

Lena added, "It is so kind of you."

I cringed inside at the stiff formality and moved to greet them, but Aunt Terry stepped in to salvage the moment. "I'm Angie's Aunt Terry. Pat, don't let them stand there. Take their coats." Wukowski helped his mother and handed her long wool coat to Papa. Aunt Terry lifted the canvas bag, took Lena's arm and guided her into the room. "The men all sit in here to watch the football game, but I prefer the kitchen, don't you?"

I reached Wukowski as he took off his down jacket and handed it to Papa. "Hi, there," I said, smiling at the sight of him. He stood, as out of place as a rugby player at the opera. I put my arms around him and gave him a quick kiss. Then I turned to Papa. "Papa, meet Ted. Wukowski, this is my father, Pasquale."

They eyed each other for a moment, then Papa smiled and clapped Wukowski on the shoulder. "Call me Pat. Come in. The game will start in a few minutes." Under his knit Henley, I felt Wukowski's arm muscles relax.

I made introductions all around. When I got to the grandchildren, Angela gave him a most serious look and said, "*Nonna* loves you. Do you love her?"

The room went silent, except for the pregame hoopla on the TV. Wukowski squatted down and said, "I do, Angela. I hope that's okay with you." The question wasn't really aimed at little Angela, who nodded solemnly. Wukowski rose and gazed at Papa.

"Have some wine," Papa said. "Or maybe a beer?" He steered Wukowski to the mudroom and the Corny keg. Time for the talk that

Papa had with every guy I ever dated—be good to my Angelina or you'll live to regret it. I left them to it.

In the kitchen, Lena sat at the counter while Aunt Terry set out the snack food for the game. I approached Lena with care. "Mrs. Wukowski, Lena, I'm Angie."

She beamed at me and gestured toward the living room. "I am so happy that my son has found a good woman to love."

"I'm happy to have found him, Lena. He's a good man. You must be proud." I reached out and we hugged. The noise level rose in the living room. "Must be kickoff time," I said. "We get pretty boisterous around here."

"It's happy noise."

Singly and in twos, my family found time during the game to wander into the kitchen and meet Wukowski's mother. I watched her for signs of being overwhelmed. She seemed calm and happy. She and Aunt Terry emptied the contents of her bag and discussed how to reheat the sauerkraut and kielbasa.

When the doorbell rang again, I went to greet Lily and Bobbie. Lily settled into a discussion with Angela, who had the second Harry Potter book in hand. Bobbie groaned with the other men when the Lions made a first down. "Defensive line is not pulling its weight," he said, to affirmations all round.

Papa and Wukowski returned and joined the fray. Patrick and Donald were engaged in a furious game of Hot Wheels on the floor. After a moment of intense whispering, Patrick got up and approached Wukowski. Donald was the instigator when something untoward was going down. Patrick, bless him, hadn't learned yet that his brother was manipulating him.

"Sir," said Patrick, "do you carry a gun?"

"When I'm on duty, I do. A police officer has to be ready for any situation."

"Are you packin' now?"

I choked on Chex mix. Wukowski gave Patrick a serious look and said, "No, I never carry a gun when I'm off duty and there are children around. I wouldn't want a kid to get curious and have a bad accident." He held Patrick's gaze. "Guns are dangerous. It's not like TV. That's why gun owners need to be trained in the use of a weapon."

Patrick nodded. "Okay." He resumed playing with his brother.

I was impressed with Wukowski. It was obvious that he wasn't around children a lot, but he treated them with respect and was honest with them. I'd trust him with my grandkids, and that was saying a lot.

I went back into the kitchen, where Aunt Terry and Lena were peeling potatoes at the sink. "Angie," Aunt Terry said, "Lena and I are going to make some calls on those who are sick or homebound in her parish."

Ah, Aunt Terry, always drawing the best out of someone. "That's such a nice thing to do, Lena. There are so many people who can't get out anymore and welcome company. I'm sure you and Aunt Terry will brighten their days."

Wukowski stood in the doorway with his empty beer glass, his mouth open in surprise. He walked over to the sink, set the glass down, put his hands on his mother's shoulders and gave her a kiss on the cheek. "Mama, you amaze me."

She laughed and shooed him away. "Just like your papa. He always wanted to snuggle when I was in the kitchen working." He picked up the glass and headed to the mudroom for a refill.

The afternoon passed quickly. The men moved from the living

room to the kitchen and back again, for drinks and snacks. The children played in the den or outside. Lily, Elaine and Emma got into a discussion on romance novels. Apparently, Lily liked Old West, Elaine was partial to contemporary and Emma sighed over historicals. Aunt Terry and Lena worked together on the final meal preparations. I gave a hand as directed. The kitchen smelled of turkey, sauerkraut and marinara.

There were fifteen of us at the big dining room table and the smaller children's table. The side dishes were all out when we sat down. Papa carried in the turkey platter and set it in the place of honor at the head of the table. When he sat, Aunt Terry said, "We have a Thanksgiving tradition in our family. We don't say the usual grace before a meal. We each say what we're most grateful for at this moment. Of course, anyone who finds that uncomfortable can just say 'pass.' Pasquale, why don't you start?"

"I give thanks for my family, for you, Terry, and Angelina, for my grandchildren and their spouses, and for my great-grandchildren." The thanks went around the table. Almost everyone spoke of the blessing of family.

Then it came to Bobbie. "I'm thankful for those who accept me as I am."

Lily said, "I'm thankful for having a good mind."

I didn't quite know what to say when it was my turn. But heck, everyone heard our earlier declarations. "I'm grateful to have a special love in my life."

It was his turn. All he said was, "Ditto."

At that, a ripple of laughter went around the table. Papa carved the turkey and we ate. Lena tried the spaghetti Bolognese and said, "Mmm." Aunt Terry took a second helping of sauerkraut and kielbasa and asked Lena for the recipe. "We'll trade," Lena said.

After the main meal, the women cleared the table and brought in desserts. *Zabaglione, budyn*, pumpkin pie. It was a merger of cultures through food, the way America ought to be, but often isn't. I had a little of each and promised myself to get back on my running game now that the soreness was almost gone.

After we pushed back from the table, Lena started to gather the dessert dishes. I put a hand on hers. "We have another tradition, Lena. The men clean up."

"Oh, I like that tradition."

Lena and I settled on the couch with glasses of wine. "My family must seem strange to you."

"No. No, it's not that you're strange. I'm...sometimes, I'm afraid. It's hard for me to be where there is violence." She looked at me. "My son, his life is about violence. I worry."

"I understand that. I worry, too." I held her hand for a moment. Then Angela wandered over.

"The boys are outside playing football again. Would you please play a game with me, *Nonne*?"

I whispered to Lena. "I'm her *nonna*, her grandmother. But she just asked both her grandmothers—her *nonne*—to play."

"Sweet child," Lena said. "Where are the games? I hope they're not those video games. I can't play those." She and Angela went into the study to assess the board games.

For a moment, all was right in my world. Then Wukowski came into the room, wiping his hands on a dishtowel. "Angie, I just got a call from the Lieutenant. There's a dead body on the Lakefront Trail. Sorry. I'll take Mama home."

"She can stay," I said. "I can drive her home later."

"You can ask."

I was surprised that Lena decided to leave with Wukowski, given how excited she seemed to play games with Angela. Apparently, she wasn't as comfortable with us as I thought, but I hoped that would come, in time.

Aunt Terry rose and bustled into the kitchen, calling that she'd pack some leftovers for them. I walked to Wukowski and nestled myself against him. "Be careful," I said.

"I'll call you if it doesn't get too late."

"Call me anyway," I told him.

He and Lena made their good-byes and left with her canvas bag loaded with plastic containers of food. Bobbie and Lily decided to go, too.

I thanked Aunt Terry for all her work in making the meal. I kissed my kids and grandkids good-bye and reminded them of our trip to the children's museum tomorrow. I hugged Papa and thanked him for being nice to Wukowski. He held me at arm's length and humphed. "Did you think I would invite the man to my home and then dishonor myself by being rude to him?"

"I worried a little that you might try to intimidate him."

"I did try," he said. "It didn't work." He smiled and pulled me into his arms. "It won't be easy, with that one. But I don't worry that he will be bad to you. He is a man of honor."

"He is," I agreed.

Papa, Aunt Terry and I all trooped to my car, with enough leftovers for another meal for four packaged into two carry bags. I waved and drove off toward my condo on the East Side. Close to the dead body that Wukowski was called to investigate.

If we stay together, I thought, *this will be part of my life. Emergency calls. Interruptions. Worry.*

I would accept it, for his sake and for my own. After years of protecting myself from the pain of love, love crept in under my defenses. I welcomed it.

THE END

"The best way to thank an author is to write a review."
– Anonymous

If you enjoyed this book, please consider posting a review on your favorite retailer's website. Reviews mean the world to an author, so I thank you in advance.

NOTES

Although I am not a historian, I took pains to make the impact of the Bosnian War realistic, especially in regards to Professor Kolar's memories. Of particular help in that regard is *Remember Sarajevo*, an online pamphlet with journalist Roger Richards' account of his time in Sarajevo in 1992. The photographs and his story are hauntingly real. I encourage you to read this small, but powerful, document. http://digitaljournalist.org/issue0302/rr_intro.html

In Chapter 19, Bobbie and Adriana have an adventure in the underground tunnels of Milwaukee's Third Ward. I took literary license with those tunnels. They do exist in downtown Milwaukee, but I'm not sure, and could not find data to tell me, if the old Third Ward was similarly equipped. I decided to use them anyway. After all, this is fiction!

Read on for an excerpt from the first Angelina Bonaparte mystery, *Truth Kills*.

Truth Kills–Chapter 1

Hold faithfulness and sincerity as first principles.
—Analects of Confucius

I'm a professional snoop and I'm good at it. While on the job, I can look like the senior partner of an accountancy firm in my pinstriped navy business suit, or the neighborhood white-haired old-lady gossip. Off the job, I'm a fifty-something hottie—white hair gelled back, dramatic eye make-up, toned body encased in designer duds. Gravity has taken a small toll, but who notices in candlelight?

As I rubbed potting soil into the cooking oil that I'd already smeared on my Salvation Army second-hand clothes, I examined myself in the mirror. A short, plain woman (five foot, three inches) with choppy white hair and no make-up, wearing dirty, baggy clothes, looked back at me. A homeless person. I nodded and headed down the fire stairs to the parking garage, trying to avoid meeting any of my neighbors.

The beauty of being a woman, as the French say, "of a certain age," is that I can be invisible. Young people, both men and women, look right through me, unless I make the effort to be noticed. Older men look past me, too, to gaze upon the tight, toned, tanned bodies that they wish they could possess. Only older women seem to notice me, because they're judging me against some invisible standard and wondering how I measure up compared to them. It's not usually malicious, it's just how we were raised. Believe me, I do it myself. Is her ass tighter than mine? Are her boobs perkier? Any cellulite on those thighs? It's competition at the most primitive level, the female equivalent of two silver-backed gorillas thumping chests and roaring at each other.

Today, however, wasn't a hottie day. Elisa Morano, one of the aforementioned tight, toned and tanned, was suspected of playing house with my client's husband, Anthony Belloni, a.k.a. Tony Baloney. Tony's cellular phone bill listed lots of calls to Ms. Morano's apartment, coincidentally located in one of Tony's many real estate holdings. His credit card statement showed purchases of lingerie, perfume and a fur coat, stuff that his wife, Gracie, had yet to see. To top it off, Gracie was eight months pregnant with their fifth child and spitting mad. She hired me to find out whether Tony was indeed cheating with Elisa Morano.

Which brings me back to my bag lady persona. Dumpster diving is legal. Once the trash is on the curb, it's public property. The Supremes ruled on it, and I mean Scalia and company, not the group Diana Ross fronted. People like me make a good living, finding out stuff from the trash. The problem is getting to it. The super will stop an average Jane from digging through the garbage, but if he sees a bag lady, he'll likely turn the other way. No harm in recycling, right?

So on this hot Thursday morning in August, I parked my car a block away, shuffled up the drive to Elisa's building and jumped into the dumpster that squatted behind it. My short stature made it easy for me to hide in there as I searched for something with her name on it. These people were upper class, everything was nicely bagged and I didn't think I'd have to worry about getting crap on my car seat when I was done.

It took about twenty minutes to find the bag, full of paper that was run through a shredder. I couldn't be sure until I put it all back together, but there was a piece with an "El" still intact. Maybe it was "Elisa." It was all I found that even remotely fit, so I tossed it over the side and heaved myself out, straight into the path of a hulk in a black suit.

"Watcha doin' there, lady?" Tony Baloney's bodyguard, Jimmy the Arm, asked as he grabbed me and pinned me to the side of the dumpster. Jimmy's sleeve-defying biceps compensate for his tiny mental gifts.

I realized that Jimmy didn't recognize me, despite having seen me on numerous occasions, both social and professional. My bag lady persona was my best defense. "Nothin.' I ain't doin' nothin.' Just lookin,'" I responded.

"For what?"

"Stuff ta sell. Clothes. Shoes. Books. Cans. These rich folks toss out good stuff." I pulled a face. "But not much today, one bag. Just my luck."

"Well, leave it and get goin' and don't come back to this building. Unnerstan?" He gave a little shove for good measure, not enough to hurt. His mama must have raised him well. Of course, he'd toss a rival into a cement mixer with no qualms. But I'm not averse to using whatever advantages come my way. I earned all the white on my head, and if it gets me out of a jam, it's just one of the perks of being slightly older.

I sloped off down the driveway, looking behind me as if scared that Jimmy was following. Actually, I was checking that the bag was still lying next to the dumpster. Sure enough, Jimmy ignored it and entered the building by the super's door. Guess Jimmy's mama never taught him to pick up trash. I scuttled back, grabbed the bag, and sprinted down the street to the lot where I left my car, to drive back to the office.

I share office space on Prospect Avenue, on Milwaukee's east side, with the firm of Neh Accountants. The "s" on the end is misleading. It's a one-person company run by Susan Neh, a third-generation Japanese American. Susan and I met when we both worked for Jake Waterman. She conducted his financial investigations and I did his legwork—computer searches, tails, background checks. It didn't take Susan long to earn her CPA and go out on her own. I joined her when I got my P.I. license and needed a place to hang my shingle. Most of Susan's clientele are of Japanese descent, but lately, she's working with a few Hmong and Vietnamese. I was glad to find that Susan was out on a client call today. It saved me from explaining my less than glamorous appearance.

It took me six hours of tedious, neck-straining, eyeball-screaming work to piece the shredded paper from the bag back together. Luckily, Elisa didn't have a cross-cut shredder, just the kind that produces long strips of paper. I can reassemble cross-cut, too, given enough time and motivation. The only way to be absolutely sure that no one can read your letters is to burn them and pulverize the ashes, or soak the paper in a pail of water mixed with a half-cup of bleach to destroy the ink. Then you can toss the blank paper with no worries.

Like most people, Elisa simply put a plastic bag into the can and shredded it into the bag. When she lifted it out and discarded it, the remains were in distinct layers, making it easier to separate and reassemble. It helped that the paper had different colors and textures. It's like working a jigsaw puzzle, without the picture on the box for a guide.

Six hours later, I had a pretty fair understanding of the woman—vain (online article about Botox, with list of local practitioners), fertile (Ortho-Provera drug interaction statement from a mail-order prescription company), savvy (year old Vanguard mutual fund statement showing a 70K balance), cautious (no intact papers with her name in the dumpster, she apparently shredded everything).

I wasn't any closer, though, to discovering if Tony was indeed making it with the beauteous Ms. Morano, and my back was screaming from hours of bending over the office work table. My skin itched, even though I'd changed out of my clean dirty clothes, and it was already six o'clock. I made copies of the pieced-together papers, tossed them in my briefcase, and headed for home in my Black Cherry Miata convertible. There aren't enough top-down days in southeast Wisconsin, but this was one and I felt good, tooling down Lincoln Memorial Drive with the cool air of Lake Michigan on my skin. Heaven.

The Miata, like my condo, was a gift to myself following my divorce. The decree restored both my self-respect and my maiden name—Angelina Bonaparte, pronounced Boe-nah-par-tay, not Bo-nah-part. Napoleon was a Corsican-*cum*-French wannabe, so he left the last syllable off, but I'm one hundred percent Sicilian and I pronounce it the way it was meant to be pronounced.

I love my car. It symbolizes my post-marriage financial and emotional independence, and the sense of personal daring that I kept under tight wraps while I was Mrs. Bozo (I call him "your dad" when the kids are around, even though they're grown and have their own kids). I still shudder to think of twenty-five prime years spent trying to fit the pattern of wife, lover, mother, housekeeper. Picture June Cleaver wearing a sassy red thong under her demure shirtwaist dress.

Bozo started playing around when he turned fifty. Funny, whenever

I heard about some guy running around on his wife, I always told my best friend, Judy, that the door wouldn't hit my butt on the way out. When it happened to me, though, I decided that I owed a twenty-five year marriage at least one chance. Or two. Three was when I changed the locks, packed his clothes and put the suitcases on the front lawn. I reminded him of Papa's toast at our wedding – "There are no divorces in our family. There are widows, but no divorces." It scared him purple.

Of course, we did divorce and I did manage to dissuade Papa from having Bozo fitted for lead sneakers, or seeing to it that his body was made unfit for further nookie. The Miata was my first indulgence after the proceedings. I went down to the dealer with a check in hand that very day. Then I put the house on the market and signed the papers for my East side high-rise condo. I heard the whispers about "middle-aged crazy" and "trying to prove something," but I ignored them. This was me, the real me, not that convention that I'd tried to squeeze myself into all those years.

I stepped into my foyer and locked the door behind me. Shedding clothes as I walked, I tossed the dirty duds into my bedroom closet's built-in hamper and walked naked into the bathroom. If driving the Miata is car heaven, standing under a steam shower with five heads massaging from toes to crown is surely water heaven.

Thirty minutes later, moisturized, gelled, dressed in yoga pants and a tee shirt, I sipped a glass of Chardonnay and stared into the fridge. Then I glared at the goods in the freezer. Why is it that there's never anything to eat when you just want to stay in? It would have to be another deep dish Milwaukee special night—cheese, sausage, mushrooms, onions, the famous "SMO." I was either going to have to step up my exercise program and cut back on the fat, or buy a bigger wardrobe. While I love shopping for clothes, the second option didn't appeal. Bozo used to pinch my waist and smirk when he could get an inch between his fingers. I love to see him assess my figure now, when we attend family functions like birthdays and baptisms. There's no way I'm gaining back that inch, so I resolved to do some grocery shopping soon. Just for good measure, I did twenty minutes of yoga/Pilates while waiting for the pizza. A couple chapters of the latest Sue Grafton (I love that Kinsey, but, jeez, one black dress for her whole adult life?) and I was ready to pound the pillow. Solo.

It's been months since my last serious involvement. He thought I wouldn't find out about the bar-time pickups. "Honest, Angie, it doesn't mean a thing. I just like a little variety." Sometimes I wish I was a lesbian, it would make life so much easier. I hear they're more than ninety-percent faithful. What a concept!

I met Kevin, my current guy, four weeks ago. My neighbor Sally and her son, Joseph, introduced us. Joseph was diagnosed with Muscular Dystrophy at age six. Kevin is his physical therapist. Picture Harrison Ford as Han Solo in the first *Star Wars* movie—a little rough, killer body, redeeming lop-sided smile that gets him out of all sorts of trouble. He's thirty-eight, so, yes, he's a few years younger than I am. Given the actuarial tables and my energy level, that's good.

We've been doing that painful boy-girl dance ever since, the one we all first learned in adolescence. Is he available? Cute enough? Is she needy? Pretty enough? Will he want to go to bed right away? Do I want to? Should I? Add today's refinements—STDs? Last HIV test? Last lover? *Ad infinitum. Ad nauseum.* Even my best friend Judy is getting sick of me. "Just DO IT," she yelled at me last week.

"Can't," I responded. "You know me." She groaned. We've been through this a lot in the course of the five years since my divorce. I have this little hang-up. I won't deal with dishonesty on a personal basis. Go figure, someone in my line of work! So I operate on the assumption that everyone is hiding something. I run credit checks and criminal and civil court searches on the men who ask me out. I watch them for signs of fooling around—scents they don't normally wear, clothes changed in the middle of the day, long lunches when they can't be called, lots of little clues that mean nothing and everything. I'm not proud of it, but I won't be a fool again. I haven't figured a way out of the morass that women and men seem to sink into. Most nights, like tonight, I sleep alone.

The End

"The best way to thank an author is to write a review."—Anonymous
If you enjoyed this book, please consider posting a review on your favorite retailer's website.

ABOUT THE AUTHOR

Nanci Rathbun is a lifelong reader of mysteries—historical, contemporary, futuristic, paranormal, hard-boiled, cozy … you can find them all on her bookshelves and in her ereaders. She brings logic and planning to her writing from a background as an IT project manager, and attention to characters and dialog from her second career as a Congregationalist minister.  (Her books are not Christian fiction, but they contain no explicit sexual or violent scenes, and only the occasional mild curse word.)

Her first novel, *Truth Kills—An Angelina Bonaparte Mystery*, was published in 2013. *Cash Kills* is the second book in the series and was published in November of 2014. Both novels are available in paperback and ebook formats. Readers can enjoy the first chapters of each on her web site or on Goodreads. The third Angie novel has a working title of *Deception Kills*, with plans to publish in 2017.

A longtime Wisconsin resident, Nanci now makes her home in Colorado. No matter where she lives, she will always be a Packers fan.

Connect with me

My website, where you can find my blog:
https://nancirathbun.com/

Like and Follow me on Facebook:
www.facebook.com/Author-Nanci-Rathbun-162077650631803

Follow me on Twitter:
https://twitter.com/NanciRathbun

Friend or Follow me on Goodreads:
https://www.goodreads.com/author/show/7199317.Nanci_Rathbun

Check out my Pinterest boards:
https://www.pinterest.com/nancir50/

Made in the USA
Middletown, DE
23 September 2018